NICE WIVES
FINISH FIRST

NICE WIVES FINISH FIRST

PATRICIA ANNE
PHILLIPS

Kensington Publishing Corp.

DAFINA BOOKS are published by

Kensington Publishing Corp.
850 Third Avenue
New York, NY 10022

Special book excerpts or customized printings can also be created to fit specific needs. For details, write or phone the office of the Kensington Special Sales Manager: Kensington Publishing Corp., 850 Third Avenue, New York, NY 10022. Attn. Special Sales Department. Phone: 1-800-221-2647.

Dafina Books and the Dafina logo Reg. U.S. Pat. & TM Off.

ISBN: 0-7394-5119-7

First Printing: March 2005

Printed in the United States of America

This book is dedicated to my mother,
Myrtle London,
for believing in my ability to write.
Thank you, mother, for your unconditional
love for all your children.

Also dedicated to Arabya Hope Royal
and Aaren Brett Haggins.

Acknowledgments

To my sisters, Jacqueline, Diane Janice, and Stacey, and my brothers, Charles and Stanley: I love the laughter and good times we share when we are all together.

To my daughter, Cassandra; my son-in law, Chris; and my son, Darren: I am truly blessed to have all of you in my life.

To Karen Thomas, my editor at Kensington Publishing: thank you for always being so pleasant to work with.

Thank you Rosie Milligan for being the agent for this book.

Thank you Victoria Christopher Murray and Maxine Thompson for answering my many e-mails when I needed help.

And to all of the authors I've met: thanks for your encouragement and continual support.

Chapter 1

It was May 2003, and the weather in Los Angeles, California, was unseasonably warm, well over ninety degrees. May was usually overcast, with gray clouds and mist lightly dancing across the windshields of cars in the early, dismal morning, and the sun only threatening to burst through the clouds before noon. It had gotten hot early, but it was cool and comfortable in Ashley Lake's home in Playa Del Rey.

In the kitchen, Ashley stood at the center island, topped with Formica the color of concrete and finished with gracefully scalloped edges. On the sink was a silver coffeepot next to an ornate silver bell. Everything in the house shone as rays of sun streamed through the long French windows.

It was quiet in the house. Ashley could hear the leaves on the trees rustle gently in the barest breeze as she arranged ham sandwiches garnished with fresh parsley over a small bowl of potato salad, enough for two, delicately arranged on a tray to carry out to the patio. She used last night's leftovers from the meal at Marcus's fiftieth birthday party celebration. She filled two tall glasses with iced tea, a thin slice of lemon tilted over the rim of the tall, crystal glasses.

Ashley was an attractive woman, pleasant to the eye, but she was plain and dressed simply in a size twelve. She had gone on several diets but never stuck to any of them. At forty-five years old, why worry about her weight? Besides, her husband never complained about her size.

Her sleeveless brown sundress was baggy and stopped below her knees. Her caramel-colored skin was smooth and healthy and she had wide-set, dark slanted eyes and wire-framed glasses. Ashley's shoulder-length, brown hair was pinned up on top her head. She wasn't a glamorous woman, but still, one would find her quite attractive.

As Ashley picked up the tray to carry it outside, she felt a cramp creeping into her stomach. She set the tray down again, taking deep breaths, leaning against the counter. She felt weak, but just as fast the pain disappeared. She picked up the tray, straightened her back, and ambled out the two sliding glass doors that led to the patio.

Vanessa, Ashley's long-time friend, got up from the round patio table to give Ashley a hand.

"I'm starved, Ash. That ham was delicious last night."

Ashley smiled and set a glass of iced tea in front of Vanessa.

"Did you see that terrible dress that Shirley was wearing last night? Some women wear dresses with cute little flowers, but Shirley wears dresses with a whole field in hers, and so distasteful. I wonder why she always wears such big flowers in her dresses year in and year out? And the styles are always the same, and out of fashion," Vanessa said, and hooted with laughter.

"Yes, I saw it. But Shirley has been that way as long as I can remember," Ashley said, and laughed out loud. "But don't tell her she wasn't looking good. And that husband of hers couldn't keep his eyes off you, Vanessa. He made it so obvious that he still likes you. I don't think he'll ever get over you."

"That was at least twenty years ago, Ash. We were still in school." She looked at Ashley's puffy eyes. "You look tired, Ash. Are you feeling ill or is it lack of sleep? After all, it was your husband's birthday. Were you guys up late after the party?" Vanessa teased.

"Not hardly. My cramps prevented that. I'm too damn old to be walking around with cramps. And the older I get, the worse the cramps are." Ashley frowned with distaste.

"Girl, why don't you listen to your doctor and let him do the hysterectomy? I feel so much better since I had it done, Ash. I mean, what are you giving Marcus, maybe one good week out of a month? That's not good," Vanessa said, pointing her finger at Ashley as though she was chastising a child.

Ashley looked closely at Vanessa's face. For forty-five she looked young, radiant. Her smooth, creamy skin glowed, the color of a Hershey chocolate bar. Vanessa was 5'7", and jogged everyday to maintain her size-eight figure. Although they were about the same age, Ashley knew Vanessa looked five or six years younger than she did. They were so close and yet so different in character. Sometimes Ashley felt as though she was ten years older.

"Are you listening, Ash?" Vanessa asked.

"Yes, sure. I'm listening, and lately I've been thinking about having the hysterectomy. But I still haven't decided yet."

"What's there to decide? You're not feeling well, so what's stopping you, honey?"

"I don't know. Have you ever heard of a woman going around sounding happy or bragging about having a hysterectomy? I just feel so old when I think of it."

"Come on, Ash. It's happened to women younger than you are. You have to admit some good will come out of it." Vanessa flicked the crumbs from her fingers and dabbed at her mouth with the dainty, white cloth napkin with lace trimming around the edges. She carefully folded it and lay it back across her lap.

"Marcus ran into Larry last Friday," Ashley said.

"Oh. Where?" Vanessa's voice echoed with interest.

"At the DMV. Marcus said that he invited Larry over to see the game one Sunday. But Marcus knew he would never come. He's too afraid of running into you here. Anyway, Marcus says he looks well, too."

"Yeah, but you know Larry was an old couch potato. I truly hope he finds someone that will make him happy, because Gary was the best thing that could have happened to me. Since we bought the house in Pasadena, I don't run into any of Larry's friends."

"You don't seem to have a hang-up about the age difference anymore. I don't know why you let eight years bother you in the first place," Ashley said, taking a bite out of her ham sandwich.

"Gary doesn't seem to mind it at all. Once we reach a certain age, eight years doesn't make any difference. Besides, he knows more than I do about life in general, and he's as settled as any older man. It's been four years, Ash, and we're still in love, and it only gets better.

"I never told anyone that sometimes a month would pass before Larry wanted to make love to me. I was beginning to lose any desire for sex. I even began to think that I wasn't desirable enough for anyone to want me. Don't ever let a man make you feel that way, Ash. How can a husband and wife sleep in the same bed for a month and not make love?

"Oh, honey, I didn't know."

"No one knew. When we did there was no cuddling before or after. No intimacy or emotional fondness that two people feel when they are in love with each other. Girl, when I first met Gary, I used to melt when that man touched me. Still do, all the time."

Ashley watched Vanessa as her face glowed when she spoke of her husband.

The phone rang and Ashley jumped up. "Be right back, it's probably Marcus."

Vanessa slipped out of her shoes and stretched her feet out in the chair opposite her. It was always so comfortable and peaceful on Ashley's patio. She took a deep breath, inhaling the scent of the lemons on the tall lemon tree. The flowers and thick green grass were so perfectly manicured; the plants looked green and healthy in large white pots surrounding the patio.

Ashley came back and took her seat again. "That was Marcus. He's in a bar in Hermosa Beach with a couple of guys watching the game on the big screen TV." She looked at her watch. It was only four-thirty.

"Well, you know how men are when they get together watching any kind of game," Vanessa said. But she knew better. She knew all the signs. Hell, she had lied when she was still married to Larry and sneaking around with Gary. Vanessa remembered watching Marcus the night before at his party. For a while it seemed as though he wasn't all there. His heart was someplace else, and he seemed restless, agitated. He and Ashley didn't dance together and didn't seem to have very much to say to each other. Then, finally, as the night wore on Marcus seemed to loosen up.

Ashley returned with a refilled pitcher of iced tea.

"Like I was saying before Marcus called, Larry had gotten too complacent with our marriage. With Gary, I feel loved and beautiful, Ash. The sex is hot, and I realized I had missed the excitement of being in love. It had been lacking in my life."

"I think married couples fall in and out of love," Ashley mused, as she thought of her marriage.

"You may be right about that, Ash. But it wasn't that way with Larry and I. The love didn't return in our marriage."

Ashley sighed as she listened to Vanessa. "Marcus is fifty and I'm forty-five now. We're too old to miss any excitement in our lives. We're married, and Lori is twenty-three-years-old. What more can I ask for?"

But as Vanessa listened to Ashley, she didn't sound too convincing. Or was she trying to convince herself? And she didn't look too happy either. But that could be because she wasn't feeling well.

"You're going to sit there and tell me that you don't need anything besides a house, a husband and a daughter? Don't you miss the rest, Ash? Doesn't he?"

Ashley didn't answer for a few seconds. Her eyes squinted as she looked up at the sun. Sure, she and Marcus still loved each other and without a doubt she was still in love with her husband. The long, passionate kissing and holding hands no longer existed, but they were together and comfortable with their lives.

"We're not kids anymore, Vanessa. We have all we need. I don't care about the excitement we used to have when we were younger. I'm still in love with Marcus. After twenty-five years, I don't know what I would do without him." Just the thought of losing Marcus was frightening. No, she wouldn't think of it. And besides, Marcus was still in love with her, too. He didn't want her to give a party, but in the end he always gave her what she wanted, and always took care of home and her.

Lately, she hadn't been feeling well. The fibroid tumors that were in the wall of her uterus were causing her to bleed more frequently, and the cramps were getting worse. Marcus understood; he was a patient man.

Vanessa looked at her watch. "I enjoyed our little chat but I have to leave. Gary should be home soon and I have to get up early tomorrow morning."

Ashley stood up and placed the plates on the tray with one hand and held her stomach with her free hand. Vanessa carried the pitcher inside for her. Ashley put the tray on the kitchen sink.

Vanessa touched her shoulder. "Should I stay until Marcus gets home, Ash?" And heaven only knows what time that would be, Vanessa thought to herself. "I don't feel right leaving you alone." Vanessa placed her hand against Ashley's forehead. "I think you're running a light fever, Ash."

"No. It stopped hurting. The pain just comes and goes quickly. But at least it's fast."

"You better go and make arrangements for that hysterectomy, girl. Life is too short to go around hurting and uncomfortable."

"I will, I will. You just stop worrying so much."

Ashley walked Vanessa to the door, and the two women embraced. I'll call and check on you tomorrow."

"If I'm not here, call me at the office."

"Okay, Ash. Go to bed and get some rest. You were up late last night." Vanessa smiled and sauntered out the door, her pink sundress revealing the top of her smooth back.

Once the patio door was closed and locked, Ashley placed the dishes into the dishwasher. It was only six o'clock, but she undressed, got into bed, and turned on the TV, with a magazine lying beside her. Ashley flipped through the magazine and watched television until she fell asleep.

Finally, at eight-thirty she heard Marcus turn the key inside the door. She could never sleep soundly until she knew he was safely at home. She thought that once Lori had left home she wouldn't have that problem any longer. But now she has it when Marcus wasn't home.

Marcus heard the TV going and went to the bedroom. He stood at the door and looked at his wife. "You're in bed so early, Ash."

"Yes. I was still tired from the party last night." She sat up and watched him as he undressed.

He placed his shoes neatly inside the closet. She was tired, Marcus thought, but he hadn't wanted the party. Just a quiet night, a good movie on TV, and a nice dinner would have suited him just fine. "I think I'll go in the den and watch TV for a while. Go back to sleep," Marcus said and grabbed the *TV Guide* on his way out.

Thinking of the earlier conversation with Vanessa, Ashley sat up in bed. "You can watch it in here, Marcus," she yelled behind him.

"No, baby. I don't want to keep you awake. You get yourself some sleep."

Ashley did fall asleep. Later, she slightly opened her eyes as Marcus climbed into bed. It was past ten.

The next morning Marcus was up first. He had already showered and almost finished dressing by the time Ashley got out of bed.

She went into the kitchen and turned on the coffeemaker, went into her bathroom and showered. They each had their own bathroom, which Ashley had decorated using the same colors: navy and light blue. By habit Marcus had her coffee waiting for her when she got out the shower, and he gave her a quick kiss on the cheek as she brushed passed him. They were in their bedroom, Ashley was sitting on the bed sipping her coffee, and Marcus was standing in front of the mirror.

On the bed was a blue oversized comforter, pillows piled high, made with silk material that Vanessa bought for them in Hong Kong. The furniture was crafted in pine. The rest of the house had eggshell-colored blinds, but Ashley liked having drapes for her bedroom, which were the same color as the blinds.

She looked at her husband again as he opened his closet and pulled out a brown-and-tan striped tie to match his tan suit. Feeling Ashley's eyes on him, Marcus looked in the mirror, and their eyes met and held for a fraction of a second.

Ashley loved watching him dress. Everything had to match perfectly. His shoes had to be shined, the tie and shirt had to complement the suits he wore.

"You didn't sleep well last night, Marcus. Aren't you tired this morning?" she asked with concern, wondering if she should be worried about him. "For the last two weeks you seem to be having trouble sleeping."

Seeing her still watching him, Marcus smiled and winked at her. "I'm just a little tired. Probably need a short vacation."

"We can go someplace if you like. We haven't been away together in two years now. Not since we went to your aunt's funeral in Dallas, Texas."

He made no comment. "Are you feeling better, Ash, or are you considering the surgery anytime soon?"

"I've been thinking about it, Marcus. But I'm not ill. We can still go away together if you can get away from work. My workload isn't too heavy at my office right now. We need to go away together for a change, just the two of us."

He didn't answer and looked as though he was concentrating on tying his tie.

As Ashley looked at him in the mirror, again he was frowning as though he was distracted. He was always so gentle and concerned about her. God, she thought to herself. What a lucky woman she was to be married to a good man like her husband. He was a man that was always there for his family.

Marcus finished tying the knot in his tie. "We won't go anyplace until you are feeling better, Ash."

"I'm all right, Marcus. Don't worry about me." She got up, went to her closet, and pulled out her gray suit. Ashley saw Marcus turn around and look at her with a frown creasing his forehead. He hated the colors that she selected. Whenever he bought her clothes, they were always so colorful and bright. To please her husband she hung the suit back in the closet and pulled out the purple one he had bought for her two years ago.

"Marcus, are you sure that you're all right?" she asked.

"Sure. Why wouldn't I be, Ash? Don't worry about every little thing. I'll get a good night's sleep tonight and tomorrow I'll be like new again." He picked up his empty coffee cup and headed for the kitchen.

Ashley looked at his back as he was walking out. He was so testy this morning, she thought. But lately he was working longer hours and taking on more responsibilities. She could see Marcus standing in the kitchen staring out the glass doors to the patio. At fifty he was even more handsome than he was ten years ago. The gray hair at his temples and down his sideburns gave him a look of distinction. His dark chocolate-colored face was smooth with deep, penetrating eyes. He kept his body trim by working out in the gym at the brokerage office downtown on 5th and Spring streets, where he was employed as vice president of marketing. He was medium height and well dressed. Marcus had broken his arm when he was in college. As a result, he felt the stiffness when the weather was cold and stretched it often for more flexibility. He had a weakness for shoes and bought a pair to match every suit in his closet.

Ashley and Marcus had separate closets. On one side of Marcus's closet was a row of suits and ties of different colors. In Ashley's closet were also suits, but they were all the same style in dark, boring gray, navy blue, brown, dark green, and black. Marcus and Lori bought the brighter colors.

The door shut and Ashley knew Marcus had left. She shook her head, remembering that when they were younger he would kiss her when she awakened and again before he left. She sighed out loud, remembering the times when they had made love in the early mornings and both were late for work. It all seemed so long ago. Maybe she would have the surgery soon. She would like to bring those days back into their marriage again. But she was lucky that Marcus was pleased with their life and never complained.

After Ashley was dressed she grabbed her purse, briefcase, and car keys. She took one last sip of her coffee and hurried out the door. The drive to the large health care insurance company in West Los Angeles took twenty minutes. Ashley managed the strategic-planning department and had been there for eighteen years.

* * *

It was noon, and Ashley knew she couldn't stay at work the entire day. As she sat at her desk she felt cramps in the lower part of her stomach and her back felt as though it had cracked in two. And to make matters worse, she had to keep going to the restroom.

After throwing her reports in her briefcase, she left a voice mail for her secretary, Julie, saying that she was leaving for the rest of the day. As Ashley started to walk out her office, she stopped and decided to call Marcus. He had looked as though he was worried about her before he left for work that morning. She knew that if he called her office and Julie said she left ill, he probably would rush home to see if she was all right. Ashley called but his voice mail was on. She left a message that she was tired and not to worry.

When Ashley got home Marcus's car was parked in the driveway. She knew immediately that he had called her office and wanted to come home and see for himself that she wasn't seriously ill.

Instead of parking in the driveway behind Marcus's car, Ashley parked on the street. He would need to get out, and she didn't feel like coming back out to move her car.

Getting out of her car, Ashley felt a cramp that was increasingly worse than the one before. But the pain was short and Ashley rushed inside the house.

"Marcus," Ashley yelled from the living room.

"I'm in the bedroom, Ash."

As Ashley walked inside the room she saw Marcus rearranging clothes in the large suitcase that was lying open in the middle of their bed. Ashley sat on the edge of the bed and eased out of her black high heel pumps.

"The company is sending you away again, Marcus? You were sent to Florida only a month ago." The disappointment in her voice was obvious.

Not looking up at her, he kept packing. "It's not the

job, Ash." He had loved her for such a long time. But now, things were different. He tried to look into her eyes, but it was too difficult. A few seconds elapsed before anyone spoke.

"If it's not the job, then what is it, Marcus?" She looked baffled.

"Ash—"

"I know," she said, her eyes dancing with excitement. She felt better already and was sorry she had spoiled the surprise by coming home early.

"You have two tickets to Florida or someplace that we can go away together." She hopped off the bed and kissed him on the cheek. Her spirit had heightened in only a matter of seconds. She was elated; they would be alone in some romantic place, just she and her husband.

"So that's what all that talk was about this morning when you said you needed a vacation. Well, I do, too, sweetheart. Honey, I'm so sorry I came home early and spoiled the surprise. When we went to San Francisco you had packed our suitcases by the time I got home from work, just like today." Her eyes were bright; the disappointment she felt only minutes ago was replaced with overflowing joy. "Oh, honey, I'm so happy. I love you so much, Marcus." She kissed him again. "Oh what a lucky woman I am," she said.

Marcus shook his head. This was going to be harder than he had anticipated, much harder on both of them.

He grabbed her free hand and pulled her back down on the bed. "Ashley, listen to me. We are not going anyplace together." He held his head down; held her hand, noticing the new bright fingernail polish she was wearing. Her hand was cold, and her fingers were slender and long.

"Ashley, I'm leaving you . . . we have to end this marriage. I have to go, Ash. It's just not working for me anymore. . . ." He started to continue, but he could feel her body stiffen beside him. First, he noticed there was no change of expression on her face. She looked at him as though she hadn't comprehended anything he had said. But he was sure it was just the calm before the storm.

Ashley closed her eyes, feeling the life draining from her body, leaving her empty, only half-alive. She stared bemused, waiting for him to say more. But he just stared at her. Ashley was sure that she was caught up in some kind of dream, a bad nightmare. Was this really her husband, Marcus? Was he really ending their lives together, all their dreams and plans to stay together for the rest of their lives, through sickness and health, the promises they had made to each other? She turned around to face him a second time.

"Marcus, what are you saying?" She felt confused and now she could feel the anger building. "God, this is real. It is all so real," she whispered to herself.

"Are you crazy, Marcus?" she asked and looked around the room, noticing for the first time that two other suitcases were shut and placed next to the door. There were suits piled at the foot of the bed and his shoes in a tall box against the door next to the suitcases. Why hadn't she noticed them before? There were no clothes on the bed that were hers. They were all Marcus's. He was leaving. God, he was really leaving, and now it hit her like a ton of bricks. The image would be forever seared into her memory.

She couldn't look at him, closed her eyes tightly, trying to remember their conversation earlier that morning. Had there been something she had missed? Was there something different about Marcus? He had, she remembered, looked sad. Now she knew it wasn't because she wasn't feeling well, and it wasn't because he was tired. He was only tired of her.

For the first time she noticed her hand resting on his thigh and pulled it away as though she had touched a hot stove and was severely burnt.

"But why, Marcus? I don't understand. Why?" she pleaded, mortified at the thought of living without him.

"Ash, you're a nice woman, a good mother to our daughter. But I need more. The excitement is gone, Ash, and replaced with emptiness and boredom. Don't you want more for yourself?" he asked.

"No, Marcus, I don't. I had all I ever wanted, to have your child and be a good wife." Her voice had gotten shaky. She cleared her throat, folded her arms in front of her.

"Well, I'm sorry, Ash. But I don't have all I want, anymore." The pain in her face tore at his heart. Marcus hated hurting his wife and felt sick inside. But he couldn't live this way any longer. And as he looked at Ashley he was sorry to admit it, but she had become so predictable, and she didn't do anything to change it. The same hairstyle, the same dull clothes. Even their sex together was always the same position with Marcus on top. No, she hadn't done anything to change herself. To her, everything was fine as it was. As it had been for twenty-five years.

Ashley's hands were trembling uncontrollably, her stomach cramped. "It's another woman, isn't it? Tell me, Marcus. It's another woman. Some tramp you've gone crazy over," she yelled, standing up and stomping her foot. "Tell me, Marcus. Who is she?" she demanded loudly. She was getting hysterical, crying, yelling. "Who in hell is this woman, this tramp you're leaving me for? Someone to wreck our home," she exclaimed. He didn't answer and for a moment she thought of striking him, to make him feel a taste of the pain he had inflicted upon her. He just stood there looking as though he felt sorry for her. He was too composed even in this difficult situation. Right now, she was sure that she hated him. He was always so damn calm and composed.

Marcus looked at her in shock. Her disparaging remarks took him by surprise. In all the years they were married, he had never heard her speak this way. But, he had never hurt her this way either. Ashley was always so soft-spoken, even when she was angry.

"Ashley, there is another woman. But that's not the reason I'm leaving. She only made me realize that I'm not happy enough to stay. Even if we stop seeing each other, I couldn't stay here. I still love you, Ash, but I'm no longer in love with you. We both deserve so much more." He was all out of words. There was nothing more to be said. Marcus stood up again, ready to leave.

"You two-timing bastard. How could you, Marcus? I'm forty-five years old. I have given you the best years of my life. How can you just walk out on twenty-five years of marriage? Twenty-five years I've loved you. You've waited until I got old to leave me."

"I'm older than you are, Ashley. You see, we think too differently. I'm fifty but I don't feel old. I'm at the age where I want to be in love and live the rest of my life happily. We think so differently in so many ways." He shook his head, amazed at how different they really had grown. "We haven't anything in common anymore, Ash. Surely you can see that."

"We don't have anything in common?" she bellowed. "Look around you, Marcus. We have this home, a daughter, and twenty-five years together. What more can we have in common?"

She unbuttoned the top of her blouse. It was too tight, and she felt as though she was choking. But she knew it wasn't the blouse, it was her nerves, and the annoyance she felt building deep inside her, the burning pain in her heart.

"Correction, Ash. We have a mortgage together, a daughter who is now an adult and has her own life to live. What you just said isn't enough for me to remain in a marriage with a woman I'm no longer in love with. Let it go, Ash."

Just hearing those words made her want to die inside. "Okay, Marcus. The onus of breaking up our home now falls on you," Ashley said, and sat back on the bed. She held both hands over her face as though she couldn't look at him any longer. And with shocking clarity, she realized it was over and swallowed the lumps of memory of the years they had shared.

He closed the last suitcase just as it occurred to Ashley that he wouldn't have been home if she had gotten home at her regular time. When he started to the door, Ashley jumped off the bed and grabbed his arm. She was screaming, crying out, flinging her arms, and hurled herself against him.

"You coward, you were going to leave before I got home. You had no idea I was coming home early. How could you, Marcus? Why?"

Marcus grabbed both her wrists. "I was packing to get my clothes out before you got home. But, Ash, I would have come back so I could tell you. I just thought it would have been easier if you didn't watch me pack." He felt as though he wanted to cry for hurting her this way. Nothing had gone as he had planned.

"Make it easier? Make it easier for whom? How can you make it easier? You say you don't love me, and you want to make it easier? I don't know who you are, what you are. I hate you, Marcus Lake. I hate your guts," she hissed between her teeth. But he was still leaving her. God, what could she do to make him stay, to make him understand? She closed her eyes with a silent prayer, asking God to help her, to stop her heart from breaking piece by piece like all her dreams had.

With one last-ditch effort she had to try again. "Marcus, I can forgive you. Everyone makes mistakes. I'll change, do whatever you want. Just change your mind and stay home with me." She laid her head on his shoulder and cried.

Marcus held her close against him. "Please, Ash. You're making it harder than it already is." He pulled her arms from around his neck. "I've got to go now."

Ashley's arms fell by her sides. She didn't know anything else to do or say to make him change his mind. She started to turn her back to him, but instead she slapped him hard across his face.

Marcus hadn't seen it coming and pushed her away. "I'm so sorry, Ash." Angry, he turned away, grabbed the suitcases and strode brusquely out the door. He was back in less than five minutes and grabbed the rest of his clothes.

She followed him to the door. "Go on," she screamed behind him. "Go to her. I never want to see you again, Marcus." She followed him outside as he took out the last box.

Ashley stood on the steps. She wore no shoes, her blouse was hanging from under her blazer. "You'll be sorry for this, Marcus. Do you hear me? You'll be sorry. Go on, go to her and never come back here again," she screamed at the top of her voice, but he ignored her as though he hadn't heard a word she was saying. And he didn't look back.

Ashley rushed back into the house, slamming the door behind her so hard that the windows in the living room vibrated as though they would crack.

She threw herself across the bed and cried when she heard Marcus's car back out the driveway. Twenty-five years had blown away like the wind blows from one place to another and disappeared into thin air as though it had never existed, or was forgotten. She closed her eyes and cried for hours. It had gotten dark before she decided to get up and close all the blinds and turn on the lamp beside her bed.

Ashley tottered through the house as though she was in a daze. She went into the kitchen and got a glass of water and brought it back to her bedroom. She set the glass on the nightstand. Still completely dressed, Ashley crawled in bed between the sheets. She turned off the lamp, closed her eyes, and tossed and turned, cried, until she was drained and finally fell asleep at four in the morning.

Ashley opened her eyes to the sound of footsteps. *Thank God, Marcus was back.* But before she turned over in bed she realized it was only a dream. She felt a cold chill; a hard cramp in the pit of her stomach working its way around her back. Her face was moist with beads of sweat forming on her forehead. The chill had left and was replaced with a warm, strange feeling. She felt dizzy and the room was spinning as she tried to sit up in bed.

She placed both hands against her stomach. She pulled the sheet and comforter down her legs, and cried out when she saw her own blood seeping through her skirt, onto the comforter and light blue sheets. She tried to stand again, but again the dizziness overpowered her. Everything she was wearing was soaked.

Too weak to stand, Ashley fell back on the bed. The pain was insufferable. She tried to reach for the phone, but it wasn't close enough. Finally, with all the strength she could muster, she stood again, blood gushing down her legs. Ashley felt herself slowly collapsing to the floor, and struggled to grab the phone cord to pull the phone closer to her. Her vision had blurred; she could hardly see the numbers clearly as she managed to dial 911.

"Blood, blood is everywhere," she whispered, taking in deep breaths. "I'm bleeding to death." Her voice was barely audible; she had to repeat her name and address twice before she was understood.

Ashley knew she had to get to the door, to open it before the paramedics arrived. She walked slowly, leaving a trail of blood behind her. Unlocking the door, her head reared back, spinning, the house seemed to be moving with her as she crumpled against the wall, and, realizing she was alone, she cried out loud, "Marcus!"

Chapter 2

It was Tuesday morning, and Ashley heard a strange woman's voice. The light was so bright that she could barely open her eyes and kept drifting back into a deep sleep.

"Mrs. Lake, wake up," the nurse purred softly, but it sounded far away.

The sound of the woman's soft voice woke her again, again the light was too bright, and she couldn't open her eyes. She could hear movements around her, footsteps, voices of more than one person. She felt the hands of someone adjusting something on her arm that felt like plastic.

"*Marcus,*" she called out, barely able to lift her tongue in her mouth. Her mouth was so dry that she choked, the words seeming to get stuck in her throat. "Marcus, Marcus," she croaked. She waited for Marcus to answer. Then she remembered: the puddle on the floor that led from her bedroom to the living room, and Marcus, Lord, Marcus had left her. He was gone and she was in the hospital, alone. He wasn't there with her. *Oh God,* she thought. *Why did I wake up?* Her body jerked, and her eyes opened while the memories of his leaving angrily floated back. The yelling, crying. It all came back, hitting her like an oncoming truck.

Ashley shut her eyes tightly as though it would make her forget. After a few moments, she felt herself sinking back into a deep sleep.

* * *

It was Tuesday evening before Ashley opened her eyes again, this time to the sound of her mother, Doris, and Lori's voices. They were sitting in chairs beside the bed waiting for Ashley to wake up. She slept the entire day, and every time she stirred she called Marcus's name. She placed her hands against her stomach where she felt the pain. Without realizing it she was crying, and she felt a tear roll out the corner of her eyes, leaving wet tearstains on the pillow.

"Mom, how are you feeling?" Lori asked. "I called Dad twice today, but he hasn't returned my calls. I don't understand why. It's not like him. And I was sure he would be here."

"He's out of town," Doris said. "What other reason would he not return your calls?" Doris looked at Ashley. "Ashley, he should make his trip short and come home right away. Have you even called him? I don't know what happened between you and Marcus, but he should be home."

Feeling the lump swelling in her throat, Ashley could hardly get the words out. What a bad time to break the news to her daughter, and even a worst time to have a hysterectomy when her husband had left her for a younger woman. She felt old, ill, and unwanted. Ashley laid her hand on her stomach again and reminded herself that she was also fat. Three reasons to make her feel old and unattractive.

"Marcus and I are not living together anymore. And I don't think he's out of town. He knows I don't want him here with me, ever," she said more to herself than to Lori.

Lori stood up so fast she knocked over her chair. As she looked at Ashley the frown deepened across her mother's forehead.

Ashley closed her eyes to give Lori ample time to digest what she had said. She opened her eyes and looked at Lori again. Shock was written all over her face, and Ashley was sorry that there was nothing she could do to soften the blow.

Lori was tall and thin with her father's dark, smooth complexion; slanted, wide-set eyes; and black shoulder-length hair that she had tied back into a ponytail. She walked with her head high, easily swinging her body. She had been married since she was twenty-one, on her parents' twenty-third wedding anniversary. But now, as Ashley looked at her, she looked like a wounded child.

"Mom, why? I don't believe this. You and Dad not living together?" she asked, looking from Doris to Ashley and back at Doris again. "Then where is he living? When did this happen?" She felt as though she wanted to cry, but she couldn't. Lori couldn't believe her parents were no longer together. They had had very few arguments, nothing serious, or so she thought.

"I don't know where he's living, Lori," was all Ashley could say.

"He'll be home in a week or so, Lori," said Doris. "Your mother and father have never lived apart since they were married. I'll bet he'll be home when Ashley gets there."

But Ashley wouldn't give her daughter any false hope. "He'll never be home again, so don't look forward to it." It hurt her to look at Lori's face.

"Ashley, you're not feeling well right now, don't say that," Doris said.

"It's true, Mother. I never want to see Marcus again. So don't say he'll be back in a week, don't say we've been married for twenty-five years, and please don't call his name in my presence." Ashley was getting hysterical, loud, and began coughing uncontrollably, rocking back and forth. The coughing caused pains in her stomach that made her cry out for help, and she grabbed the cord to summon the nurse.

Lori stood in horror as she watched her mother holding her stomach and crying out, strenuously pulling the cord that was hanging over her bed.

Doris helped Ashley sit up in bed as Lori ran to the door for help. The nurse was rushing down the hall and into Ashley's room. She was short, in her mid-sixties with short, salt-and-pepper hair. She grabbed a pillow and placed it against Ashley's stomach. Once Ashley had stopped coughing, the nurse gave her a glass of water.

"When you have to cough, press the pillow against your stomach," the nurse said. "It helps the pain and gives your stomach the support it needs." She smiled warmly. "You'll be better by tomorrow. The day after tomorrow you may go home if you don't have a fever. Now, I'll leave you alone." She adjusted the pillow behind Ashley's back and walked out.

"Mom, I know you don't feel well right now. Why don't we wait another day or two before we talk about Dad again." Lori didn't want to upset Ashley any further. She kissed her mother on the cheek. "Do you want any magazines or anything? I can bring some back."

"No, Lori. I don't need anything. You stay home tonight and come back tomorrow. I need some sleep tonight." She didn't want to talk about Marcus. Ashley just wanted to sleep her life away.

"You too, Mother. Have Dad bring you back tomorrow."

"Okay, sweetheart. Try and get some sleep," Doris said. She didn't want Ashley to be alone, and she was concerned about the breakup with Marcus at a time when Ashley needed him so badly.

Lori and Doris left quietly. Once they were out of the room Lori faced Doris. "Do you really think she'll be all right, Grandma? She looks terrible and she's in so much pain. I've never seen her in so much pain before." Lori stopped at the elevator and looked down the hall where Ashley's room was.

"Come on, Lori. She needs to be alone. And as for the

pain, the nurse will give her pain medication. But for now, she needs to be alone and think rationally." She didn't want Lori to know that she was just as worried about Ashley as she was. And what will Daniel say when he finds out? Doris wondered. How did all this happen?

"I'm sure that in time Marcus will go home."

"What if he doesn't, Grandma?" Lori asked, as they stepped off the elevator.

"He will, Lori. By the end of the week, he'll be home as though nothing had happened."

"But something has happened, Grandma, and I'm not totally convinced if things can be put back together the way they were before." They were quiet as they walked to Lori's car.

"Ash, are you awake?" Vanessa asked, and took a seat in the chair next to the bed.

Ashley opened her eyes. "Yes, I'm awake. What time is it?" she asked, feeling the dryness in her mouth. She reached for the glass of water and Vanessa got it for her.

Vanessa looked at her watch. "It's five-forty. I tried to get here earlier, but I had to stop by a client's house on the way, and as usual the 405 Freeway was slow as hell. Why didn't you call me last night, Ash? I would have come to be with you."

"There wasn't time. And I had no idea another break-through of blood would be so sudden with so much of it. The doctor said the fibroid had grown bigger than a grapefruit. I should have listened to you and had the surgery months ago." She wondered if it would have made a difference in her marriage.

"I was surprised when you phoned and left me the message about Marcus. Have you heard from him?"

"No, and I never want to hear from him again," she said, and started to cry. "I don't know why I'm still crying. It's not helping and it's too late for us now."

"Are you sure it's too late, Ash?"

"Much too late. He's been cheating, Vanessa. I could never go back to him." Ashley looked at Vanessa's face. "You knew, didn't you?"

"No, but I did suspect it. Remember, Ash, I know the signs. After all, I cheated myself. I'm just sorry that it had to happen to you."

"I wish you would have said something to me about it, Vanessa."

"I have never seen Marcus with another woman, and I wasn't going to speculate, because I only suspected and wasn't completely sure of it. You know me better than that." Vanessa looked at Ashley's face. It had gotten thinner since the surgery. She frowned every time she moved, and her eyes were swollen with dark circles under them. Vanessa noticed that Ashley kept wiping her eyes with the tissue she kept balled up in her hand. The tray of food that was sitting by her bed was untouched.

"Ash, I know it's a shock for you, and I don't know what to say except take one day at a time and try to get better. I'm sure you want to get out of here and go home."

Ashley closed her eyes. "Go home to what? There's nothing to go home to, Vanessa. I'll just remember walking in on Marcus when he was packing. I wonder how long had he planned to leave me?" she asked, her voice strained. Her world had shattered and it would be a struggle to get it back on track again.

The doctor walked in, and Vanessa got up and went to stand at the window so he could examine Ashley. When Vanessa stood his eyes lit up, he smiled, and nodded at her. She was wearing a white knit suit that clung to her well-proportioned curves and stopped above her knees, revealing long coltish legs that most women would die for. Her pumps were white and her pearl earrings dangled on her ears.

"Mrs. Lake, we took blood from you, and I'm sorry to

say that right now your body is a walking time bomb, set to explode any day."

Ashley looked perplexed, bemused at whatever he was talking about. "What do you mean?" she asked, and tried to sit up.

"Your cholesterol and blood pressure are too high. And you're overweight. Right now your life is in danger. You could have a heart attack or a stroke at any time. I'm going to put you on medication for both and a diet for your cholesterol. As soon as you are strong enough, I suggest you go to see your physician. I'm so sorry to give you this news when you've only had surgery last night," he said. As he looked at her face, he wondered if she understood the seriousness of her condition. Somehow, she looked as if she didn't really care. She looked stony-faced, until she heard the doctor's voice again.

"Do you understand what I'm saying, Mrs. Lake?"

Again, the tears were rolling down her cheeks. Ashley felt as though her life was over. She was old, ill, and without a husband. What more could go wrong in her life? "Yes, doctor, I understand what you are saying. How soon should I start my diet?"

"I've already spoken with the nurse. You'll start right away. Exercise, take long walks, and watch what you eat. But do it soon, Mrs. Lake," he said firmly.

She nodded as the doctor walked out.

"Did he say it looks all right, Ash?" Vanessa took her seat next to the bed again.

"Yes, sure. It looks good. My blood pressure and cholesterol are both too high. I should have gone for regular checkups. I've got to change my eating habits and go on medication." Ashley forced a smile as she looked at Vanessa. "And I saw the way he looked at you."

"The best thing you can do for yourself is to get well. You still have a whole life ahead of you. You're only forty-five years old. Honey, you'll lose weight, look good, and feel much better about yourself. Take what the doctor said seriously, Ash. High blood pressure isn't anything to play with."

"Yes, but I feel much older." She sighed and closed her eyes again. When she opened them she had to wipe away another tear. "If only I had known Marcus didn't love me anymore. He said the excitement was gone out of our marriage, and we haven't anything in common anymore. He even said that he's not in love with me anymore, Vanessa. I could have died when the words came out his mouth." She shook her head. "You know what was crazy? They weren't cruel words, but they were so damaging. If Marcus ever wanted to come back, there's no way I could ever forget the words he said to me. I hope he knows what he's done. It's really all over now."

"I know, love. But you have to keep going. When you are stronger you can go back to work. That should help a little. And if you want to go to a movie or just come over so we can talk, I'll be there for you. God knows you were there for me and you never judged me, Ash. I appreciate that."

"Every day I go home from work, cook dinner for me and Marcus, take a shower, and read a good book or watch TV and go to bed. Now what do I do in the evenings when I get home?"

"Any damn thing you want to do. Ash, you don't have to cook unless you want to or even make your bed up. You just do whatever you want." Vanessa hugged Ashley. "Now, eat your food and get some sleep. I'm leaving so you can rest. But I'll be back again tomorrow."

Chapter 3

It was Wednesday morning, and Ashley had just finished dressing when her mother and father stepped out the elevator at Daniel Freeman Hospital in the Marina.

Beside her bed, her overnight bag was packed with her gown and bathrobe that Lori had brought to her the morning after her surgery.

Daniel walked in first, and Ashley looked up at the brown hat he was wearing. Daniel never left the house without a cap or hat on his head. Ashley smiled as she noticed the brown shirt, the same color brown as his chocolate brown hat. His hats had to be the same color as his clothing. Daniel was a large man, over 6'2", thickly built, well over two hundred pounds. Doris's head barely touched his shoulders. His skin was dark, and his hair was thinning.

"You're all ready to go home, Ash?" Daniel asked as he looked at his daughter. She looked ill, her eyes were weak, and she moved slowly. If he saw Marcus he would place both hands around his neck. Marcus had hurt his daughter. If only he could see the bastard now, he would make him feel the pain that he had inflicted on Ash.

He stood in front of the bed looking at his daughter. "Your mother was out of bed at five-thirty this morning to make sure your room was ready, not that she has changed anything in there since you left."

Ashley sat on the edge of the bed without moving. "I had planned to go home, Dad. Everything I need is at my house. My mail, lots of food in the refrigerator that was left over from the party." She stopped talking, wondering if Marcus had been home for anything he had left behind.

Doris walked into the room. "I can stay at your house with you, Ash, if it's more comfortable for you. It's no trouble at all for me."

"You really don't mind, Mom?"

"Of course she doesn't mind," Daniel answered.

Ashley didn't acknowledge Daniel's answer. He always made decisions for her mother without consulting her, answering every question as though she couldn't answer for herself.

"Of course not," Doris answered, picking up the three magazines that Vanessa had bought.

"Good. Dad, you can take some food home. I have lots of ham left over."

Daniel put both hands up in front of him. "No, my doctor says my blood pressure is a little on the high side. I'm staying away from pork. Just fish and chicken for me."

The nurse came in with the wheelchair and wheeled Ashley to the lobby while Daniel went out to park the car at the entrance. Doris walked in back of Ashley, carrying her overnight bag.

"Be sure to follow the doctor's instructions, Mrs. Lake. You don't want to end up back here."

"No, I don't want to end up back here. But thanks for your help."

Ashley watched the nurse as she walked away, her back straight, taking long strides back inside the hospital lobby.

"She was nice," Ashley complimented.

"She sure didn't seem so nice to me. As a matter of fact, she seemed pretty cold," Doris said, and looked toward the lobby where the nurse had disappeared.

Daniel helped Ashley into the front seat of the car.

Doris sat in the back seat. "Are you all right, Ash?"

Doris asked. "And Daniel, don't drive too fast," she warned her husband.

"Mother, I'm fine. And please don't worry about Dad's driving." She sighed, in a hurry to get home. Even though there was no one home waiting for her, she wanted to go to her bedroom where she could be comfortable. And she had so many things on her mind: the surgery, her high blood pressure, her cholesterol levels, and what would she do with the rest of her life, and so on and so on. She frowned as she thought of being home, unable to do much of anything for herself, thinking of Marcus and what they used to have together, how they lost it all.

Daniel unlocked the door and held it open for Doris and Ashley to go inside. Doris held Ashley's hand to help her inside the house.

She picked up Ashley's mail off the floor and opened the blinds and windows in the living room.

"Sit down, Ashley, and rest," Doris said.

Ashley looked around the living room. "You did a great job cleaning up the mess I made, Mother. I'm sorry you had to see it."

"Don't be sorry, Ash. I didn't want you to have to come home to it, baby. Lori and I came over yesterday. Daniel, I'll make lunch. There's got to be more than ham here."

Daniel nodded and took a seat on the sofa, placing his hat on the coffee table in front of him.

"Look in the refrigerator and find him something. There should be some sliced turkey in there, too." Ashley went into her bedroom and dropped the mail on her bed. She flopped down and held her hands to her face, closed her eyes, feeling the quietness, the loneliness in her room that she had shared with Marcus. As she looked around the room, it seemed cold and empty, no love or warmth in the air. Everything about her bedroom profoundly depressed her. She wanted to get up and scream. If Marcus were still home, he would be doing everything to make her comfortable. But he wasn't home, and sooner or later she had to get used to it.

The phone rang and Ashley jumped. She heard her mother answer from the living room.

Doris rushed to Ashley's room. "Ash, it's Marcus. He wants to speak to you." Her eyes were dancing with excitement. She knew Marcus would come home again.

Ashley nodded and waved her hand. "Tell him I'm all right, Mother. I haven't anything to say to him."

"Ashley," Doris said, taking on an edge to her voice. "It's your husband and he's worried about you. Why don't you just see what he has to say?"

"Mother, please tell him I don't want to talk to him." Ashley held her head down. Her heart was breaking in two. If she talked to Marcus, she would only cry on the phone. No, she wouldn't let him hear her cry.

"Ashley!"

"Leave the girl alone, Doris. She says she doesn't want to speak to Marcus. Although I should tell him a thing or two, the son-of-a . . ." Daniel's deep voice resonated through the room. But he stopped when he saw his daughter's teary eyes. Doris and Ashley jumped at the sound of his boisterous voice.

Ashley looked at Doris as she rushed back out the room. Why didn't her mother believe her when she says it's over between her and Marcus?

Doris came back into Ashley's room. "Well, I told him," she said, and sat next to Ashley. "He said if you need anything to call him."

"Yeah, right. Like I would really call him. Marcus Lake is the last person in this world I would call for help, Mother."

"Don't say that, Ash," Doris said in a low voice that her husband couldn't hear.

"Why not? I mean it. Without opening the mail, she picked it up off the bed and placed it on the nightstand, and lay across her bed. "You can sleep in Lori's room. I'm tired and need to lay down for a while." She just wanted to be alone, to try and make some sense out of her life.

Daniel had finished his turkey sandwich and leftover potato salad. "Do you ladies need me to go to the store for anything, Doris, Ash?"

"No, Dad. I got everything I need."

"Okay, I'll check with you ladies later. I think I'll finish painting the gate in the backyard today." He bent over and kissed Ashley on her cheek. Doris walked him to the door.

"You can come back for dinner since we're only fifteen minutes away, Daniel."

"Ash is hurting, Doris. I can see it in her eyes. Even as a child she's never been able to hide her feelings from me. I'll eat at home. Just can't stand to see my daughter hurting. And see that she eats, Doris," he ordered.

The phone rang again, and this time it was Lori. "Mom, I'll leave work an hour early and stop by to see you."

"Okay. I'll be here. I don't think that I will be going out shopping today," Ashley said and smiled.

Ashley took two sleeping pills and fell into a deep sleep. She was dreaming and woke slowly as she snuggled against her pillow. She opened her eyes and burst into tears as reality jerked her wide awake, making her remember that she was alone. Marcus would never sleep with her again. She had been in bed for two hours when she heard Lori's voice in the living room with Doris.

Together, Lori and Doris walked into the bedroom. Doris had a cup of tea for Ashley.

Ashley sat up in bed. "How long did I sleep, Mother?"

She pushed her hair from her face and lay her head back against the headboard.

"Two hours. While you were asleep I read one of those magazines you brought home from the hospital."

"How are you feeling, Mom?" Lori asked, adjusting the pillow in back of Ashley.

"I'm glad to be home. It's still a little hard to move around, though."

"I can stay as long as you need me, Ash." Doris pulled a chair near the bed while Lori pulled the other chair from the corner of the room.

"What smells so good, Mother?" Ashley asked. She sniffed, trying to guess what her mother was baking.

"Bread pudding?" Lori asked.

"You're right. It is bread pudding," Doris said and laughed as her granddaughter wiggled her nose and sniffed. She wiped her hands on the yellow-flowered apron tied around her waist.

The phone rang and Doris walked out the room to answer.

"I'm angry with Dad. I don't know if I want to go around him anymore," Lori pouted.

Ashley took a sip of her tea, and with her free hand she touched Lori's hand. "I don't want you angry at your Dad, Lori. What has happened between us hasn't anything to do with you."

"Yes, it does, Mom. He's breaking up our family. How can you say that?"

"I can say it because he's been a good father and he loves you. Your father doesn't love anyone in this world the way he does you. He probably waited until you were an adult before he made this decision. This is between Marcus and me. Stay out of it, Lori."

Lori sat up straight on the bed. "How can you blather about how good he is after what he's done to you?"

"Because he did it to me, not to you. He wants to live happily the rest of his life. You can't fault him for that.

As for me, I can take care of myself. And as for you, well, you stay out of it. Hear his side of the story. I'm not defending him and I'll never forgive him. But, he is still your father."

"You really mean that, don't you? What if I think he's wrong for leaving?"

"Yes, I really mean it. If you think he's wrong for leaving, then, that's your opinion, and mine, too. But don't let it ruin what you and your dad have together. Too many kids wish they had a dad as good as the one you have. Too many kids never see their dads; some dads left when they were still too young and never came back. Yours waited until you became an adult."

"What are you two talking about in here?" Doris asked. "I was talking to Cora on the phone."

"Oh, how is she?" Ashley asked.

"She's okay. She called to see if you were all right." Doris sat back in her chair and looked at Ashley and Lori's faces. Must have been talking about Marcus, she supposed. What else could make the two look so miserable?

Chapter 4

Drinking two cups of coffee in an hour was unusual for Marcus Lake. One cup every morning was all he needed. But this morning he had asked his daughter to stop by his office on her way to work. It was Lori's first year as a court reporter, and the courthouse was only a few blocks from Marcus's office.

Marcus was sitting at his desk, tapping an ink pen against his coffee cup. Going over the conversation in his head that he had with Lori the night before, she sounded angry that he had left Ashley. At first she was remote, had nothing to say except to answer whatever questions he asked her. She'd made it clear that she had nothing to say to him. But Marcus tried to explain that his separation from Ashley has nothing to do with her. After all, she's an adult with her own life to live. But Marcus realized he had to handle the situation with Lori delicately. He didn't want to lose his daughter's love or the closeness they shared. He loved Lori and had to convince her that he always would—even if he loved another woman.

"Dad?" Lori stuck her head inside the door.

"Come in, baby." Marcus got up and came around to the chair next to her in front of his desk. "You look like a real businesswoman in your smart green suit." Where has the time gone? he wondered to himself, as he looked at his daughter, now a young, married woman. He noticed that she had started to resemble Ashley with her smooth skin and high cheekbones. She reminded him of Ashley when she was younger.

"How's Ash feeling?"

Lori looked at him as though she couldn't believe what he had asked. How did he think she was feeling? "What do you mean, Dad?"

Marcus crossed his leg. He could feel the strain between them. "I mean with the surgery. Does she need anything at all?"

"No. Grandma is there with her if she does. And I'll be stopping by in the evenings."

"Good girl. Now, I know you only have a few minutes, but I wanted to tell you how sorry I am for what happened between me and your mother."

"I'm listening," Lori snapped, and crossed her arms in front of her.

"When you are young and get married, you're in love. But sometimes it doesn't last and it takes a real effort to keep it together. With some couples, one outgrows the other one, and in some cases they grow apart and no longer have anything in common. And when the children leave home, there isn't anything left. Lori, that is what happened to your mother and me. It's no one's fault. It just happened. I'm sorry about that."

"Why can't you and Mom patch things up and start over again? People do it all the time. Don't you still love her, Dad?"

"Yes, but not the way I should to stay married to her. Don't misunderstand me, honey. Your mother is a terrific woman and mother. But, Lori, it's too late for us." He looked at Lori, waiting for her response.

Feeling sick to her stomach, Lori's eyes started to water. "You don't want to try, do you, Dad?"

"I've tried, Lori. It just doesn't work anymore." He got up and closed the blinds to prevent the sun from shining in their faces.

"So what about us? If you get married again, what if I

don't like your new wife or she doesn't like me? I'm so damn angry at you—"

Marcus put his hand up to stop her. She was questioning him like a child. "Wait a minute, young lady. You don't have anything to be angry about. You and Keith are married and have a life of your own. You are happy, so why is it so hard to understand that I need the same thing? I can honestly say I've been a good father and husband. I gave you and your mother everything you wanted. Our relationship doesn't have to change, Lori. You will always come first in my life and in your mother's life."

She listened to him and he was right about one thing: he was always a good father to her and a good husband to Ashley. But now everything was so different. She just didn't know how to handle this. It had never occurred to her that her parents would get a divorce. And she sounded like a child, she knew, but she was hurting. Why couldn't they understand this has everything to do with her? They are her parents.

"What if your new wife doesn't like me?"

"You sound as though I'm getting married tomorrow. Your mother and I haven't filed for a divorce yet. Nobody's talking marriage but you, Lori." He took her in his arms and held her close.

Lori wanted to cry, but she had to show her father that she was no longer a child. And she loved both parents. "Okay, Dad. I guess somehow I will have to get used to not seeing you and Mom together. But right now it's just too new, and it happened so suddenly. The fact that you left her for another woman disturbs me. No matter what you say to make it sound better, well, it's just the facts. You left my mother for another woman." She turned her head stubbornly and faced the window.

Marcus placed his finger under Lori's chin so she could face him again. He kissed her on the forehead. "I'm so sorry, baby. I know it hurts because it hurts me, too. You must know I hate myself for hurting your mother." He was smart enough not to introduce another woman to his daughter right now. Like she said, it was still too soon, which was why he was moving into his own apartment. If Lori happens to drop by and he has company, he was sure she could deal with that. After all, he was human, and it's not like he was moving in with his new love or marrying her in the next six months. He had planned to wait a year before he marries again. He felt that he owed that much to Lori. Maybe it would soften the blow so that she would continue to come around him.

Lori looked at her watch and grabbed her purse. "Got to go, Dad. Maybe one day next week we can have dinner together. Keith won't be working overtime. The three of us can go out together." She got up and picked up her purse off his desk. She wasn't pleased at all with the way he talked. He had made it clear that the marriage was over. And to think that he didn't love her mother anymore thoroughly disgusted her, and he showed no remorse.

Marcus walked Lori to the door. "Please try and understand, honey. And if your mother needs anything, call me. It will be our secret. But I need to know, Lori." He kissed her on the cheek.

"Oh, all right, Dad. I'll let you know."

"Promise?"

"Yes, I promise. But Mom wouldn't be too happy if I call you because of her."

Marcus watched Lori as she walked out the door. Looking at her as they talked, he knew that she was disappointed with him. He had to find some way to make it up to his daughter. They had always been so close and could talk about anything together. He sighed and went back to his desk.

"Mother, relax and stop fussing over me. I'll take it easy, I promise," Ashley said. "You've cooked enough already, and what about all the food in the freezer?" Ashley was sitting in the den and Doris had just fixed her lunch.

"But, Ash. You only came home yesterday. I should stay at least a week with you. Besides, Daniel will have a fit if I leave you so soon." Doris sat at the table and watched Ashley as she played with her soup. She had been home since the day before and still hadn't eaten anything except a slice of cake, coffee, tea, and half a bowl of hot cereal.

"You know, if you just eat one meal I'll feel better. I'm just afraid when I leave you won't eat anything and make yourself sick." Doris didn't know what else she could say to convince Ashley to eat. "You're hardheaded just like Daniel. Can't tell either one of you nothing for your own good." Doris got up and watered the plant on the kitchen counter.

"Mother, now you're getting upset, and for nothing." Ashley placed the spoon in the bowl and set it aside. It was a hot day and every bone in her body ached, which made it impossible to get comfortable. She just wanted to be left alone and have time to herself to think about what she would do with the rest of her life, what she would do next. When she was married she had never given it a second thought. First mistake, she thought. Second was placing her life in Marcus's hands and doing everything to please him. Had she ever just sat and thought about what she wanted? No, of course not. Everything was to make Marcus happy.

"Okay, Mother. Stay another night. But, tomorrow night I will stay alone. Believe me, if I need you again, I'll call you. You and Dad can come over and check on me every day until I get stronger. Now, sit down and eat some lunch yourself. You've been fussing around here all morning."

The phone rang; it was next to Ashley and she answered. She was glad to hear her daughter's voice. "Hi, I was just telling Mother that after tomorrow I can take care of myself."

"I went to see Dad today."

Ashley's throat went dry and she swallowed hard. "Oh, how did it go?"

"It went okay. I guess I'll have to get used to it unless you two get back together. And you both seem to have made up your minds." Lori wanted to cry, but she couldn't while her mother was on the phone. And last night Keith was shocked by the news, too. Her parents had kept their unhappiness well hidden from everyone. But as she thought of it, her mother never seemed unhappy.

"We won't be going back together, Lori. I don't want to give you any false hope. I'm sorry, honey, but your dad and I have our lives to live now, and separately."

"I know, Mom. I was just hoping. I better get back to the judge's chambers."

Doris watched Ashley as she hung up the phone. She looked as though she was lost, hurting deeply inside, and there wasn't anything she could do to ease the pain.

Doris and Ashley went back to the den where Ashley could relax on the sofa.

"You know, Ash, couples break up all the time and get back together again. Marcus will be back. This is his home. He's not used to staying away."

Ashley looked at her mother in disbelief and shook her head. Doris was always so afraid of making decisions of her own, and admitting that sometimes, life doesn't always end up good for everyone. Sometimes you have to take a stand and go your own way, face what's in front of you. Poor Mother, Ashley, thought. She was so weak, so servile.

"Mother, stop thinking of Marcus and me getting back together. Don't you think if there was any chance of it I would have taken his phone calls, or I would be calling him? It's over for us. Marcus said he doesn't love me anymore. He's in love with someone else. I can never take him back. I don't even want to get into this conversation with you again. It's over and done with," she said, her voice getting louder as she explained it.

"But Ash, you need to talk about it. Somebody has to talk some sense into your head. Marcus is your husband—"

Ashley turned around fast and faced her mother. "Mother, please, please listen to me. Marcus and I will never get together again. You're giving me a headache talking about him," she said in a rush of words. She was getting upset and before she realized it, she got up too fast and placed her hand over her stomach as it seem to knot into a pain that made her groan.

"Ashley, I'm sorry if I upset you."

"It's okay, Mother. Just please don't speak of this anymore. I have all I can handle." She threw both hands up in the air. "I think I should lay down for a while." She went into her bedroom and closed the door behind her.

Ashley stayed in her room the rest of the day, pretending to be asleep. Daniel came over for a while and left. At eight that night, Ashley took two pain pills and went back to bed, praying she would sleep through the night.

The next morning, Ashley could smell the coffee from the kitchen. She got up, brushed her teeth, and washed her face. She looked at herself in the mirror and sighed. Another day, she thought.

Ashley went to the kitchen. Doris had set the table and was filling her bowl with oatmeal and two slices of wheat toast on the side.

"I thought you would be hungry. You went to bed last night without eating anything."

"Thanks, Mother. I am a little hungry this morning. Guess what?"

"What, Ashley?" she asked, as she looked at Ashley's face, seeing her daughter smile for the first time since her surgery.

"I got on the scale and I've lost thirteen pounds. Does my face look slimmer?"

"Yes. And it looks good. I noticed it yesterday." Doris got up and got a bowl of oatmeal for herself.

"Ten more pounds and I'll be the size I want. I intend to stay at least twenty-five pounds lighter. Like I was when I first got married," she said, trying to keep her voice as placid as possible. "And I have to watch my blood pressure and cholesterol. I'm older now."

"Just don't make yourself sick, Ashley. Eat some food but less fatty foods. That's what I keep telling Daniel. His eating habits are improving."

"Oh, I will. I should have done this sooner, Mother." She had let herself go too long and was sure that Marcus had seen it, too. He hadn't looked at her or complimented her the way he used to. But she had been sure that their marriage was only experiencing a dry spell; after all, they had been married for a long time. Sad, she hadn't thought of it in time. What a blind fool she was.

"Mother, I love having you here, but you can go anytime now. I feel better today."

"I'll wait until the afternoon so you will be sure that you are all right, Ashley."

After breakfast, Doris cleaned the kitchen and washed a load of clothes, put fresh towels in Ashley's bathroom, and made lunch. At three Daniel came over to take her home. Ashley promised that she would call for Doris to come back if she needed her. But for now, she needed to be alone.

Chapter 5

It had been five weeks since Ashley's surgery and she was getting around better. For the last four weeks Doris and Daniel came over during the day, and Lori stopped by to see her on her way home from work. But this week she had told them she could do for herself.

Ashley stood in front of the long mirror in her bedroom and admired her new body. Her stomach was still a little swollen from the surgery, but she had lost five more pounds and proud of it. She wished she had lost weight sooner. Maybe Marcus wouldn't have left her. She stayed inside day and night, which gave her more time to think of Marcus and wonder what he was doing. Did he ever think of her, did he feel guilty for leaving? An hour didn't pass without her thinking of him. And every time she did, she cried and wondered what would she do with the rest of her life.

Vanessa and Gary had gone on vacation for two weeks, so she didn't have anyone she could talk to. But they returned last night, and Ashley was waiting for Vanessa to come over today. She sat back in the chair and smiled to herself. When Marcus was home, this was his chair. He would sit in it and watch TV or read the newspaper. Sometimes he would lay his head back with the newspaper folded across his lap and nod. Everything, every sound, every smell reminded her of Marcus.

The doorbell rang and Ashley was glad. Vanessa understood what she was going through. They knew so much about each other and felt the freedom to be honest and open with their opinions.

"Hi, girl, come on in. I was sitting in the den waiting for you." Ashley led Vanessa to the den. How was your vacation?"

"Fun. We ate, stayed up late at night, and were going from one place to another all day. Now, how are you feeling, Ash? You look good."

"I'm finally getting around. I have some apple juice, or want some Coke? My dad bought a case, so it will last forever."

"Apple juice. Here, I brought something back for you. There are so many places you can shop in New York."

Ashley opened the bag and pulled out a beautiful gold purse. "Oh, how pretty. You remembered that I needed a gold bag to match my shoes. Thank you, Vanessa."

"Yes, I remembered. And Ash, how much weight have you lost? You look seven years younger in the face and well rested."

Ashley turned around and held her dress tighter to her body. "What do you think now?" she asked with pride.

"You look so good, girl. Too bad most people can't get ill and look better. How much have you lost?"

"Nineteen pounds, to be exact. I weighed myself this morning. Wait, let me get the apple juice."

She could talk to Vanessa from the kitchen. "I still want to lose about eight more pounds. When I can get into a size eight, I'll feel better. I want to be a new person, Vanessa, a better person. I even want to look different." She looked at Vanessa. The woman was always so glamorous—shoes, lipstick, everything had to match. Her nails and hair were perfectly in place. She looked as though she had just stepped off the front cover of a fashion magazine.

"No one is going to know you when you go back to work, Ash."

Ashley got up again and turned off the TV. She had

been listening to the news and was tired of hearing the same thing on each channel.

"I'm not sure if I'm going back to my job, Vanessa. Ever since I got home from the hospital, I've wondered what I'm going to do with the rest of my life. When we were going to school together, you took interior decorating and did something good with it. I took up dress designing and was good at it. But you were smart. You finished school and went right into it. Unfortunately, I listened to Marcus and went to work in an office. I guess he didn't think I was clever enough to run a business of my own. Remember when I was in the hospital and you told me that I can do whatever I wanted to?"

"Yes, I remember," Vanessa answered, and sipped her juice.

"Now I will do it, Vanessa. All I've had time to do is think and it's what I want."

Vanessa watched Ashley as she held her head high with an air of confidence that she hadn't seen in her in a long time. "It's about time, Ash. I say do it," Vanessa said, placing her glass on the coffee table in front of her. "Life's too short to satisfy everyone else and not yourself."

"I can put most of my retirement in the bank and use some to start my own business. I'm looking forward to it, Vanessa, at last."

Vanessa jumped off the sofa and kissed Ashley on the cheek. "I'm so proud of you, Ash."

"Well, wait. I haven't done it yet." The phone rang and Ashley got up to answer it. "Ever since I've been home from the hospital, everyone is calling to see if I'm all right."

From where Vanessa was sitting, she could see the kitchen and dinning area. Vanessa looked at the table on the right side of the sofa and noticed Ashley and Marcus's wedding picture was missing and replaced with her daughter's wedding picture. The two pictures used to be side by side, but now there was only one. There didn't seem to be any other changes in the den, except Vanessa very seldom saw Ashley sitting in Marcus's brown leather chair. Vanessa smiled to herself as she remembered when Ashley and Marcus had gone shopping and bought the chair. They used to race like two young children to see who would get to it first. She had still been married to Larry then, and the four of them did so many funny things. She slipped her shoes off, feeling the plush gray carpet under her feet.

"That was a friend of mine from work. As I was saying, I've had time to sit around and think a lot about starting a business of my own."

Looking into Ashley's eyes, Vanessa could see that she hadn't been getting enough sleep. Her eyes were puffy, and even though she was excited about starting a business, it didn't change the sadness in her eyes. She looked tired.

"Ash, it's fine to lose weight, but are you eating well?" she asked with concern.

Ashley sighed. "Sometimes. And sometimes it's hard to get food past the lump in my throat. Sometimes I think my life has rushed past me while I was still sleeping. You wake up one morning and you're older and all the good years are gone. My whole life has changed. Too bad I didn't wake up sooner. But I'm awake now and I know what I have to do."

"Not many of us wake up in time, Ash. I know Larry didn't."

"You're the only person I can talk to, the only person that understands, Vanessa. Lori thinks I can just push a button and her father will come back to me. And my mother, well, that's a different story altogether." Ashley picked up a napkin off the coffee table and dabbed at her eyes.

"My mother thinks my life should stand still until Marcus comes back. She doesn't understand that I have my pride, too. The truth is, I can't take him back, and to be realistic, he has no intentions of ever coming back, I am sure of that. I know him, Vanessa. All I want at this point is to get a good night's sleep and stop thinking of him every minute of the day. I want to forget him."

"Well, honey, I'm afraid you won't forget, but you won't hurt as much as time goes by. Right now it's a shock to you, your mother, and Lori. It just takes time to heal and go forward. Starting your business is a good start, Ash. You'll have so much to do that you won't think of him as much."

"Have you had lunch?" Ashley asked.

"No, have you?"

"No, but I can make a couple of sandwiches." Ashley stood up with her glass in her hand.

"No, no, Ash," Vanessa said, and raised her hands. "You sit down and I'll make the sandwiches. I know where everything is." She walked to the kitchen in her bare feet.

Ashley sat back in the chair and watched. The kitchen was one step down into the den. They could still see each other and continue their conversation.

"In three months I'm going to an award dinner with Gary. Maybe you could make my dress, Ash. Do you think you'll be set up and ready to go by then?"

"Sure. All I need is a sewing machine. My old one doesn't work and I gave it away."

"I have all afternoon to hear your plans. You've got me excited now, Ash. I'm so happy you are doing something to make yourself happy. Remember Gary's friend, Thomas?"

"Yes, I remember him. But it's been at least a couple of years since I've seen him."

"Well, he died. Fifty years old and died of a massive heart attack. I say enjoy life while you can. You never know when it will be your turn."

"You got that right," Ashley answered.

Vanessa and Ashley laughed and talked until three-thirty that afternoon. After Vanessa put the dishes in the dishwasher, she left.

In the backyard, Ashley could see her roses blooming and hear the birds singing. It was a beautiful summer day. She had to fight the urge to jump in her car and drive to the beach. She lay her head back, feeling herself falling into a deep sleep as she thought of her future plans; but before she was completely asleep the last thing she thought of was Marcus.

Chapter 6

Seven weeks had passed, and the doctor had told Ashley that she could go back to work. But she had already mailed a certified letter of resignation to the company.

Today, Ashley was going shopping for a power sewing machine. The doctor was in Santa Monica, and as she drove down Lincoln Boulevard she spotted a Singer sewing machine company on Venice and Lincoln Boulevard. Ashley pulled into the parking lot. The sun was hot and the back of her sundress was cut low. She could feel the heat against her skin.

As Ashley walked into the store, the saleslady greeted her with a warm smile.

"Can I help you, miss?" she said, folding some material and placing it on the stack on the table. Her bleached blond hair was piled high on top of her head, and her thick, black-framed eyeglasses were resting on her nose.

"I'm looking for a power sewing machine. What about the one over there?" Ashley pointed and the woman led her to it.

"This is a good one, one of the best we have. It runs real fast, if that's what you want."

"That's exactly what I'm looking for." Ashley opened the walnut cabinet and looked inside.

"Let me set it up so you can see how well it works. Yes, it's a real nice piece, miss." The woman turned it on. "Here, try sewing on this thick piece of material and see how fast and smooth it goes," she said convincingly, trying to make her first sale of the day.

Ashley tried it and grinned. "You just made a sale, Miss Schwab," Ashley said, as she looked at the name tag the woman was wearing. "Do you deliver?"

"Yes, we sure do. What about Saturday morning?"

"Saturday morning is fine with me." Ashley paid for it with her Visa. She had taken her first step of going into business for herself, she thought, with a spring in her step. Ashley smiled to herself as she walked to her car. She stopped when she realized that she was actually smiling and not crying. She started to go home but instead she got on the Marina Freeway and made a left turn, exiting on Slauson Boulevard. She decided to pay Vanessa a visit. Ashley adjusted her sunglasses and turned the air conditioner on high. Ten minutes later she was parking in front of Yee's Chinese restaurant and ordered lunch to go.

"Hey," Ashley called out as she peered through the door.

"Come on in. I just called your house and here you are. What's in the bags?"

"Fried rice, garlic chicken, and egg rolls. I'm starving." Ashley went into the small kitchen and took paper plates and plastic folks out of the cabinet. She knew where everything was kept.

"The doctor said that I can go back to work and do everything I was doing before the surgery. And when I left his office I stopped by Singer's and bought me a power sewing machine," she said, walking back to the long table where Vanessa was looking through a thick book of sample materials.

"That's good, Ash. I'm glad you are getting started. And you look good, too." Vanessa looked at Ashley's loose-fitting dress, with her hair pinned up on top her head. She wore no makeup, not even lipstick. But she did look rested and relaxed.

"Come on so we can eat." They went back into the kitchen, and Vanessa took two Diet Pepsi's out of the refrigerator, flipped on the answering machine, and took a seat at the table.

"That's a cute pantsuit you're wearing, Vanessa. None of my clothes fit me anymore, and my hair, I don't know what to do with it. But I'm lucky I can sew. Can you imagine if I buy more clothes to fit me? It'll cost me an arm and leg."

Vanessa was glad that Ashley brought up the subject of the outdated hairstyle she wore. "Do you have to go straight home now, Ash?"

"No, not really. When I go home all I'll do is watch TV and walk around the house, trying to think of ways to make it look as though Marcus had never lived there. But, of course, that's impossible. He has lived there too long. Even though I've packed away what belongs to him, his presence is still lingering in the air."

"Okay. So when we finish eating I'll call Charlie, my hairdresser. He will do wonders with your hair, Ash. New hairstyle, new clothes, and you'll make all heads turn."

"You really think so?" Ashley pushed the top of her hair from her face. "Do you think he can do it today? I need something to make me feel alive again. Lately, I just want to look different so I can like myself again."

"Oh, Ash," Vanessa said sympathetically. "We'll find out. Bringing lunch was a good idea."

They finished eating and Ashley helped Vanessa clear the table.

"I'll call Charlie now." Vanessa went back to the front room and was still talking when Ashley walked in.

Vanessa hung up. "Charlie says for us to come in now. He just finished with his last client. Now, his name is Charles, but he calls himself Charlie. He's real good, you'll like him."

"Charles, Charlie, whatever. Let me get my purse so we can go. I need all the help I can get." Ashley stopped and looked at herself in the long mirror that hung on the door to the supply room and frowned. Vanessa was so fashionable. And she looked like an old maid.

"Yes, look now because baby, you're going to be beautiful. The next thing we have to do is go shopping. That damn dress is too big, too long, and the color is dull as hell, Ash."

"Oh, no. I can't buy any new clothes until I lose at least seven or eight more pounds," she said, still facing the mirror.

"Seven, eight? What's the difference. Why, Ash?"

"Because by then, I will be able to get into a size eight. Because for years, I've been old and boring. Can you believe I'm going from a twelve to an eight? Half from the surgery and the diet the doctor put me on and the other half from depression, thanks to Marcus Lake. I tried on one of my old size-eight dresses and it's just a little too tight."

"I think it's pretty magnificent. You're going to be irresistible, honey. That beautiful face of yours is going to get some lucky man's attention and one that will deserve it, too." Vanessa stood beside Ashley. Her skin was clear, smooth, the color of caramel candy, her eyes slanted. She was a beautiful woman and didn't know it, yet. What a pity, Vanessa thought. She looked at Ashley's eyes and saw such sadness, such earnestness that Vanessa had to hold her breath to prevent herself from crying.

"I'll bet Marcus's girlfriend is a small woman. But it's what it is, and I was about twenty-five pounds too late."

Vanessa went to her desk and pulled out her purse and car keys. "Too late for your marriage but not too late for a happy and loving life, Ash. Now, let's get out of here. Charlie is waiting."

* * *

"Hi, Charlie. This is Ashley," Vanessa said, looking around the shop. Three of the beauticians were working, and four women were sitting under hair dryers, two were lying back in chairs getting their hair shampooed.

Charlie was a small man with a small waist and close-cut brown hair. He had light skin with freckles across his nose. He was wearing a pair of tight-fitting jeans and a blue T-shirt with torn-off sleeves. He was friendly, always had everyone laughing in the shop. Whatever he had on his mind, Charlie had no problem saying it. Charlie loved talking about his wife and two daughters.

Charlie stood in front of Ashley. "Do you always wear those glasses?" he asked in a playful tone.

Vanessa coughed and took a quick glance at Ashley. She knew by the expression on her face that she was appalled by the insult. But she had warned her that Charlie was very straightforward.

Charlie looked from one woman to the other. "Sorry, did I say something wrong?"

"No," answered Ashley. "I was planning to go and have laser surgery on my eyes so I can throw these ugly old glasses away."

"I didn't know, Ash," Vanessa answered. "When did you decide that?"

"Just yesterday. I told you I want a new look."

"Good, now that we have that out of the way, let me get a good look at this hair," Charlie said. He pulled the hairpins from her hair, letting it fall through his manicured, long fingers. He led her to the chair and circled the chair, looking at her head from all angles, feeling the texture and the ends that needed trimming.

Charlie raised both hands in the air. "Ashley, the bangs can stay since you can always comb them back when you want to. But I have a cute cut for the rest. I'll leave a little length to it so you can wear it up when you want to.

"I know how to style hair. You should see my wife's.

When I finish with your hair, you'll love it, and so will the men," he said and smiled. He looked at Vanessa as she stood back and watched. "So, what's going on, Miss Beauty Queen? Every time I see you, you're decked out in a bad outfit. You look good in whatever you put on that pretty brown figure."

Charlie started to comb out Ashley's hair. "Are you married, Ashley?"

"I'm separated, soon to be divorced. He may have already filed for all I know." She sighed as Charlie turned her chair around to face him. "I was married for twenty-five years." That phrase had begun to sound like a broken record to her.

"So sad. A good man is hard to find. I know, honey. My youngest sister is a pretty woman and her old man left her three months ago, and for another man. I don't think she'll want him back this time. Your husband will probably be back, too, Ashley." He stepped back, opened the drawer, and pulled out a plastic cap. "It's hard living alone and going home to an empty house after you've lived with someone for so long."

Vanessa sat in a chair and waited for Ashley while flipping through a magazine, looking at hairstyles and fashions. She placed the magazine back on the rack. "I'm going to walk over to the mall for a while."

"Now, Vanessa, I know you're not going shopping. Don't return with new clothes," Charlie yelled behind her.

Vanessa yelled back. "No. I Just wanted to have something to do while you're doing Ash's hair."

Charlie looked at Ashley. "She'll come back with something new. I know Vanessa. Go on and be good to yourself, baby, is what I say."

Charlie and Ashley were left alone except for the two operators in the back, shampooing hair. "What made you want to do hair, Charlie?" Ashley asked.

"I always loved pretty hair even as a child, and it's a

way to always make a living. Women will spend money to look good. You can't look good if your hair doesn't, right?"

"Yes, absolutely," Ashley agreed.

An hour had past. Ashley was nervous as she watched her hair falling on her lap and to the floor. How much was he cutting? she thought to herself. Once Charlie had finished, Ashley stood in front of the mirror and she hardly recognized herself. Charlie had left her bangs but her hair was shorter and hung down her neck. She ran her fingers through her hair and it felt as soft as feathers. Charlie gave her a mirror so that she could see the back. Ashley hadn't seen Vanessa standing in back of her.

"You look lovely, Ash," Vanessa complimented. "At least six years younger."

"Turn around, girlfriend, so we can see the front," Charlie said, grinning with pride. All the ladies loved what he did with their hair.

"Oh, Charlie, I love it. And I love the way it bounces with so much body. Her face lit up as she admired herself in the mirror. "You are so talented."

Vanessa drove Ashley back to her car. "You made my day, Vanessa. I love my new hairstyle."

"It looks good, Ash. Now drive carefully, girl." Vanessa went inside her shop and Ashley drove off. She started to go home but decided to go over to her parent's house and show off her new look. Besides, it was sunny and warm outside, and she hadn't felt this good since she came home from the hospital. She smiled to herself, thinking of the expressions on Daniel and Doris's faces when they saw Ashley for the first time with a new hairstyle and pounds lighter.

"Ashley, what a surprise," Doris said, opening the door for her daughter to come inside. "Wait a minute, there's something different about you." Doris circled her daughter slowly trying to figure out what was different. There was a glow in Ashley's face that she hadn't seen for several weeks. "It's your hair, Ash. What did you do to it? It's so cute."

"Do you like it, Mother?" she beamed, feeling good about herself for a change.

"Yes, I love it. It's so becoming, honey. You look younger." Doris went to the hall and called Daniel and Cora to come into the living room to see Ashley's hair.

"Mother, it can wait."

"No it can't. I want them to see how good you look. Are you feeling better, too, Ash? You're beginning to get your color back into your cheeks."

"Yes, Mother. I feel much better." Ashley listened to her father and aunt asking each other, "What has Ash done to herself?"

"Oh, look at her. Ash, how much weight have you lost? You can put any movie star to shame with that figure," Cora said. Ashley hugged her and kissed her on the cheek.

"I like your hair, baby," Daniel said. He smiled, standing back with both hands in his pockets.

"How long are you going to stay in L.A., Aunt Cora?" Ashley asked.

"As long as I'm welcome," Cora laughed, as she pushed the front of her black wig back and scratched her head. Then she tried to straighten it, but it was sitting on her head like an ill-fitting hat.

Cora was Daniel's only sister. She was tall, with large round eyes. She had been married only once to a man that used to knock her around every time he had too much to drink. The last time he hit Cora, he turned to walk away and a bullet glazed his butt. Once he was released from the hospital, he returned to an empty house. Cora had left and came to Los Angeles to stay with Doris and Daniel for three months before she received word that he had gone back to New Orleans to live. She moved back to Kansas City and never remarried. That was twenty years ago. Now she's sixty-five, and as far as Cora was concerned it's too late for marriage. She was happy with her life as it was. So why change it now and be sorry later? she always said.

"I've just finished frying chicken," Doris said to Ashley.

"Okay, let me go and put my teeth back in my mouth," Cora answered. "The last time I bit down on a chicken bone with no teeth, it cut my gums something awful." She pulled off her wig, turned it around, and placed it back on her head.

They all sat around the dining room table and talked. Ashley laughed more than she had in weeks. But she knew that the minute she got home, the memories of the day Marcus left her would be there waiting for her like a disease with no cure.

"When do you go back to work, Ash?" Daniel asked.

Ashley placed her drink on the table in front of her. "I've decided to go into dress designing, Dad. It's what I went to school for. Since I'm alone, I've decided to do what I've wanted for so long. I even bought myself a power sewing machine today."

"Ash, you're not serious?" Doris asked, and sat straight up in her chair, her back stiffened. "You've been on your job for a long time. It's stable, you have all the benefits you need." Doris looked at her husband. "Daniel, help me," she pleaded. "Talk some sense into her."

"It's what she wants, Doris. Don't you think she's old enough to make her own decisions? She knows what's best for her. Damn, she's forty-five."

"Ash! Think about what you're doing. You're forty-five years old. What if it doesn't work out? Then what will you do?" Doris asked.

Ashley sighed. She knew her mother would overreact this way. Doris was so afraid of everything. Everything she wanted to do, she needed Daniel's approval. She had been that way as long as Ashley could remember.

"Mother, it's what I've wanted to do all along. It was Marcus who kept me from doing it. Why do you think I went to school?"

"But Marcus will be back. What will he say when he finds out you are out of a job?" Doris asked, her stomach beginning to ache in reaction to her daughter's seemingly poor decision. She propped her elbows on the table with her face resting in her hands.

Cora looked at Ashley and back at Doris. She decided to stay out of their disagreement.

Daniel listened to his daughter. This was what she wanted and he would support her all the way. When Ashley leaves, he would speak to Doris about her behavior. This wasn't the time to discourage Ashley when she needed support from her family.

"Mother, for the last time, Marcus won't be back, and I've already quit my job. I'm going into business for myself. Now, I don't want to argue about it." Maybe it was time to leave, Ashley thought. She couldn't go through this with her mother at a time when her life was already in shambles.

"You are making a mistake, Ashley."

"Let me be the judge of that."

"All I've got to say is, be happy, Ash. If this is what you want, then grab it. But just be happy," Cora interjected.

All heads turned toward Cora. Had she said the wrong thing?

"We all can't be happy, Cora. What does happiness mean anyway when you have no husband and are too stubborn to listen?" Doris snapped, more to Ashley than to Cora. She just didn't understand her daughter. Stubborn, just stubborn, like her father, Doris thought. As for Cora, she is crazy, just crazy like an old bat.

Doris got up from the table and went into the kitchen to wash the dishes. She knew that Ashley would do what she wanted. *Besides, Ashley never listens to anything I have to say anyway.* The only person Ashley had ever listened to was Daniel, and of course he would agree with whatever she wanted. Where did I go wrong as a mother? Doris wondered, as she put the dishes into the dishwasher. Nothing had changed since Ashley was a child. It seems that it was always the two against her. What made her think it would be any different now? Tears were streaming down her cheeks. She grabbed a napkin and wiped her face.

"How is John, Aunt Cora?"

"That cousin of mine is the same. Dumb as dirt, I tell you, he'll never learn any sense. Do you remember when he was a boy, Daniel? Always stealing and selling cars. He's changed but only because he's too old to run from the law. Your cousin John is an old man now."

Ashley didn't really care. She just wanted the conversation changed.

Doris came back into the dining room with a bowl of fried chicken. She went to the kitchen and returned with cornbread and bowls of brown rice and collard greens.

Ashley got up and helped her place all of the food in the center of the table. She looked at her mother's face and smiled, touching her gently on her hand.

Ashley took her seat next to Cora. "I just want a small piece of chicken. I ate lunch with Vanessa today before I had my hair cut." She touched her hair and smiled when she saw her father looking at her.

"You look real pretty, honey," Daniel said to Ashley.

"Thanks, Dad. I needed the change."

After dinner Doris and Cora cleared the table, and Ashley grabbed her purse and car keys.

"You should go straight home and get some rest, Ashley. You just had surgery eight weeks ago. Don't overdo it," Doris said, and walked Ashley to the door. She kissed her mother on the cheek.

"Don't worry so much about me, Mother. I am going straight home. Thanks for the dinner. Everything was delicious." She blew Daniel a kiss.

Chapter 7

It was a hot, sultry day in midsummer, and Ashley could feel sweat soaked into her sleeveless, white T-shirt. She stood in her bedroom looking at the boxes lined against the wall, wiped the moisture off her forehead, and took long gulps of her diet cola. She placed the cold can against her forehead, sighed, savoring the relief she felt.

Ashley had just finished gathering everything that belongs to Marcus—his colognes, books, shoes, everything that was left behind—and neatly packed it in boxes. The last box, she thought, taking a deep breath, wiping her forehead again. She perched on the edge of the bed to catch her breath. It must have been the hottest day of the year. She felt the heat under her skin quickly spreading up her neck, face, and forehead. "Damn hot flashes," she said out loud. It was already hot enough without them. High blood pressure, cholesterol, now hot flashes. God, she felt old.

Finally, she got up and carried the last box through the kitchen to the adjoining garage. Luckily, she could just open the door inside the kitchen and step down. She went back to her bedroom and stood in the center. There were no signs of Marcus ever sharing the bedroom with her, she thought as she looked around to see if she had missed anything. She had even hung some of her clothes in his former wall-to-wall closet. When Lori visited, she could take all Marcus's boxes and store them in her garage until he could get them.

Back inside, Ashley pulled out a box of her old drawing board. There were drawings of dresses and suits she had created while going to school. It was time she got started with new ideas that were playing around in her head. And tomorrow she would rearrange the guest bedroom into her sewing room. The sewing machine was already there. She placed all her drawings on the floor next to the chair. She would select the ones she wanted after she showered and ate lunch.

Ashley finished eating and sat in her favorite spot, facing the backyard. The birds were singing on top of the patio roof. She started sketching suits and making changes to her older sketches. After she finished working on a suit she started sketching a dress. When she stopped again it was past six. Ashley held up the sketches and admired her new creations. Feeling the joy of her accomplishment, she knew she could achieve exactly what she wanted as a second career. Just looking at what she had done in one afternoon motivated her more. This was something she needed in her life, and she was now determined to do it more than ever. If Marcus was home, she thought, he would never allow her to quit a job that she had had for eighteen years. Ashley could hear him now, "Ash, you're too old to start a business you know nothing about. Do you realize how long it's been since you went to school for it?"

"Well Marcus, I'm doing what I want for a change and there's nothing that you can do about it," she whispered to herself, and smiled.

She had walked at least two miles on the walking trail at Stocker and La Brea Avenue. Ashley was now walking four days a week and loved watching the view from the high, hilly walking path, the homes that sat high on the hill, and she loved the feel of the damp grass under her shoes. She watched people walking fast around her; some in twos and threes, and like she, some were alone. Ashley was always alone. She smiled at familiar faces that she had seen every morning, but still she preferred to walk alone. Walking in the early mornings gave her time to clear her head and think of all the things she wanted to change in her life. Sometimes she wondered why she hadn't started the early-morning routine before now. Marcus didn't have to walk to maintain a figure of a younger man. He had the same body as he did when they were in college. She now realized she should have started years ago, too.

The air was refreshing and crisp. The weather hadn't gotten too hot yet. It was only six forty-five, and she still had the remainder of the day to do whatever she wanted. She stopped, moving aside to tie her white Reeboks. She was wearing a pair of navy blue shorts and a white T-shirt. And as she ran around the track and down the hill, a leaf on a tree brushed against her shoulder as she headed for her car.

Three weeks had passed and Ashley had the laser procedure performed on her eyes. Although her eyes felt tired, she was amazed that it took only one full day to recover. She could see perfectly without her glasses. Ashley's new look was complete.

She was ready to start her business, but first, she had to think of a way to get word out and show people her newly designed fashions.

Sitting in her sewing room, Ashley heard a car drive up the driveway. Must be Vanessa, she thought. She looked at the clock; it was past one, and Vanessa said she would be there around one.

Ashley stood at the window and watched Vanessa as she got out of her gray BMW. She looked elegant in her navy blue suit and pumps. Her hair was cut shorter and combed back from her face. A smile curved her red-painted lips as she saw Ashley open the door for her.

"I was just admiring you, Vanessa. You look stunning in that suit." Ashley closed the door and led her into the den. "How can someone look good in everything they wear?" Ashley asked.

"I try, girl. You look good, too, Ash. How does it feel without glasses?"

"Good. When I sit down to read the newspaper, sometimes I forget and reach for my glasses," she said and laughed. "I don't know why it took me so long!" She shook her head in wonderment. "Do you know it never even occurred to me to have the surgery done. Boy, was I boring."

"And you are small enough so we can do some shopping for you now. Get rid of all your old clothes. They're too big for you now, Ash. You can get into a pair of tight jeans and show off your little butt."

"I know I should go shopping soon. When you have time to go with me, I'm ready. Would you like a glass of iced tea while I finish the salad?"

"Yes, that'll be fine. I'm glad you called. Would you believe I'm tired already and it's just past noon? That new client can't make her mind up if she wants white for her blinds. I had to take some samples for her and her husband to go over." Vanessa sat on the sofa and slipped her feet free of her shoes.

Ashley gave her a tall glass of iced tea with a thin slice of lemon tilted over the edge of the gold-rimmed glass. Ten minutes later she was placing the salad on the table. "Come on it's ready."

They ate and talked about Ashley's new business. When they finished Ashley cleared the table and Vanessa stepped down into the den.

Watching Vanessa from the kitchen, Ashley sensed that she had something to say. Vanessa kept looking at

Ashley as she placed their plates in the sink. Ashley dried her hands with a paper towel and took a seat in the chair facing Vanessa, where she sat on the sofa.

"Well, are you going to tell me or not? I always know when there is something important you have to say."

"You're too much, Ash. I can't keep any secrets from you, can I?"

"No. So remember that." Ashley kicked off her shoes and curled her legs under her.

"I was pumping gas early this morning and guess who I saw?" Vanessa asked.

"I have no idea. Who?"

"Marcus. He looked quite surprised when I spoke to him. I wondered if he would have seen me first, would he have spoken to me? He looked at me as though I were a ghost. And I'm sure I was the last person he wanted to see."

Ashley sucked in her breath and closed her eyes, picturing Marcus in her mind. "Was he alone?" she finally asked, holding her breath as she waited for Vanessa's answer. She felt as though her salad would come up.

"Yes, he was alone. And he didn't look too happy to me, or maybe he just wasn't too happy to see me. And you need to try and stay healthy, Ash. You look ill at just the mention of Marcus's name," Vanessa said with concern, as she watched Ashley's face glowing red. Vanessa got up and refilled her glass again. "Do you need a refill, Ash?"

"No. I'm all right. Marcus called me a week ago but I didn't return his call."

"I wonder what he wanted?" Vanessa asked.

"Hell if I know. I can't stand hearing his voice. He sounds so calm and natural as if nothing has changed between us. And besides, hearing his voice still hurts too much." She stood up and sat down again as though she didn't know what to do next. "That one message kept me from getting any sleep that night. I was tossing and turning, wondering what he wanted. But whatever he wanted I'm certain it wasn't me."

"I know you want to forget him, Ash. But keeping busy is all you can do. You were too good for him, anyway. Maybe now he knows it."

The phone rang. "I'm going to take it in my bedroom. It's probably personnel returning my call about the stock in my pension plan." Ashley rushed to her bedroom.

Vanessa returned to her seat. Everything was pristine. Even the oatmeal-colored floors shined in Ashley's kitchen. Vanessa took a peppermint from the crystal bowl on the coffee table and popped it into her mouth.

Ashley returned to the kitchen. "That was personnel all right. My stock was converted to an IRA account." She looked at the small water spot in front of her T-shirt that had splashed from rinsing the dishes before she placed them in the dishwasher.

"Good. Now I want to see some of your sketches. You know it's only two weeks before that award dinner. I need something elegant and a little sexy, if you know what I mean." She winked and laughed out loud.

"Come on in the back room and see the changes I've made. Tell me what you think."

Ashley led the way. Vanessa stopped at the door. "It looks good, Ash." She looked around at all the changes Ashley had made. The sewing machine was in the left corner, a mannequin stood against the wall waiting to be dressed, a daybed with multicolored pillows was alongside the wall. A long cutting table and entertainment unit with a CD player were on the center left wall.

Vanessa looked at a drawing of a suit hanging on the wall. "This is different, Ash. I like the sleeves." Looking at the length above the ankles, Vanessa stood back to get a better look. On the drawing board she saw a dress that she was sure she wanted. "Show me some sketches of all of your dress designs."

"Sure, have a seat, girl. I'm going to have a fashion

show for you. We can look at some dresses, and I'll make whatever changes you like. I can change the sleeves, make them short or long; the neckline can be even lower, and the length. Just whatever you want." Ashley had seven sketches of dresses, long and short.

Vanessa stood up again. "Oh, I like that one. How does it look long with no sleeves?" Vanessa asked, anxious to see the changes.

Ashley picked up her pencil and eraser and started to draw the dress all over again. She stood back, tilting her head to the side. "Vanessa, I'm sketching what I call a buckle-back dress with a boat neckline that opens up to a full scoop back, and a silvertone metal clasp at the neck. Now, look at that. It's going to be subtly shaped with front and side darts. Maybe it can be long with a slit on one side to show off those shapely legs of yours. And make Gary jealous," Ashley teased.

"Get out of here. Girl, you should have been doing this fifteen years ago, Ash. I think I want it without the sleeves."

"Let's see how it looks." Ashley erased the sleeves. "Yes, it does look good without the sleeves," Ashley said, setting the picture against the wall. She and Vanessa stood back about six feet and looked at the beautiful creations.

"That's the look I want Ash, that's it. I couldn't have bought it in a store. At least not the exact way that I want it." Vanessa threw both hands in the air. "That's it, girl."

"You're sure?" Ashley asked. "I can make more changes."

"I'm sure. That's the look I want. I'm impressed, Ash. I know women at the award dinner are going to ask me where I bought it. Now I can say Ashley designed it and give your phone number."

"I think black will be the perfect color," Ash suggested.

"Yes. I want it in black."

"I'll go out tomorrow and look around for some mate-

rial and get started. I'm excited about making your dress,"
Ashley said happily, and clapped her hands together.

"I guess I better go back to work. I have an anxious
client who is ready to spend her money."

Ashley and Vanessa walked through the dining room
and into the living room. Vanessa stopped in front of the
gold-framed mirror that was hanging on the wall. With
both hands she smoothed her hair back on both sides.

After Vanessa left and Ashley placed the rest of the
dishes in the dishwasher, she dressed, combed her hair,
and left. She saw a fabric store next to Singer's sewing
machine store. She had two weeks to finish Vanessa's
dress, and it had to be perfect.

Ashley turned the air conditioner on in her car,
squinted her eyes against the bright sun, and put on her
sunglasses.

As she drove she whispered a prayer, "Lord, please let
this be the right decision in my life." Even though she
felt she had made the right decision, starting her business by dipping into her pension still frightened her. But
she had to try.

Ashley did find just what she wanted for Vanessa's
dress. She even picked up a small piece of black silk or-
ganza material. It was light enough to keep the wind
from blowing her hair out of place, and the ends could
hang over her shoulder.

Once she arrived home, she placed the materials for
Vanessa's dress in her workroom and went to her bedroom to listen to her messages. Her first reaction after
hearing Marcus's voice was to turn off the machine and
throw it against the wall, but she changed her mind and
sat on the edge of the bed to listen to what he had to say.
The last time he left a message for her she didn't return
his call. As she listened she felt her stomach cramp, her
heart thump.

"Ash, the bank account at Wells Fargo Bank has
twenty-six thousand dollars in it. Take whatever you

need. I won't touch it. It's all for you to keep up with the house and your car note, not that you don't make enough money to do it on your own. But I just thought you should know." She waited, listened, but after a few seconds he hung up.

She wondered why he held the phone without saying anything more. Maybe he thought she was listening and would pick up, she thought to herself. "But if that's what he thought, he was dead wrong," she whispered, without realizing she had spoke out loud. She will never speak to him again. "Guilty conscience," she said out loud again. "Just pure guilt. Eating you up inside, huh, Marcus," she said, and switched the machine off. Well, thanks for upsetting my day, she thought, and lay back on her back.

The first fitting of Vanessa's dress was perfect. She had been pleased and didn't want Ashley to make any changes. Ashley had to admit that it was a stunning creation. As Vanessa had walked across the room, the crepe material flowed around her ankles.

The phone rang, Ashley answered, and it was Vanessa. "Ash, I'm still waiting for my client to arrive. It may be later before I get there."

"Don't worry about it. I'm not doing anything and I'll bring it to you." Ashley pulled a plastic bag over the dress and hung it in her car.

While driving to Vanessa's shop, Ashley decided to stop at the bank. The weather wasn't as hot as it had been the week before. After working so hard with her exercising, Ashley looked lean and fit, wearing a pair of white slacks and a red cotton blouse, red sandals with straps that tied around her ankles. Her white earrings dangled as she strolled inside the bank.

Ashley passed the line at the safe deposit department and saw a tall, handsome gentleman standing in the line. He looked at her and smiled. Ashley returned his smile, trying to remember the last time a man had really given her such an admiring smile, watching her until she had disappeared into a line clear across the other side of the bank. What a good day it had turned out to be, she thought. The line Ashley stood in had only about ten people ahead of her.

Ashley made a withdrawal from her savings account that had the twenty-six thousand dollars in it. After all, Marcus did say it was hers. As she started to walk away from the teller window, she stopped. Her heart was beating so fast she was afraid that she would pass out.

Marcus was standing near a line at the new accounts department when a woman came from behind the counter and walked up to him. He kissed her on the cheek, and the woman smiled up at him. Ashley stayed on the other side of the line so that she wouldn't be noticed. As his eyes lingered on the woman's face, it was apparent that they were in love with each other. It had been so long since she saw that look on Marcus's face. Somehow, he looked different, younger. What was so different as she looked at him? Then it hit Ashley right between her eyes. It was a look of lust that she hadn't seen in a long time. The same look he had when they were younger and couldn't get enough of each other. But Marcus wasn't younger, he was . . . in love.

Her heart sank, and she felt weak. Ashley turned her back when they started to walk out the bank. Once they were outside, Ashley went to the door and watched as they walked to Marcus's car. The woman looked to be in her midthirties, short black hair, slender, and in spite of how much Ashley hated to admit it, she was a lovely woman.

Feeling as though she had been hit with a ton of bricks, Ashley slowly walked to her car. All the times she said it was over between her and Marcus. But seeing him today, and with another woman, she was hurting more than ever. Why was she feeling as though she were dying inside? It was really over between them. Marcus looked happier than she had seen him in years. Was he so unhappy with her?

Once inside her car, she lay her head against the steering wheel. She whispered, "Damn you, Marcus. Damn! Damn! Damn you for hurting me." Then she lay her head back against the seat, tears trickling down her cheeks as she indulged in the memory of the happiness and love she saw in Marcus's face today, and in the memory of the first time they met and the first day she came home from the hospital with their daughter in her arms. She saw it all, felt it all as though it were right in front of her. Ashley swallowed the lumps of memory in her throat. Now she was older and alone. Why did he wait until she was older? Marcus had aged, too, but he had a lovely young woman in his life. She had no one.

Ashley sat alone in her car for a half hour before she drove off.

She parked in front of Vanessa's shop, but all of a sudden she was frightened. She didn't remember driving herself there, didn't remember stopping for any red lights or stop signs. "Oh, God," she whispered, feeling her nerves jittering inside.

Vanessa was on the phone when Ashley walked in. She smiled and motioned for Ashley to sit down.

Ashley hung the dress on a coatrack against the door and took a seat.

Vanessa hung up. "Girl, this new client is going to worry me to death. Finally, we agreed on the color she wants to use for the blinds all through her house. Hey, Ash, in two months another space will be available if you want to lease one," she said, starting to take the plastic bag off her dress. "I can't believe what a good job you did with this dress." She pulled the plastic all the way off. "It's beautiful, Ash. I certainly couldn't have bought one so pretty in a store. Girl, you have my business." Vanessa looked at Ashley, and saw that her eyes were red, and that she looked as though she hadn't heard a word Vanessa had said to her. "Are you listening, Ash?" Vanessa frowned and looked at Ashley's face again.

"I'm sorry. Bad day, my mind is drifting off. What were you saying?"

"I said a space next door will be empty soon and I love my dress."

"No. I better work at home until I see how it goes. Anyway, for sure, you won't see anyone else wearing a dress like yours."

"I know. Let me get my checkbook. Get yourself a Coke or a can of juice from the refrigerator." Vanessa went in back to her office. In less than five minutes she was back and gave Ashley a check. "Gary is going to love this dress, Ash." She sat in a chair next to Ashley.

"Okay. Now tell me what's wrong, Ash. You haven't heard a word I've said to you." Vanessa looked genuinely concerned.

Not knowing what to do with her hands, Ashley folded her arms in front of her, then placed her hands in her lap. "I saw Marcus and his girlfriend today." Her eyes had begun to water, and she felt the nagging ache in the center of her heart.

"Where did you see them?" Vanessa led her to the small sofa and took Ashley's hand in hers.

"On my way over here. I stopped at the bank." Unable to continue, Ashley shook her head. "I started to wait until tomorrow. Lord, I should have waited. But no, I had to go today. If only I would have waited," she repeated. "Knowing it is one thing, but when you see it . . . it just hurts so much."

"What did he say to you?"

"Nothing." She sat up straight and blew her nose. "I turned my back so he couldn't see me. I figured since I'm smaller and don't wear glasses anymore, he wouldn't recognize me anyway. But you know what, he couldn't see anyone else but her. She works in the bank, and she's cute and younger than me."

"And you are beautiful inside and out. Let's hope she looks as young as you do when she gets your age." Vanessa took Ashley in her arms and felt her body tremble, then crumble as she cried.

"I don't even know who Marcus is anymore. We were married for twenty-five years and I don't even know him."

"I know, honey. But I'm glad he didn't see you this morning. That would have been too awkward for both of you. Mostly you, Ash."

Ashley stood up and picked up her purse. "I'm just glad that I saw him before he saw me. I wouldn't have been able to stand on my feet if Marcus saw me."

"Where are you going now?" Vanessa asked.

"Home. No, over to my mother's house. Aunt Cora is visiting again." Ashley started to the door and turned around to face Vanessa again. "You're going to be the prettiest woman at that award dinner. Gary won't be able to keep his eyes off you." She smiled at Vanessa, wiped her eyes, and said good-bye.

Vanessa stood at the window and watched Ashley as she drove off. She remembered the day she had seen Marcus and a woman at Macy's in the Sherman Oaks Galleria. But he didn't see her, and she never mentioned it to Ashley. Actually, she didn't think it was her business to mention it to anyone.

Vanessa remembered the day she told Larry, her ex-husband, that she wanted a divorce. It wasn't easy, and Larry only made the situation worse. In nineteen years, that day was the only time he had raised his hand to strike her.

Vanessa had met Gary at Helen Graham's book signing. Gary was her agent. That Saturday Vanessa and Larry had had a terrible argument, and she needed to get out of the house for a breath of fresh air. Listening to the radio, Vanessa heard that Helen Graham would be doing a book signing, and she decided to take her book to be signed. It was a novel she had bought two weeks prior.

The line at Borders Books was long. As Vanessa got closer to Helen, she felt someone staring at her. It was Gary, standing behind Helen. She was flattered and surprised that with all the younger, prettier women in line he couldn't keep his eyes off of her. When it was finally her turn to get her book signed, Gary gave Vanessa his business card. He left Helen's side and walked Vanessa outside. He was so handsome. So friendly, and obviously quite attracted to her. He was a nice man, but Vanessa had no interest in calling him. She even wondered how many business cards he had given out after she left. A month later Vanessa happened to walk into Zahra's Books-N-Things on La Brea Avenue. She was flipping through a home magazine when Gary walked up to her.

"Hello, Vanessa," he said in a deep, smooth voice.

It was odd that after meeting someone a month prior for the first time, and for only ten minutes, she remembered his voice and he remembered her name. Vanessa closed the magazine, at a loss for words. "Hi, what a surprise to see you here," she said, feeling her face glow with heat from embarrassment. Just by giving her his business card, surely he didn't expect her to call him, a complete stranger.

"It's a surprise seeing you here, too, but the best surprise I've had all week," he said, smiling. His teeth were so even and white, his black shirt was opened at the top, and he wore black trousers.

"Are you always in bookstores?" Vanessa asked.

"Pretty much. I'm Helen Graham's agent and friend, plus I represent other authors here and in New York. I see you read a lot, too." He noticed the novel she had set aside to flip through the magazine. He also noticed that she was a very attractive woman and one with a wedding ring on her finger. Why hadn't he noticed that before? He wondered if she was happily married.

"I'm an interior decorator. Home magazines help give me the latest ideas." Why was he standing here wasting her time and his? Couldn't he see that she was married and didn't really feel like talking? She was here because she was lonely and unhappy, not to pick up some single guy who was in search of a one-night stand. But for some bizarre reason she couldn't move her feet. So the conversation continued for fifteen minutes and became a luncheon date. A month later a love affair had blossomed and they were madly, completely in love.

She was no longer in love with Larry but tried not to tell him until he forced it out of her, by slapping her across her face. That was four years ago. As Vanessa thought of that day, she inadvertently touched the side of her face where he had slapped her as though it still stung.

It had been raining on that Sunday morning in January. Vanessa waited until the holidays were over. But leaving Larry was something she had to do. After all, with Larry her life was empty, and she merely existed from day to day.

As usual, Larry was siting on the sofa in front of the television, watching a football game. And as usual, he acted as though she wasn't even in the house with him.

Vanessa sat in the chair opposite him and cleared her throat, hoping to get his attention.

"Larry, we need to talk."

"What is it, Vanessa? Can't it wait until later?" he asked, still watching the TV.

Nineteen years, she thought. And she couldn't even get his attention because his football game was apparently more important than she. Surely she deserved more.

"No, Larry, it can't wait till later. We have to talk now." She knew that if she didn't tell him now, it would be another month before she could drum up enough courage. Besides, when he had fallen asleep the night before, she had put some of her clothes in her car. Yes, she had to tell him now. She looked around the room as though she was suffocating. The beer cans, a line of three on the table in front of Larry, the remote control by his side and the protruding beer belly that hung over his shorts. God, she hated all of it.

"Well, what's so important that it can't wait, Vanessa?"

"Larry, we're not living like a happily married couple, at least I'm not happy. I want a divorce. I haven't been happy for a long time and I don't think you have either." She didn't move, or breathe, and it took forever for him to react to what she had said.

Larry sat up straight, looking at her as though he was waiting for her to laugh or say she was only joking. But when he looked at her face and watched her dab at a tear that had rolled down her cheek, he realized she was serious.

"What brought this on, Vanessa? We have a nice home. I make a good income. Sure, we don't have any children, but that's not my fault. The doctor said you're the one that couldn't produce, not me."

"Produce is what you call it, Larry? How insensitive you are." She looked at him as he took a quick glance at the TV again.

Larry wasn't the handsomest man Vanessa knew before they were married, but he used to be so kind and caring. He had light brown skin, was medium height, and had sandy hair. He looked better with his mustache, but he had shaved it off the week before, which made the scar across his chin more obvious. He got the scar from an injury when he was in high school playing football and fell on a piece of glass that was stuck in the grass.

"So, what is it, Vanessa? What's with this divorce talk all of a sudden?"

"It's not all of a sudden, Larry. It's been a long time coming. I just didn't have the courage before. I need more in a marriage. I don't understand why you need so little." She looked sad; telling him wasn't as easy as she thought it would be.

"No, Vanessa. I don't need more. You are my wife and I have enough right here."

She held her head high, determined to get it out in the open. "Well, I don't," she snapped. "And I won't continue to settle for this kind of life. Sometimes I feel as though I'm dying inside, just like our marriage. I'm leaving today, Larry—"

He got up quickly, too quickly, and switched off the TV, throwing the remote at the end of the sofa. Larry was beginning to wonder if he'd just awakened from a bad dream. How did this happen? Why is it that the one who is left behind never sees it coming?

His large hands hung at his sides, and he was breathing hard like a maniac, his face frowned in a distorted twist. "What can I do to turn things around and make it like it used to be between us? Just tell me what to do and I'll do it." He was flexing his fist open and closed as though he was nervous and desperately afraid.

Vanessa was still sitting in the chair watching him as he stood in front of her, too close. She had to strain her neck to look up at him.

"It's too late, Larry. The love between us died years ago. I really should have left before now. You just never made any effort to make our marriage work. I did try, now it's too late, I'm sorry." She got up from the chair, but before she could make another move, Larry grabbed her arm. Vanessa looked at his face. He looked angry and perplexed. She had never seen him look as hurt before. For a heart-stopping second, she touched his face with her free hand. She wanted to cradle him as she would a child. Seeing the pleading in his eyes tore at her heart.

"Is it another man? Tell me, Vanessa. Have you been seeing another man?" He held her wrist tightly.

She tried to twist her arm from his tight hold but couldn't. He only held her tighter.

"No, Larry. It's not another man. Let me go," she said loudly. "You're hurting me."

He didn't let go and slapped her hard across her face. "Tell me!"

Her eyes were wide and she tried to pull away, but he slapped her again, and again.

"I said tell me, Vanessa," he yelled, still holding on to her as she cried and tried to pull loose.

"Yes, Yes," she screamed. "I'm in love with someone that can love me back. I'm sorry," she cried out. "But, yes. You should have tried, Larry. You should have been here when I needed you."

The answer he heard snapped him into more rage. He pulled her closer to him, his mouth fell open, tears rolling down his face, and his eyes were wide with rage. "Sorry? You're sorry? We've been married for nineteen years and all you can say is that you're sorry?" He slapped her again and again till he saw blood gush from her nose and felt it in the palm of his hand, and his head jerked up as though he had been in a state of shock. He let her go, and Vanessa landed on the floor in front of the chair that she had been sitting in.

Larry walked out the house, and an hour later when he returned, Vanessa was gone. Half of her clothes were left in the closet, but she never went back to get any of them.

Vanessa moved in with Gary. One week later she filed for a divorce, and six months later she and Gary were married. Being married to Gary was like a dream come true. She never knew her life could be so complete.

Chapter 8

"Hi, Mother. Where's Dad and Aunt Cora?" Ashley asked.

"Daniel took her shopping. Come on; let's go into the kitchen. I was baking a chocolate cake for Cora's birthday. The woman eats sweets and fatty foods excessively. She's your daddy's sister all right. Stubborn, won't listen to nothing anyone tells her."

"Then why are you baking her a cake?" Ashley asked, as she poured a glass of water and sat at the table. Doris was standing at the sink mixing the batter for the cake.

"So she won't keep asking me, I guess. Have you heard from Marcus lately?"

"No, but I saw him today."

Doris quickly wiped her hands on her pink-flowered apron and took a seat at the table. "How is he, Ash? Is he ready to come home?" Doris waited anxiously for Ashley to answer.

Ashley sighed. "Mother, no. Actually, it's time I file for a divorce. Marcus was with another woman." If only she could hate Marcus, then maybe it wouldn't hurt so much. But she still loved him, and she was hurting like hell.

"She probably doesn't mean anything to him, Ash. He'll wake up soon. I know he will," Doris said, dusting the flour off her apron. "He's from a good family. Marcus is just like any other man, Ash. You know, he married young and just needs to air out a bit, that's all. Just be patient and he'll come around soon enough." Doris stood up and started to mix the chocolate frosting with her back turned to Ashley.

Ashley could feel her body tremble with frustration and anger. Why was she even discussing Marcus with her mother? "Was airing out what you thought Dad was doing, Mother?"

Doris quietly set the mixing bowl on the counter as she listened to Ashley.

"When Dad left us for three months, did you really think I believed his job had sent him away on some project, as you called it? Was he just airing out, Mother?" Ashley was so filled with anger that she jumped from her seat and stepped closer to her mother. Although she could see Doris's back stiffen, she didn't move. Doris just stood there with her back to Ashley.

"When he was younger, as long as I can remember, he cheated on you. I knew he was sleeping with Ruby Miller until she got too sick and died. All of my friends knew it, too. Everyone who knew us knew he was sleeping around on you, and you waited for him and took him back." Ashley wanted to stop but she couldn't. Her anger had ballooned to a point where she couldn't help herself. She had wanted to say this to her mother for a long time, but couldn't bring herself to hurt Doris. But today she was livid, overflowing with rage and had to get it out of her system.

"Ruby's son and I look alike, Mother. Doesn't that mean anything to you? What I don't understand is that Dad taught me to grow into a strong woman with pride and dignity. Maybe he didn't want me to be like you. You are too weak, Mother. With you, it's turn the other cheek. I don't understand that at all. Were you afraid of him, afraid of being alone, what?" she yelled, jumped from her chair, and stood in back of her mother. She waited for Doris to answer.

Doris bowed her head. Her shoulders jerked, but still

she didn't speak. And she couldn't let her daughter see her face streaked with tears.

"I won't be weak. I tell you . . . and I won't wait for Marcus."

The words rang in Doris's ears as she wiped tears from her eyes with her apron, and turned around to face her daughter. "And what did I teach you, Ash? I certainly didn't teach you to speak so cruel and heartless to your own mother," Doris said, her voice quivering. "Since you are recalling the past, maybe you should think about some of the good things. Your father was a good man. Don't you ever speak of him that way in this house again. Who paid your college education, made sure you wore the best clothes, made sure you wanted for nothing, Ashley? He always loved you. But men are men and one day you will learn that. You are a fool to divorce Marcus. When will you—?"

Ashley stopped her by throwing both hands up in the air. "I'm divorcing Marcus, Mother. I'm not scared to step out on my own." She picked up her purse and walked through the living room on her way out. Ashley turned around and Doris was walking slowly behind her. When she got to the door she turned to face her mother. "I will divorce Marcus and I don't care what anyone says." She turned around, sauntered out, and slammed the door behind her.

Once outside, Ashley saw her father's car turning the corner. But not wanting to talk to anyone else, she got inside her car and drove off as if she didn't see him. After seeing Marcus and arguing with her mother, she was in no mood to see anyone else that day.

Doris sat at the table and wiped her eyes with her apron. She lay her head on the table and cried for Ashley. She was suffering and Doris knew it.

Doris heard Daniel and Cora come inside. She stood up and filled a glass with ice and water. Ashley was right about one thing, she was a weak woman. But she was only sixteen when she and Daniel were married.

Doris was from Jackson, Mississippi. She was the oldest of three girls. Their father walked out when they were babies. Her mother worked at home, doing laundry, sewing, baking homemade breads and pies for the local restaurants. She had a fatal heart attack and died when Doris was in high school. Doris and her two sisters stayed on a farm with their aunt and uncle. The only reason they took them in was because they could help work the farm, and their uncle wouldn't have to pay anyone. Doris and her sisters were miserable.

The girls began to drift apart, all three going in different directions. But luckily Doris met Daniel, and they fell in love, and two months after they met, they were married. Doris had never been with a man, and never had to work another day of her life. Daniel made her stay home and supported her so she wouldn't have the life she had on the farm. She stayed home and took care of their home and Ashley, and did what she was told with no questions asked. After eight years of marriage he moved his family to Los Angeles. Doris wanted to find a job but Daniel wouldn't hear of it. She owed her life to her husband.

The other women in his life were just women, nothing more. Except Ruby, she thought, as she dabbed at her eyes with the paper towel she held in her hand.

Daniel walked into the house first. "Doris," he called her name from the living room.

"I'm in the kitchen, Daniel." Doris went back to the counter to finish the cake when she heard Daniel's footsteps coming to the kitchen.

"I saw Ash rush to her car. You didn't upset her, did you Doris, with all your talk about Marcus returning home? Personally, I hope the bastard stays away. Ash is doing well for herself without him."

It surprised Doris that he felt that way. But it shouldn't

have, especially after Ashley said she was not taking Marcus back. Doris heaved an exasperating sigh. "No, Daniel, I didn't upset her. Ashley was in a hurry to go home." She lied—God, how she hated lying.

Ashley got home and changed into a pair of shorts and a T-shirt. She sat in the leather chair and tucked her legs under her. Now she was sorry for the impetuous words she had said to her mother, but once she started, she couldn't stop. She knew that she had said too much. Thinking of how her mother must feel, Ashley placed her hands over her face and cried. She was just so angry that she had to lash out, release the anger and hurt, but it shouldn't have been her mother that she released it on. She would have to find a way to make it up to Doris. She would start by calling her tomorrow and apologizing. But Doris was Doris, and she would always be weak and afraid to make a change in her life. And at her age she didn't have to. But it was different for Ashley. She had no choice. Marcus had made the choice for her.

Ashley went into her sewing room, picked up her drawing board, and placed it against the wall. She drew a suit, a long skirt and short-waist jacket. Standing back, she looked at it from all angles and decided which changes she wanted to make. Maybe she would make one for herself—after all, what better way to market the clothes she was designing? She had designed a blouse and gave it to Vanessa to wear.

Hours had passed, and it was dark when she looked at the clock.

"Mom, are you here?" Lori yelled from the living room. She and Keith had just returned from the Bridge Theater in Westchester. The living room was dark and Lori turned the lamp on while Keith closed the blinds.

Ashley was concentrating so deeply on her drawing that she hadn't heard Lori open the door. "I'm coming."

Ashley slipped her feet into her slippers and went into the living room.

"So where are you two coming from?" she asked, as she hugged Keith and kissed Lori on her forehead.

"A movie. It was so dark I didn't think you were home," Lori said.

"I didn't realize that I had been working so long. I'm really enjoying it. Are you guys hungry or would you like something to drink?"

"I'll take a Coke. I know you have one, Ash," Keith said.

"Lori, get your husband a Coke," Ashley said, and took a seat on the sofa.

"I think it's good what you're doing, Ash. So many people talk about going into business for themselves, but they are either too afraid to take the chance or never get around to doing it," Keith said. "And I never got a chance to tell you, but I'm sorry about you and Marcus separating. Lori says he has already filed for a divorce." Keith was waiting for her reply; she acted as though she wasn't going to answer him.

So much for filing for the divorce, Ashley thought. Marcus seems to be in a rush. She should have known he would be. Ashley shook her head. Lately, she'd gotten one slap in the face after another and today was a day from hell.

"Thanks for all your support, Keith. But life goes on. The good and the bad of it. Now, how is your mom?"

"She's all right. Right now she's in Texas visiting my sister. She just had another baby. A girl this time."

Ashley really did love Keith. He was a good guy. He was medium height, well built, with dark chocolate-colored skin, black hair, and most of all, he was kind. He still had a slight limp from the motorcycle accident he had had six months earlier. They thought they had lost him, but he came out of it alive and was back to work again. Keith was an engineer at a large aerospace company in El Segundo. He was recruited right out of college, where he and Lori had met.

"Here's your Coke, Keith," Lori said. She had one for herself, too. "Mom, we thought we would take a couple of Dad's boxes out of the garage." She bounced on the sofa next to Ashley. "How are Grandma and Granddad?"

"They're both okay. I'm going to see them tomorrow."

"When is Helen Graham coming over?" Lori asked.

"Helen Graham! You don't mean the writer?" Keith asked in awe.

Lori laughed at the expression on her husband's face. "Yes, Helen Graham the writer."

"How did she find out about you, Ash?" Keith asked.

"At Anita's bookstore, Helen saw Vanessa wearing a blouse that I made and loved it. And Helen wants me to make her the same blouse but in another color. Vanessa loves my work. Looks like she's going to be a repeat customer."

"I'm going to call you tomorrow, Mom. I just have to know if she's nice and as pretty as she looks on her book covers. Lynn, her daughter, is very down-to-earth and friendly. I haven't seen her since we graduated, but I heard she's an editor for the *Los Angeles Times.*"

Lately, every time I see Lori it seems she looks more like Marcus. The more I try to forget the man the more I think of him, she thought to herself. But they had been together too many years and everything around Ashley reminded her of him.

Keith stood up. "I have to get up early tomorrow, Lori. Why don't I start putting the boxes in the car?"

Ashley got up. "Let me show you which boxes belong to Marcus, Keith. I really appreciate you doing this for me."

Lori looked up at Ashley and placed the magazine back on the table.

"You seem to be feeling better, Mom. Dad asked about

you yesterday. He wanted to know if you were feeling okay."

"Tell him that I'm just fine. Does he know that I'm working from home yet?"

"Yes. He was surprised but he says he wishes you well. I think he really means that, Mom. Oh, and he says you haven't returned any of his phone calls."

"No, and I'm not going to." Ashley stood up.

Lori saw how tense Ashley had become and knew it was time to change the conversation. The wounds were still too fresh. "Do you go walking every day, Mom?"

"Yes. I like it, too. Sometimes I need to get out and clear my head. When I'm walking, I can think of all kinds of ideas for my business, plus it's good for my health. My life has taken quite a turn."

"Yes, it certainly has changed," Lori answered.

Keith walked inside and sat next to his wife. "All finished. Are you ready?"

"I'm glad you guys came over. I needed the break."

"One day we have to go to a movie or do something together, Mom. Just the two of us."

"We will soon. I promise. My business is keeping me pretty busy these days. Soon I'm going to have to find help."

Ashley walked outside with them. She looked up and the stars were shining. It was a beautiful night. She looked at Keith and Lori holding hands as they walked out. A beautiful night for lovers, she thought.

"Hang in there, Ash. You look good," Keith said.

"Thanks, honey. Now drive carefully." Ashley went back inside.

Chapter 9

It was cool and windy the first week of September, and a sinus headache had awakened Ashley at three in the morning. She went into the kitchen and made herself a cup of tea and went back to bed, but after tossing and turning for two hours she decided to get up again. Once she was awake it was always difficult to go back to sleep.

Sitting in the chair in the den, with the TV on, she pulled the plastic off a dress she had been working on the night before, and finished sewing black beads around the neckline. Ashley had made two other dresses since she had finished with Vanessa's. The one she was working on was the fourth. She had to work hard and fast with this one, but at least it kept her mind off her current problems. And she had to ask around for a divorce lawyer.

At eight, Ashley was standing in the hot shower, feeling the tension release from her body. Her headache was gone and she was finished with the dress. It was green velvet, beautiful for the holidays.

At one o'clock the doorbell rang. It was her one o'clock appointment, Helen Graham.

On the way to the living room, Ashley took a quick glance at herself in the mirror and rushed to the door.

"Helen?"

"Yes. How are you?" Helen asked.

"Good. Come in. We can go to my sewing room and look at some drawings." Ashley led her to the room.

Helen Graham was a real class act, and beautiful. She

was about 5'8", thin, wearing a blue silk pantsuit and the same color blue sandal shoes. Her brown hair flowed past her neck. Ashley noticed that she wore very little makeup. But with a face like an angel, she didn't need any.

"Would you like a cup of tea or something cold to drink, Helen?"

"No, thanks. I have a lunch engagement later. If I drink anything now I'll lose my appetite." She stood in the middle of the room feeling the coziness and warmth surround her. "You have a beautiful home. I'll bet you decorated it yourself?"

"Yes. I love decorating," Ashley said with pride. She had just met Helen and knew that she liked her.

While Ashley set up her design presentation on the table, Helen walked around the room and stopped, picking up a picture of Ashley, Lori, and Marcus at his company picnic. One they took six years ago. "You have a lovely family, Ashley.

Ashley turned around quickly. "My husband and I are separated. That's our daughter, Lori." She sighed. She had placed all the pictures away that included Marcus, but every time she picked up that one she couldn't seem to put it away. Now it was time she did.

"I guess I should start looking for a divorce lawyer soon." For a moment she felt foolish telling her business to a complete stranger.

"I'm so sorry, Ashley." Helen looked embarrassed. She knew too well what it was like getting a divorce. She had gone through one herself with her first husband. Helen felt as though she was the luckiest woman in the world to get a second chance with a wonderful man.

"Okay. Let's get an idea of what you're looking for. These are some of my favorite styles."

"I'm going to be a speaker at the Book Expo in Chicago. I want a pantsuit, something comfortable and unique."

"I have a drawing in the closet you may want to see."

She pulled out a large pad and stood it against the wall. "I've had this for a long time. You know, I told my daughter you were coming over. She says that she loves your writing. Lori graduated from USC. As a matter of fact, she says she knows your daughter."

"Lynn did graduate from USC so I'm not surprised they do know each other." Helen took off her jacket and Ashley hung it in the hall closet.

"I should have brought my sister along with me. She loves to shop."

"You're lucky, Helen. It gets lonely sometimes being an only child. How many sisters and brothers do you have?"

"Only one sister. My older sister, Harriet, died four years ago." Helen's smile slowly disappeared. Although she and Harriet were never close, and Harriet hated her, it was still hard for Helen to speak of her without feeling remorse about their relationship.

"I like the slacks, but without the pockets, and I would like the legs straighter. Excuse me while I get this phone call." Helen opened her purse and took out her phone. She talked for only about three minutes. "That was my lunch date. She had to cancel so now I can take the time I need."

"How about a cup of tea now?" Ashley asked.

"Great. I'll take it."

"Honey or sugar?" Ashley offered.

"Honey, please."

Ashley was back in ten minutes, carrying a tray in her hand with two cups on it, lemon slices, and honey.

"When I lived in Atlanta a friend of mine used to serve honey and lemon with her tea. I don't drink tea as much as I used to." She shook her head. "I still miss her. Miss Lettie was an old, wise woman."

They returned to the drawings. Helen stood back again looking at the pantsuit. "You know, I like the jacket but what if it was longer and the pockets were a little higher?"

"You're good at this, Helen. You know exactly what you want."

"I didn't until I saw this drawing," Helen said, sipping her tea.

Ashley erased the pockets and drew them higher, and made the jacket longer. She drew the jacket on top of the pants so that Helen could see what it looked like as a suit.

"Perfect. Just absolutely perfect," Helen complimented.

"Are you sure? I can make as many changes as you like."

Helen shook her head, stood back, and took a longer look. "No, don't change anything. I love it just the way it is. I'll take it in taupe, the same color as the shoes I'm wearing."

"You've got good taste, Helen." The doorbell rang and Ashley excused herself. "I'm not expecting anyone else today," she said, rushing to open the door.

It was the mailman delivering a certified letter. Ashley signed and closed the door. Assuming it was a letter from her previous employer, she started to drop it on the coffee table and read it when Helen left, but when she flipped the letter over, it was from a lawyer. Furiously, she opened it and pulled out neatly folded pages. As she read the heading she felt a lump in her throat. She tried to swallow, but couldn't; she tried to hold back the tears, but they were escaping against her will, like gray clouds bursting in the sky. She had been served with divorce papers. Marcus had filed for a divorce.

She held her breath and closed her eyes. "God, he is actually divorcing me. Marcus is divorcing me?" she asked again, as though she had to say the words to believe it. She had to say it out loud to believe it was real. Just looking at the papers didn't seem realistic to her.

Ashley had to pull herself together, put the papers away, and finish reading it later. Ashley went into her bedroom and placed the papers on her dresser, then went to the bathroom and wiped the tears away with a damp towel. She stood at the door, squared her shoulders, sighed heavily, and flounced out.

"It was just the mailman delivering a letter. So, is there anything else, maybe a blouse to go with your suit?" God, she was trying to keep herself together, but her stomach was quivering and her hands were shaky.

"No. I'm thinking of wearing just the jacket and slacks." Helen put her jacket back on and picked up her purse. "I really love your creativity, Ashley. Believe me, I will refer other women." She looked at Ashley as she nodded her head. "This has truly been a productive day for me because I couldn't seem to find a pantsuit that I really wanted."

Ashley forced a smile, but she couldn't reply. She knew if she tried to speak she would only make a fool of herself. God, why didn't Helen come tomorrow instead of today? she thought.

Helen looked at Ashley's face and wondered if she had said anything that may have offended her. The woman looked as though she wasn't hearing anything. Was she in pain, Helen wondered? Helen noticed Ashley's hands trembling as she placed the drawing board on top of the cutting table.

Helen stood in front of Ashley. "Are you all right?" she asked with concern. She took Ashley's hands and pulled her down on the sofa. There was no way she could leave without knowing if Ashley was really all right, or if there was anything she could do before she left.

"No, it's just a headache, Helen, but thanks for asking." She felt foolish. A complete stranger and this would be her first impression of her, just foolish. She stood up with Helen and as they started to the living room, the dam broke, and Ashley burst into tears.

"I'm so sorry, Helen. I feel so ashamed that you had to see me like this. My husband just had me served with divorce papers. I wasn't expecting a divorce so soon. Although I knew it was over between us, I just hadn't prepared myself. And I knew it was coming so I don't know why I wasn't." Her hands were covering her face, her shoulders shook, and she felt as though she were dying inside. "He's making it final."

Helen placed her hand on Ashley's shoulder. "Don't feel foolish, Ashley. I know what you're going through, and I'm glad I'm here with you. At a time like this, you need someone who understands."

Ashley raised her head and grabbed the box of Kleenex on the table beside the sofa. "Guess I really have to find myself a lawyer now. No use waiting any longer," she said, sniffling, and blew her nose. "Helen, did you say your husband is a lawyer?"

"Yes, but he's a criminal lawyer." Helen looked inside her purse and pulled out a business card and wrote on back of it. "Here's a divorce lawyer's number with the same law firm as my husband. He is very good. If you ever want to talk, Ashley, give me a call." She stood up. Helen was sure that Ashley was embarrassed enough with her being there.

"I'm so sorry, Helen, and I'm going shopping tomorrow morning for the material. Your suit will be ready on time." She walked Helen to the door.

"Remember, you haven't anything to be embarrassed about. I've gone through the same thing, and other women have, too." Helen walked out and Ashley closed the door behind her and went to her bedroom.

Once she was in her bedroom, she took the divorce agreement out of the envelope and nervously glanced through it. She placed the papers back into the envelope, stood up, and threw the envelope across the room. But she felt no gratification in throwing the papers to the floor. Then she jumped up and stomped the papers.

"That's what I think about your fucking divorce, Marcus," she hissed between closed teeth. She stormed out the room, grabbed the phone, and went into the den.

Ashley dialed Marcus's work number, but before he could answer, she changed her mind and hung up. Tomorrow she would call the lawyer. "Marcus wants a divorce, and a divorce is what he'll get, damn him," she said out loud. He had become such a jerk.

That day Ashley couldn't concentrate on her work or Helen's pantsuit. She paced the floor, picked up the phone at least five times to call Marcus, and changed her mind. She had to do something before she climbed the walls with anxiety. She wanted to cry, to strike out at anyone. Frantically, Ashley combed her hair and decided she needed some fresh air. Maybe if she went out and walked in the mall, she would get tired enough to return home and sleep the night away.

Ashley drove to the Beverly Center and walked into a small dress shop. She saw a purple pantsuit in the window and went inside as she caught a glance at matching shoes.

The saleslady saw her walk in and met her just as she stood in front of the rack where the suits were hanging. The woman was short with gray hair, and well dressed in a gray suit. "Can I help you, miss?" She smiled and hung two suits on the rack.

"I would like to see the purple suit that's in the window. A size eight and a ten. I've lost weight so I'm not sure of my size."

The lady looked at Ashley. "I'll say an eight might fit you. The color will look good on you, miss."

Ashley looked at the label: it was Jones New York, but what the hell, Ashley thought. It was only $325. "And I like the black one also. Oh, let me see the gray one, too. I have a pair of gray pumps that match." She looked at the price tags and the gray one was $359, the black one was $349. Then it hit her, she would buy everything that looked good on her for a change. The credit card was in Marcus's name, so he was still responsible for the bill. Picturing the expression on his face when he opened the bill made her smile.

Wearing the purple suit, Ashley walked out of the fitting room and stood in front of the long mirror. She turned from side to side, amazed at how well it fit her. And it was only a size eight, a perfect eight, she thought. She was so happy to be able to say she was only an eight instead of a twelve, and her last checkup indicated that her blood pressure had lowered. Her arms, thighs, and waist had gotten smaller. You go, Ash. She looked in the mirror and beamed with delight.

"You look beautiful, miss," the woman said, standing back to see how well the suit really fit her. "Nice figure and a pair of legs like yours, you should wear all your suits and dresses that length."

Ashley bought sweaters to match each suit. "Oh, I need shoes. I would like some sandals with the heel and toes out."

"Right through here, my dear."

Every color Ashley wanted, they carried. "I'll take the purple and a pair of black. Oh, what about the red pumps?"

Ashley tried on the shoes and decided to buy every pair she asked for. The shoes were $195 a pair and she still didn't care. All the years she worked and never asked for anything, never wanted anything but to be a good wife and mother.

The saleslady was excited about the commission she would get by waiting on Ashley. She grabbed a red purse to match the shoes and a purple scarf to match the purple suit.

"I'll take the red purse, too. I need a black and a gray one, also. Now, may I look at a pair of gold-and-sterling silver earrings?" Ashley followed the saleslady to the jewelry counter.

After she selected the earrings, they were placed on the counter with the rest of her items. "Now, I need a couple pair of slacks."

The saleslady helped Ashley select the slacks. She left the clothes on their hangers and pulled a plastic bag over them. She neatly placed the shoes and purses in a large shopping bag. When she rang up the total, it was well over $3,000. She had charged the credit card to the limit.

Ashley ambled out with a wide smile across her face. She was ready for a new look and a change of life. *It was time.*

Elliott Douglas hated this case. The only motivation he had was knowing that his client would win. The relentless headache that pounded in his left temple plagued him, as did a persistent head cold that kept him up late last night and caused him to oversleep this morning.

Elliott would have postponed the appointment this morning if Robert Wilbertson had not recommended her as a favor to his wife, Helen. Now he had to wait another hour for her arrival.

Looking at the stack of papers on his desk, he sighed, and took another bite out of the club sandwich his secretary had brought back from lunch. After Elliott gulped down the remaining root beer soda, he still had time before the woman arrived and decided to go over some notes for a pending case.

Elliott had been married for twenty-one years. The first twelve years were happy ones. The second nine years were busy with one case after another, but it provided him and his wife with a comfortable life financially. Janet started to complain about his work and the late hours he was spending at the office. She was a beautiful woman but very selfish. Janet complained that Elliott didn't take her on vacations as often as she liked, but she spent money as fast as he could make it. Her taste was extravagant, she shopped often in expensive stores, and everything she bought was costly name brands. When she wasn't shopping, she was going to expensive restaurants for dinner with her friends and picking up the tab. When Elliott confronted her about spending so much money, her excuse was always the same: Elliott worked too many hours, and she spent money only to replace what she was missing in their marriage. But whenever he came home early, Janet was always out. Lately, they were always going in separate directions. He wondered why he went home at all.

Elliott was a handsome man, exceptionally so, tall, over six feet. His skin looked healthy, the color of beach sand, and he had a square chin and a full sexy mouth. He was dressed in a brown suit, white shirt, and brown tie.

By habit, Elliott ran his long fingers through his crop of wavy black hair, waiting for the potential client referred by Robert. Ashley Lake—hope she doesn't come in crying. So many of them came into his office crying because their husbands took everything. Made their ex-wives sell the house because most of the wives couldn't pay the note alone. Some women had no work experience or skills. Some didn't even know how much money their husbands made, or how much they had saved in separate accounts they didn't know about. They never looked at their husband's paystubs and didn't know what deductions were taken out. He expected another forty-five- or fifty-year-old woman to come in confused and desperate.

Again, Elliott sighed as he thought of his own marriage. Why wasn't he filing for a divorce himself? he thought. There was no love left between him and Janet, except the love she had for money. He had brought up the subject of divorce several times, but she threatened to clean him out, take everything he had worked hard for. And why would she want a divorce when she had everything she wanted, including her freedom? All Elliott had was his work. What a life, he thought, stacking papers aside for the receptionist to file away. He looked at his watch. In thirty minutes, Mrs. Ashley Lake would be walking into his office.

Terri, the receptionist, stuck her head into his office. "Mr. Douglas, your one o'clock appointment is stuck in traffic. She says she'll be about fifteen minutes late."

"Thanks, Terri," Elliott answered. He slumped back in his chair. Fifteen minutes late, probably more like thirty minutes. Her first consultation and she's late. Elliott sat behind his large oak desk; the pain in his right temple stabbed him again, reminding him that it was still there.

Elliott refilled his glass with water, opened his desk drawer, grabbed a bottle of aspirins, and popped two into his mouth. He closed the blinds halfway to prevent too much sun from glaring into his eyes.

The intercom on his phone buzzed and he answered.

"Mr. Douglas, Mrs. Lake is here to see you." Elliott looked at his watch. It took her only ten minutes. Good, he thought. After she leaves he would go home and crawl into bed.

Showing no sign of perturbation, Ashley Lake ambled leisurely into his office. Stopping only inches from his desk, Elliott looked at her from head to toe. The affliction he felt only minutes before her arrival dissipated and was replaced with a burst of energy he hadn't had for days.

"Please sit down, Mrs. Lake. Would you like a cup of coffee or a glass of water?" he asked.

"No, thank you." She didn't smile. Ashley wanted only to get this part of her life over with as soon as possible. She pulled the thick white envelope from her purse. "Here are the terms of the divorce decree that my husband filed. I don't have the perspicacity with fancy words that a lawyer would use. So I need your help."

Elliott pulled the papers from the envelope and started to read them. Except for the shuffling of papers the office was quiet. Ashley noticed the expensive paintings, diplomas, and certificates on the wall. It was such a beautiful day that she couldn't help but wonder why the blinds were closed at the large window to the right of Elliott's desk.

The view on Century Park East was gorgeous. Ashley stood for a moment, poised at the window, looking over the city. She felt a deep sadness inside her, standing in a divorce lawyer's office forced her to accept that her marriage was finished.

From the corner of her eyes, she could see Elliott watching her. He was handsome enough to make a woman want to stay in his office and look at him forever. She felt an overwhelming urge to reach out and smooth the gray along his sideburns, and feel the texture of his hair against her hand. She hadn't wondered what he looked like before she arrived.

As Ashley stood at the window with her back to him, Elliott looked at her. She wasn't too tall, but she had a slender figure and long, coltish legs. Her physical attributes, and her ability to wear clothes well and in good taste, gave her an elegance of appearance that was quite singular.

He cleared his throat. "Do you agree with refinancing the house and buying your husband out so soon, Mrs. Lake? He seems to want it sold as soon as possible."

Ashley returned to her seat in front of Elliott's desk. "I plan to sell the house and buy myself a townhouse." She crossed her legs and placed her hands in her lap, wondering what he was thinking as he read the terms of the property settlement. He made notes as she answered his questions.

"And your husband's pension? Do you agree that neither one of you will ask for any of the other's pension?" He took off his glasses and rubbed his eyes.

She cleared her throat. "Yes, I agree."

"But, Mrs. Lake. You can get payments from his pension or a lump sum when he retires. Are you willing to give it all up?" This was not what he expected of this client. Most women who hired him wanted to take everything their husbands had worked for. They were all hurt and angry, and wanted revenge.

"Mr. Douglas. I'm not trying to hurt or rob my husband out of anger. I have just as much pension as he does. He has his life and I have mine. I just want to let it go and get it over with. I've decided to start a business of my own." She wanted to cry out but held her head high. *Don't make a fool of yourself, girl,* she thought, taking a deep breath.

"Mr. Lake doesn't seem to be asking for anything either. He says you can have everything in the house except his personal belongings. As far as the highlighted paragraphs, it's just the legal way to write out an agreement between two people who are getting a divorce." As he talked, this was the first time he noticed that her lips were painted purple. The same color as her suit. Her eyes were slanted, fringed with thick lashes. She had been hurt deeply; he could see it in her eyes. Even though she had no intention of robbing her husband or getting even, her demeanor was cold, unreachable. Every time he mentioned her husband, her eyes turned cold and calculating. They revealed so much. Sure, she tried to hide it, but Elliott had met them all, though Ashley Lake was different. In some inexplicable way he felt her pain, as though they had met before. Maybe it was because, like him, she held her pain inside. And there were no tears; she knew what she wanted.

"Mrs. Lake," he repeated.

She looked in his face as though she had just returned from a long, distant journey. Ashley wondered if he had called her name more than once. "I'm sorry, Mr. Douglas. You were saying?"

"As I was saying, I can draw up another agreement that states you can stay in the house for another year before it goes up for sale. That will give you enough time to decide if you really want to sell it or not. The one thing you don't want is to make hasty decisions. How does that sound to you, Mrs. Lake? Remember that it's in your own best interest. It will give you enough time to work and find yourself a place."

"Okay, maybe you are right, Mr. Douglas, about selling the house in a year, though I plan to do it sooner," Ashley said, looking skeptical.

"You've been very agreeable, Mrs. Lake. Extra expenses could occur for your business. You may even need to hire an extra person to help you. I can only advise you, but I really think you should give the advice about the bank accounts more thought, and ask for more."

"Okay, I'll have to agree on that, too. You could be right. After all, he makes enough money to take care of himself. The thirty five thousand is the emergency account for both of us. You see my husband was very good with saving money. I'll agree that two of the other bank accounts are mine. He can keep the twenty two thousand dollars, and the other account that has twenty six thousand dollars. The one hundred thousand dollar portfolio at Fidelity Investments belongs to me. That's what I'll agree to."

Elliott buzzed for Terri, and she answered. "Terri, please put Mrs. Lake down for next Tuesday." He placed his hand over the phone. "Is that all right with you, Mrs. Lake?"

"Yes, anytime next Tuesday is fine for me."

Ashley stood up and Elliott walked her to the door. He was about the same height as Marcus. She would have to tell Vanessa what a sexy-looking man he was. "Thank you for everything, Mr. Douglas. I appreciate you seeing me on such short notice."

"My pleasure. If you have any questions at all, don't hesitate to call me."

Ashley smiled and left his office.

Once she was outside she looked up at the building; Elliott's office was on the tenth floor.

Ashley's next stop was the bank. As she walked inside and passed the teller window she noticed that the bank wasn't crowded. The lines were short, and she could get out fast.

First Ashley went to the new account's desk. There were two but she knew exactly which desk she wanted to go to. She took a seat, and pulled her passbook out of her purse and completed two withdrawal slips for the balance of the account that had $26,000 and the other account with $28,500.

The young woman picked up the passbook and held it in her hand for a few seconds before she spoke. "Hi, can I help you, miss?" she said in a rush of words as she stumbled to get them out. She looked at Ashley's face; their eyes met and held.

Ashley gave the woman the slips and her identification. "I want to close out my account please," she said, and watched the woman as she checked her accounts on the bank's computer. The woman walked away, and Ashley waited patiently for her return. She imagined the woman had gone to the vault to bite down on her fingernails, or to call Marcus to inform him that his wife was in the bank.

The young woman came back and gave Ashley two cashier's checks for the amount of each account.

Ashley could sense that she was nervous. "You can tell my husband that I closed my personal accounts. No, correction, our personal accounts. Everything that is his is mine."

"Excuse me?" The woman replied.

"Excuse me, my ass. My husband, Marcus Lake," she said, enunciating each word clearly. "You know, the man you've been sleeping with? If you have a hearing problem, I can say it louder. My husband that you've been sleeping with. Did you hear that?" Ashley yelled out loud.

The woman looked around, obviously knowing that someone must have heard. She saw her coworker sitting at the desk near her, staring; three customers in the teller line were staring, whispering to each other.

"Okay, okay," the woman said, looking around nervously.

"I thought you heard." Ashley snatched the cashier's checks from the woman's hand and pushed them down into her purse. "The rest of my money and his will be transferred to another bank, and I suggest you take care of it personally so you won't have to see me again. I will create a scene if my husband doesn't comply with my wishes. I'm sure he doesn't want to see you embarrassed, Miss Brown," Ashley said, looking at her name tag.

Miss Brown opened her mouth but no words emerged. Ashley gave her one look before she smiled and sauntered out the door.

"Ashley, look how good you look. Doris, come out here and look at your daughter," Cora yelled from the living room.

Doris dried her hands with a dishtowel. "Where have you been all dressed up, Ash? And you've been shopping, too, I see."

"I'm going to take my water pill. If I don't I'll feel like a hot air balloon," Cora said and left the room.

"Mother, I have something to say before Aunt Cora comes back. I'm so sorry for what I said to you the last time I was here. I've been so angry. But that's no excuse for the harsh words I said to you. Anyway, it's over now."

"What do you mean by that, Ash?" Doris took a seat on the sofa and Ashley sat next to her.

"Marcus had me served with divorce papers. I went to see a lawyer today."

"I can't believe he would do such a thing. Has the fool lost his mind?"

"No, mother, he left me because it's over between us. I told you that but you refused to believe it."

"I thought Marcus had more sense, the fool."

"Mother, I just wanted you to know. You have to realize that everyone's marriage is different. Marcus says he's no longer in love with me. So why wouldn't we divorce?"

"He actually said that to you, Ash?" Doris asked, stunned at such cruel words.

"Mother, I've told you all of this before," she said, trying to hide the irritation she felt. "Why would I even want him back? But, that's not important anymore." She sighed as though she was tired. "I really came over to apologize. I'm sorry."

"I knew you were just hurting inside, Ash. But looking at you all dressed up, and looking like a different person, you don't look hurt at all. If Marcus saw you now—"

Ashley put both hands up in the air. "Mother, don't start on me and Marcus again, please."

Cora walked back into the living room. She wasn't wearing her wig and had small, nappy, salt-and-pepper braids all over her head.

"Where is Daddy?" Ashley asked.

"He went to the doctor's office to have his blood pressure checked. The doctor wants to check it every month," Cora answered. "I've told that man about adding so much salt to his food."

Ashley looked at Cora. "Is he all right?"

"He's just hardheaded that's all," Cora said. "Now why would he decide on his own to stop taking his medication just because he thought he didn't need it? Daniel was obstinate when he was a boy and still is, if you ask me," Cora said, shaking her head. Cora scratched the top of her head and folded her arms in front of her. She was sitting on the love seat opposite the sofa where Doris and Ashley sat.

"He'll be all right, Ash. At least he's getting his monthly checkups like the doctor ordered," Doris exclaimed.

Ashley didn't say so out loud, but her father doing what the doctor ordered was what concerned her. It wasn't like Daniel to take orders from anyone. Going to the doctor's office every month wasn't like him at all.

"Ashley, you still haven't said where you've been. Dressed like that, honey, some man is gonna follow you home," Cora teased. "I like that new hairstyle on you, too. I've known you all your life and I wouldn't have recognized you in a crowd."

"Thanks, Aunt Cora. I went to see a lawyer about my divorce."

"Was he good-looking? I bet he couldn't keep his eyes off you," Cora teased again.

For the first time that day, Ashley laughed out loud. "Yes, as a matter of fact, he was good-looking. And he could certainly keep his eyes off me."

Ashley worked her feet out of her new shoes and put them on the floor next to her. She glanced at the family pictures that her mother kept on the table next to the sofa. Her wedding picture was still there—she in her white wedding dress and Marcus in his white tux.

The living room was neat and comfortable with light green drapes, carpet, and a small antique walnut coffee table in front of the green sofa.

Doris got up and opened the drapes wider, letting in the warm sun. "Now, that's better. This room is too dark for a nice sunny day."

They chatted for a while and Ashley slipped her shoes back on.

Finally, Ashley stood up with her purse in her hand. "I

have so much to do. I better leave now." She looked at her watch; it was almost four. "I wanted to wait for Dad but tell him to call and let me know how he feels."

"Now Ashley, don't go worrying about Daniel. He wasn't feeling ill when he left. If he was, I would have gone with him," Doris scowled.

Doris and Cora kissed Ashley on her cheek. All three women walked outside.

"Oh no, Cora," Doris said. "Daniel says he's going to take us to see a movie."

Ashley entered her car, waved, and drove off. She looked through her rearview mirror and saw them walking inside.

What a hell of a day, Ashley thought.

Ashley stopped by the supermarket and headed for home. She stuck the key in the door from the garage as she heard the phone ringing. With an arm full of groceries Ashley ran to the phone. She set the bags on the kitchen counter and picked up the phone. Before she could answer, she heard his voice.

"Ashley, what the hell did you think you were doing today? What's gotten into you?"

"What do you mean, Marcus? Would you explain yourself?" she asked, knowing full well what he was speaking of.

"Don't be funny, and don't play games, Ash. You know damn well what I'm talking about."

"Okay. It's like this, Marcus. Right now you're wondering how I knew who you're screwing around with. I saw you two together, Marcus, and all of a sudden I don't like the service that bank gives. I don't want to look at that little tramp's face every time I go there. Now, if you don't have the other two bank accounts transferred to a bank of my choice, I'll just have to talk to my lawyer again about the terms of the settlement. So, I'm warning you, Marcus. Don't mess with me. I will be banking at

Wells Fargo Bank on Jefferson and Sepulveda Boulevard."

"For Pete's sake, we've been banking at Bank of America for fifteen years and now you're telling me to change banks? You're losing your mind, Ash. This is petty and you know it."

"Maybe it is, but you weren't screwing the bank's employees for fifteen years. Change the bank, Marcus and make it fast."

Her voice took on an iciness that Marcus had never heard from her before. She was trying to make his life miserable any way she could. But he wouldn't have it. No, she wouldn't continue to get her way. He took the receiver away from his ear and looked as though he was trying to see her face.

"And why do you need a lawyer, Ash? The divorce papers were easy enough to understand. Even you can understand it," he said sarcastically.

"I'm not stupid, Marcus. Do you really think I would agree to everything you want without consulting my own divorce lawyer?" she snapped, again her voice coated with ice.

"How will I know the account numbers and how will I get my new checks? I have bills to pay, Ash. You are making me angry with this little game you're playing."

"Well, it's just too damn bad you're angry, Marcus. As for you getting checks, that's not my problem. Now, please don't call me anymore. My lawyer will be in touch with yours once he has modified the settlement." She heard him sighing.

"What in hell didn't you agree with? I was fair, Ash. Why are you being so difficult? And incidentally, what is this Lori told me about you retiring from your job to start your own business? You are forty-five years old. You moved out of your parents' house and right into marriage. You have never been out on your own. Keep things simple, Ash. Don't—"

"Don't be stupid? Is that what you were going to say, Marcus? When I wanted to do this before, you said that I was too stupid. Now, I can do whatever the hell I want."

"As I was saying, you have never been out on your own. How the hell do you expect to pay the bills while you are wasting time and money trying to start up a business? Hell, you haven't even paid a house note alone in twenty-five years."

She sat on the barstool at the counter feeling a sob stuck in her throat, but she wouldn't let it escape. Instead, she closed her eyes and swallowed hard.

"Wait for my lawyer to contact yours, Marcus. In the meantime you can go to hell." She hung up but her hands were still shaking, hurting from the tight grip she had had on the phone. He talked to her as though she was too stupid to have a successful business. "You just watch me, just watch me, Marcus," she said and held up her middle finger to the receiver, giving Marcus the four-letter sign.

Marcus sat behind his desk. "Damn," he said, banging his fist down hard on the desk. What in hell was Ashley up to? he wondered. Up until now, she hadn't accepted any of his phone calls and refused to return any of them. He didn't understand why she disagreed with the divorce settlement. And what did Monique Brown mean when she said that Ashley was pretty, but evil? "Ash, pretty?" he said out loud. "Women, they never know what they're talking about. Ash? Pretty?" He laughed out loud.

Chapter 10

Elliott Douglas was surprised when he drove into his driveway in Ladera Heights and saw his wife's car. There were times when he came home in the middle of the day and she wasn't home. It was only three-thirty, and he was lucky that he didn't have to fight the five o'clock traffic. His body and head ached. He would have been home an hour earlier if Ashley Lake hadn't been in his office. Although her case was an easy one, he still needed to go home early, undress, and get into bed. Elliott walked in and went straight to the bedroom.

Janet was on the phone talking to one of her sisters. She turned to face him and knew immediately that he was ill. "What's wrong, Elliott?" she asked with concern. "You don't look too well," she said, and felt his forehead with the back of her hand. "And you're running a temperature, too. But not too high." Janet hung his jacket in his long, wall-to-wall closet.

"It's just a touch of the flu, that's all. I just need to lay down and get some sleep." He slumped down on the bed, his head hitting the pillow.

"Take your clothes off and get under the covers. I'll make you a steaming cup of lemon tea and honey, with a little bourbon. That should knock you out."

Coming home to his wife made him feel better already. She was home and concerned about him. Every time he thought Janet didn't care about him, she always surprised him. Elliott knew that Janet still cared for him but was sure she was no longer in love with him. They had been married for twenty-one years and the love was gone. Now they were two married people with a reciprocal respect for each other. When he came home and she was there, she still cooked his dinner, kept the house clean and comfortable, made sure his clothes got to the cleaners when needed. But, the love had disappeared years ago. All that was left were years of routine boredom.

It was frightening when Elliott first discovered they were no longer in love, and it was apparent that Janet was the first to fall out of love. He was certain that one day he would walk into an empty house or would be served with divorce papers, delivered to his office. But Janet didn't do either of those things. She loved her big beautiful house, the Mercedes Benz, shopping in any store she wished to, weekend cruises with her friends. She no longer nagged when he worked late or brought work home, as long as Elliott didn't question her about her comings and goings.

After Elliott finished with his tea, he lay still with his eyes closed, feeling the bourbon slowly traveling to his head. This was what he needed, to just lay still, beneath the warm blanket. And after only minutes had passed, he was in a deep sleep.

Elliott awoke to the ringing telephone. Why didn't Janet answer? It was probably for her, anyway. He turned over in bed, his eyes still closed, but no one answered. Elliott sighed, wiped the sleep from his eyes, and answered.

"Hi, Elliott, this is Sharon. Has Janet left yet? Our meeting starts at six-thirty."

Elliott tried to clear his head. Thinking it was morning, he looked at the clock, then looked at the window; it was still daytime. With one hand over his mouth, he yawned. "What meeting, Sharon?"

"My investment meeting. Janet said she would be over. If she's not there, then she must be on her way."

"I haven't the slightest idea where Janet is," he answered, feeling disappointment creep up on him. "Maybe she is on her way."

"Oh, Elliott, she's walking in now."

The phone clicked hard in his ear. Elliott got out of bed and went into the kitchen, opened a can of chicken-and-rice soup, and sat at the dining room table, alone.

It seemed to him that being alone was becoming the story of his life, but what else was new? He thought of Ashley Lake. *Was she lonely tonight, too? Does she cry at night?* When he asked her why her husband walked out of their marriage, she looked as though she wanted to dissolve into thin air. But he had to ask. And he could have helped her more than she wanted. She was a woman with pride and morals. No one could rob her of that. What a lucky man her husband was. Elliott wondered how long they had been in love.

Elliott placed his spoon back into his bowl. He wasn't hungry. He closed his eyes and envisioned Ashley dressed in purple, and walking into his office. Her hair was shiny and black in a pageboy style with thick bangs lying across her forehead. Her eyes were sharp but melancholy as she searched his face for answers and advice. She pranced into his office as though she was keeping in step with soft, slow music; her pear-shaped face glowed with a distinct beauty. As Elliott looked at her, he became more enchanted. He was sure there was much more to her than he could guess.

Elliott opened his eyes and went back into the bedroom, flipped on the TV, and closed the drapes. He had to stop thinking of Ashley. She was only a client, nothing more, he tried to convince himself. He crawled back into bed. Why would he think being sick would make any difference to Janet? So much for coming home to a loving wife. That was over years ago.

* * *

"How good it is to see you again, Helen," Ashley said, leading Helen into her sewing room.

"Elliott said you went to his office. I hope he can assist you. He's really quite good and has a heart of gold," Helen said, taking off her jacket. She was dressed in a pair of green jeans, matching blouse, and black sandals.

"He was very helpful, Helen. Thank you for referring him. I felt very comfortable with him." Ashley went to the closet and pulled out Helen's suit. "How do you like it?" She gave Helen the jacket to try on first.

"Oh, Ashley, it's more than I expected. It's absolutely beautiful. I don't have to worry about anyone else having one like it." She slipped into her jacket and stood in front of the tall mirror that was installed on the closet door for the customers.

The phone rang. "I'm going to answer it in the living room while you try on your slacks." Ashley ran to the phone. Out of breath, she managed to answer before it rolled over to her answering machine.

"Ash, what are you doing?" Vanessa asked.

"Helen Graham is here trying on her suit. I finished it yesterday."

"I won't keep you. But I have a woman that wants to see you. She needs a pantsuit, too."

"Good. Give her my phone number." She was walking to the front door. The mailman was dropping the mail inside the mail slot on the door.

"I did already. Just to warn you, she needs it next week."

"If she comes over soon enough I can finish it," she said. "Anyway, I'll call you back when Helen leaves." She hung up and went back to her sewing room.

Helen was standing in front of the mirror turning from side to side. "I love it, Ashley. It's a perfect fit. Looks like you have yourself a repeat customer."

"Good, Helen. Let me put it back on the hanger and wrap it in plastic."

"I'll be leaving in two days. But when I get back, I'm having a small dinner party. I would like for you to come, Ashley."

Ashley looked surprised. "I would love to. Just call me when you get back and tell me when and what time. I'll be there. All I've been doing lately is working." She was so pleased that Helen Graham invited her. *Just wait until I tell Vanessa and Lori,* she thought. But it seemed so strange to go to a dinner party alone, and without Marcus. The only places she went without him were the supermarket, cleaners, and shopping. She would have to start sooner or later. She would have to get her hair and nails done. Maybe even shop for something fancy to wear. Alone or not, she wouldn't miss it for the world.

"I'll get my receipt book while you're changing."

When Ashley came back to the sewing room, Helen was finished dressing and had written Ashley a check.

Ashley gave Helen a receipt and walked her to the door. "I'm so glad you're happy with your suit, Helen. And the color looks incredible on you."

"I'm excited about wearing it. Day after tomorrow I'll be leaving, and for once, Robert will be going to the Book Expo with me. He's been working so hard lately. I convinced him to take a week of his vacation."

"I'll call you when I get back. In the meantime, hang in there, Ashley. Elliott will take good care of you." Helen left and waved good-bye as she got inside her car.

When Helen departed, Ashley went to the kitchen and grabbed a Coke. Realizing she had been drinking too many Cokes, she changed her mind and poured herself a tall glass of water. She went back into the den and sat down. Soon she had to move out of her house. She knew that Marcus would wait a year, but she didn't want to. The second thing she had to do was to rent a space for her business. She needed a place with a large window so that she could display her clothing designs. And she had to think of a name for her business. Ashley smiled to herself. "I'll let Marcus sweat a little before I locate a house. Let him think I'm going to wait a year."

Ashley had left her old life and had stepped into her new one. She loved the clothes she was now wearing, her new hairstyle, and her independence. She felt new and improved. This was the second half of her life, and she was going to live it. With that thought in mind, Ashley smiled.

Chapter 11

"Ash, since you've been walking every morning you look toned and fit," Vanessa said, taking two steps back to get a better look at Ashley from head to toe.

Ashley twirled around and looked at herself in the mirror. "How do you like my hair?" She turned her head so Vanessa could see the back.

"It's beautiful, too. When I arrived for my appointment, the first thing Charlie asked me was if I had seen your hair. It flows and bounces when you walk. And you did a terrific job on that dress."

Ashley looked in the mirror again. Seeing herself was like looking at a different person. She was three sizes smaller than she was before Marcus left her.

Her dress was black and stopped right above the knees, sleeveless, with a deep V-neck in front. She had never worn a dress cut so low before. Her sheer hose were black and she wore black slip-on shoes.

"I'm amazed, Ash, at how far you've come. Glamorous is all I can call you." Vanessa picked up her purse off Ashley's bed. As they walked into the living room she picked up her jacket from the sofa. "I promised Gary that I'd cook tonight so I better go."

"Is he feeling any better?" Ashley asked.

"He was up during the night. That cold really got him this time and I'm doing all I can so I won't get it from him."

"Wait for me. I'm leaving, too," Ashley said, and sauntered out the door with Vanessa.

Robert Wilbertson watched his wife as she stood elegantly, wearing a beige pantsuit and matching shoes that she had bought when they were in Chicago. He looked down at the strip that went across her perfectly painted red toes. Was it possible that he could actually love Helen more than he had the year before? He smiled to himself, and emphatically answered yes, and every day he loved her more. And after a long, hard week in court, seeing his wife looking so beautiful was like a breath of fresh air. He was a lucky man.

Robert looked at his watch. It was time for Elliott and Janet to arrive soon. Elliott had discussed with Robert the divorce he was doing for Helen's dress designer. Robert had been out of the office when Ashley consulted with Elliott, and he was looking forward to meeting her tonight. Helen had mentioned that getting out of the house and meeting new people were what Ashley needed. Boy, he felt fortunate to come home to the woman he loved every day. The only regret Robert had was that he and Helen had no children of their own. Helen had had Lynn by her first husband.

The doorbell rang and Robert answered it. "I was just wondering when you guys were going to arrive," Robert said, and kissed Janet on her cheek.

"You look lovely as usual, Helen," Janet said. "I just love this house. The décor is so warm and cozy. Is there anything you can't do, Helen?"

"No, there isn't," Robert answered, and kissed his wife on the cheek.

Just as Robert was closing the door behind them, he saw Dan and Elaine's car.

"Honey, why don't you introduce Elliott and Janet to

everyone who doesn't know them? I'll wait here for Elaine and Dan."

"Okay," Helen said.

Another couple walked in behind Dan and Elaine. It seemed as though everyone was walking in at the same time.

Soon Helen was back by Robert's side to greet more guests.

A half hour later everyone was laughing and talking. The music was slow and soft. Two couples were in the corner telling jokes and laughing out loud. The door to the large den was open and a couple was sitting on the white leather sofa with plates in their hands.

"Janet looks pretty tonight. But I still don't like her, Helen. I don't care what anyone says, that woman is evil. She has a way of talking down to people." Elaine looked at Elliott and shook her head. "How does he put up with her? He is such a nice guy."

"He's not happy, Elaine. I think he has learned to live with it. They don't do much of anything together anymore. For a while they went out together for appearance's sake. But that has changed." The doorbell rang again and Helen went to answer it.

"Ashley, don't you look beautiful tonight. Come in, honey." Helen held her hand. "Do you know that I didn't recognize you when I first opened the door?" Helen took her jacket and led her to where Elaine was standing. "Ashley, this is my sister, Elaine."

Ashley held her hand out to Elaine. "It's nice to meet you, Elaine. I'm your sister's new seamstress."

"So I've heard. I would like to see what you can do for me, and soon, too."

"That's a lovely dress you're wearing. Red looks good on you," Ashley said.

"Come on, Ashley. Let me introduce you to the rest of the people here," Helen said.

Helen and Elaine guided Ashley into the living room

with everyone else. "First, I would like to introduce you to a dear friend of mine. Anita, can you come here for a minute?" Helen asked. "This is Ashley, Anita. The lady who made my suit."

"You did a great job, Ashley, and it's nice to finally meet you. Did you design that beautiful dress you're wearing?"

"Yes, I sure did. I went shopping and couldn't find anything I liked. So I made my own."

"You are good, girl. I'll see you soon about making me a couple of outfits. You know, Vanessa buys all her books at my bookstore. So if you can't find a book you want, call me; if I don't have it, I'll order it for you."

"I've been in your store before, but I'll keep that in mind."

They were standing in the middle of the room when Helen announced, "Hey everyone, this is Ashley Lake."

Robert walked up to her and Helen held his hand. "Ashley, this is my husband, Robert." Helen's face lit up with love and pride when she introduced her husband. It was always that way with them. And everyone who knew them knew they were inseparable.

"I'm sorry I missed you when you went to see Elliott. I was in court all day."

"It's quite all right. Mr. Douglas took very good care of me."

All Elliott could do was look at Ashley. He hadn't realized that she had such a shapely, sexy body. And that face, she looked like an angel. Her dark hair was up in back with ringlets of curls against the back of her neck. The V-neck in front of her dress—just low enough to keep a man wondering what she looked like underneath. The dress certainly accentuated her figure. She was a stunning picture and as Elliott looked around he saw other men watching her as well.

"Elliott, Elliott?" Janet had called his name twice. She looked in the direction where he was looking, and she knew he was looking at the woman that Helen had just introduced to everyone. Who was she? Janet wondered. She had never seen her before. She looked at Elliott again. This time he wasn't looking at the woman, but he didn't look happy, either. He was looking inside his wineglass as though he was lost.

Elliott looked at Janet and smiled, but he had to force it. He felt empty, only existing from day to day, without love or the feeling of being wanted. He had been thinking of his empty life quite often, but until tonight, he thought that he had learned to live with it. And he had for years. Ashley Lake had that affect on him. What a mysterious woman, he thought, and was sure that she had no idea what affect she had on others.

Looking at all the strange faces, Ashley knew only Helen and Elliott. For a few seconds their eyes met and locked, but she smiled and looked the other way. The woman that stood next to him probably was his wife. She was tall, expensively dressed in a beaded black dress that dropped to her slender ankles. Her hair was black in a fashionably short cut. She had small eyes and full lips painted dark red. As she talked and moved her hand the large diamond on her ring did not go unnoticed.

Elaine came back and stood next to Ashley. "Helen tells me that your daughter and Lynn went to USC together."

"Yes. My daughter remembers Lynn."

"Come on, let's go into the den and get to know each other. My husband is talking about sports so he won't miss me for a while," Elaine said.

Just as Ashley and Elaine started toward the den, Elliott stepped in front of them. "It's nice to see you, Mrs. Lake."

"Thanks, it's nice to see you, too. I didn't tell you, but I appreciate you seeing me the day after I called you. I've had better days, believe me," she said, looking at Elliott's wife. She was talking to a couple but Ashley could see from the corner of her eyes that Janet was watching her.

"Mrs. Lake?"

"Call me Ashley. We don't have to be so formal with each other, do we?"

"No, Ashley, of course not. My secretary is back from her leave of absence. Why don't you call my office Monday morning and she can see what kind of schedule I have. I'll tell her to work you in so we can go over the draft I have for your approval. Sorry I had to cancel the last appointment." The smell of her perfume lingering in the air only drew him closer. And as he watched her full red lips he felt an ache in his heart. But his relationship with her was only business and Elliott never mixed business with pleasure.

Elaine and Ashley were talking in the den when shortly after Janet came in.

"Hello, Elaine. I didn't get a chance to say hello to you tonight. And you look lovely," Janet said.

"Thank you, Janet. This is Ashley. She's a friend of Helen's. Can you believe she made this adorable dress she's wearing?"

"Really? Did you really make it?"

"Yes. I also made Helen a suit that she needed to take to Chicago," Ashley said.

"Oh, but Helen could have found anything she wanted if she would have looked in the stores where I shop. She loves to shop, you know. Why would she want a dressmaker to make her suit?" Janet looked at Elaine and back at Ashley, the corners of her mouth turning up into a smirk.

"I think Helen did find what she wanted, and she wanted something different and just as elegant," Ashley answered. "Also, dressmakers make the clothes that are in the stores," Ashley said in a chilly voice that made Janet take a step back.

"I was just telling Ashley that she has another client. I want her to design a dress for me," Elaine said.

"Well, in that case, I guess I should take a look at what

you can do. Can you come to my home, Ashley?" Janet asked.

"I guess I could but I have so much you can pick from at my house. Whenever you want to see what I have, just call me."

"Thanks, I will. I really should be getting back to my husband. He's so jealous when other men are around." Janet gave Ashley one last smile and went back to the living room.

"She's what you call an artificial, snooty bitch," Elaine hissed. "Phony, phony. I keep telling Helen."

Ashley looked at Elaine, and they both laughed out loud.

"I do agree," Ashley commented. "She is phony, and one doesn't have to be around her that long to know it."

"Now, take Anita and the other three ladies, all down-to-earth. But Janet, she makes my skin crawl," Elaine snarled.

Everyone went into the dining room for dinner, and Ashley sat next to Elaine; they were instantly friends.

After dinner was over, Helen played more music while three of the couples danced in the center of the living room.

It was midnight and the only ones left were Raymond and Anita, Dan and Elaine, and Ashley. Elaine convinced Ashley to stay longer.

Ashley felt good. She had made another step into the second half of her life, with new friends, a new surrounding, and, of course, a pending divorce.

Chapter 12

It was a chilly morning. To warm up, Ashley jogged faster. As others ran toward her, she could see the sun streaming across their faces, their eyes squinting against bright sunlight.

Since Ashley had fallen into a routine, she jogged four mornings a week; soon she could jog faster and worked up to an extra mile. She passed a man she had seen twice a week since she had started jogging. Acknowledging her, he smiled and nodded his head. Without slowing up she returned his smile. All the joggers's faces had gotten familiar.

As she jogged around the park for the fifth time, she looked at her watch. One more time around, she thought.

Fox Hills Park was busy this time of the morning because some of the joggers were there before going to work. Ashley liked it better than the track off La Brea and Stocker Boulvard, where she first began jogging. She ran around the park one last time and kept running until she got to her car.

Once she got home, Ashley had a glass of orange juice and stood at the kitchen sink looking out onto her back yard. She finished her juice and went to the bathroom to shower, lingering under the running warm water, feeling muscles relaxing all through her body.

* * *

"Was there a full house at Helen's party?" Vanessa asked.

"No, not exactly. Four couples, but a gentleman and I were the only ones alone without a date. And they were all married couples, too. I had a nice time, but I felt a little out of place being alone," Ashley said, following Vanessa from the dining area to the living room. "I guess I'll have to get used to going out alone."

"You won't forever, Ash. You've met new friends, and you've taken the first step of going out alone. That's a start, Ash."

"I guess so. Girl, you can look in that man's eyes and see the love he has for Helen. And you can see she feels the same for him, too. Like you and Gary."

"I'm a lucky woman, I know. It'll happen to you one day, too, Ash."

"Maybe, one day." She felt sad and decided to change the conversation. "When will Gary be back?"

"He still doesn't feel well but he'll be back tomorrow morning. His mother is feeling better and can move her left arm. That stroke scared Gary to death. A call at midnight will scare anyone to death."

"I'm sure." Ashley rubbed her hand along the arm of the chair that she was sitting in. The leather was as soft as a glove. She looked at her watch. "I better be going so I won't be late. Elliott's secretary squeezed me in this morning."

"Elliott, huh?"

"No use being so formal. He's a nice man and so down-to-earth. But that wife of his, I don't know about her. Elaine, Helen's sister, says she is superficial. You know, if I had talked to her longer, she would have made me feel stupid."

"How is that, Ash?" Vanessa asked and placed her cup on the table. She was still wearing her robe and her hair was in rollers.

"Well, she made a comment about not having time to

go to a dressmaker when one can shop at one of the better stores. Can you believe one can be so ignorant?" Ashley stood up, and picked up her car keys and purse.

Vanessa walked her to the door. "To hell with her, Ash. And you look nice in that green suit you're wearing. I can't get over the change in you."

"Thanks," Ashley said. "The only regret I have is not making the change in my appearance years ago. All this time my health was going bad. The doctor says I've been walking around like a time bomb about to go off." Feeling lucky, she shook her head in amazement that she was still alive.

Vanessa stood outside watching Ashley walk to her car. Her entire wardrobe was different from what she had before she lost thirty-five pounds.

"Mrs. Lake, Mr. Douglas will see you now," the receptionist said.

Ashley walked in back of her. From the back she looked like a small Barbie doll. Her skirt was short, about a size four, with long dark hair. She was tall, walked in high heel shoes, higher than any Ashley dared to walk in.

Elliott stood at the large window, hands in his pockets as he looked out. He was very distinguished-looking, dressed elegantly in a gray pinstriped suit that fit as though it was tailored for his well-built body. The sun was shining and Ashley could see his hair was lighter than she had noticed before. It was brown, not black at all.

He turned around when he heard her walk in. "Good morning, Ashley," he said, extending his hand as he sat behind his desk. "I hope you had a nice time last night."

"Yes, very nice," she said, taking her purse off her shoulder and placing it on her lap.

"The Wilbertsons are good people. Now, I want you to go over the divorce settlement and see if you want any more modifications made." He opened a folder and placed it in front of Ashley.

"Take your time. I'll be right back. Would you like a cup of coffee?

"Oh, no thanks. I'm fine."

Elliott stood up. "I'm going to the office next door. Just take your time." He watched her for a few seconds before he turned around and walked out.

As Elliott walked down the hall, he felt the same stab at his heart that he felt two nights before. Today she was all business, but there was still something warm and loving about her, something that made a man realize what he needed in a woman. She was like a magnet that drew you closer against your will. But he knew that he had to get over it. He was married, and she was unhappy over her divorce, and probably still loves her husband.

On the way back to his office Elliott stopped in Robert's office and picked up a brown envelope that was left out for him.

Ashley had finished going over the divorce settlement and was waiting patiently for Elliott's return.

"Is there anything you want me to change, Ashley?" He sat back at his desk.

"No, it's just the way I wanted it to read." She clicked her tongue at the roof of her mouth. "I guess I can sign it and make it final. It's really over now," she said, still holding the agreement in her hand. She shook her head and looked as though a dark cloud was lingering over her.

Elliott looked at his watch. He couldn't stand to see her look so unhappy. "I could use a bite to eat and I hate eating alone. Why don't you join me, Ashley?"

For a moment she started to say no. But she needed someone to take her mind off her divorce, and she had felt so good the day before. Why not go to lunch? After all, it was only a lunch. "Yes, right now I sure could use the company."

"So could I," he answered. "There's a restaurant on the corner. We can walk there."

Ashley followed Elliott, who returned the receptionist's smile as he passed her desk.

He led Ashley to the elevator.

Walking to the restaurant, Ashley wondered if it was a wise decision to have lunch with Elliott. She wasn't in a happy mood. But, he was her lawyer and was beginning to feel like a friend, which she needed today. As they walked she wondered how many women had he been so kind to, to help ease the pain. And as they walked he started discussing her new business. The fresh air felt great, and the stress she felt inside his office began to diminish.

"I eat at this restaurant quite a bit. It's convenient and the food is good."

"I guess as busy as you are, it is convenient by being so close to your office."

"Here it is. The Steak House, and they have great steaks, too." He held the door open for her.

"Hello, Meg," Elliott said. The waitress's smile lingered as she looked at him. She took them to a corner table. She knew that Elliott was a lawyer and liked privacy with his clients, so that they could talk and not be overheard by others.

Elliott ordered a steak, medium-rare, a baked potato, and small salad. Ashley ordered the same. The restaurant was nicely decorated with snow-white tablecloths and a fresh red rose in the center of each table. There were a few people but it was quiet.

The waitress left and returned with two tall glasses of water. Ashley noticed that as the waitress bent over Elliott, her large breast just happened to brush against his shoulder. Elliott didn't seem to notice, but how could a size forty breast rub against a man and he not notice? Yeah, sure, Ashley thought.

Twenty-five minutes later the waitress was back with

their orders. No one spoke until she placed the plates on the table and left.

"You have one daughter, Ashley?"

"Yes. She's married and happy. Lori is the one good thing that came out of my marriage."

"I always wanted children, but my wife couldn't have any. We discussed adopting one but never got around to doing it. Sometimes I wish we would have. You see, I have my work and my wife has the social life." He squeezed a sliced lemon into his glass of water and sipped it. "I always wanted a couple of kids. But life has a way of taking a turn in the opposite direction."

"I understand. I used to dream of owning my own business as a dress designer."

"Now you haven't anything to stop you. In the beginning I worked long hours to accomplish what I have today. I'm afraid my wife never understood that. After I made a name for myself, I joined the law firm where I am now. Then I had to work long hours with cases that the last lawyer had left behind before he died. There has to be a strong foundation to hold a marriage together when one is always so busy," Elliott said.

Ashley looked in his eyes as she listened intensely. Looks like she wasn't the only one that had a marriage on the rocks. She placed her fork on her plate.

"So here we are in the prime of our lives—you have a problem marriage and mine has fallen apart. Sometimes I wonder: when did mine fall so hard? I didn't see it. Where was I when it happened? But I'm tired of trying to figure out when it happened, how it happened. It did, and that's that. It's time I get on with my life." She sat up straight, squared her shoulders.

He was surprised to hear her make that statement. "Everyone asks that same question when they come into my office. But life goes on, Ashley. I promise you."

It was strange how he felt so close to her. She was someone who listened and understood what he meant.

He could sit and look at Ashley all day. Elliott didn't have to touch her or make love to her. He just wanted to look at her, inhale the scent of her perfume, watch the graceful way she held her head high with such a young and lovely smile. The truth was, he was overwhelmed by her charm and her strength to forge ahead with her life after a devastating divorce. She was still hurting, he knew. But one day she would fall in love with someone else. Not many men could be around her and not want to know more about her.

They finished lunch and went back to his office so that he could validate her parking ticket.

As Elliott and Ashley got out of the elevator, they were laughing when they entered his office, and Janet was sitting in a chair, waiting.

Janet looked from Elliott to Ashley. "I take it your lunch went well?"

Chapter 13

"Mom, Grandma, I'm six weeks pregnant. Keith and I are going to have a baby." Lori beamed, her face was glowing, and her eyes were gleaming with happiness. Keith was by her side, equally happy.

Ashley jumped from her chair and hugged Lori, then Keith.

Doris's eyes watered and Cora laughed out loud and clapped her hands.

"I'm going to be a grandmother? I can't believe I'm going to be a grandmother, Lori." Ashley was so happy and so excited she almost cried.

"You're a grandmother," Doris said. "I'm going to be a great-grandmother. But I've been waiting for this moment."

Daniel walked into the living room. "All my girls are here at the same time. What's all the fussing about?" he asked, as he looked at Ashley wiping her tears.

"Did you hear, Granddad?" Lori beamed, standing in front of him as he took a seat on the sofa next to his wife.

"Hear what?" he asked.

"I'm going to have a baby, Keith and I are going to have a baby."

Daniel jumped up off the sofa and gave Lori a big bear hug. "Hot damn. A baby is on its way, Doris." He was so happy to see both his girls at his house today. Usually, he would see one and miss the other.

"This calls for a celebration," Daniel said. "Doris, we

have to take Keith and Lori out to dinner soon," he said, and held Doris's hand. "I knew you could do it, son," Daniel said to Keith.

Doris looked at Daniel's face. He hadn't been feeling well lately, but today he was looking well and happy. Maybe she had been overly concerned about him.

"Honey, you've made my day," Ashley said. "Have you told Marcus yet?" Before she realized it, she had already included Marcus. And as she looked at Daniel, he was staring at her. Was he afraid she would cry? Old habits are hard to stop, Ashley thought.

"No. I'll call him when I get home. I wanted you guys to be the first to know." Lori looked at her mother. Ashley had gotten her hair frosted with light highlights. Lately, it seemed that every time she saw her mother, she looked more stylish. She just wished her father could see Ashley now.

"I know what I'm going to do, Cora," Doris said. "Come and help me. I'm going to get a cold bottle of apple cider out the refrigerator and five champagne glasses so we can toast to Lori and Keith. This calls for a big, big celebration. But all we have is apple cider." Cora followed Doris to the kitchen.

Ashley, Lori, Keith, and Daniel were left alone in the living room.

"How are you feeling today, Dad?" Ashley asked.

"Just fine, daughter. I was at the doctor's office the last time you were here. Cora said I had just missed you."

"And your blood pressure?" Ashley asked.

"Good, Ash. Don't you go fussing over me. Now, we're going to have a little one running around here soon."

"Lori, have you and Keith told his parents yet?" Ashley asked.

"We will when we get home. We just left the doctor's office. Do you think Grandma will babysit when I go back to work? I don't want a stranger keeping my baby."

"I'm sure she will feel the same way. You know Mother.

She'll love babysitting and Dad will, too. Won't you, Dad?"

"I'll be here, but Doris and Cora will have to do the babysitting. But, I'll be here."

"How is business, Ashley?" Daniel asked.

"I have three dresses and a suit to make. And I got another order today. Also, I have to talk to a lady that Elaine referred to help me."

"That's great, Ash. I knew you could do it," Daniel said.

Ashley's eyes watered. "Thanks, Dad. You've always supported me in everything I do. I'm lucky for having you."

Daniel placed Ashley's delicate hand in his.

"Here we are," Cora said, setting down the six glasses on the coffee table. Doris began to fill them. They all took a glass and toasted to the new addition to the family. They laughed and talked about Lori and Keith's baby.

An hour had passed and Ashley, Lori, and Keith left, going their separate ways.

Driving home, Ashley wondered how Marcus would react to the news. She thought they would always be together to share news of a grandchild coming into the world. Things sure had changed in her life, but she was taking it in stride.

The doorbell rang. Ashley was expecting Joan, the woman Elaine had referred. Ashley opened the door and the woman introduced herself.

"Come in and have a seat," Ashley said, leading her into the den.

"You have a lovely home, Mrs. Lake." Joan was a short woman, about 5'2"; her hair was in long French braids; her eyeglasses were round with wire frames. She had a pleasant face and a warm smile. Ashley guessed her to be in her early fifties.

"Would you like something to drink—coffee, tea or some apple juice?"

"No thank you, Mrs. Lake."

"Please, call me Ashley."

"Okay, and call me Joan." Joan took a seat on the sofa in the den and Ashley sat in the chair facing her.

"Now, first I'll explain what I'm doing. My business is just starting to get off the ground and I have a feeling it's going to be too much for me to handle alone. I need someone to cut the material in patterns, do some of the hemming, placing shoulder pads, and sewing bottoms on the clothing.

"I have to think of a name for my label," she said and sighed. "I have so much to do, and I'll be selling this house and moving into another, and also, I'm going to lease a space soon. It won't be too far from here, but that's not right away. Where do you live, Joan?"

"I live in Inglewood, right off 6th Avenue and 78th Street. I'm not far at all. And I'm dependable, too, Ashley. I can come anytime and leave anytime. I learned to sew when I was fifteen years old."

Ashley nodded her head. "You're exactly what I need, Joan."

"I'm the oldest of seven girls. We were poor and had to learn to make our clothes."

"I think we will get along just fine together, Joan. Can you start the day after tomorrow?"

"Yes, oh yes. Just tell me what time and I'll be here."

"Nine will be a good time. Make sure you dress comfortably, and feel free to use the phone whenever you need to, and the kitchen can also be used including the microwave." Ashley liked Joan and wanted her to feel comfortable in her home. After all, Joan was her first employee.

"Do you have any grandchildren, Joan?"

"Honey, I have six already. I have four children and

three of them have two kids each," she said and smiled. "I take it you do or have one on the way."

"My daughter is pregnant now. I'm so happy."

"You don't look like a grandmother, Ashley. You look so young, honey."

"Thank you, Joan. But I feel older than what I am. My life changed abruptly. I'm going through a divorce, a new business, and soon a new place to live. But I'm coping the best way I can, and I keep busy."

"That's all you can do, Ashley. Keep that head up and start living life to its fullest to make yourself happy."

Two days later Ashley was sitting on a barstool in her kitchen, making a list of foods she needed from the supermarket. The phone rang; she dropped the pencil on the counter.

"Hello," Ashley answered. It was Elliott.

"Ashley, your husband agreed with all the terms of the settlement. He wanted the property to be sold right away but after his lawyer and I discussed it further, he backed down and agreed. But don't be surprised if you get a telephone call from him. From what his lawyer says, he's not too happy."

"Oh, I'm sure I will get one from him. I'll probably put the house up for sale next week. But I won't tell him that. Let him squirm for a while."

"I must say, this is the cleanest divorce I've done since I've been a lawyer." But Elliott didn't expect anything but "clean" from Ashley.

"Incidentally, he was pretty pissed off about the $3,000 dollars' worth of clothes that was charged on his Visa. He says it was a card that was only used for emergencies."

Ashley wanted to laugh out loud, but she didn't. Instead, she rolled her eyes up at the ceiling. "So let him stay pissed. He'll get over it, Elliott." She walked to the kitchen sink with the phone resting on her shoulder and picked brown leaves off a plant.

"Anyway, once it's recorded, you'll get it in the mail."

"I appreciate everything you've done, Elliott."

"It was my pleasure. You are a free woman, Ashley. Call me if you have any questions. Better yet, when you're in my neck of the woods stop by and we can have lunch."

Elliott held the phone. A few seconds passed before she responded and Elliott was afraid that his suggestion was inappropriate. But it was only lunch and only if she was near his office.

"Lunch sounds good. I'll certainly keep that in mind."

He released a sigh, relieved that she wasn't offended.

"Thanks for everything, Elliott. And I owe you lunch."

"You're welcome, Ashley. Take care of yourself." That was the end of the conversation, but he was sure that he would see Ashley again. He would make sure.

Chapter 14

"Joan, you can cut a pattern faster than I can draw one," Ashley said. She was sitting on the floor, stacks of brown paper lying unfolded that she drew her patterns on. As she drew a pattern, Joan was instructed to cut it out, fold it, place it in a large envelope, and label it by the name that Ashley had given it. They were now working on the Ruffle Blouses.

"In two months I have to make thirty dresses for a church celebration. It will be twenty-six years since the church was built, not to mention that it will be around the holidays and other customers will be coming out of the ceiling." She laid down her pencil on the floor in front of her. "What am I going to do, Joan? We'll need more help. And to make matters worse, I may have a buyer for this house. I'm going to look at a town house for myself tomorrow." Ashley took a long shallow of her diet cola, feeling it tickle at her throat.

"Honey, don't you worry about help. I have a sister who is two years younger than I am. Her name is Renee. She doesn't have nothing to do all day but sit up, eat, and watch television. She would love to help us out and could use the extra money, too. Who couldn't use extra money for the holidays? Renee could even pack for you while we're sewing, not that she doesn't know how to sew because she does. But you'll need help with packing, too."

"You really think she'll want to help us out, Joan?"

"Yes. When you're ready I'll bring her over one morning." Joan sensed that Ashley was skeptical but wanted to make her feel comfortable. "Now, don't you worry about anyone that I refer to you. You're not sure about having strange people in your house. And I don't blame you. But Renee is a decent woman like me. Nothing will be missing after she's gone," she said convincingly. "You can also call Elaine and Helen. Renee did some work for both of them. She still helps Elaine out when she needs her."

"Elaine spoke very highly of you, Joan. If Renee worked for her and Helen, then she must be as dependable and trustworthy as you are."

"Thank you, Ashley."

"Well, then it's settled. When I'm ready you can speak to Renee. I'll pay her the same as you. I guess I must be doing something right to be lucky enough to have someone like you."

Joan smiled.

"Do you have any brothers, Joan?"

"No. My mother always said she wished she had had one son. But my father seemed to be happy enough with all girls."

The phone rang and Ashley picked it up on the first ring. It was Marcus; Ashley excused herself and took the phone in her bedroom.

Ashley perched on the edge of the bed and crossed her leg as though she had positioned herself for an argument. "I expected to hear from you sooner." She heard him sigh.

"When are you going to sell the house, Ash? You could just buy me out, you know."

"I know I can, Marcus. But I'm not going to buy you out until I'm good and ready. I can't handle two notes right now."

"Then sell the damn house. Why are you holding onto the past, Ash? What are you trying to prove? Oh, I know what you're up to. You want people to feel sorry for you.

You hold onto the house, you cry and make everyone say, 'poor Ashley has that big note to pay by herself.' Is that it?" He sounded cruel, he knew. But he was tired of her games, her trying to get even.

"Why would I want people to feel sorry for me, Marcus? I'm just getting my business off the ground. I'll sell when I find the time or when it's convenient for me. So get over it." She started to hang up. Why listen to anything he had to say? Hadn't she listened for twenty-five years?

"Look, Ash. I've tried to be fair with you because of all the years we have behind us. I've respected all your wishes whether I agreed or not. But you're going too far. I want to go forward, Ash. And leave the past behind me."

Ashley cringed at the sound of the icy tone in his voice. "Well, Marcus, you got the woman and the freedom you wanted. Sorry, honey, you can't have it all. If you can't get over it, take me to court. I can do whatever I want, whenever I want to. And you know what I just discovered, Marcus?"

"No. What have you just discovered?" he asked, and whirled his chair around to face the window.

"I'm no longer angry with you. I just hate you, Marcus." She hung up and tried to compose herself.

Ashley opened her hands and held them in front of her. They were trembling, her palms red from holding the phone too tight. Why did she still let him upset her so? she wondered. She hated him, but yet she still loved him. Oh, it was all so confusing, she thought. She forgot to ask him how he felt about becoming a grandfather. Five-and-a-half months and two days since Marcus walked out of her life. She blinked, felt tears rolling down her checks. She had to get out the house and get some fresh air. She had to clear her head, clear the hurt, if only for a short while.

Ashley changed clothes so that she could run a couple

of errands. "Joan, you can finish cutting the patterns. I shouldn't be gone too long."

"All right, Ashley," Joan said, without looking up at her. She knew Ashley's eyes would be red from crying. Joan had seen it more than once in the short time she had known Ashley.

"There's some cold cuts in the refrigerator. You're welcome to whatever you see."

The first stop Ashley made was at the bank. She had been carrying around a thousand dollars in checks. Thank God she didn't have to look at Marcus's girlfriend or watch Marcus coming in to see her. Changing banks was a good idea, plus, it gave her a good reason to inconvenience Marcus.

Ashley stood in the line behind two other customers and was out in less than twenty minutes.

Her next stop was at the Beverly Center at a large fabric store. She picked out the material she needed and left. That should conclude her errands for the day, she thought.

As Ashley walked through the mall, she heard a familiar voice calling her name, and she turned around. He looked tall, dressed in a pair of navy blue slacks and a light blue shirt with no tie. He was handsome enough to make a woman breathless.

Elliott was carrying a bag from Barnes and Noble bookstore. Ashley smiled as he walked toward her. "Playing hooky from the office, Elliott?" She had to look up at him—he looked taller than she had noticed before. And his eyes were light.

"Yes. I'm playing hooky today. I thought I would buy myself a good book." Lately, a good book was all he had for entertainment.

"There's a Starbucks over there. Have time for a cup of coffee?" he asked.

"Sure. Coffee sounds good."

She sat at a table and waited while Elliott got the coffee. Ashley watched him as he stood in line. She had to admit that she was glad to see him. Most of the friends she and Marcus had were his. And ever since they had separated, his friends had gone with him. She watched Elliott carrying a cup in each hand.

"Here we go. It's a lovely day. I'm going home and read and watch TV like normal people do. I didn't take any of my cases home with me yesterday. So I have a free day."

"Do you really know how to do that?" Ashley asked. They both laughed out loud.

"Not very well, I'm afraid. What do you do when you're home, Ashley?"

"Work on my business, draw suits, dresses, blouses. Then I make the patterns to go with each one, cut them out. I hired a lady to help me. I make some of the clothing just to show clients. Right now I can play hooky, too. I needed the break."

"I've listened to you speak about your business before. You have a good head for business," Elliott said. He looked down at her delicate hands.

"I'm going to have to find a space to lease. There was one in the same unit where Vanessa has her shop. But I waited too long and someone else got it. I just didn't think I would have so much work so soon."

"Did you meet Anita and her husband, Raymond, at Robert's house?"

"Yes, but briefly."

"Well, Raymond owns some spaces in the Ladera shopping center. Why don't you give him a call? Helen can give you his phone number." Elliott couldn't take his eyes off Ashley's face. He was sure that after the last time they talked, there was a chance that he wouldn't see her again. And again, he felt the same loneliness nag at him. Would he feel this way every time he was near her?

She took on a serious tone. "You are always so helpful, Elliott. All I can say is thank you for all your advice."

He reached across the table and touched her hand. "I'm always—"

"Elliott?" the woman's voice was behind him. Elliott turned around to see who it was.

"Cheryl, good to see you. This is Ashley Lake, a friend and client. Would you like to join us?" he asked, hoping she would refuse. He wanted to be alone with Ashley.

"Nice to meet you, Ashley. I just ran in here to look around. Sorry, I can't stay any longer."

The woman smiled, and Ashley noticed that as she talked to Elliott she kept looking at her. And as she walked away, Ashley noticed she looked back at her twice.

"Nice woman," Elliott said. "Now where were we?"

"I was just thanking you for all your help. My husband never had enough confidence in me. I appreciate that you do." She looked at her watch. "I better be going. Joan probably needs me about now. But I'm so glad that I ran into you, Elliott."

Elliott couldn't think of any excuses to keep her any longer. Damn Cheryl for her interruption, he thought. All he wanted to do was to talk to Ashley, look at her, touch her hand as he had before Cheryl came along and broke the spell. He got up. "I think I should be going myself. It was good to see you, Ashley. Don't forget, we still have a pending lunch date."

Ashley stood and looked up at him. He was such a nice man, a good-looking one, too, but she had no intention of calling him for lunch. He was a married man, and why start something she couldn't finish? Janet was indeed a lucky woman.

"Thanks for the coffee, Elliott, and thanks for giving me the tip to call Raymond." She smiled and walked away.

Elliott watched Ashley until she was out of sight.

* * *

Three days later Elliott came home from his office at about seven. He was tired from the long day in court. He had had a late lunch so he wasn't hungry. All he wanted was to get comfortable, slump into his large chair, and close his eyes until the pain lessened in his left temple.

He heard Janet come into the den and take a seat on the sofa opposite him.

"I talked to Cheryl today, Elliott. She says that she ran into you and Ashley three days ago. Is she the dressmaker?" She crossed her leg and waited for his response.

"Dress *designer*, and yes, Cheryl did stop and say hello to us. And yes, it was Ashley Lake." He closed his eyes again, both legs stretched out on the table in front of him.

"Elliott, did you arrange to meet her? Because if you did, I won't have it. I won't have you humiliating me in public by sneaking around with trash," she hissed, and sat up straight.

Elliott opened his eyes and looked at her. "First of all, if I had arranged to meet her, Janet, rest assured it would not be in a mall. I can think of better places. Secondly, why the hell do you care?"

As he stared at her she felt uncomfortable. She saw something in his eyes that she hadn't seen before. Was he in love with someone else, or did he just hate her?

"Elliott, I've never been unfaithful to you. I deserve the same respect. Like I said, I won't have you humiliate me in public."

Elliott sighed. "I didn't come home to hear this conversation or your false display of concern for me, Janet. Do I question you about anything you do or anyplace you go? Do you really think I care? Don't start this jealousy thing so late in the marriage. And if you're worried about me cutting your allowance, don't worry." He looked at her again, waved his hand as if he had dismissed her, and closed his eyes.

He was too calm and that infuriated her. Nothing she said seemed to bother him any longer. But she wouldn't let Ashley or anyone else take what's hers. Although she had more skills than a dressmaker did, she had never worked. She had gotten used to staying home and doing what she wanted to, and still got what she wanted. Knowing Elliott, why would he want less than she? A man in his position wouldn't want the woman.

"When does Ashley, or whatever her name was, get time to date a man in the mall?" She looked away when Elliott opened his eyes and looked at her.

Janet looked at the painting on the wall that had been in the same spot for years. She would buy new paintings for this room, but she would take care of that later. Besides, first things first, and getting back to the business at hand was first. "Is she the best you can do, Elliott? Surely, you can do better than that."

He sat up straight; the pain in his temple throbbed from the sound of her unwelcome voice.

"I'm telling you once and for all and this will be the last of this conversation. Ashley and I both happened to be at the mall, so we spoke, had a cup of coffee together. Now don't bring it up to me again. You know, Janet, don't think for one minute that I haven't divorced you because I'm afraid of losing everything I have. There are ways to get around that, dear."

His eyes pierced through her as she felt the frosty chill of his presence. But she couldn't stop. "Do you think for one minute that influential people such as Helen and Robert will always invite someone like her to their house? She makes clothes for people, for Pete's sake, Elliott."

Elliott looked at her in disgust, raised his hands up in the air in an angry gesture. "It's not what a person does that makes them someone, Janet. I mean, look at you. You could be doing something to help people, but you would rather make people think you're something that you are not. You have no heart, no soul, you're just an empty shadow walking around and pretending you're more than you really are. We both know what we mean to each other." He turned his head, and again waved his hand in dismissal as though he couldn't stand to look at her any longer.

"You just don't understand, Elliott. I'm trying to protect your reputation. Maybe you really don't have any interest in Ashley. But there are women out there that will do anything to get a man like you." She waited for his response but he just laid his head back, kept his eyes closed as though she was no longer in the room with him. He was so unapproachable lately. But she would keep a close check on his attitude. Could it be sex he wanted from Ashley? Well, if it was only sex, she had nothing else better to do tonight. If that was what he needed she would accommodate him. She sighed and went into their bedroom.

After a few minutes had passed, Janet called for Elliott to come into their bedroom. When he walked in she was lying naked in the middle of their king size bed; her arms open to him.

Surprised, Elliott came to a halt and stood in the middle of the room. They hadn't made love in over a month. Now, Janet wanted to smooth things over. He started to walk out, but what the hell. It had been a month and he hadn't had a woman. Besides, it wouldn't take long. Janet wasn't the kind of woman that had much of an appetite for making love, except when it suited her. He unbuttoned his shirt and stepped out of his trousers.

When Elliott entered Janet he moaned, closed his eyes, and saw Ashley's sweet face, felt her hands slowly, gently, caressing his back, her lips pressing sweetly against his. When his name purred from Janet, Elliott's body stiffened; it was over.

Chapter 15

"Mother, what did the doctor say about Dad this time?" Ashley asked with concern. "When I came over last week he didn't look well. He said that he was only tired, but I'm concerned."

"That hardheaded brother of mine didn't go to the doctor last week. You know how stubborn he is," Cora answered.

"Maybe if you talk to him, Ash, he'll go," Doris said. She knew that if anyone could convince Daniel it would be Ashley. Doris was worried about him today. He couldn't even remember where he had placed his cap this morning, and Daniel never forgot where he puts his caps. He had hung them in the same spot for thirty years. Every time Daniel walked in the house he would hang his hat or cap on the brown wooden coat rack that was kept in the corner of the living room.

"Okay, let me go in and talk to him," Ashley answered, walking fast past her mother and Cora.

First, Ashley stood at the door and watched Daniel sleeping. She walked in the bedroom; he was nodding off into a light sleep.

Daniel heard Ashley's footsteps and opened his eyes and smiled.

"What brings you this way today, daughter?" He sat up in bed and fluffed his pillow.

Looking at her father's face, Ashley saw him strain. She was genuinely worried because it was rare that one of her parents was ill. Her father was always so strong, showing no sign of illness. Seeing him in bed in the middle of the day was Ashley's worse fear. Daniel was ill. "Dad, when was the last time you went to see your doctor?"

"I think I just went to see him two weeks ago." he said, trying to remember.

"He didn't give you an appointment to see him since?" she asked, looking at Doris as she walked in. "I'm concerned about you and with good reason." Ashley got out of the chair and sat on the edge of the king size bed. Looking at the colorful comforter with the faded orange flower in the middle made her remember when she took her mother shopping and bought it as a birthday gift.

"I'm just a little tired, Ash. Remember, I'm an old man now," he said jokingly.

Daniel feeling tired didn't quite set right with Ashley, and she couldn't shake off the ominous feeling settling in her chest. It had haunted her for three days.

"You're only seventy years old. That's not old. But at that age you have to keep your appointments, Dad. I would feel much better if you let me take you to the doctor's office. I know that Mom would, too. You know how she worries about everyone." Ashley tried to sound calm, but she was just as worried as her mother was. "Please, Dad, for me."

"Okay, okay, we'll go. But he'll just tell me to get some rest and take vitamins." He got out of bed, wearing the bottom of his red-and-blue strip pajamas and a white T-shirt.

"Okay, Dad, I'll wait in the living room." She went back to the living room while Daniel got dressed.

Ashley had gone back into the living room with Cora and Doris.

"Mom, he's getting dressed. Why don't you and Aunt Cora go for the ride? I know you would feel better if you could talk to the doctor." Ashley sat down on the sofa.

She had been up sewing until two that morning. Luckily, she had someone she could depend on like Joan.

Finally Daniel was ready. Ashley insisted on driving her car.

In the doctor's office, Doris went in with Daniel. But a half hour later, she walked out slowly, wiping tears from her eyes with a tissue. The minute Ashley and Cora saw her they jumped up at the same time.

"What is it, Mom?" Ashley asked. "Tell me, what is it?"

"Dr. Martin isn't completely sure but he wants Daniel to be tested. He says his blood pressure is high. That's why I called and asked you to come over, Ash. Daniel couldn't remember where he hung his hat, and he only hangs it in one place." Doris shook her head. "We got to take him to the hospital, Ash, so they can run tests to find out. What if it's a deadly disease? I don't like the feeling of not knowing," Doris whimpered.

Cora sat back on the sofa and held Doris hand. "We'll take care of him, Doris. Don't worry, honey. His blood pressure has been up before. But it goes down, besides, the Lord won't take him until he's ready."

"I'm going in there and talk to that doctor." Ashley marched right into the room where her father and the doctor were talking. "Dr. Martin, what do you think is wrong with my father?"

Dr. Martin was standing in front of Daniel and stopped talking when he saw Ashley. She looked so different from the last time he saw her that he almost didn't recognize her.

"I'm not completely sure yet, Ashley. But his blood pressure is high and I want to have a couple of tests run on him. I'll call the hospital so they will know what to do."

"But what kind of tests?" Ashley asked.

"His heart, and of course he'll stay in the hospital until

his blood pressure is lowered. I need to know why it keeps going up so high."

Dr. Martin had been Daniel and Doris's doctor for twenty years. He was a short, middle-aged man with small blue eyes and a nose too large for his too-slender face.

"And he should go right now?" Ashley asked, looking at Daniel. He stood up and put his brown cap on his head.

"I would say so," Dr. Martin answered. "Or no later than tomorrow morning, first thing."

"We can go tomorrow morning," Daniel stated. "Who's to say I'm really ill or if I can't wait to go then? I'm staying home. Doris looks frightened and I'm staying with my wife," he said more to Dr. Martin than to Ashley.

Dr. Martin nodded in understanding and looked at Ashley. "Okay, but take him early in the morning so he won't have to go too long without eating. He's not to eat anything after midnight or before he goes in tomorrow morning. Don't even drink water or coffee before you go."

"Okay, Dr. Martin. I'll have him at the hospital first thing tomorrow morning," Ashley said, and went back into the waiting room. Daniel was behind her.

On the way to her parents' house, Ashley thought of Lori and decided she would call her as soon as she got home. She hadn't talked to Lori at all today and had been checking on her every day since she got the news of her pregnancy.

The ride back was quiet. Doris sat in the front seat, and Ashley could see out of the corner of her eye that her mother was worried. Every time she looked at Doris, she was looking back at Daniel. Lord, Ashley thought. They had been married for forty-six years.

"Well, here we are," Ashley said as she parked the car. "You're okay, Dad?"

"Ash, don't worry. I'll be all right, baby." Daniel got out the car and opened the door for his wife and Cora to get out. They all went inside.

"Okay, Dad, I'm leaving but I will be here around seven-thirty tomorrow morning. So be ready."

"I'm going, too, Ash," Doris said.

"So am I. Don't leave me out," Cora said, snatching off her wig. She shook it out as she would an old rag. "I'll be ready on time, Doris, and sit down and rest. I'll cook dinner today. You don't want to stay for dinner, Ash?" Cora asked.

"No thanks, Aunt Cora. I need to get back before Joan leaves so I can leave her instructions for tomorrow." Ashley kissed her mother and father on the cheek. "See you all tomorrow morning, early."

Driving home Ashley felt as though her brain was running on overload. It's funny, she never thought of Daniel getting old until today. He was always so in charge of everything, but today, she had to take charge. What would happen to Doris if anything ever happened to him? Well, she wouldn't let herself think that way.

The minute Ashley walked in Joan met her at the door. "Ashley, call your mother, honey. She just called a minute ago. I was going to call you on your cell phone."

"Did my mother say what she wanted?" Ashley asked, running to the phone. Her purse fell to the floor. Her fingers fumbled as she punched in the numbers on the phone.

"Mom, it's me, what's wrong?" she yelled into the phone and held her breath.

"The paramedics are here, Ash. They think it's a stroke—"

"Ash, this is Cora, meet us at Westside Emergency." Cora was yelling loudly into the receiver.

For a few seconds Joan was sure that Ashley would collapse. She fell against the sofa, one hand open against her chest. She looked at Joan, but no words emerged.

"Ashley, are you all right? Can you drive alone?"

"Yes, yes. I can drive alone." Ashley grabbed her purse and ran to the door, then stopped as though she had forgotten something. "Joan, you can leave now so I can lock up."

"Are you sure you can drive, Ashley? I can go with you."

"No, I can make it. Oh, God." They ran out the door. "I'll call you tomorrow, Joan. Take the day off." Ashley ran to her car, dropped her purse in the driveway, picked it up, and sped off.

Joan watched as Ashley's car disappeared around the corner.

At the hospital, the emergency parking lot was full. But a car was pulling out and Ashley beat the car that was waiting before her. The man who was waiting cursed at her but she didn't care. When she hopped out her car, she took a quick look at him, stopped, flipped her middle finger up in the air, and ran inside the hospital. Cora was waiting and met Ashley as she ran inside.

"Aunt Cora, how is he? Where is Mother?" she asked, breathing and talking fast, looking beyond the closed doors where she saw nurses and doctors walking in and out, and wondered what was waiting for her back there. Two police officers brushed against her as they walked fast and disappeared behind the doors. Ashley jumped, and cursed under her breath.

Cora took both of Ashley's hands in hers. "It's bad, honey. But you never know, he might come out of it all right. Come on and I'll go with you."

"Oh God, Aunt Cora."

They rushed down the hall, Ashley running, preparing herself for the worse. Oh, why didn't she insist on him going to the hospital as soon as they left the doctor's office? So many terrible thoughts were going through her mind, her mother, herself. How would she react if he doesn't come through? And once again, she thought of Marcus. If only he was there with her, to tell her Daniel would be all right, reassure her that she wasn't alone.

When Ashley got to Daniel's bed she stopped in her tracks. Her mother was sitting in a chair rocking backward and forward. Her father's eyes were closed, tubes hooked up to his veins. He didn't look like the same large man she had seen less than an hour ago. Instead, he looked weak and tired, and his face looked darker. Ashley shivered as she came close to kiss him on his cheek and saw his face twisted to one side. She turned to Cora, buried her face into her shoulder, and cried softly so that Daniel wouldn't hear her. Ashley felt Doris's hand tightly around hers.

The doctor walked in behind her. "I'm sorry, but if he lasts through the night I'll be surprised. He had a massive stroke. It's bad."

Ashley's legs almost crumbled under her but she had to pull herself together and be strong for Doris. She stood beside Doris, placing her hands on her shoulders to reassure her that she was there.

Doris placed both hands over her face and cried softly. She didn't want her husband to hear her crying. Where did she hear that if you talked to someone who was unconscious they could hear? She placed Daniel's hand in hers. "You've got to wake up so we can take you home, Daniel. And I'm going to sit here until you do. You won't like this hospital food. Now get well, Daniel," she said and looked up at Ashley. "Say something, Ash," she whispered, and pulled Ashley's hand toward the bed.

Deep inside her heart, Ashley knew it was too late for Daniel, but who knows, talking may help, anything that would make him open his eyes and smile again.

"Dad, you've got to get well so I can drive you home, besides, you have a great-grandchild on the way in just a few months. By then you will be well. Please open your eyes, Daddy." Feeling a lump rise in her throat, it was almost impossible to continue talking, but Doris motioned for her to continue. "Dad, please open your eyes." Ashley's weak voice was fading, but she kept talking, pleading for Daniel to wake up, move his hands, touch her, anything. "Please, Dad," Ashley pleaded, and placed both hands over her face.

Cora stood in back of them and cried. Daniel was the last of her three brothers and her favorite. All that would be left are the nieces and nephews, and she didn't like any of them. But thank the Good Lord, she had the chance to spend some time with Daniel before he dies . . . no, she wouldn't think of him dying. Lord, he had to live, he just had to.

Doris held her husband's hand and knew the moment Daniel stopped breathing. She felt his hand move, saw his eyes flitter, and heard a low groan, almost as though he was trying to squeeze her hand for the last time, to let her know that he was leaving, and to say good-bye. Doris knew her husband for forty-six years. Now he'd gone on to a better place. His time had run out.

Doris rocked back into her chair with a loud squeal that resonated throughout the room. She cried out loudly, and the nurse and doctor rushed to Daniel's room. The doctor went straight to Daniel while the nurse asked the family to wait outside. But Doris knew that Daniel was already gone, and there wasn't anything left for the doctor and nurses to do for him.

"Wake up, Daddy. It's time to wake up so I can take you home." Ashley fell to her knees in front of the bed and grabbed one of Daniel's hands. "No! Daddy, don't. Please wake up, Daddy. Please, please, don't leave me now, please Daddy, don't . . ." She looked up at the ceiling. "God, please, wake him up—"

"Get her out of here," the doctor ordered.

"Please, just let me sit with him, please." Ashley was

getting hysterical looking at Daniel lying still in the middle of the bed.

"Ash, he's gone. It's time for Daniel to rest in peace," Doris whispered. But she was crying, too.

Cora had to hold Ashley's hand to guide her out the room. Once outside, they sat on a bench and waited for the doctor.

Ashley couldn't stand the waiting. She paced backward and forward in front of Doris and Cora. Ashley stopped and looked at Doris. Her head was leaning against the wall, her eyes closed. Ashley went over and sat next to her. Doris had never looked so helpless. Ashley wondered what Doris would do without her husband, and what she would do without her father. Daniel was always there when she needed him. As a child, she never wanted for anything, and had no doubt that her father loved her unconditionally, as she did him.

Daniel had always taken care of Doris, made all the decisions for her, made sure she was taken care of. She never had to do anything but be his wife and Ashley's mother. At sixty-three, what was she to do after a marriage to a man who did everything for her?

The doctor walked out. "I'm so very sorry but we did all we could. It was another stroke and his heart was weak. Sorry," he said, and walked away, leaving behind him their faces filled with grief and disbelief.

Oh God, she had lost her father. She looked at Doris for help but knew she had to endure her grief alone. Doris was in no condition to help her. She looked as though she was in shock.

Cora sat next to them, murmuring a soft prayer.

There wasn't anything else they could do at the hospital.

That night Ashley stayed with her mother and aunt. Cora called long distance to other family members to give them the news of Daniel's death. Ashley gave her mother a drink of Jack Daniels, which her father used to drink, and helped her to bed.

As Ashley sat on the sofa, the door flew wide open. "Mom, when did it happen?" Lori burst into tears as her husband circled his arms around her.

"I didn't tell her until we were parked outside, Ashley. With the pregnancy, I didn't want Lori to get too excited."

"Thanks, Keith," Ashley said, and walked over to Lori. "Don't cry, Lori." She held Lori in her arms like she was a child. She would have to grieve later when she was alone. Ashley knew she had to be strong for Doris and Lori. She looked at Cora, who had pulled her wig off her head. She sat on the sofa, her hands folded in her lap.

"I had no idea that Grandpa was so ill. He was fine when I came over three days ago." She couldn't believe that he was dead.

"I know it's hard, Lori. It is for all of us. And Mother, I don't know what I'm going to do about her yet."

Ashley looked at Cora. "You're not planning to leave anytime soon, are you?"

"No. Doris is like a sister to me. I'll be here as long as she needs me. A month, year, two years, as long as Doris needs me. I'm going to make some hot tea. And Lori, you relax and calm down," Cora ordered. "Daniel wouldn't want anything to happen to the baby. Now, we're going to make the arrangements and go forward. That's what Daniel would want," she said as she took charge.

"She's right, Lori. You're carrying a baby," Ashley said.

Ashley and Lori looked in on Doris. She was still awake with the lamp on beside her bed. She held her arms open, and Lori lay down on the bed beside her.

Keith walked in and kissed Doris on the cheek. He loved her as though she was his own grandmother. She was always so meek and so kind to everyone.

"I'm so glad my family is here with me tonight," Doris managed to say.

"Mother, I'm staying tonight. I'll go home for an hour to wrap things up and tomorrow we can make all the arrangements. You won't have to do anything but rest."

"No, Ashley. I'll be right by your side to help. I can't stay in bed forever." Doris picked up her husband's picture on the nightstand and held it close to her heart. Large teardrops rolled down her face, falling on her pink-flowered gown. Lori held her grandmother close to her.

"Here, drink this tea down, Doris," Cora said. She sat in the chair opposite Doris. "It's nice and hot just the way you like it.

It was night when Lori and Keith left. Doris had gotten back in bed, and Ashley and Cora were in the living room.

"Aunt Cora, do you realize that I've lost my husband and father in the same year? I don't know how much more I can take. How much more do I have to take before I can get some stability in my life again? Every time I take one step forward, it looks as though I take two steps backwards." They were sitting on the sofa. It seemed so strange: no TV was on, her mother was in bed, and her father wasn't there at all. The house was cold and lacking the warmth and life that Ashley was used to.

"Ash, you have lost your father. But, honey, you sound as though Marcus is dead, too."

"I feel that way—what's the difference, he's gone." she snapped.

Cora's mouth fell open. "Now, don't talk that way. You may hate him now, but in time that'll pass." Cora placed her cup back on the tray. "Everything seems dark and ugly now, but darling, it won't be this way forever. You are much stronger than you think you are, Ash."

"I don't know, Aunt Cora. I'm at my limit. I'm trying

to get my business going and Dad supported me. It made me want to prove to him that I could do it."

"No, Ash. Just prove it to yourself. That's what Daniel would have wanted."

The next morning Ashley went home and called Joan.

"Ashley, do you need me to go over to your mother's house with you? I'm here if you need me. I can even finish cutting the patterns if you want me to. Remember, Ash, business goes on."

"You're absolutely right. I'll leave the key in the white flowerpot on the patio. I appreciate the offer, Joan. Today is Tuesday. I should be back in business once my father is buried. In the meantime, we'll be talking by phone. Maybe I can get my mother and aunt to come over and help us for a couple of days. It may get my mother's mind off things." But Ashley knew it wouldn't be so easy. It was hard enough on her, and she hadn't depended on her father as much as Doris had.

The next thing Ashley did was call Lori to make sure that she was all right. After she talked to Lori she called Vanessa. She was crying when she hung up, went into her bedroom, grabbed her checkbooks and a change of clothes, and left. "Marcus, where are you when I need you the most?" she whispered.

"Ashley, I don't care what you and Cora say. I'm going with you to pick out my husband's casket." The night before Doris had drowned in a sea of tears. But today she had to make arrangements for Daniel.

"Okay, Mother. I just thought—"

"Well don't. I'm ready, and I'm going. Daniel is gone now and I have to start thinking for myself," she snapped, holding her head high and walking right past Ashley and Cora.

Doris stopped at the door and turned around to face them. "Are you two coming?"

"Yes, yes, Mother, we're coming. Come on, Aunt Cora. Don't just stand there," Ashley said. "Well, I'll be damned," Ashley whispered under her breath.

The day was long and they were tired when they arrived back at Doris's house. Ashley had suggested that they stop on the way home at a little deli near her house and buy some sandwiches, which was a good choice. They were all too tired and grief-stricken to try and cook or eat very much of anything.

That night Ashley was up at one o'clock, standing at the living room window looking out. She had heard Doris crying but decided not to go in and disturb her. She had to release the hurt and pain that she was feeling, and maybe she wanted to be alone. They all had their own way of coping with grief. Cora was quiet for the first time that Ashley could remember.

Ashley went back into the bedroom that was once hers and got back in bed. She tossed and turned, and at three-thirty she fell asleep.

Three days had passed. Ashley looked at her watch. In three hours it would be time for Daniel's funeral. Ashley wanted a graveside service but Doris insisted on having her husband's ceremony in a church.

Ashley stood in the living room watching the sunlight piercing through the closed eggshell-colored drapes. Distressed, she walked in circles in the living room. The suddenness of her father's death was weighing her down. Since his death, five minutes hadn't passed without her thinking of him. The pain, the regret came from not having the chance to say good-bye to him. When was the last time she had told him that she loved him? She couldn't remember.

Ashley walked around looking at pictures, glancing

out every window she had passed. She couldn't seem to sit in one place or in one room. Every room she walked into seemed as though her father should have been there, smiling that warm smile when he looked at her. She loved seeing his smile, so happy and so natural.

Ashley went to her mother's bedroom and knocked on the door.

"Come in," Doris yelled. She was completely dressed, sitting on the edge of the bed. She looked up at Ashley. "Marcus called this morning. He asked if you were all right. I told him you had been strong, Ash." She waited for Ashley's response, but there wasn't one.

Ashley sat on the edge of the bed and held Doris hand. "Would you like a cup of coffee and toast, Mother? You didn't eat much yesterday."

"I guess I can use some coffee. You know, Ashley, I keep wondering if I should have noticed anything different about Daniel. He hadn't been feeling well for two weeks. I was trying to remember what day he started to complain. Two weeks and I didn't see any signs that he was sick enough to die. I should have seen something."

"If he was that ill mother, he wouldn't have told you anyway. And maybe there weren't any signs for you to see. I didn't see anything unusual either," Ashley said, trying to sound convincing.

"I didn't see anything out of the ordinary," Cora said. She walked in and sat on the bed beside Ashley and Doris. "You know, just about all my family are dead now." Cora wiped a tear from her eye.

The sound of the doorbell caused all three to jump. "They're here, Mother, Aunt Cora. It's time to go." Ashley went to her room and took her black jacket from the closet. When she opened the door, she saw the long black limousine parked in front of the house. She gasped, placing her hand over her mouth, and took a step back.

Doris and Cora walked into the living room and saw

Ashley standing at the door waiting for them. As soon as Doris looked at Ashley's face she knew it would be the longest day of her life.

The three women walked outside and quietly climbed into the limousine, and Lori and Keith joined them. No one spoke as they rode to Mt. Tabor Baptist Church at Western Boulevard.

The ride was long and mournful. As they climbed out of the limousine, people were standing outside the church, all heads turning as the family walked passed them. Ashley was holding Doris by her arm and Cora was on the other side of Doris. Lori and Keith walked in back of them.

They were seated on the front row. Ashley could smell the scented flowers that were on the casket in front of them. As she looked in back, her eyes met with Jason's, the son her father never spoke of. Ashley turned her back to him, then looked at him a second time—the resemblance was uncanny. He was virtually her double—the same brown hair, slanted dark eyes, high cheekbones—and both looked like Daniel.

Doris followed Ashley's gaze. When she saw the man, her stomach felt as though it was tying into knots. Her eyes narrowed as she gave him one long stare. The hurt she felt was as fresh as it was the first time Daniel told her about the boy. But they never told Ashley. Doris often wondered if she knew but was unable to initiate the conversation. Ashley mentioned it the day she got angry, Doris remembered. She turned around in her seat and listened to the pastor speak about her husband.

Ashley was waiting for someone to sing her father's favorite song, "Lord You Been Good to Me." She instructed the pastor to make the service as fast as possible. Say a speech, pray for her father and his loved ones, sing the song, and be done with it. No one needed to sit and listen to the whispers, the crying, and the speeches.

The pastor started to sing and the crying began. Ashley held her mother in her arms and Cora cried softly.

Now the marching and viewing the body had begun. When Ashley stood up, Marcus marched and stopped in front of her. He looked Ashley up and down in disbelief. It seemed like he had forgotten where he was and that people were in back of him.

"Ash!" he called out her name in a whisper as though he wasn't certain that it was she.

As though Ashley didn't know him, she looked at his face for a few seconds, turned her back to him, and continued to comfort her mother. Marcus Lake was the last person she wanted to see.

Marcus kissed Lori on the cheek and squeezed Doris's hand. When he held his hand out to Ashley, she completely ignored it.

Ashley looked up, and Vanessa and Gary took a seat next to her.

Marcus got back in line, keeping in step with everyone else, but he kept looking back at Ashley.

The pastor spoke again, but he made it short, as promised. Daniel was not a churchgoing man, but his funeral service was held in the church because Doris faithfully came to church every Sunday. It was the same church that Ashley went to with her mother when she was a child.

The pastor was a tall, thickly built man, with slanted dark eyes and a large mole on the bottom of his chin. "All rise," he instructed. He held his arms out and began to sing. Once the singing was over, he excused everyone and said he would see them at the cemetery.

The ride to Inglewood Park Cemetery on Florence Avenue seemed long to Ashley. But she knew it wasn't. In the long black limousine, they were all seated just as they were before, quiet, sad.

A quiet movement in a seat could be heard or a mere whimper.

At the cemetery, the first person Ashley saw again was Jason. Their eyes met and held, and again his presence was disconcerting. He looked as tired and grief-stricken as Ashley did. He was tall like her father, well dressed in a black suit and white shirt. When Ashley looked at him again he walked slowly across the cemetery as though he was forcing his legs to move.

Ashley held Doris's arm and looked at her when she stopped walking. She had stopped to look at Jason. And looking angry as she held her lips tight, she turned on her heels to continue walking to the grave where the casket was being taken.

The first line of chairs in front of the casket was for the immediate family, and Jason stepped aside so that they could sit down. Vanessa and Gary stood in back of Ashley, Vanessa's hands resting on Ashley's shoulder.

Jason didn't claim himself as part of Daniel's family. Out of respect for his father he would never do anything to embarrass him or his deceased mother. But he would have his day, it just wasn't today, that's all. He looked at Ashley; she had gotten prettier. He used to watch her when they were younger, but they were never friends, even though they went to the same school. No one knew that they were sister and brother. It was a conversation that never came up.

Before his mother died of cancer, she told Jason what he already knew, that Ashley was his sister. Looking at the bitter expression on Ashley's face, Jason wondered if he had ever hated her. They were both in their forties. Maybe if they had been told when they were children, they would have built a relationship. But all he felt was resentment for the girl that his father lived with and protected. When he was younger he even envisioned her sitting on his father's knee, calling him Daddy. Jason looked up as he heard someone yell out loud. It was Daniel's wife.

"Mother," Ashley whispered, and held Doris in her arms. She could feel her mother's body tense and stiffen, tears wet against Ashley's face.

Ashley held her head up, her eyes closed against the warm sun.

Cora sat on the left side of Doris and held her hand. Lord, she thought. *My brother was a good man in so many ways, but he could be the devil in others.* But the one thing she could say, Daniel took care of his family, always made her welcome in his home. Cora shook her head and prayed softly for Daniel's family. He was in the Lord's hands. Cora looked at poor Doris. *It's going to take her forever to get over her despondency about Daniel's death.*

As everyone walked back to the cars, Doris stopped and gave Jason one last look. Why does that man insist on invading their lives? And she didn't like the animosity in his eyes every time he looked at Ashley. It was apparent that he didn't like her.

Doris was glad to be back home. Her spirit was dampened and the sorrow she felt was overwhelming. Every time she looked into Ashley's tear-stained face she felt even worse. The poor child had lost her husband, now she has lost a father, and he meant everything to her.

Although only a few people came to the house, Doris tried to stay to herself. She just wanted everyone to leave and be left alone with her family. She sat in her bedroom and finally everyone left.

Ashley and Vanessa walked outside into the backyard. "When are you going home, Ash? You look so tired, honey."

"I'm not sure yet. But even if I sleep here at night I have to go home during the day. I have a business to run and orders to fill. I'm going to have to work double hard when I go back to make up for the time I've lost."

"I saw the look that Marcus gave you, Ash. Girl, you shocked the hell out of him. That black suit you made looks good on you and your hair looks good up. You look marvelous, Ash. You better believe Marcus thinks so, too," Vanessa said with a teasing glint in her eyes.

They were sitting in the two wicker chairs. Ashley reached over and picked a rose from the rosebush and inhaled the scent. "Sweet," she said. "I feel like I've lost so much time during my marriage, Vanessa. I gave Marcus much more than I gave myself. Now I have time to improve my life and live it the way it makes me happy. And yes, I hope I did look good to him. That's the only way I can get even with the jerk. Do you understand what I mean?"

"Yes. I understand perfectly. I felt the same way when I left old dull-ass Larry." Vanessa got up. "I'm going home and lie down for a few minutes. This day was not a happy one. Besides, Gary is probably ready to go, too."

Ashley got up and walked Vanessa and Gary to their car. "Thanks for coming, Gary." They drove off. Ashley folded her arms in front of her. She heard the neighbor across the street call her name. "Hello, Miss Payne," Ashley said and waved. She was eighty years old and because of her wheelchair, she was unable to attend the funeral. Ashley ambled back inside the house.

"Mother, everyone is gone. I told Keith to take Lori home so she can get some rest. She's a pregnant woman now." Ashley walked over to the bed and took Doris's hand as she got up. They went to the living room where Cora was sitting on the sofa looking through a magazine.

Cora laid the magazine on the coffee table in front of her. "Doris, I've made a decision," Cora announced.

"What is it? I hope you're not leaving so soon, Cora?" Doris asked with disappointment written all over her face. "I was so sure you would stay longer. I want my home to feel like home to you." Doris and Cora were more like sisters. The thought of Cora leaving made her want to cry, especially when she needed her most.

"No. You know we're like two peas in a pod. I've been thinking of living here with you if you don't mind. Or if you like, I can continue to come out here every year. I just think you may need me, Doris. And I know that I need you."

Doris and Ashley let out a sigh of relief. Doris held both hands to her chest. "I'm thankful for that, Cora. Please stay on and live here with me. I've never lived alone except the two months many years ago." She laid her head back on the sofa feeling the tension easing from her body.

"I'm so happy, Aunt Cora. Mother needs you," Ashley said, and kissed Cora on the cheek. Ashley went to the kitchen and came out with a Coke in her hand.

"Why don't you go home, Ashley? You've been here since Daniel—" Doris swallowed hard. "Since he died," she choked out.

"Are you sure, Mother? I was planning to stay."

"Yes, I'm sure. Go home. You have a business to run. Cora is here with me." Doris looked at Cora. She was a sister to her in every sense of the word. She hadn't heard a word from any of her sisters in twenty years. She wasn't sure if they were still living or not. What a shame, she thought. What a sad, sad shame.

Chapter 16

"Joan, I should be back in a couple of hours. It's time for me to get back into the swing of things."

"You will, Ash. I know what it's like to lose a parent."

Ashley spread the silk material on the wide table and pinned the pieces of pattern to it. When she finished she took the last sip of her coffee, rinsed the cup, and placed it in the dishwasher. She watered her plants and went back to her workroom to get her purse.

Thinking about going to the reading of her father's will was beginning to wear on her nerves. As she looked at the clock her heart started to beat at a rapid pace. What was Doris doing now? she wondered. *She must be as fidgety as I am.*

Doris and Cora were waiting on the front porch when Ashley drove up the driveway. As they climbed in the car, Ashley could see that they had been crying, and, although the distance to the lawyer's office was only about fifteen minutes, this would be another long drive for all of them.

While they were in the reception area waiting for the lawyer, Jason walked in and took a seat. Ashley and Doris looked at each other. Seeing him there had confirmed what Ashley had known since she was a child: he was her brother. Why couldn't he be the brother that her mother could have had? The situation wouldn't be so repellent.

Ashley watched as Doris moved around impatiently in her chair. She folded her arms against her chest, then unfolded them again. Her eyes shot daggers as she watched Jason ease into a chair as if he had every right to be there.

Ashley took one of Doris's hands and leaned over to whisper in her ear. "We've known all the time, Mother. Don't let it upset you so."

"Yes, but I wonder why he's here? Daniel never said anything about leaving him something in his will," she whispered.

Before Ashley realized it, Doris stood up; her purse fell to the floor.

"Mother, you have to stay. Don't let him upset you so. What's done is done," Ashley said, trying to keep Jason from overhearing her. And where in the hell did Cora and Lori go? Ashley wondered as she looked around. They said that they were just going to the ladies room, twenty minutes ago, it seemed.

Ashley stood up, alarmed when she saw them coming down the hall. "You look ill, Lori," Ashley said with concern and touched Lori's arm.

"Morning sickness, Mom. Everything I ate last night came back up." She felt miserable and slowly eased back in her chair.

"Stay here with Mother. I'm going to buy you a Ginger Ale from the 7-Eleven store across the street."

"But what if the lawyer comes out before you get back?" Doris asked. She was frantic. And from time to time, she still looked to her right at Jason. But luckily, he didn't return her stares. And as she looked at him again, his resemblance to Daniel was stunning. She felt a hard lump in her throat as a reminder of the earlier years of their marriage.

"Tell Mr. Browne to wait until I get back, Mother. After

all, we've been waiting a half hour for him." Ashley went to Cora where she sat quietly in the chair opposite Doris. "Please watch Mother until I get back."

Cora nodded. "She's just nervous, Ash." But Cora sat in Ashley's seat beside Doris.

Feeling sorry for her mother, Ashley hurried down the hall and out the glass double door. She dashed inside the store and was back in less than ten minutes.

Ashley rushed through the door and right past Jason, but he only looked through her, and didn't speak or acknowledge that he even knew her. She wondered what had happened to him over the years. For Pete's sake, they went to the same school, grew up in the same neighborhood, and they were sister and brother. She was sure he blamed her for being the child her father lived with. Well, it wasn't her fault that his mother had him out of wedlock.

Again, Ashley noticed that Jason was dressed expensively and wondered what he did for a living.

"Here, drink the Ginger Ale, Lori. It should help." Ashley sat close to Lori.

Cora was sitting next to Doris, holding her hand. "Doris, stop worrying about the boy. You're going to make yourself ill."

"Mr. Browne is ready now," June, the receptionist said. Her voice was high-pitched and Ashley frowned.

Jason heard the receptionist and walked ahead of them as Ashley and her family stopped to watch him.

In the office there were chairs for them lined in front of the lawyer's desk. Ashley and Cora sat on either side of Doris. There was an empty chair next to Lori but Jason sat in the chair on the far end. It was clear that he didn't want to associate with Ashley in any way.

"I'm sorry we have to see each other under these circumstances, Doris, Ashley," Mr. Browne said. He looked in all their faces; they looked as though they were at

Daniel's funeral all over again. Mr. Browne looked at Jason and then back at Ashley and nodded.

"I won't keep you all no longer than I have to so I'll just get right to the matter at hand. It won't be easy one way or another." He looked from Jason to Ashley again and cleared his throat.

It wasn't easy for Edward Browne to stop looking at Ashley's face; she was lovelier now than she had been five years ago.

"Daniel left two life insurance policies." He picked up the will and began to read. "I, Daniel Taylor, leave the house, my pension income and the one hundred thousand dollar policy, all the savings accounts, my car and everything in the house to my wife, Doris, except the savings account at Union Bank in the amount of ten thousand dollars to my sister, Cora." Edward heard Doris whisper something under her breath, and stopped for a few seconds, then proceeded again.

"My two hundred fifty thousand dollar policy is to be divided. One hundred thousand dollars to my daughter, Ashley. Fifty thousand dollars to my granddaughter, Lori, and one hundred thousand dollars to my son, Jason—" There were movements, whispers, and Edward stopped, looking in the faces of each one of them.

"What do you mean, one hundred thousand dollars for him?" She turned and pointed her finger at Jason. "That money belongs to Ashley—"

"Stop it, Mother. This is what Dad wanted." Ashley looked at Jason but he stared straight ahead.

"I won't stand for this!" Doris yelled. Impulsively, she stood up in front of Edward's desk, pointing her finger close to his face. He was sure she would touch the tip of his nose. "When did Daniel sign that will?"

"It was signed two years ago, Doris. I'm sorry, but he divided it equally."

"I'll contest it before I see that man with anything that

belongs to my husband." She turned to face Ashley. "And Ashley's father. It should go to her."

"Mother, please, let it go. It's what Dad wanted. Please let Edward finish reading the will."

Cora and Lori's mouths were open as they looked at each other in shock.

"Also," Edward continued. "Here's a letter that Daniel left for his son in case of his death." Edward gave the letter to Jason. "There's one more thing, Daniel's gold watch goes to Jason, too." Edward took a deep breath. "Ladies and gentlemen, I guess this concludes it." There was a knock on the door, and June asked him to come out.

"Excuse me, this won't take long." Edward welcomed the interruption. He felt as though he was suffocating. And the animosity was thick enough to slice with a knife.

Lori was now staring at Jason. "I can't believe this. Mom, this is your brother. Did you know about him? Did Grandpa tell you that you had a brother?" Lori moved closer to Ashley.

"Yes, I knew but he didn't tell me."

"I wonder how much older or younger he is than you? Maybe about three years? Hot damn, no wonder he never said anything."

Ready to leave, Jason stood up but Doris jumped up in front of him. She pointed her finger in his face. "You'll never get away with this. You will never get your hands on my husband's money," she hissed between closed teeth, both hands resting on her hips. "You come parading in here like you're one of the family. But you're not. You're nobody, you hear me, nobody."

"Mother, please don't," Ashley said, surprised that her mother would say such a thing. She had never seen her this angry.

Jason stood tall and only stared down at Doris. He turned to walk away and stopped when he heard Doris call his name again.

"You hear me, that money belongs to Daniel's daughter." Her fists were closed, now hanging by her sides. "Expensive clothes or not, you came from a whore . . . a whore." Doris stopped when she saw Ashley place her hand over her mouth.

Jason took a step closer to Doris, his eyes full of hostility. "Miss, that same whore birthed your daughter, which was more than what you could do." The expression on his face was mean, lifting the corners of his mustache into a smirk as he saw the shock on Ashley's face, the disbelief in her eyes. He took so much pleasure in hurting her. He had waited for years to do this and his day had finally come. He only wished his mother were alive to see the old bat stifle as though she couldn't breathe.

Ashley looked at her mother and back at Jason again. She looked helpless, like a small child. "What do you mean, Jason?" she demanded. "What are you talking about?" She took a step closer to him. "Tell me!" she screamed at the top of her voice.

"He's crazy, just like his whore of a mama, Ash!" Doris yelled. Now she regretted everything she had said. And how was she going to stop him from talking?

"I said, what do you mean?" Ashley demanded again, yelling even louder. Her voice was cracking and she reached out for Lori's hand.

"Nothing, I tell you." Doris said loudly, and looked at Cora for help, but Cora was at a loss for words, and held her head up, tilted her wig to one side, and stretched her head.

"Come on, Ash, I got a terrible headache. Let's get out of here." Doris repeated.

"No," Ashley said firmly, pulling her arm from the hold Doris had on her.

"Tell her, miss. Tell her the truth. If my mother was a whore, so was hers . . ."

Shaking her head from side to side, Ashley dropped

her purse to the floor and slumped back into her chair. She had forgotten that Lori was holding her hand until she felt the long fingers tighten around hers.

"Somebody, any one of you, please, help me. Tell me it's not true," Ashley pleaded. "Mother, please, tell me it's not true." She felt ill, too warm, and wiped moisture off her face.

Cora sat next to her, placed Ashley's hand in hers and squeezed it. It was time she knew the truth, but Cora was sorry that Ashley had to find out in such a cruel way.

Jason took a step closer to Ashley and she hopped out of her seat again, but Doris pushed at him. Standing between Jason and Ashley, Doris screamed from the top of her voice. "I said, let's go home, Ash. He's crazy. Can't you see how crazy he is? Lord, let's get out of here. We got what we came for." Doris burst out in tears and pushed at Jason once again. "You bastard, get out of my sight," she screamed loudly. Her head was spinning; she was beginning to feel dizzy and crumpled into the chair.

"Since you wanted it all, old woman, tell her the truth. You started it so tell her," he said as though hurting Doris made him happy. "You look like our Dad, Ashley. *But you look more like our Mom.*"

He was very matter-of-fact about it, indifferent almost to the point of arrogance. And he smiled as he saw Ashley placing both hands against her ears.

Doris's anger was getting out of control. She raised one hand and came closer to Jason, stopped in front of him, and slapped him hard across his face. "How could you do this to her? What would Daniel say if he could hear you now?"

Jason looked at Doris; his smile faded away as though Daniel was near him and saw what he had done to Ashley. Then he quickly strode out the office. He didn't even look back at Ashley.

Ashley couldn't get up, or move. Her purse dropped to the floor. Her mouth fell open as she stared at Doris.

She felt Lori's hand resting on her shoulder. Again, her life had turned upside down.

Lori looked at Ashley's face and was afraid that she was having a heart attack. Her hand was against her chest, and her breathing became labored, and she shook her head as if she could dislodge what she had heard. She looked at the door that Jason had exited and turned around to face Doris.

Cora was sitting with her head down looking at the designs in the carpet. She couldn't even look Ashley in the face. She had told Daniel more than once to tell Ashley, but he always reminded her that Ashley was his daughter, not hers.

Finally, Ashley was able to speak again. "Mother, how can this be true? How can you not be my mother?" She started to cry and Lori held Ashley in her arms.

"Oh God, tell me, Mother. Please tell me it's not true." She rocked back and forth begging for the truth. But as she looked in Doris's eyes, deep inside she knew it was true. It had to be. The door opened, and Edward Browne came bursting into his office and saw Ashley crying.

"What happened, Ashley?" He looked around and didn't see Jason. What he saw wasn't very pleasant; he knew what had happened, but how, he wondered, and knew it had to be Jason who told Ashley at this time of sorrow. What a cold-hearted jerk he had turned out to be.

Trying to speak, Doris stood in front of Ashley, and just nodded her head until she was able to speak. "Let's go home so we can talk, Ash. We need to be alone, just the two of us."

Ashley looked at her mother's face. Somehow she looked smaller, older, and mentally beaten. But she couldn't say anything to Doris. Besides, it was her life that had changed so suddenly.

Doris slowly walked to the door as though all her strength were gone, her brown purse hanging off her shoulder, almost touching the floor. Walking beside her, Cora had to hold her arm for support.

Ashley was staring at Doris as though she didn't know her. She felt her hair on her face and pushed the untidy mane that had fallen out of place.

"Mom, can you drive?" Lori asked Ashley.

"Yes, I think so."

"Are you sure? I can drive and bring you back to your car. I really think I should drive you guys. I can call in sick for the rest of the day. We all need the rest of the day off," Lori said, taking Ashley's hand and guiding her to the door.

Ashley looked at her daughter's face. "Yes, we sure do need the rest of the day off."

Ashley got in the front seat with Lori. Doris and Cora sat in back.

Ashley turned around in her seat so that she could face Doris. "You didn't answer me, Mom. I'm forty-five years old and just finding all this out? Why is it at forty-five my life is falling apart?"

"Ash, can't this wait until I get home? I'm so tired, I feel as though I have no strength left."

"Yeah, Ash. Let's get home, get comfortable, and sit down and talk," Cora said, looking at poor Doris. She looked so beaten.

No one spoke on the ride home. But luckily, it took only fifteen minutes to get there.

Once everyone went inside, Doris went straight to her bedroom, slammed the door, and hung up her jacket. She got down on her knees and prayed for the Lord to give her the strength she needed to get through this day. This was all Daniel's doing, and she was left to clean it up behind him. She had pleaded with Daniel to tell Ashley the truth when she was twenty-one, but he refused, and told her she had better not say anything about it. Doris had never seen Daniel so angry. And she was too afraid to mention it to Ashley. So, as usual, she did as she was told. She balled her fist, opened her eyes, and looked up at the ceiling. "I hope you are watching, Daniel. Haven't I suffered enough?" she bellowed. She lay both elbows on the cold floor, held her head down between her arms, and cried.

When Doris walked into the living room, they were all waiting for her. Ashley was pacing back and forth as she does when she was nervous. Lori was drinking a glass of 7 UP and Cora was holding a cup of tea in her hand. She had pulled off her wig and left it in her room.

Ashley stopped in her tracks when Doris came near her. All eyes were on Doris, waiting, watching.

"Well, Mother?" Ashley asked.

"Sit down, Ash." Doris took a seat on the sofa next to Cora. "Before me and Daniel came here to L.A., he knew Ruby, Jason's mother."

"And mine," Ashley intervened.

Doris looked at Ashley with wondering eyes. "They had dated even before he married me. In the beginning we were so in love." Doris took a deep breath and wiped a tear with the white handkerchief that she held in her hand.

"Daniel decided we could live better here. So he was transferred from the plant and had a job waiting for him when we arrived. In the beginning, it was good between us. I didn't know anything about Ruby at the time, but she followed Daniel here. He started seeing her again. I felt desperately unhappy and betrayed. We wanted a baby but I couldn't get pregnant, and I began to feel helpless." Doris looked in all their faces; they were listening profoundly.

"I knew that Daniel was having an affair, but I had no one or no place to go. So I stayed and tried to do everything he asked, tried to be the perfect wife, perfect housekeeper, and cooked everything he liked, hoping he would be faithful and things would be good again. One day, out of the blue, he came home with this tiny baby in his arms. She was ill with a bad cold and as soon as he uncovered her face, I knew Daniel was the father." She looked at Ashley, but Ashley was just listening, waiting for more information.

"I cried as Daniel told me about the affair. But he said that Ruby couldn't afford to raise a baby by herself and didn't want a child to tie her down. The way he looked at you, Ash, his eyes told me that he loved you. He said if we raised you he would have no reason to see Ruby again and the baby was ours, his and mine. He said that Ruby had even considered giving you up for adoption. I wanted a child so badly and I really wanted you, Ashley."

Doris stopped to wipe her eyes again. She looked at Ashley's face but couldn't read what she was thinking. Did she hate her? Could she ever forgive her? The questions were killing her inside.

"But, Grandma, weren't you angry enough to leave him?" Lori asked. "I would leave Keith if he was ever unfaithful to me."

"And go where, and to who? I was young and had no family. No work experience except for the work I did in a department store downtown, and that wasn't for very long. Yes, I was angry, but I also wanted Ashley.

"For three years we were happy and we both loved Ashley more than anything. She was the center of our lives. It was as though I had birthed her into this world. She was mine." Doris placed both hands over her face and stopped for a few seconds.

"And what happened after three years, Mother?" Ashley asked. But she knew the answer. She just wanted to give her father the benefit of the doubt by hearing it from Doris.

"Your father told me that Ruby was pregnant again. I almost died because I thought they would take you away from me. That time I told him to leave and go to her. And they would not take my baby away from me. We had adopted you, and you were my daughter. I would have fought for you with my life. You got to believe that, Ashley. Daniel didn't know what to do when I spoke to him so bitterly. That was the one time that I spoke up."

Ashley wiped a tear from her eye and cleared her throat.

"He and Ruby didn't see each other as often. I think they were both convinced that I would win custody. They even broke it off for a long time. They went back together again but there were times he didn't see her for months. I knew because he didn't leave the house unless he was going to work. Other times, he took you and me with him. He did all he could to make up for all the hard times he gave me.

"Ruby raised Jason, and we kept you, Ash. Daniel never left home again for many years later. I had no choice but to stay with your father. No way I would have left you. But later, their affair ended. He did pay child support for Jason and paid for his education. He loved that boy. But you were always his little girl, Ash."

Ashley had stopped crying. But she felt strange, as if she didn't belong. But when she looked at Doris again, she was looking at her mother. Nothing she felt for Doris had changed, not her love or fond memories, and Doris was her mother. And how could it change after forty-five years? Doris was the one who raised her, took care of her when she was ill, bandaged her cuts and bruises, and told her that she loved her more than life. Doris was her cherished mother who took care of her, and for the first time, Ashley realized how she truly felt about her.

"I don't understand why I wasn't told. Why did I have to find out who I am this way? It's not fair, Mother. I should have been able to go and see Ruby, after all, she was my mother, too."

"What do you mean, too, Ash?" Doris asked.

"Because, to me, you are my real mother. She was just the one who gave birth, and giving birth doesn't make you a mother. You're my mother but I still should have had the right to see her if I wanted to." Ashley got up and went to Doris, got down on her knees before her, and lay her head on Doris's lap. Ashley cried the way she used to when she was a child.

Doris cried alone with Ashley. Cora and Lori joined in with them. Doris and Ashley had gone through so much together. Both had lost their men: Doris had lost Daniel and Ashley had lost her husband and father.

Cora wiped her eyes. What a terrible week it had been. "You did it and got away with it, didn't you Daniel?" Cora thought to herself.

Chapter 17

"Girl, what is going on with Ashley?" Charlie asked. "She was in here today. I talked to her but she didn't hear a thing I said. She looked totally depressed, Vanessa."

"Of course she does, Charlie. Her father just died and she was close to him. Is there any soda in the vending machine?"

"Yeah, sweetheart. The man refilled it yesterday. Have you ever seen him, Vanessa?"

"No, I'm afraid not, and I like the color of your shirt," Vanessa said, feeling the material between her fingers. Charlie's mint-green shirt was sleeveless. He wore brown sandals and tight-fitting jeans that showed his nice butt.

"Ashley been very busy since her father's death. She's been working hard and trying to make up the time she lost. Anyway, I had better go and see her when I leave here."

"Somebody better. She's tore up from the floor up. Walking in here looking like plain Jane or somebody. No lipstick, not that any would have helped with that ugly dress she was wearing. And I don't know what she had done to her hair. It looked like she'd been sweating in it. She's down in the dumps, if you ask me. My wife's sister went through the same thing when she lost her husband. It took two years before she stopped grieving and could take care of herself again."

Vanessa sighed. "Well, when you finish with me, I'm

going straight over there. I called her mother's house this morning and she said Ashley was at home."

"Maybe she was beginning to feel the full impact of her father's death. Ashley and Lori were his heart. I mean, think about it, Charlie. First her husband leaves her for another woman, and now she loses her father. Sooner or later that would get to anyone." Vanessa closed her eyes, feeling Charlie's fingers working their way through her hair.

Ashley and Joan were working quietly in the workroom. Ashley was only going through the motions, moving like a hard wind sweeping through a small city. She refused to think of anything except her work. If she worked hard and fast she wouldn't have time to think of anything else. She couldn't sleep the night before—thinking of her father, her maternal mother—then her mind would drift back to Doris. What kind of family did she come from? She stopped and sighed. When she saw Joan looking at her strangely, she started back to work.

"It looks almost like rain today," Joan said. She placed the pattern on the table and walked around the table to where Ashley stood. Joan placed a hand on her shoulder.

"It's none of my business, but you are hurting inside. If you need an ear, I'm here for you, Ashley."

Ashley patted her hand. "I know, Joan. This is something I have to work out on my own. It's three-thirty, why don't you go on home? I'll pay you for a full day's work." Although there was still a lot of work to be done, Ashley had to be alone.

"All right, Ashley. I'll be back first thing in the morning. Maybe we can finish with all the cutting and you can start sewing on the dresses the day after tomorrow."

Ashley stood on the front porch and watched Joan as she drove off. She had turned to go back inside when she heard another car driving up. It was Vanessa. Ashley waited for her to get out the car.

Vanessa got out and started toward Ashley. "I called you yesterday. Were you home last night, Ash?"

They walked in and Ashley hung Vanessa's blazer on a hanger. "Would you like a glass of wine, coffee, or tea?"

"No, I'm fine." They walked into the den and Ashley closed the patio door.

"You look tired, Ash. And how is Doris?"

"I am tired and Mother is getting along okay. Aunt Cora will be staying on so Mother won't be alone. I'm glad Cora is staying with her right now."

As Vanessa watched Ashley, she knew that there was definitely a problem. "Ash, you want to tell me about it? I know you must be hurting over your dad's death. But is there something else?"

"Yes, there's a lot more to it. I'm going to miss him terribly. But there is more. I don't even know how to say this. I'm still trying to figure it out myself. My mother, Doris, is not my real mother."

Vanessa just sat and looked at Ashley; she was waiting for her to burst out with laughter. Had she and Doris had an argument?

"Well, what?" Vanessa asked.

"I'm not joking with you. You know how I always said that Jason and I looked so much alike? Well, we have the same mother and father. Jason and I are whole sister and brother. My Dad got Ruby pregnant with me first, then he and Doris raised me." Ashley told Vanessa what happened in the lawyer's office and what Doris had told her when they got home.

"Suddenly, I don't know who I am anymore. Who was my mother, what was she like? Vanessa, I thought that I knew my dad but I didn't. Now I have a brother that hates my guts. If only my father was here to explain it to me."

"How is Doris, really?"

"She's just as devastated as I am. What happened in

the lawyer's office was what she had always feared. They should have told me the truth long ago. Why wait? Did my dad think it would just go away?"

"Ashley, I don't know any of the right answers. But at least you do have Doris. If your real mother didn't want you, you were lucky to have someone love you as much as Doris does. You couldn't have had a better mother, Ash." Vanessa took one of the peppermints from the crystal bowl on the coffee table in front of her. After she opened it, she kept playing with the paper.

"I realize that, but I'm so angry, Vanessa. Mostly at my father." Ashley unbuttoned the top of her blouse. "I'm having hot flashes, too. What a bad time for those."

"You know what you need to do, Ashley? You need to have a long talk with your brother. He can answer some of your questions about your mother. Who knows, you two might even become friends. You're all he has left."

"You should have seen the way he looked at me," Ashley said, shaking her head. "He took so much pleasure in telling me, seeing my hurt and shock. I don't know if I can talk to him, Vanessa. I don't know why at forty-five years old I find all this out. And he must be at least forty-three by now. I don't need this at a time like this." She stood up and got herself a tall glass of cold water. "Are you sure you don't want anything?"

"No, thanks. Charlie said you might need someone to talk to. That's why I'm here."

"Hey, I bet I could make that suit you're wearing." Ashley reached over and felt the material.

"I bet you could, too. Ash, we know how controlling your father was. Doris probably wanted to tell you, but Daniel wouldn't hear of it. You are all she has left." Vanessa stopped and waited for Ashley to respond. She had been doing so well with her business. Before her father died she had even stopped talking about Marcus every time they saw each other. Now it seemed as though she was sinking back into a depression. Vanessa knew she had to find the words that would inspire Ashley to stop sinking and find a way to live with the truth.

"I have a new respect for my mother. Do you realize how many women aren't strong enough to do what she did?" Ashley said.

"Do you know how many women that weren't strong enough to even accept a child that their husband had while creeping out? But Doris took you in and raised you, Ash. You are sitting around here crying and feeling sorry for yourself when you should be worshipping Doris."

"I'm glad you came, Vanessa. You know what I'm going to do?"

"What, Ash?"

"I'm going to cook dinner Sunday and have my family over. Why don't you and Gary come over, too? I'm so tired of being depressed and unhappy. I have a family who loves me and a best friend."

Ashley stood up and hugged Vanessa. "It's time that I go forward with my life. The worse is over now, I think."

Chapter 18

Ashley was almost finished setting the table when the phone rang. "Hi Ash," Vanessa said. "I picked up two bottles of wine. Do you need anything else?"

"No, you guys come on over. I have everything I need."

"Okay, see you in a few minutes." Vanessa hung up.

Ashley started back into the dining room when the phone rang again. She frowned when she heard Marcus's voice.

"What is it, Marcus? You caught me at a bad time." She was standing at the kitchen table with a Coke in her hand.

"I'm sorry about Daniel, Ash—"

"He died almost two weeks ago, Marcus. So cut the small talk and tell me what you really want." She heard him sigh through the phone, and she smiled, hoping she had aggravated him. But she didn't care. There were still some last-minute things she had to do before her guests arrived.

"I signed the divorce decree two days ago. I was wondering if you are really going to wait a year before you sell the house?"

"Are you broke, Marcus, or is this just a way to bug the hell out of me?"

"Look, Ash. I got my life to live and you have yours, whatever that is—"

"Whatever it is, you just pissed me off." She banged the phone back in its cradle. Ashley picked it up and

looked at it a second time to make sure she hadn't broken it. She took a deep breath, closed her eyes, and
counted to ten. "I won't let Marcus ruin my day."

Ashley took off her apron and took one last look at
the beef roast with white potatoes and carrots around it.
The two sweet potato pies were beautiful. All she had to
do was toss the salad when everyone arrived.

She looked in the mirror and smoothed back her hair.
As she looked closer, she gently rubbed her hand up and
down her neck. It was still smooth and unwrinkled.
While still standing at the mirror, Ashley turned from
side to side to see if her green jeans weren't too tight.
"Good," she said, "I haven't gained any more weight."
She beamed with pride, and her blood pressure had
gone down, too. She loved her new size. The doorbell
rang and she rushed out her room.

It was Doris and Cora. "Here is a lemon cake, Ash.
Your favorite," Doris said.

"Mother, you didn't have to do this. I made sweet
potato pies and there's ice cream in the freezer. But you
know I love your lemon cake. Now, come in the dining
room and get comfortable. Lori, Keith, Vanessa, and
Gary should be here any minute now."

Doris went to the bathroom and Cora got up and went
to Ashley. "She was so happy when you called and invited
us to dinner, Ash. She's been so worried about, well, you
know. About you finding out that Ruby was your mother."

"Yes, but Ruby only birthed me, Aunt Cora."

"You're a smart girl, Ash. I'm proud of you."

"What are you two talking about?" Doris asked as she
entered the room.

"Aunt Cora was just admiring my plants, Mother.
Would you like a glass of wine?"

"Yes, that sounds good, don't you think, Cora?"

"Yes, Doris. I could use a glass after all the packing we
did yesterday."

Ashley started into the kitchen and turned around. "What packing are you talking about?"

"Cora and I packed some of Daniel's clothes yesterday. We put them in boxes and I put them inside the garage until I figure out what to do with them."

"Oh, okay," was all Ashley said. But she wondered if she should ask her mother to see if Jason wanted any of them. She wouldn't today, but maybe she'll call her tomorrow morning and ask. After all, Daniel was his father, too. And as she thought of it again, maybe she should leave well enough alone. Daniel was Doris's husband, and it was her decision, and hers alone.

The doorbell rang. "Would you get the door for me, Mother?" Ashley yelled from the kitchen. It was Keith and Lori, and Vanessa and Gary behind them.

Ashley felt better than she had in weeks. Everyone she loved was there with her, except Marcus, of course. She lived for the day that she would wake up one morning and not think of him.

"This was such a good idea, Mom," Lori said. They were all sitting in the den. The men were watching sports and the women were chatting about Ashley's new suit that she had completed.

"Maybe you guys can help me think of a name for my label that goes inside the clothes."

"Why not just Ashley's," Lori suggested.

"Yeah, Ash. Why not?" Vanessa interjected. "I think it has a classy ring to it."

"Ashley's, Ashley's," she repeated twice. Well, I guess, Ashley's it is," Ashley said.

Dinner went well. Everyone laughed, ate, and told jokes. Ashley and Doris acted as though nothing had changed between them, except they seemed closer. Every once in a while Ashley would pass her mother, touch her shoulder, or kiss her on the cheek. Everyone missed Daniel, but no one spoke much about him. It had been a while since everyone was happy at the same time and no one wanted to dampen the happy day.

Ashley looked at Vanessa and Gary, and she could tell that they were still deeply in love. Gary had grown a beard and was wearing a nice-fitting pair of brown slacks, which showed off his slim waist. His black hair was cut close, with gray around the temples. Every time he laughed, Ashley looked at the deep dimples in each check. He and Vanessa complemented each other with their good looks. And as Ashley watched them, for the first time since Marcus had left, she missed the affinity that she and Marcus had once shared.

"Everything tastes so good, Ash. I have to take a slice of sweet potato pie home," Keith said. He had already eaten two slices.

"So do I, Ash," Gary said, and kissed Ashley on the cheek. "You look good, woman, and you don't need any pies in your refrigerator," Gary whispered against her ear. "You won't be a single woman for very long."

"You don't think so?" Ashley asked, laughing out loud. "Take the pie, Gary."

They were all getting their jackets or purses. By six everyone had left.

Ashley finished cleaning the kitchen, closed all the blinds, went into her bedroom, and slipped into a thin, purple gown. Feeling tired, she flipped on the TV and lay across her bed.

The next morning Ashley was up and dressed early, sitting at the table with a cup of coffee and writing out checks to pay her monthly bills.

"Are you sure that you don't want anything to eat, Joan?" Ashley asked.

"No thanks, Ashley. Just coffee will be fine. Working for you is the easiest job I've had. But I love it."

Ashley set a cup of coffee on the table in front of Joan

and went over what they had to do that day. Joan worked hard and Ashley was relieved to know that she could trust her in her home.

"By the end of the week, I'll be ready to start on the dresses for the church. I went there two weeks ago and took the measurements of all the women. We have lots of work to do, Joan."

"I'm ready whenever you are, Ashley. But I think you will need a larger place soon."

"I agree. A larger place is next on my list."

They went into the workroom and got more done that day than Ashley had anticipated. After Joan left, Ashley made herself a grilled cheese sandwich and kept working.

As Ashley was folding material the phone rang. She sighed, wondering who it could be. She was dead tired.

"Ash, it's Sheri. How are you?"

Ashley smiled as she listened to the high-pitched familiar voice. "Hi, Sheri. It's good to hear from you. I had just asked Lori about you a couple of days ago." Sheri was Lori's closest friend.

"Ashley, I want to give Lori a baby shower, but first I wanted to check with you. Were you planning anything?"

"I had thought about it but hadn't made any plans yet."

"Good. And I'm so sorry about your father. Mr. Daniel was always so nice to me whenever I went to their house with Lori. I hope Miss Doris is all right."

"She is, Sheri, thank you." Ashley took a seat at the counter facing the backyard. Looking out, she could see two birds pecking at her roses. "How is Jada and your mom?"

"Jada and Mom are both well, Ash. Can you believe that Jada will be three years old in six months?"

"My, how the time flies," Ashley answered, hoping Sheri would make the conversation short. It always took so long for her to get to the point.

"I'll call you back, Ash, as soon as I speak with Lori about the shower."

"I'll look forward to hearing from you, Sheri." Ashley hung up. Good, she thought, as she set the phone aside.

Ashley placed the dishes in the dishwasher, and wiped off the table and counter. The phone rang again. Ashley sighed and shook her head. "Will this phone ever stop ringing?" she said out loud.

"Hello Ashley, this is Elliott."

She smiled as she heard his voice. She already knew who he was when he said hello.

"Hi Elliott. How are you these days?"

"I'm all right. Just working day and night. My receptionist forgot to have your divorce decree mailed to you and instead it was recorded and mailed back to us. I was wondering if you wanted to pick it up, or should I have her mail it to you?" He held his breath waiting for her to answer. A month had past and he couldn't think of any other excuse to see her.

"Sure, I can pick it up. Is tomorrow morning okay with you?"

"Tomorrow morning is good. I was in court all day today, otherwise, I would have called you earlier."

"You have a receptionist, Elliott. Make her work. I could have picked it up today." She was sure that he was personally handling everything for her because Helen had referred her. But she didn't want him to feel that he was obligated to give her any special treatment.

"I know she could have. But I wanted to. You are a good client, Ashley. We all have our favorites," he said and laughed.

"Thank you, Elliott. What time should I come?"

"Let me look in my appointment book." He put her on hold for a few seconds. "What about eleven-thirty?"

"Eleven-thirty is good for me. See you tomorrow, Elliott. And thanks for everything." Hoping no one else would call, she went into the den and turned on the TV to the six o'clock news.

    Elliott sat back in his chair and turned around so that he could look out the window at the stars and the lights. The view from his office was exceptionally beautiful at night. It was already dark outside and inside his office was quiet; everyone had already left. His head had cleared from the long day in court but now clogged with thoughts of Ashley. He was a fool for seeing Ashley again tomorrow. It would take another month to get her out his mind. And he could sense by the way she talked, she had no idea how he felt about her. She was just coming out of a marriage that left her brokenhearted, besides, she was still in love with her husband. He could see it in her eyes when she speaks of him. Elliott closed his eyes. Maybe in time she would want to be in love again.

    "Good night, Elliott," Terri said as she stood at the door.

    He turned around to face her. "I thought you were gone, Terri. But have a nice evening."

    Terri smiled and walked out the door. She had to call his name twice and wondered what he was thinking of. Terri was thirty years old, tall and leggy like a Barbie doll, long black hair that fell below her shoulders. She had been working for the firm for three years and was perfect at everything she did. But there was one flaw with Terri: she was never on time. Janet had even told him what a wise choice he'd made by hiring her. It was hard to believe Janet liked Terri because she didn't like any of the other receptionists or assistants in the office.

    Today was Terri's birthday and Elliott had had beautiful red roses delivered. One of the other partners gave her a gift certificate to Macy's department store, and the other partner was in court and would bring her a gift when he came back to the office.

* * *

The next morning Elliott didn't have to go to court and was in the office early.

"I went to Starbucks and got coffee, Elliott."

"Thanks, Terri." He pulled a bill from his wallet and paid for their coffee. "Hey, that's a sharp watch you have there. Did your boyfriend buy it for your birthday?"

"Yes. It is beautiful, isn't it?" She held her arm out and blushed all over. "Is there anything I can do for you before I get started?"

Elliott looked at her short skirt. It was green and black. Her sweater was tight fitting, the same color green as her skirt. "You must have a luncheon date?" he asked.

"Yes, I do. The watch and now lunch. I've been a good girl," she teased.

"I can handle things here. When you go to lunch, take all the time you need. Just leave my door open so I can see Mrs. Lake when she comes in."

"Gee, thanks, Elliott." Humming, she ambled out his office and closed the door.

Elliott worked for another half hour and had forgotten the time until he looked up and saw Ashley standing at the door.

"Hi there," she said, and stepped into his office. "You were far away when I walked in."

Elliott stood up and watched as she sat in a chair and crossed her legs. There was something quite calm and collected about her today.

"You just brought the sunshine to my office, Ashley. You look beautiful in yellow. It's a good color on you." He looked at her as though he was enthralled by her presence.

Ashley was wearing a pair of green slacks and a yellow cotton blouse. Her hair was combed back, which accentuated her perfectly sculptured face. She actually blushed as he looked at her. How long had it been since

NICE WIVES FINISH FIRST 193

a man made her feel so young and vibrant, even giddy? Lately, she had noticed, there were other men who looked at her, but she felt something stir inside as Elliott's eyes riveted across her face.

"I started to mail this to you but thought if you were in the area, you might want to stop by." Elliott handed Ashley the neatly sealed brown envelope.

Ashley's hand trembled as though she was reaching for a signed death sentence. Twenty five years of her life had expired, wrapped neatly in a plain brown envelope.

"I've been so busy this week that getting out of the house was a pleasure. Tomorrow a realtor will be coming by to put my house on the market. Now I'm going to need a place for my business. I'll call Helen for the number of what's his name that owns the commercial building."

For a moment it seemed as though Elliott didn't know who she was speaking of. "Oh, you mean Raymond, Anita's husband? As far as I know it's still vacant. Her bookstore is on the other end of the parking lot. As a matter of fact, they met when she was looking for a place to lease for her bookstore."

"I'll give him a call as soon as I get home." Ashley glanced at the picture of Elliott and his wife that sat on the corner of his desk. And then she remembered Helen's party. Elliott and his wife were always separated at the party. There seemed to be no attachment between the two. But there was a time that Ashley thought she and Marcus were close, and now she held a divorce decree in her hand. Six months from now, she would no longer be a married woman. Not that she considered herself a married woman anymore, anyway.

"Ashley!" he repeated.

"Oh, I'm so sorry, Elliott. You were saying?"

"Are you all right? You seem a little preoccupied today."

"Yes. I'm all right." She smiled, trying to hide her embarrassment. "I've just been so busy the past two weeks."

Elliott bent forward, his hands flat on his desk in front of him. "You know, Ashley, if you have something on your mind, I'm a good listener. I don't have another appointment for two-and-half hours. How have you been, really?"

Ashley sighed and looked into his eyes. She hardly knew this man but he was no stranger to her. And being her lawyer he already knew everything about her.

"A lot has happened since we had coffee that day in the mall."

For a second she didn't know where to begin, but when she started she spilled her heart out to Elliott, all the emotions she had carried in her heart, Daniels's death, and Jason's indignation. It was all there, waiting to be unloaded.

Elliott listened, watching her eyes mist as she talked. "How do you feel about Doris now that you know the truth?"

"Sometimes angry, guilty. I always thought she was a weak woman, but now I know it was because she was afraid of losing me. I get angry sometimes because she didn't tell me sooner. I can't believe I'm forty-five years old and just learned who my mother was. If it wasn't for my brother I still wouldn't know the truth." Ashley cleared her throat and looked at the bottled water in the corner of his office. "May I have a cup?"

"Sure, Ashley. I'll get it for you." He got up, grabbed a cup and filled it to the top.

"If you had known, would you have gotten to know your mother?" Elliott asked.

Seconds passed before Ashley answered. "I would have gone to see her because there are unanswered questions."

Ashley felt relaxed with him. She could really talk to Elliott, spill all her emotions. He listened and really understood her. And he dug deep into her soul, her thoughts.

"We never really know what can happen in our lives.

But you keep going forward, Ashley, and keep your head high. Keep yourself engrossed in your business and your private life will get easier as the time passes. Good things will come to you. And you can always call me if you want to talk."

Ashley smiled. "I'll keep that in mind. The same goes for you, too, Elliott." She got up and he walked her to the door since Terri wasn't at her desk.

"Did your receptionist take the day off?" Ashley asked, as they stood in front of her desk.

"No, she went to lunch early today and needed an extra hour. It's her birthday and her boyfriend was meeting her for lunch. I told her to take all the time she needs."

"You should have been my boss when I was working in corporate America. Anyway, thanks, Elliott, for listening. I needed to say some things out loud to get a clearer view of it." She held out her hand and he took it. Ashley gently pulled her hand away, kissed him on the cheek, and strolled to the elevator.

Elliott felt a faint tremor course through him as he felt her soft lips against his cheek, and he stood back. Even after the elevator door had closed, he stood for a few seconds as though he was waiting for her to step out again. He went back inside his office wondering if his own life would ever change. How much longer could he remain married to Janet? Where and when would it end? Now that Ashley had left, he felt empty again. But what else was new? he thought to himself, and with an audible sniff and sigh he got back deeply into his work.

Chapter 19

Ashley rushed around her house to make sure that everything was in place. It was four o'clock, and the realtor would be at her front door momentarily. She went back to the den and stood at the window. Her red roses had bloomed beautifully; the buds opened up and breathed in life. She heard a movement; it was a bird pecking on a lemon that had fallen from the tree.

The thought of selling her house made Ashley feel sick inside. It was like going through her divorce procedure all over again. And she was always on the losing end. First her husband, then her father, and now her house. At first, she thought that buying a townhouse would be a welcome change in her life. But as she stood at the window she could feel her heart slowly sinking. She turned away from the window, unable to look at all the work she had put into her flower garden, all the good times and memories she'd had on the patio. To sell it now was like losing a chunk out of the happiest part of her past. As she turned away and started to go toward the kitchen she stopped. They're only memories, she thought. However, she could not dwell on the past forever. But she started to her bedroom and stopped at the room that used to belong to Lori. When Lori got married and moved out, Ashley left everything the same. It would one day be the room that Lori's children would sleep and play in. She could never bring herself to change anything in it. Even the tall black doll that Marcus bought for Lori's sixth birthday was still standing in the corner, and her purple beanbag sat between the twin beds.

Ashley jumped at the sound of the doorbell and reluctantly went to open the door. It was the realtor.

"Mrs. Lake? Tom Black." He reached out to shake her hand.

"Come in, Mr. Black." Ashley moved aside so that he could step into the entryway. She led him to the den and he stopped at the kitchen.

"Your kitchen looks like a country kitchen in a magazine, Mrs. Lake."

"Thank you," she said with pride. "You can look around the rest of the house."

He followed her from room to room, and stopped every time he saw something interesting.

"This is a beauty house. Did you do all the decorating yourself?"

"Yes, and loved every minute of it." Forcing back the tears, Ashley looked away.

As Tom followed he couldn't take his eyes off her. He smiled, and his eyes lit up and lingered on her breasts. "We can sit and go over some figures for the sale of your house. It should appraise at a good value, Mrs. Lake."

Ashley started to offer him something to drink but changed her mind. Her heart just wasn't in it. She didn't like this man or the suggestive signals he gave when he looked at her. And she would not tell him that she was going through a divorce. He wasn't anything like Elliott Douglas. The minute Elliott came to her mind, she pushed him right out again. What was she thinking? But she knew it was only because she had just left his office. And he was so warm and understanding, and in a way, a little sad.

Tom Black sat on the sofa and Ashley purposely sat in a chair that was opposite him.

"I looked over some comps before I came over, Mrs. Lake. The prices in this neighborhood are very expensive. I can get you a good price and a fast sell." He pulled out a purchase agreement from his brown leather briefcase. He then got up and went into her kitchen to see which appliances would be included in the sale. "Yes, Mrs. Lake, we can make big bucks with this house."

As he stood at a distance, Ashley could see that he was too thin, his neck was too long, and his eyes were too round. Moreover, he seemed to be a little man with a greedy mind.

Ashley watched him as he took inventory. He was medium height, very light skinned with a heavy, light-brown mustache over lips that were too small. Ashley noticed a small scar on his forehead just below his hairline.

Tom Black finished in the kitchen. "Now, I need to go into your backyard again. I noticed you have a really nice patio. Why don't you join me, Mrs. Lake? Maybe you can show me something that I might miss that may add value to your home."

"I'm sure I can't, Mr. Black," she said, without making any attempt to move. Going back to the backyard would only depress her further. It was her favorite place. It was where she used to sit with her feet up and read during the summer months, and it was where she and Marcus made love the first night they moved into the house. Ashley was almost at the point of breaking down with tears. And now this, this ignominious man that looked at her as though he could see under her clothing, and could eat her alive, wanted what she and Marcus had worked so hard for.

"Come on, Ashley. Besides, I like your company. Your husband is one lucky man," he said, and moved a step closer to her.

In an instant, Ashley was on her feet. "Mr. Black, I didn't tell you that you could call me Ashley. My name is Mrs. Lake to you," she said, enunciating each word as clearly as possible.

"But, Mrs. Lake—"

"No buts, Mr. Black. I've decided not to sell my house after all. Please leave." She walked through the living room and opened the door as he followed behind her. "Good-bye, Mr. Black."

With a deep frown between his brows and a look of complexity, Tom walked out the door and slammed it hard behind him, enough to make the windows shake. "Crazy bitch," he said under his breath, and stormed off to his black VW. He looked at the house one last time. What a good commission he could have made, he thought angrily.

Ashley walked back, grabbed the phone, and sat back in the chair. "Marcus, it's Ash." For a few seconds she held the receiver to her ear waiting for him to respond.

"Yes! Is anything wrong, Ash?" he asked anxiously.

"No more than usual." She wasn't in any mood for small talk and got right down to business, which was the only thing left to talk about with Marcus. "If the house was sold, how much money would you expect to get?"

Marcus's ears perked up. "Why? You said you wouldn't sell for a year. So why do you ask, Ash?" He wondered what she was up to.

"I said, how much, Marcus? If I get the money in a few weeks, how much would you expect?" Waiting for his answer she tapped her fingers against the phone nervously, and held her breath.

"Seventy-five thousand is fair," he answered, placing his ink pen on the desk in front of him.

"Fifty-five thousand is better. If you want it soon I'll buy you out for fifty thousand dollars. If you don't accept, then you can wait a year and get seventy-five thousand dollars. And that's if the price of homes doesn't drop by then. It's up to you, Marcus. This is my final offer. Seventy-five if you wait," she said impatiently.

He heard her tapping against the phone and pulled the receiver from his ear, sighed in frustration. "Everything has to be your way, Ash. I don't even know you anymore. You waited till you're damn near fifty and go crazy as hell."

"Look, you waited till I'm damn near fifty and went crazy, too. I won't reconsider, Marcus. It's now, or you wait a year."

"Are you selling?"

"If I were, we wouldn't be having this conversation, would we? You settle for fifty-five and I keep the house. I need the extra twenty for my business. It's growing and I need more space. But I don't really have to do anything for a year. Good-bye, Marcus—"

"Wait! Just wait one damn minute, Ash." He ran his long fingers across his forehead and sat up straight in his high-back, brown leather chair, twirling it around facing the window. "I didn't say I wouldn't take it. You can't just call me and expect for me to jump at everything you want, when you want it."

"Are you going to take it, Marcus?"

"Yes. Now, when can I have my money so I can go forward with my life?"

"I don't want to take a second mortgage on the house. I'll have to sell some stock from my retirement. You should have it in a couple of weeks. Oh, and Marcus, I'll mail you an agreement to sign stating you are in agreement with this offer."

"What the hell—?"

"Good-bye, Marcus." She hung up.

The next thing on Ashley's list was to call Helen Graham. She dialed her number and Helen answered on the third ring.

"Hello, Helen. It's Ashley Lake, you know, your seamstress?"

"Yes. And the best seamstress that I know. As a matter a fact I was going to call you this week. I'm going to New York in two months. And I want a gown that flows at the bottom." Helen went on to tell Ashley about the trip.

"Will Robert be going with you this time?"

"No, he has a court date during that week. But I promised him I'd only be gone for two days. I hate traveling without my husband." Helen had forgotten that Ashley was going through a divorce and shifted the conversation back to the kind of gown she wanted. Once she started to talk about Robert she could go on and on for hours. And with good reason, too. It took twenty-one years for the two to get back together again.

Ashley and Helen talked about the space she needed as a dress shop. It was in a good location, and not that far from Ashley's house.

"Ashley, as a matter of fact Anita and I were together when she found the space for her bookstore. It's a funny story. I'll have to tell you about that one day."

"I look forward to it. Just call me and let me know when you can come over. I'll do some drawings and see what we can come up with," Ashley said. She loved talking to Helen. She was such a class act and so inspiring.

Ashley wrote down the phone number for Anita's bookstore and her home number.

The next thing Ashley did was to call the broker that she and Marcus used a year ago, but this time she wanted to sell some of her own stock, seventy thousand dollars' worth. She felt better, as though some weight was lifted off her shoulders. She could keep the house, maybe do some redecorating here and there, but she would keep her house.

Ashley went into the bathroom to comb her hair and put on some fresh lipstick, grabbed her purse, and ambled out the front door.

As Ashley was driving to her mother's house, she went over everything she'd accomplished earlier. Deciding to keep her house was the best, she had given Marcus very little choice in her decision. For once, she had the upper hand with him and enjoyed it with victory. She smiled and parked her car in her mother's driveway.

As she stepped out the car, Ashley saw Cora peeking through the drapes.

Cora opened the door and waited until Ashley came inside. "What brings you over today, Ash?" Cora asked and hugged her.

"Just thought I would come over and visit you and Mother. Where is she? I didn't see the car."

"She went to the bank. Come inside the kitchen. I was washing dishes when I heard you drive up the driveway."

Ashley followed her and took a seat at the wooden table. Cora wiped her hands with a paper towel.

"You want some fresh-squeezed orange juice?"

"Yes, that sounds good. I can get it, Aunt Cora."

"Okay. But I'm all finished. Now, I can sit until Doris get back from the bank. Oh, she has to stop at the supermarket and buy some potatoes, too."

"How is she, Aunt Cora? Is she getting along all right without Dad?"

"She's doing all right for herself, Ash. Doris isn't as weak as you thought she was. She loved Daniel and he loved her, too. My brother just took advantage of a situation that Doris had no control over. But she'll do all right. She and I both agreed that I'll stay on here with her so this is my new home now."

"I'm so happy you decided to stay with her, Aunt Cora. You two are as close as sisters anyway, and get along so well together. Dad would have wanted you to stay."

"Ash, I'm sorry about the way you found out. I told Daniel more than once to tell you the truth. But he was always so hardheaded and stubborn. He was so used to doing everything his way. Now look what a mess he's made of things."

"Why do you think he didn't tell me, Aunt Cora?" She took a long swallow of her orange juice, felt a seed slide down her throat.

"I think after you became a woman, Daniel thought

you would never find out. Your mother had died so who was to tell you?"

"Well, I'm sure he never thought Jason would be the one. But he still should have told the truth, Aunt Cora. Right now my life is one crisis after another. It's going to take some time to build it back up again after the tumble I've taken. Can you imagine me, a forty-five-year-old woman just finding out who her mother is? It's unbelievable. I should have been able to talk to my mother before she died. But, who knows? Maybe she didn't want to see me; after all, she knew who I was and never made the effort." Ashley tried to remember how Ruby looked. But the last few years that she was alive she stayed home in bed or in the hospital.

"Ruby was a wild woman, Ash. I'm surprised she kept her son. But it was a way of keeping Daniel, I suppose."

"Maybe she kept him because he was all she had. Maybe she was tired of being wild and alone," Ashley mused.

"Her mama raised her alone because her father walked out on them when Ruby was a child. He was wild and loved to party, just like Ruby did. Her mama worked in a bar. The way the story was told, she used to take men in a dark back room for money. Looks like she learned a lot from that old mama of hers. Ruby's family lived a rough, sinful life," Cora said, shaking her head. "I used to feel sorry for Ruby when she was growing up. I'm surprised she didn't have a house full of babies."

"I wonder how she and my dad got together?"

"When Daniel was young he used to roam some of those bars, too. Plus he and Ruby went to school together. They'd known each other almost all their lives. From what I heard, Ruby loved Daniel, and Daniel loved Doris and Ruby." Cora winked one eye and smiled.

"Did she settle down after she had Jason?"

"Some, but not much. It just wasn't in Ruby's blood to be the motherly type. But she may have changed as she got older. She did the best she knew how. She wasn't the

kind of woman a man would marry. Doris was just the opposite. Dumb, shy, didn't know nothin' about men or sex.
But she was a pretty girl, and she was the type a man would
take home to mother. She was smart in school, too."

Cora stood up. "I got to take this wig off my head. For
some reason it just ain't sitting right today." Cora jerked
the wig off. "I can't get no air through this thing. Be
right back, Ash. I gotta put this wig in the box. One
night I left it on my bed. Poor Doris was walking down
the hall and passed my room. The only light on was in
the hall. Anyway, Doris glanced at my room and
screamed her head off." Cora whooped with laughter.
"She thought someone was lying on my bed, so she
screamed and Daniel cursed."

Ashley placed her glass on the table. Holding her
stomach with one hand she laughed, pounding her fist
on the table. It had been a long time since Cora had
seen her laugh so much.

"Take your time, Aunt Cora." Ashley laughed to herself. Her aunt would never change. Cora had been wearing a wig for at least ten years. Every time Ashley saw her
she complained about it being too warm, too big, or too
heavy for her head. But she kept wearing it.

Cora came back into the kitchen and picked up the
wooden spoon to stir the stew. "This is good, Ash. You
should stay for dinner."

"Aunt Cora, do you think I should have a talk with
Jason?"

"You're all the family he has, Ash. It might be nice if
you two at least talked every once and a while. You may
not ever be close, though. You should prepare yourself
for that." Cora sat back in her chair at the table.

"I'll give it some thought. I just wonder if he would
talk to me?" She finished her orange juice, raised the
glass, and placed it in the dishwasher. "Guess I was thirsty
after all."

"Have you heard anything from Marcus, Ash?"

"Yes, as a matter a fact. I called him today to make a deal about the house. I've decided not to sell it, Aunt Cora. My heart was breaking in two before I decided to keep it. It would have been like selling a part of my heart. So I made a deal with Marcus. I'm giving him fifty-five thousand. He was pissed, but I told him take it or wait a year."

"You're good, Ash. Real good. After what he done, he's lucky you are willing to deal with him." Cora looked at Ashley again and laughed out loud. "Yes, you are good, and a smart businesswoman, too. Daniel would be proud of you. Not that he wasn't already, but now you're stronger."

"Well, it works for me. Now I have to find myself a spot for my business and hire a new person to help." Thinking of all she had to do, she sighed.

"Ash, Cora, I'm home," Doris yelled as she walked down the hall with a plastic bag from Sav-on Drugs in her hand.

Ashley got up to meet her. "Here, let me take this for you, Mother."

Doris followed her back to the kitchen. "How long have you been here, Ash?" she asked, still walking behind Ashley. She stopped and hung her jacket in the hall closet.

"Not very long. I needed to get out the house and get some fresh air." She looked at her watch. She would call and check on Lori when she got home. Since her pregnancy, she hadn't been feeling well.

In the kitchen, Doris started taking everything out of the plastic bags. She pulled out a large jar of dill pickles. "Lord, Daniel used to love these things. I remember one day he sat watching the television and ate half a jar. Now Cora got me buying them for her," Doris said, her expression changing quickly from the smiling face she had when she first got home. She missed Daniel but at least she could speak of him and smile. She didn't burst out with tears every time she thought of him like she had when he died four months ago.

"Daniel and me ate so many dill pickles when we were children, Doris. You would think I'm tired of them by now. Mama used to fuss at us for fighting over the last one."

Ashley smiled as she listened to Cora. She and Daniel looked so much alike. They were both tall, dark-skinned with pointed, stubborn chins.

Chapter 20

It was the first week in December, and Ashley had found a space for her dress shop. She hired a second person, Joan's sister, Renee. Ashley should have been happy, but she was depressed with the holidays so near and Marcus so far.

Now that they had completed twenty-five dresses for the church, a wedding gown for a young bride in the church, and a black suit for the pastor's wife, business had slowed down and Ashley had time to move into her shop.

For once, everything had been going smoothly for Ashley, except that she worked every day and night. Vanessa, Doris, and Cora volunteered to help her move into her new shop. Lori wanted to help but Ashley made her promise to take it easy. After all, this was her first pregnancy.

It was a chilly Saturday morning, and Lori met Ashley at the shop. She stood in the middle of the room and looked around. "Everything looks good, Mom, now that everything's in place. Your shop is even larger than I thought it was. There's space for everything."

Ashley watched her daughter as she walked around the shop. She smiled, looking at how cute she looked in her pink-flowered maternity top and white pants. Her hair was growing, combed back into a ponytail. She never wore any makeup except for lipstick. Keith thought she looked prettier without it.

"Yes, everything is going well and I'm as busy as ever." Ashley sipped on her coffee that she had bought across the parking lot at Starbucks. She ordered Lori to go and lie down on the small sofa in the back room that was her office.

"I'm having another power sewing machine delivered on Monday. Hey, look over here at the mannequins that I'm going to display in the window." There were two of them, fully dressed. One wore a black suit that Ashley had made and the other one wore a green velvet dress that was designed for the holidays.

Lori sat up on the sofa and shook her head in disbelief. "I'm amazed at what you can do. They're beautiful, Mom. When did you find the time to make them? I would have thought the twenty-five dresses you made took up all your time," Lori said, feeling the velvet material. "You could also design something in red for the holidays, too."

"Come here, Lori," Ashley said, motioning for Lori to follow her. "Here's something I made for you." She pulled the purple velvet maternity dress from the small closet and handed it to Lori. "Something for the holidays."

"Oh, Mom, I love it." Lori placed the dress against her protruding stomach and stood at the full-length mirror. "It's just in time for Keith's company party."

Ashley remembered when Marcus got his first good-paying job. "Time flies, and lives change," she murmured under her breath.

"Come over here and sit down, Mom. I have something to tell you."

The smile disappeared from Ashley's face, replaced with fear. What else could go wrong in her life at forty-five? First, her husband leaves her for another woman, and her mother turns out to be someone else. "Now what? What is it, Lori? Is everything all right with your pregnancy? Oh no, it's not the baby?"

"No, Mom, it's not my pregnancy. It's about Dad. He

asked his girlfriend to marry him as soon as the divorce is final. I met him for lunch yesterday. He told me so himself." She waited for Ashley's response. It seemed like minutes had passed before Ashley was able to speak again.

Ashley inhaled, then exhaled, as though the news was a physical blow and she was gasping for air. "Well, that certainly was fast," she said, her voice quivering. "Our divorce isn't even final yet. I take it he had planned to marry her all along." She had to do something with her hands, started folding material. She could feel Lori's eyes on her and had to fight back the tears, the hysterics. For her daughter's sake, she had to appear calm.

Lori watched her as she folded the material, but it was easy to see Ashley's back stiffen, her hands shaking.

She took her seat again. "Have you eaten anything yet, Lori?"

"Yes. I had a bowl of Cream of Wheat before I left." She couldn't take her eyes from Ashley's face, waiting for the impact of her father's marriage proposal to hit her.

But as they talked Ashley's demeanor didn't change. After an hour Lori thought it was safe to leave her. Ashley had taken it better than Lori thought she would.

Once Lori left, Ashley slumped back into the chair. Her heart was frozen, but for the moment she didn't feel any hurt, hatred—she was just shocked and numb, which was worse. If she hated Marcus, if she felt hurt or betrayal, she could cry, curse, or even throw a glass against the wall. But no, she just felt as though her arms were too heavy to move, her heart stomped on again and again. After several minutes passed, finally, she inadvertently touched her face and it was wet with tears. Was there no end to Marcus's hurting her? she wondered. Couldn't he just move to another state or disappear into thin air?

* * *

After tossing and turning in bed, Ashley flipped on the lamp beside her bed. Knowing she would get no sleep, she got up and went to the den and flipped on the TV, poured herself a glass of white wine, and slumped into the chair. She had never drunk any alcohol when she was alone, but tonight, at two in the morning, she needed something to desensitize the anxiety she felt. Besides, every position she had laid in wasn't comfortable enough to relax and help her to get to sleep.

Ashley knew precisely what was causing her to be unable to sleep. *Marcus*—he was always there, still somewhere in her life. She was livid every time she thought of him getting married so soon. Feeling anger exploding inside her, Ashley grabbed the phone from the small table beside the chair. She was going to call Marcus and give him a good cursing out. Couldn't he wait until their divorce was final before he asked that skinny girl to marry him? Ashley punched the first three numbers and stopped, looking at the receiver as though she was waiting for his voice to come through.

"No! No! No!" Ashley said out loud to herself, and placed the receiver back in its cradle. What would be the point of calling him and humiliating herself? Why give him the satisfaction of knowing that she was still hurting and losing sleep over him? She was like an old shoe, wore out and tossed aside. What was she going to do with her life anyway? she wondered with teary eyes. Well, there's only one thing she could do. She closed her eyes and lay her head back. Finally, Ashley got back in bed, but at five-thirty she was wide awake again.

Ashley got out of bed, and as she walked to the kitchen she could see the sun shining through the blinds, and decided to go back to her bedroom. She changed into a pair of red sweats and T-shirt, stood in front of the mirror and braided her hair into one braid in back, grabbed her blue baseball cap, and strode out the door. She was running on overload and needed to jog and release the stress.

She drove to Fox Hills Park in Culver City. She could do a few laps around the track before it got too crowded. She started jogging slowly. It seemed that every man who passed her in some way reminded her of Marcus— the height, build, even the smile. Every time she thought of him her heart swelled, and she jogged faster and tasted the tears that fell from her eyes and dried against her face. No longer jogging slowly, Ashley began to run faster as though she was running for her life. As she ran, she heard herself repeating, "Marcus getting married." She repeated it over and over again, her heart pounding as though it would pound out her chest. Her breathing became labored, but she couldn't stop. She had to clear her head. She had to run from her broken heart, the memories of the earlier years, the hurt that was stuck in the pit of her heart. And all of a sudden she felt sick, dizzy, and almost threw up. She stopped and leaned against a tall tree. Gulping for air, Ashley limped to the ground, and sat against the tree trunk, and closed her eyes. Knees up, she placed both hands to her face, taking deep breaths. She had run too fast, too hard, and got too overheated. *"Why, why did it have to be this way, to end this way? Marcus, why?"* Burying her face against her knees, she cried.

Two men jogged along the path and stopped when they heard the woman cry out. They ran and stood in front of Ashley. "Are you all right, miss? Did someone hurt you?" one man asked with concern. The second man looked around but didn't see anyone near Ashley. From the position she was sitting in, they wouldn't have seen her if she had not cried out loud. "Are you ill, miss?"

Ashley slowly stood up and pulled her cap down on her head. "No, I'm not ill. Thanks for stopping." Embarrassed, she couldn't look them directly in the face and couldn't say another word. Ashley took off running back to her car. Once she was inside, she lay her forehead against the steering wheel and sobbed more.

The first thing she did was shower. She thought of her life as she stood under the hot water, still feeling weak by exhausting herself. She didn't know what came over her, running and overheating herself. But as she thought of her life she knew it had to change, had to get better, and she had to do it for herself. She started to speak out loud. "Right now my business is inchoate, but it won't always be. I'm going to work night and day to accomplish what I want, which is to make my own line of clothing and place it in department stores."

Ashley dried off and went into the kitchen. As she leaned over to set the empty glass on the table, she felt dizzy again, and her body felt as though she was floating in a pool of water. It was still early, and she felt relaxed enough to sleep for a couple of hours, and slowly walked to her bedroom. She climbed in bed and covered herself. As she closed her eyes and began sinking into a deep sleep, the last thing she remembered was getting even with Marcus. And what better way to do so than being successful with her business? He thought she couldn't do it on her own.

As the weeks passed into the holidays, Ashley had developed a routine. She ran in the early mornings and was at her dress shop from seven in the morning to seven or eight in the evenings, and all day on Saturdays. The only day she stayed home was Sunday. Once she got home, she ate and made herself comfortable and she drew pictures of more styles for her shop.

Ashley began to live and breathe to make a success of her business, develop some prospective in her life again, and leave the past behind her. She had family and friends who loved her, but it wasn't enough. The void in her life seemed to be with her everywhere she went, like it was part of her life. She now had enough customers to keep her busy day and night.

It was seven in the morning, and Ashley was already working in the shop. She pulled her sweater tightly around her, flipped on the coffeemaker, and undressed one of the mannequins. She replaced the black suit with a navy blue silk. Ashley even placed a wide-brimmed hat on the mannequin that was dressed like a movie actress or model. She stood back with a cup of coffee in her hand. Someone shook the doorknob and she almost jumped out her skin. She looked toward the door and saw Joan peeking through the window. Ashley smoothed her hair with her hands and opened the door. Joan and her sister, Renee, were such terrific workers and Ashley felt lucky to have them. She had forgotten they were coming in early that morning.

Joan stepped in first, carrying a small brown bag in her hand.

"The coffee smells delicious. We stopped and bought warm muffins," Joan said, holding the bag up in her hand.

"Yes, and the muffins smell luscious. The only thing I ate last night was one slice of bread with some jam on it," Ashley said, grabbing for the bag.

"Honey, you got to stop eating like a bird. You look great, but you need some good home cooking to stick to your bones." Joan looked at Ashley's glowing brown face. "You work day and night. You have to take care of yourself, Ash," Joan said, and Renee agreed. As Joan looked at Ashley, she noticed Ashley looked thinner than she was last week. "Lord, if I could only keep my weight down like yours."

"When I found out that my cholesterol was high enough to cause a heart attack I cut back on so many foods. But I didn't give up my Cokes. Plus, when I get home I'm so tired, Joan. I just curl up in a chair or draw ideas that I've thought of during the day. And I've been coming in at seven. I can't rest until my business is what I want it to be. One day I would like to expand and get a larger place," she said, and looked around at the space she had.

"Don't worry, Ash. At the rate you're going, it won't be long," Joan replied.

"Look who's talking," Renee said, with her hands resting on her wide hips. "Joan, you go home and work when you should be resting, too." Renee was in her midthirties, about 5'2" and heavy in the hips, brown skin the color of light chocolate. Her hair was in French braids and hung down her back.

Finally, they sat down and had coffee and blueberry muffins. The phone rang and Ashley got up and answered.

"Ash, what are you doing there so early? I called your house and got no answer," Vanessa said. "I thought I would find you at the shop."

"I have orders to fill. As a matter a fact, I'm going to find out what I have to do to land a contract with one of the major department stores. Oh, and I have to call Charlie and find out when he can trim my hair this week, too. So much to do," she said.

"Well, I have some good news for you, Ash."

"Like what? Did Marcus drive off a cliff?"

Vanessa laughed. "No, silly. I wore that last pantsuit at a meeting of the L.A. Chamber of Commerce Businesswomen, and incidentally, you should go to the next meeting with me. Anyway, this woman was there who owns a small dress boutique. She wants you to call her, Ash. She told me that she could use something different in her boutique that's not in the large department stores."

"Oh, Vanessa. Do you really think she might have me make a few outfits for her boutique?" Ashley asked with so much excitement that Joan and Renee looked at each other, then looked at Ashley with interest.

"Yes, I'm pretty sure she will, the way she talked, and she really admired my pantsuit. She had other women looking at it, too."

"Oh, Vanessa, you just made my week. This is my dream, to put clothes in different stores." Ashley felt an eruption of energy and hopes she needed for her business. She had been striving so hard and now it was paying off.

"Well, just don't overdo it, Ash. Hire more help if you need to. Besides, the holidays have crept up on us again. And you'll probably be invited out." Vanessa hesitated for a few seconds but she had to tell Ashley before she found out through someone else. "And Ash, I ran into Gloria yesterday. Have you heard the news about Marcus getting married? Gloria got a kick out of telling me."

"Yes. Lori told me. Last night I had to almost get drunk to get some sleep. I can't believe I was ever married to him, Vanessa." She got up and walked into the front of the shop still holding the phone to her ear. "I wouldn't be surprised at anything Marcus does now. Next you'll hear they're having a baby."

Vanessa laughed out loud. "As for you, you need to go out and start dating again."

"I'm not ready yet, Vanessa. I have so much to do with my business before I have time for a man in my life. My luck, I'll find one that wants the world centered around him, like Marcus did. I can't give anyone that again."

"One day you will, Ash. Maybe not now, but one day you'll love again, and hopefully it will be with someone who'll appreciate you. Now, get a pen and pad so you can write down the woman's name and phone number.

Her name is Abbie Davis and her boutique is on Overland Boulevard and Washington Street."

Ashley wrote the phone number down as Joan and Renee stood in the door listening.

"Okay, Vanessa. I'll call Abbie straight up ten o'clock. I'll call you when I get home." After Ashley hung up, she, Joan, and Renee threw their hands up in the air and jumped around in a circle. They were indeed her new friends and felt as happy as Ashley did.

Ashley did telephone Abbie, and they made arrangements for her to visit Ashley's shop the next day. That day, Ashley took out all her drawings, made sure everything she had made was hanging on a rack along with the four dresses they had finished today. She was so happy and felt light on her feet. And she worked even harder that day and later that night.

The next day as Ashley, Joan, and Renee were sewing, Abbie Davis walked inside the shop. She was a tall woman with freckles across her nose and cheeks, bleached blond hair that was too light for her complexion and hung past her shoulders.

As Ashley got up from her sewing machine to introduce herself, she noticed that Abbie's green skirt was too tight across her slender hips and wondered how she walked in such high heel shoes. They were so high it seemed like she was walking on her toes.

"Hello, you must be Miss Davis. I'm Ashley," Ashley said, extending her hand out.

"Yes, and you can call me Abbie." She gave Ashley a warm smile and looked at the rack that had at least twenty-five different dresses, suits, and blouses that Ashley had made.

"You can look on the rack to see if you like anything. And I have some drawings you might want to select from that are not made up on the rack."

"Honey, I think I've seen what I want." Abbie went straight to a purple suit with a short and long skirt.

"I have a pair of pants for that suit, too," Ashley said.

After Abbie had gone through the clothes that were hanging on the rack, she looked at all the drawings. Once Abbie had finished looking, she ordered fifteen suits, dresses, and slacks. "This is so exciting. I get to select what I want."

"I can fill the order in three weeks."

She would sew all night if she had to. She was on her way to being a full-time designer, and she intended to be the best designer in Los Angeles, and soon California.

Chapter 21

It was Christmas Day, and Ashley was invited to have dinner at her mother's house. Lori and Keith would be there, too. Last Christmas Eve she was baking and had had everyone to dinner at her house. But today was different, and it didn't seem like Christmas at all.

Ashley was up early. She cut some material for the two blouses she had left to complete Abbie Davis's order. Today, all she really wanted to do was to stay home and finish the hem in three of the dresses, but she knew she would never hear the end of it from her mother. Doris cherished the holidays. And as long as Ashley could remember her parents always had a Christmas tree, and Daniel would decorate the outside. But it would be different for Doris without Daniel.

Ashley closed her eyes wondering how she would get through the holidays, and she still had New Year's Eve to contend with. Old habits had to be broken; her entire life had changed. But how many New Year's Eves would she be alone? she wondered.

Ashley got up off the floor and went to her bedroom to decide what she would wear. She pulled out a dress, hung it back in the closet, and pulled out a pair of black slacks and a green satin blouse. She was in no mood for pantyhose or a dress.

Ashley arrived at Doris's house with an armful of presents. Thirty minutes after she got there, Keith and Lori walked in. They all hugged and kissed, laughed and talked. But this Christmas was different. Daniel wasn't alive and Ashley thought of him constantly, and she was sure that Doris felt the same.

Doris's Christmas tree was tall and green with white-and-gold decorations and a large black angel on top, the pine scent floating through the house. They were sitting in the living room drinking eggnog. Ashley had brought a tray of pastries that Keith couldn't seem to keep his hands out of.

Lori was now seven months pregnant, and Doris and Cora made her stay put in one place as they waited on her when she needed anything.

"Mom, next month Sheri is giving me a baby shower at her house. Is that all right with you?" Lori asked, not wanting to hurt her mother's feelings. She didn't know if Ashley had planned to have it at her house.

"Sure. She's your closest friend. And you gave her a baby shower. Tell her to give me a call and I'll take care of the expenses. Every time I think of you having a baby I get happy enough to cry."

"Every time I think of you having a baby I think of the baby clothes I want to buy," said Cora. "They have these little baby clothes that aren't as big as my hand."

Ashley looked in her mother's face. Doris was trying to be happy but Ashley could see the sadness in her eyes. Ashley had to think of a way to make her mother feel better. Not that she felt any happier herself. It was Christmas, and they still had to get through New Year's, and it was meant to be happy.

She stood up. "Dinner will be ready soon so let's open our gifts," Ashley suggested.

Lori was the first one to jump from her seat. "I was hoping someone would suggest that," she said happily. She was the first to grab a present and gave it to Ashley. "This one is for you, Mom." She gave Doris and Cora their boxes. And then she and Keith started to open theirs.

Ashley opened one of the boxes from Lori and Keith. She pulled out a beautiful black Guess purse with a gold handle; a pair of black boots was in the second box. "Oh, Lori, they're beautiful." Ashley went over and kissed Lori and Keith. She held her purse up again before placing it back inside the box.

Everyone was talking at the same time. And finally, Doris was so excited about her gifts that it wasn't long before she was laughing along with everyone else.

For a second Ashley wondered how Jason was spending his Christmas. Was he alone? Did he have someone to love him? She was beginning to think of him quite often.

Dinner was delicious, with a lot of chattering and laughter. And, as always, Cora said something funny to make everyone laugh even more.

"I'm going to have to run an extra mile tomorrow morning," Ashley said, taking a bite out of her monkey bread that Cora had baked. She still had to remember that her cholesterol might go up again, especially during the holidays.

It was past four, and Ashley and Doris were alone in the kitchen.

"Looks like you made a wise choice by starting up your own business, Ash. Daniel said you could do anything you put your mind to. He would be so proud of you." She kissed Ashley on the cheek.

"I miss him, Mom. I know you do, too." Ashley dried the last dish and put the stack of plates inside the cabinet.

"I do miss him. There's not a minute in a day that I don't think of Daniel. But it's something that I will have to live with and learn to adjust without him, Ash. I just thank the good Lord for Cora. We go shopping together. And we are going to go on a bus trip to Vegas. You know how she loves those slot machines."

"If memory serves me right, you do pretty good at those machines, too, Mother." They both laughed.

Once everyone was back in the living room Ashley stood up. "I hate to go so early, but I still have some dresses to hem."

"But, Mom, it's Christmas," Lori said.

"I know, Lori. But I can't relax knowing I have work at home waiting for me. It won't be this way always." Ashley picked up her neatly stacked boxes that were in the corner. "Did you like your leather coat, Lori?" Ashley asked.

"Mom, I love it."

"I love mine, too, Ash," Keith said and kissed her on the cheek. "I got the best mother-in-law in the world."

Ashley looked at him and smiled. He still looked like a kid with his thick glasses.

Ashley walked inside her house and dropped all her boxes on the sofa in the den, went to the refrigerator, and opened a Diet Coke. She had gone from regular to diet. Knowing she was drinking too many Cokes, she looked at the one in her hand. She couldn't eat all the foods she loved but she wouldn't give up her Cokes. She lit the fireplace, went to her bedroom, and changed into an oversized T-shirt and sweats.

Ashley started hemming one of the dresses for Abbie Davis. The crackling fire broke the silence in the den.

The entire day Ashley had tried so hard to smile and to hold back the tears that were now beginning to flow freely. God, she was lonely. If only Marcus could have loved her, if only Daniel was alive. She took a deep breath . . . but she kept hemming the dress.

Three weeks had passed, and Ashley had delivered the order to Abbie as scheduled. Abbie was very happy with the clothes and promised that whenever the order got low she would call Ashley for more. But three weeks later she reordered the same as before. And along with her order Ashley had five orders from women referred by Helen and Anita. Ashley hired Joan's niece, Brenda. Now she had three in the same family working for her and all three were dependable, hardworking women.

Chapter 22

It was five in the afternoon, and Elliott Douglas decided to leave his office for the day. He'd been seeing clients since morning. At noon, he had a client to debrief, which took three hours.

Terri had left at ten with an upset stomach. That morning she had moved around the office as though she was moving in slow motion. With her monthly routine he suspected she had cramps. Robert was on vacation with Helen, and the other partner was in court all that day.

As Elliott took the elevator he wondered if Janet was home. He never knew from day to day what to expect from her.

Elliott got off the elevator on P2, and went to his car. He drove off into the traffic on Century Park East, and sighed at the thought of the busy traffic. His headaches and marriage were one and the same, a pain that ate at him constantly. When a man hated to go home every evening, something had to be done. How much longer could he live with such dejectedness day after day? Didn't he deserve more out of life? He had asked himself that question a thousand times. Tonight, if Janet was home he had to speak to her. For the past few months they hadn't even been sleeping in the same room. She lived her life, and so did he.

The traffic was barely moving until Elliott reached Pico Boulevard. Within twenty minutes he was driving into his driveway. And just as he figured, Janet wasn't home; her car wasn't in the driveway.

Elliott grabbed his jacket and briefcase and went inside the house. He set his briefcase on the floor in his home office and hung his jacket in the closet.

After taking two aspirins he sat on the sofa, lay his head back, and closed his eyes. Finally, after a half hour, the pain in his head dwindled into a nagging reminder of the throbbing he felt only thirty minutes ago.

He had taken off his shirt and released his feet from the new brown shoes, the color of his suit. He was left wearing a T-shirt and slacks.

After working at his desk, Elliott looked at the crystal clock; an hour had passed quickly. He heard the front door open and shut.

Janet was walking down the hall and peeked into Elliott's office. "You're working as usual?"

"Yes, I'm working," he answered, and looked into her eyes. "Have you been drinking, Janet?"

"No, Elliott. You know I don't drink and drive. Not alone, anyway." She gave him a long, singular look and wondered why was he watching her so closely. What was on his mind? Elliott was so unreachable lately, she thought, as she took her jacket off and folded it across her arm.

"Are you having an affair, Janet? You're never home anymore and when you are your mind is preoccupied. You and that receptionist of mine are one in the same. Never around when you're needed."

She pondered his jeering remark before she answered. "Really, Elliott. Must you compare me to a simple receptionist? When did you get such a low opinion of me?" She kicked one of his shoes in the corner and turned her back to him. "You can move out if you want to, but don't take anything except your clothes." She pranced out his office.

Elliott sucked in his breath and wondered why she

had gotten so pissed off all of a sudden? But never-theless, he would give a lot of thought to her sugges-tion. He got up and leaned against his desk when he heard Janet's footsteps coming back to his office.

"So, talk to me, Janet. Are you having an affair, do you want a divorce, what?" Getting angry, he threw his hands up in frustration. Looking at Janet, she was still an attractive woman, but over the years she had changed. And she spent money exorbitantly. She had become a snob and acted as though she was better than anyone else.

"No! No divorce," she said, and threw her hands up to fan him off. She pushed her hair back as though she was getting too warm. Why in hell did he choose now to dis-cuss their problems? She had lied about drinking and had had three glasses of wine. All she wanted to do was undress and lie in their comfortable bed. But no, tonight Elliott had to whine about a divorce, she was thinking as she stood in the doorway glaring in his face.

"What are you talking about, Elliott, and why this sud-den interest in me and a divorce?"

"I've always been interested in you, Janet. But what's going on with you? You're not happy with me. You don't want a divorce, and you say you're not cheating. So, what? Talk to me," he demanded, looking her straight in her eyes. She would not get off so easily this time.

Janet sat in the chair two feet from his desk. "Every time you feel I'm not being the little homemaker you want for a wife, you accuse me of cheating, Elliott. You work all the time. Even when you're home, you're work-ing." She slipped her feet out her black, high heel shoes, and straightened the side of her black dress.

It hadn't gone unnoticed by Elliott that her dress clung seductively to her breasts for all to see. And for a fraction of an instant, he wondered who was she wearing it for. Certainly not for him.

"I may be working, Janet, but at least I'm home. You

don't do anything to make me want to come home anymore without my work. You're either coming in or going out. What kind of marriage is this?" he said sensibly, and rubbed the stiffness out of his neck. "I can't live this way any longer, so you think about it, Janet. I advise you to think hard on it," he said and dashed out, leaving her looking behind him. He had gotten angry, and was tired of living a lie, and most of all, tired of hardly living at all.

Janet jumped up from her seat. "You advise me?" she yelled back at him while walking to the door. "Don't talk to me as though I'm one of your clients, Elliott. Do you hear me . . . ?"

Chapter 23

January had been a long, hardworking month for Ashley. Joan had been ill, first with the flu that developed into a terrible cough, leaving Ashley, Renee, and Brenda carrying a heavy load; and then Ashley worked long hours to fill an order. She took work home to keep her business growing. Most of all she needed to know that she had accomplished what she had set out to do.

The news of Marcus getting married was a blow to Ashley's ego. She felt a pain in her chest every time she thought of it, which was constantly. She had gotten thinner since she was working so many hours a week, but she was still a forty-five-year-old woman, nothing she could do to change it, and in two months she was going to be a grandmother.

The weeks passed fast from Monday to Saturday and Helen was signing her new novel at Anita's bookstore. Ashley still had work to do but Vanessa insisted on picking her up at one that afternoon, and she had better be ready to go. At least she was meeting new friends, and a bookstore was the last place she would run into Marcus. They were going in different circles. She had her friends and he had his.

Turning from side to side, Ashley stood in front of the long mirror looking at her new creation that she was wearing. It was a suit: black Capri slacks with cuffs and a short-waist jacket with red trim around the collar and cuffed sleeves, simple in design yet rich in texture.

She stepped into a pair of black slip-on high heel shoes. There, she thought, this suit has the perfect touch. She stepped back, turned so that she could see the back of the jacket. The corners of her full mouth turned up into a smile as she had to admit that it was a stunning creation.

The confidence she felt was new to her and gave her a sense of power and independence she had never felt while she was married. Maybe that's what it feels like to become a woman with a purpose in life.

She had struggled through the holidays with old memories haunting her from every direction. Everything she saw reminded her of the earlier years. Now, she worked hard and tried in every way to adjust to her life as an unmarried woman, a fatherless daughter. And next week would be the final blow; her divorce would be final. Twenty-five years, and six months to end it.

Ashley swiveled on her heels and walked into the living room to wait for Vanessa. Today she didn't want any old memories to cloud her mind or turn a smile into a frown. She wanted this day to be a good one. Besides, it was time to accept what was, and what wasn't anymore.

A horn blew and Ashley peeked out her large French window. In the driveway Vanessa was waiting for her. Ashley grabbed her purse, and flounced out the door and climbed in the car with Vanessa. This time she was driving her two-seater gold Benz.

"Now, aren't you a pretty one today," Vanessa said, admiring the nice fitted suit. Looking into her rear view mirror, Vanessa drove off. She was dressed in a tangerine-colored pantsuit.

"Nice suit, Ash. When did you have time to make it? You've been working day and night since Joan's been ill."

Ashley looked out the window at the puffy gray clouds traveling slowly across the sky. Vanessa always knew what to say to make her feel good about herself.

"It only took me a couple of days to make it. Boy, I

sure will be glad when Joan is well enough to come back. Her sister is good, but Joan can hem faster." Pulling a tissue from her purse, Ashley wiped off her sunglasses.

"Gary is going to meet me at the bookstore. Later, we plan to go to a movie with his new client."

"You were lucky to marry him, Vanessa. I used to think that you should have stayed with Larry because he was your husband for so long. But you had enough courage to move on to a better life. Gary was a good choice." Ashley turned her face to the window to hide the sad expression that she was wearing. Damn, she said that she wouldn't do this today.

"You know what, Vanessa?"

Vanessa glanced at her. "No, what, Ash?"

"I'm just so tired of thinking of Marcus," she hissed between closed teeth.

"One day it will get easier, Ash. You'll go all day and not think of him. When night comes you'll realize that you went an entire day without thinking of Marcus. Now, you look too pretty to be thinking of him today. Hey, look, Ash. I see the balloons in front of the store. And there's Gary's car." Vanessa pointed at the gray SUV.

The line ended outside the bookstore and Ashley and Vanessa went to the end.

Ashley was looking at a group of five women walking to the end of the line when Elaine came outside and told her and Vanessa to come inside. They walked fast around the people in line and slipped inside.

Helen was sitting at the table signing books for two women who had come together. Gary and Robert were standing at the counter talking to Anita, and Lynn was unpacking another box of books for Helen to sign.

The bookstore was large and fancy with brown paneling on one side of the wall; there were a coffeemaker and two long tables lined with refreshments and assorted cookies.

"You ladies are like a breath of fresh air," Gary said,

and kissed Vanessa and Ashley on their cheeks. "It's good to see you out for a change, Ashley." Gary held Vanessa's hand, his eyes roaming her entire body in just seconds.

"How are you, Gary?" Ashley said. "It's good to see you, too. I haven't been able to get out much these days."

"Have you been to a book signing before, Ashley?" Gary asked, looking around at more people as they came inside the store. "And you look too good to stay inside all the time."

Ashley laughed at Gary again. "I do think your husband is flirting with me, Vanessa."

"Honey, I see someone else looking at you even harder," Vanessa replied. "There's talk that Janet is on her way out. It's been a long time coming," Vanessa whispered against Ashley's ear. Then she and Gary walked toward the door where the crowd was.

Ashley sped around as Elliott came strolling up beside her. For some obscure reason, Ashley felt her heart jolt, and her hands were moist as she tightly held her purse. She could feel heat increasing beneath the skin in her face and prayed that it wasn't a hot flash. She would have to phone her doctor first thing Monday morning, she thought.

"What a pleasant surprise, Ashley. Gee, don't you look stunning in that suit you're wearing. Did you design it yourself?" Elliott asked with interest, standing back to get a better look at her. But he had seen her when she first came into the store; she just hadn't seen him. And again, he wondered what would it be like to hold her in his arms, protect her so she would never experience the pain again that her husband had inflected upon her.

In a way their lives were the same. Marcus walked out on Ashley because he didn't love her, and Elliott stayed home, but there was no love.

For the first time, as he stood facing Ashley, he knew

the truth that he had been avoiding; he no longer loved Janet at all. And now all Elliott could imagine was to slowly and leisurely peel, piece by piece, Ashley's clothes off that sexy, brown body of hers. And as he looked deeply into her eyes he even wondered what she was wearing underneath. He looked away, trying to block the image from his mind. He hadn't imagined anything so libidinous about a woman since he was a younger man, and he had been around many women.

"It's good to see you, too, Elliott. And yes, I made this suit for myself." She looked at him peculiarly. Had he heard a word she had said to him?

Elliott turned his attention back to Ashley. "You did a wonderful job, Ashley. Tell me, how are things going with you? You are almost a single woman again. The time passes so fast, doesn't it?"

"Yes, I know. Marcus will soon be getting married again." Damn, she thought. Marcus was the last person she wanted to talk about.

"One day, my dear, you will get married again, too. Trust me."

"Marriage? Not for a while anyway. I have my business to get off the ground."

"And when your business is going the way you want, what then, Ashley?"

She cocked her head to one side and wondered what he was pondering inside his head. "I have time to think about it." Ashley stopped talking and looked in another direction for a few moments.

"Do you come to all of Helen's book signings, Elliott?"

"No, but today I wanted to do something different. I'm glad that you're here, and it's good to see you are among friends."

She wondered if he realized how appealing he really was. "Thanks Elliott, and I'm glad that you are here among friends, too, and not stuck inside your office."

Elliott looked at the long line again. What was wrong

with him today? He was a married man for Pete's sake.
And he cared too much for Ashley to reveal what he really felt. When did it happen? he mused. Was it her first
appointment in his office, or was it the day they had had
coffee together? He didn't remember. It seemed as
though he had known her for a long time. But all he
knew was that his blood had been brewing hot inside for
her. He would have come to Helen's book signing anyway, but he was hoping Ashley would be there if only just
to have a casual conversation and be near her.

"Barnes and Noble has nothing on Anita's store. It's
so bright, and the bookshelves are lined with so many interesting books. I like the different variety of mystery
books. I used to be a mystery reader. But that was a long
time ago," Elliott said. "I don't have time for recreational
reading anymore."

"I used to read romance novels before I started my
business," Ashley said, as she looked around to see
Vanessa and Gary talking to a couple that she hadn't
met. When did they manage to get away from her without her noticing it?

"I wonder what made Anita decide to open a bookstore?" Ashley asked. She leaned against the counter and
smiled at Anita. She was busy counting books and working at the cash register. Her husband walked in back of
the counter to give her a hand.

"I did the legal workup and contracts for different dis-
tributors for Anita when she decided to go into business
for herself. She says she always wanted a small bookstore.
Before I met her, Robert was a defense attorney for the
City of L.A., and Anita worked with him. I met her
through Robert and Helen. She found this place to
lease. Raymond owns six of the storefronts in this shopping center."

Ashley watched him intensely as he talked. He was always so sincere and so easy to be with.

Robert and Raymond motioned for Elliott, and he excused himself and walked away.

Ashley purchased a book for herself and one for Lori. She mingled among others that were in the bookstore. She gave out four business cards to women that complimented her suit. At four-thirty the book signing was over, and Vanessa and Ashley left.

"I really enjoyed it. There's so much I didn't do when I was married," Ashley told Vanessa as she was driving.

"I know, Ash. Once your business is where you want it you'll have time to socialize more. It's time you live a little for yourself. The entire time you were married you lived for your family. Oh, sure, I did the same thing with Larry. But with Gary, he's more sociable than Larry was. And of course, he's an agent so he knows how to socialize. We'll go home later and have a nice glass of wine, make a little love, and cuddle. We all need it, Ash." Vanessa turned the corner and parked her car in front of Ashley's house.

"You're making me absolutely depressed. All I have to go home to is work and more work," Ashley said laughing.

"Ash?"

Ashley turned around and looked at Vanessa, as she sounded serious. Vanessa had parked the car and rolled her window down.

"What is it?" Ashley asked with concern.

"Do you know that Elliott likes you?"

Ashley looked at her as though she was losing her mind. She still had no idea that Elliott cared more for her than as a client.

"Yes, I know he likes me. But I think Elliott likes everyone. He's a good fellow. I don't know him very well, of course, but it seems that we've known each other for a long time. I'm sure that anyone would feel the same about him. Oh, and he's so good-looking, and his debonair manner never abandons him. It's like something he was born with."

"Ash, you can be so dumb sometimes. The man really cares about you. Do you understand? Care, as in 'wants' you?"

"But how can you tell?" Ashley asked, still surprised at what she was hearing.

"When he talks to you, it's as if no one else is in the room but the two of you. Just you, and you alone. He gets this expression in his eyes like he's in pain and is trying to hide it. I can't explain it, but the feeling is there, Ash."

"Now you're the one who's dumb, Vanessa. That man has a beautiful wife."

"Yes, and she's a diabolical bitch if ever I saw one. She doesn't want anything but his money. Helen told me once that Janet said Elliott wanted children when they were younger. But having children would ruin her figure. When she was asked why they didn't adopt, she said that she kept asking Elliott if they could adopt. But when the subject came up, Elliott had no idea she had said that. Elliott is a good man and a fool. He needs a real woman, Ash, and you need a good lay about now. I mean, who knows what could come out of it?"

"Are you out of your mind, Vanessa?" Ashley asked in shock. "When he gets tired of her crap, he'll leave. Right now he's a married man. I wouldn't touch him with a ten-foot pole. Now, thanks for picking me up. Good lay? What's wrong with you, girl?"

"All right. Just don't say I didn't tell you." Vanessa turned the key in the ignition.

Ashley shook her head. "I had fun anyway."

"Good, Ash. Now aren't you glad you went? I know Elliott was," she said, and laughed out loud. "Just kidding, girl." Vanessa drove off and left Ashley standing in the driveway shaking her head in amazement. She was certain that Vanessa was mistaken about Elliott having any interest in her besides being her lawyer. Ashley smiled and went inside the house.

Another month had quickly passed. It was Friday night and Ashley was still at her dress shop. Joan was back but was working only eight hours a day until she regained her strength. Renee had taken two weeks off to go to Atlanta on family business, which meant Ashley was working even longer hours.

Ashley was sitting at her small desk going over her profits and losses. She had paid her rent for the shop, bought materials and other supplies, paid utility bills. She sighed and went over her figures again to make sure she hadn't made any mistakes, but she came up with the same figures. This time she included her house and car notes, and wages paid out. She had made a small profit. It wasn't a lot of money but it covered all her bills, and she didn't have to go into her retirement fund.

Ashley clapped her hands and jumped up in the middle of the floor. She looked up to the ceiling and laughed out loud. After months of working long hours, putting her life on hold, and wondering if she had made a drastic mistake by quitting her job and going into business for herself, she had finally made a profit. She smiled all the way home.

It was dark when Ashley arrived home and stepped in her living room, flipped on the lamp beside the sofa, and began opening her mail. The first envelope she opened was a small one: an invitation to Lori's baby shower. The invitation was white, engraved in silver. Two weeks from today. Ashley smiled as she read it. Lori's friend Sheri was giving it at her mother's house in Inglewood on Hillcrest Drive, near Manchester Avenue. Well, the house was certainly large enough, Ashley thought. Ashley had planned to buy the cake and have all the food catered.

All of a sudden the thought of becoming a grand-mother made her feel old. She was too old to keep her husband, and now she was going to be a grandmother.

To add insult to injury, Ashley was certain that Marcus would be there, alone, she hoped. She just couldn't imagine seeing him and his future wife so soon. Seeing him alone would be all she could bear. She sighed and closed her eyes, running her fingers through her hair as she lay her head back on the sofa.

Ashley fell asleep for an hour, then got up and went to bed without dinner.

She was up early the next morning and dressed to go back to her dress shop. On her way she stopped at Winchell's Donuts and bought a blueberry muffin and a large coffee.

She set the bag on her desk and switched on the TV, just to hear a voice. It was always so quiet that time of morning when she was there alone.

If she worked till noon she would take her lunch break and go check on Doris and Aunt Cora.

"Look who the wind blew in," Doris said, walking to-ward Ashley with her arms open. "Give your mama a hug, girl. I haven't seen you in three weeks. Come on, let's go to the kitchen where Cora is."

Cora was standing at the stove. "Hope you stay and eat. Ash, you look thinner than you did a month ago," Cora said. She wasn't wearing her ill-fitting wig and her hair was braided and pinned up in back. Ashley could see the top of her stockings tied above the knees in knots to hold them up. "I cooked today. You smell a meatloaf inside the oven and yams cooking on the stove."

"I was only going to stop by and check on you ladies. But how can I refuse an offer like that? I haven't had a home-cooked meal since the last time I was here."

Doris and Cora looked at each other.

"Now, don't you guys worry about me. I saw that look on your face, Mother," Ashley said, and followed Doris to the living room.

"Okay, we're not going to fuss at you this time. But Ashley, you have to take better care of yourself. And now you're working seven days a week," Doris scolded.

"I know, Mom. But I made a profit this month."

"Lori came over yesterday. She's getting bigger by the day," Cora said. "We got her invitation in the mail. And I can't wait. I haven't been to a baby shower for anyone in this family for ages."

"I guess Marcus will be at the baby shower. I hope he comes alone," Ashley mused.

Doris's heart went out to her daughter. Ashley looked as though she was going to cry. Doris knew how hard the divorce had been on Ashley. Doris also suspected that loneliness was another reason why Ashley was working such long hours every day.

"Maybe he'll come and not stay too long, Ash. And I'm sure he'll come alone. Lori wouldn't have it any other way, I'm sure," Doris said.

Ashley shook her head in disgust. Marcus was now just a person she used to know. He wasn't at all the man she was married to.

All three were sitting at the dining room table. Cora sat next to Ashley. "You need to go out on dates, Ash. You've been staying at home and at work too much." Cora turned around and looked Ashley in the face. "I bet Marcus was the last man you've had."

"Aunt Cora, Marcus was the only man I've had."

"Honey, you got a real treat coming if he was the last, and only one. Someone different might make your toes curl. Don't you know the way to get over one man is to get under another one? It's the best cure in the world, if you ask me. Now, I'm just telling you how it is."

Ashley and Doris looked at each other, mouths open, and laughed out loud. "I've never heard that before,

Aunt Cora, but I do agree. The only problem is that I don't have a man yet."

"If you get out of that house more often you would. Wouldn't she, Doris?"

"Yes, you should get out more, Ashley."

Did she have to hear this every time she came over? And then she thought about what Vanessa had said to her. And she's right; I do need a good lay. One day, she thought to herself and smiled. But it was hard to imagine sleeping with a different man than Marcus. He was her first, and so far, her last.

Ashley ate more than she had in weeks. She ended up staying until six that evening.

Driving home, Ashley decided that when Marcus arrives at the baby shower, she would simply act as though he wasn't there. She could do it, she knew she could do it. It would be only one day, maybe just an hour. Surely he wouldn't want to stay from the beginning to the end of a baby shower.

When Ashley got home she did just as she promised Doris she would. She undressed and put on a short, pink gown. Instead of working, she got in bed to relax. Ashley read until eight-thirty that night. With all the long hours of working, she slept until seven the next morning.

The day of Lori's baby shower was busy for Ashley. She was up at six and went out and jogged to calm her nerves.

Ashley started jogging slowly, and worked herself into a slightly faster pace. She passed a large tree in the front yard. The leaves had fallen on the sidewalk, and Ashley felt them crushing under her feet, some sticking to the bottom of her white Reeboks.

As she ran, tension slowly left her body, replaced by a new boost of energy. She jogged for forty minutes before she went back inside.

Ashley promised Sheri she would be at the house early to help decorate. After she showered, she popped two slices of wheat toast into the toaster. She reached for her Coke and changed her mind, poured herself a glass of apple juice, grabbed the *LA Times*, and sat at the table. She tried to read but couldn't seem to concentrate. After reading a paragraph that consisted of seven lines, she couldn't remember what she had read. She neatly folded the newspaper and left it on the table for later.

The baby shower started at two, and it was already eleven-thirty when Ashley looked at the wooden clock on the dining room wall.

She went into her bedroom closet and pulled out a navy pantsuit and a light blue blouse. Standing in front of the mirror, Ashley pulled the pins from her hair letting it tumble into curls. She sighed and began skillfully applying her makeup. Once she had finished, she stood in front of the long mirror to take one last look, picked up her navy Guess handbag, and ambled out the door.

On the way to Sheri's house, she had to stop by the bakery to pick up the cake. Twenty minutes later she was parking her car in front of the house.

She sat there thinking of Marcus for a few moments. What would she say to him? What would he say to her, and how would they react toward each other? They hadn't seen each other since he walked out on her, except for Daniel's funeral, and she didn't speak to him then. But today she had first-time jitters. She had to speak to him, for Lori's sake, and she was sure that all eyes would be on them. Ashley still didn't want him there but after thinking about it, she knew better. It was Lori's baby shower; knowing the way he felt about his daughter he would be there under any circumstances. *"Just come alone, Marcus,"* she whispered to herself.

With her purse in one hand and the cake in the other, Ashley managed to ring the doorbell.

"Hi, Ashley, I was just telling Mama that it was probably you at the door. Gee, you look great," Sheri complimented.

"Thank you, dear." They were standing in the marble foyer.

"Is that Ashley?" Jeannie yelled from the kitchen.

"Yes, it's me, Jeannie."

Sheri took the cake from Ashley, and Ashley followed her into the kitchen.

"Hey, look at you, Ashley. Lori told us that you had lost weight. Girl, what size do you wear now?" Jeannie asked, standing at the kitchen sink. She dried her hands with the dish towel and circled around Ashley. "How did you do it, Ash?" Jeannie and Ashley were the same age. She was short, about 5'1", tiny at one hundred and five pounds. Her black hair was in a short cut. She still walked with a limp from the knee replacement she had three months before. She had had complications that lasted longer than expected.

"My doctor put me on a diet for high cholesterol and high blood pressure. My life was in danger. It was hard at first but I did it. I haven't weighed myself in a while but I came down to a size eight from a fourteen. And now my size eights are fitting a little loose these days."

Sheri walked out the kitchen as Jeannie and Ashley talked. Sheri's French braids lay across her shoulders. She bore a strong resemblance to her mother. They were both very light skinned but Sheri took her father's height: tall, with dark hair. Sheri was twenty-five and single. She and Jeannie still lived together and got along well. Sheri and Lori had gone from elementary school through college together.

"Everything looks so nice, Jeannie. It's nice of you and Sheri to do this for Lori. And at a time when I'm so busy."

"Ashley, you know we love Lori. Now, let's go into the living room and see what Sheri needs us to do."

"That's why I'm here so early," Ashley said, walking behind Jeannie.

The balloons, crepe paper, and eating utensils were all blue and yellow. After Ashley, Jeannie and Sheri had decorated for an hour, the large living room looked festive and warm. Two large tables against the wall in the dining room were lined with fruits, sandwiches, punch, and cake. On the other end were pasta, salads, chicken wings, and white and wheat rolls. They stood in the middle of the living room to see if anything needed to be changed.

The doorbell rang and Sheri ran to open it. It was Vanessa with a big box wrapped in white-and-silver wrapping paper. She hugged and kissed everyone. Minutes later the doorbell rang again. This time it was Doris and Cora. Lori and Keith walked in, and afterward everyone came in, one right behind the other.

Ashley and Vanessa served punch while Sheri was directing the games that were played at baby showers.

Ashley was so proud of Lori. She was such a lovely girl, and the perfect daughter. She looked at Doris and Cora. For a change Doris seemed to be completely happy but Ashley knew she still had her moments. Daniel's death was a great loss for all of them.

"I better slice the garlic bread and warm it. They're down to two more games and we can start serving the food," Ashley said to Vanessa.

"Can I help, Ashley?" Jeannie asked.

"No, stay off that knee, you've done enough. Vanessa and I can do the rest."

Ashley was in the kitchen slicing the bread and listening to the laughter echoing throughout the house. There was so much happiness and fun, everyone speaking at the same time. The doorbell rang; someone opened the door and the laughter toned down. Ashley instinctively knew who it was. It was Marcus walking in as though he had crashed the party. But after a few seconds she heard Lori's voice introducing her dad to everyone who didn't know him.

Ashley's hands started to tremble, and her legs felt weak as her heart thumped rapidly in her chest. Except the day in the bank, she hadn't seen Marcus since he had left. Even in the process of getting their divorce she made it her business not to see him. And here he was. She was standing at the sink facing the window to the backyard, her eyes closed tightly. "I can do this, I have to do this for Lori's sake, for my pride," she whispered to herself. Vanessa had already gone out the kitchen to carry a tray to the dining room.

Ashley picked up the tray with warm garlic bread lined on it, squared her shoulders, held her head high, and strolled into the living room as though she didn't know Marcus had arrived.

Ashley placed the tray on the table and turned around to face the guests. "Everyone can eat, now. The plates, forks, and cups are at this end of the table. Enjoy your food," she announced, forcing a wide smile. Not everyone knew Marcus nor did everyone know that Lori's parents were divorced. But everyone who knew had their eyes on Ashley as though they were waiting for her to explode like a volcano that was ready to erupt. But she held her head up high with dignity. This was her daughter's day. She wouldn't let Marcus or anyone else spoil it.

Marcus turned at the sound of Ashley's voice. It was Ashley, it was really her. He had seen her at Daniel's funeral, but he thought what she wore explained how small she looked. She looked lean and wonderfully lithe. He thought of his girlfriend, the day she said his wife was beautiful. But he figured she was just upset. But as he looked at Ashley it was as though she was a complete stranger. No, she was a stunning stranger. Her dark hair looked like silk against the side of her slender pear-shaped face, which made her lips appear fuller. And that figure—he didn't know what to say. Her eyes were deep and penetrating, but as she looked at him they turned cold with hate. Someone said something to her, and suddenly her eyes were smiling again. Her mouth looked delicate, and she smiled wide when she was happy. Marcus talked to everyone he knew, but his eyes were on Ashley. She was simply irresistible. What had she done to herself?

Vanessa stood in the corner talking with Jeannie, but every time she glanced at Ashley she was smiling or speaking to someone, her head high, and she appeared calm. She didn't appear nervous at all. You go, girl, Vanessa thought, and held up her thumb as her eyes met Ashley's.

Ashley took a quick glance at Marcus. He was dressed in a black suit with a black sweater underneath. It was the black sweater she had bought for his last birthday. One would have thought the jerk would have been sensible enough to wear something different. She released a deep sigh when he kissed Lori on her cheek.

Ashley went back into the kitchen for more ice to put into the punch. As she was pouring ice into the bowl, she heard footsteps behind her.

"Hello, Ash."

"Hello, Marcus," she answered. She didn't turn around to face him, and his presence was disquieting.

"You look swell, Ash. I hardly knew who you were when I walked in. I mean, really elegant. I'm stunned, I really am."

She slowly turned around to face him. "I'm sorry I stunned you, Marcus." She started to walk away, but he grabbed her hand.

"Don't be sorry, Ash. I like surprises and this is the best of all."

Without any change in her expression, Ashley looked at his face, looked at his hand on her arm, and lifted one brow.

Marcus quickly released her. She had never looked at

him with so much confidence. As though she could walk on water if she wanted to. And all she had to do was give that look of authority, raise her brow, and turn her eyes from warm to cold. It did work for him, and he liked it. Marcus was amused by this new Ashley. She wasn't the homely wife he was married to. And when he looked at her again, he swore there was a tug in the corner of her mouth as though she was going to smile at him.

She gave him one last look, their eyes locked and held, and she walked out the kitchen. But once she got to the dining room table she was sure her legs would give out from under her. And as she stood with her back to the kitchen, she could feel his eyes on her back, and feel hairs standing up on the back of her neck. He had come to his daughter's baby shower—why didn't he leave now?

"Aren't you going to eat, Vanessa?" Ashley asked.

"In a minute. Right now I'm enjoying the view. Marcus looks at you like he doesn't know who you are, Ash. He's looking like an outdone fool if you ask me."

Doris had her plate of food in her hand when she walked up to Ash. "Are you all right, honey?" Doris asked with concern.

Cora came over to the circle where they were standing. "Yes, she's all right, Doris. Ashley is a strong girl. She'll live through this. Now come on and have yourself a good time. They want to play a game that I've never heard of before. If you forget and cross your leg you have to give them the clothespin that Sheri is passing out to everyone."

"It's not a new game, Aunt Cora," Lori said, walking up behind her.

Ashley hugged Lori. "Everything is so nice, Lori."

"Thanks to you, Jeannie, and Sheri." Lori turned around when she heard Marcus call her name.

"I'm leaving now, baby." He kissed her on the cheek. "Looks like I'm the only man that's here."

"I'm sorry, Dad. Keith dropped me off and went to see the game with his friends."

"Which is exactly what I'm going to do. Are you going to work tomorrow?"

"Yes, at my regular time," Lori answered.

"Call me. Let's do lunch." She walked him to the door.

Marcus took one last look at Ashley and closed the door.

"Thank God," Ashley thought. He was gone and she could relax and enjoy herself.

Chapter 24

It was a month after the baby shower on an early Saturday morning in April. Ashley was just crawling out of bed for her early-morning run. The phone rang; she lay down again, reached over to the nightstand, and answered the phone.

"Ash, it's Keith. I'm at the hospital with Lori—"

Ashley dropped the phone, jumped out of bed, and stood up straight. She picked up the phone again and Keith was still there. "I'll be right there. Wait, is Lori okay, is she in a lot of pain?"

"She's in pain, Ash." Keith sounded like a new father. His voice was shaky, and he sounded excited and nervous.

Running to the closet to pull out a pair of jeans and a sweater, Ashley turned around and ran back to the telephone again. She dialed Doris's number and she answered, and one minute later Ashley hung up the phone.

After she was dressed, she looked in the mirror and brushed her hair. She would have to get it cut again, she thought. She had no time for makeup. She grabbed her purse and keys and ran out the door.

By the time it took Ashley to reach the hospital emergency parking lot, Doris and Cora were parking their car. They ran to catch up before Ashley got inside. They had never seen her walk so fast.

"We thought that we were slow but we got here the

same time as you, Ash," Doris said, out of breath. "And please, slow down so I can breathe and keep up with you."

"And I didn't have time to comb my wig so you have to excuse my appearance," Cora said.

Ashley looked at Cora's wig, and it did need styling, but who cares at a time like this? Her daughter was having a baby.

"I'm going to be a grandmother. I can't believe I'm going to have a grandchild today," Ashley said, as they hurried to the third floor of Kaiser Hospital on Cadillac Street.

All three rushed out of the elevator and saw Keith walking out of the room into the hall. He looked worried and had started to pace the hall. When he looked up and saw Ashley coming, he rushed to her.

"Is she all right, Keith?" Ashley asked in a rush of words.

"Yes. I told her that I'd see if you were out here yet. She wants to see you."

"Okay. Be right back, Mama." She went into the room with Keith.

"Did Ash call you 'Mama'?' Cora asked Doris.

"Yes. She only calls me Mama when she's afraid. The girl is really nervous, but so are we. My great-grandchild is on her way out."

"No, Doris. *He's* on his way out. It's going to be a big-headed boy," Cora argued.

"All right, you'll see. It's a girl, a pretty little girl," Doris argued back at her.

After a few minutes passed, Ashley came back out. "She'll be all right. It's going to be real soon now." Ashley saw a man get off the elevator. No, she thought, it couldn't be. Yes, it was Marcus, she thought. Ashley sighed and took a deep breath as he got closer.

"Hello, ladies."

"Hi, Marcus," Doris said without looking up at him. She and Cora were sitting on a sofa.

"Can I see her, Ash?"

"I think you will have to wait until Keith comes out. Did he call you, too?"

What a stupid question, she thought. If they hadn't called he wouldn't be here.

"Yes. Keith called me after he talked to you. I'm glad we could be here together."

"Why?" she asked, still facing him.

"Because we are her parents. Now we're going to be grandparents."

"Yes, so we are," she answered, and walked away from him.

All Marcus could do was look at her. She was calm and in control. He was the nervous one and needed her there with him.

Ashley quietly walked up and down the hall until Keith came out again.

"You two can come in," Keith said, taking Ashley by her hand. "She's asking for you again, Ash. She'll be happy to see you here, too, Marcus."

"I'm happy to be here," Marcus said, and looked at Ashley.

Ashley walked in front of him to their daughter's bed. Lori was moaning in pain, screaming out loud. The nurse ran over and pulled Lori's gown up to examine her.

"You're ready now, Mother. It's time for the baby to come." She called out for the doctor and pushed Ashley and Marcus away from the bed. Keith stayed with Lori.

"It's time now, Mother," Ashley said to Doris.

"Ash?"

Ashley heard Keith call her name, and her heart began to beat rapidly inside her chest. "Is she all right, Keith?" Ashley rushed by Keith's side.

"Yes. Lori keeps calling for you and the nurse said you could come back."

"Fine, let's get back in there." Ashley rushed passed Marcus without looking at him.

Ashley and Keith went back into the delivery room just in time. After Lori gave three hard pushes the baby started to come out. Ashley looked at Keith's face and was sure he would faint. But he only held his wife's hand.

The baby was coming, and Lori was still screaming in agony. Ashley pushed Lori's hair back from her face and felt moisture on her own face.

"It's a beautiful baby girl," the nurse said, holding the baby in her hands.

And Ashley cried as she looked at her beautiful granddaughter with black hair like Lori and Marcus's. It was a night that she would always remember. And then she remembered how old she felt only days ago that she was going to be a grandmother. But tonight was one of the happiest of her life. In a way, she felt as though she was becoming a mother again.

She walked out the room and into the hall where Marcus, Doris, and Cora was waiting.

"Is my baby all right?" Doris asked, holding a tissue to her eyes.

"Yes, Mother, Lori is all right. She's overjoyed over her new eight-pound daughter."

Doris burst out crying. Cora chuckled and held her hand.

Marcus smiled. But Ashley saw him wipe a teardrop from his eye.

Marcus slowly walked over to Ashley and stood in front of her. "We're grandparents now, Ash. Why can't we put the past behind us and be friends? Just think about it, Ash."

She looked at him for a few seconds without saying a word. And when she spoke her voice was level to a degree that made him take a step back. "Friends, Marcus?

You want me to think about being friends with you? To think about being your friend will take a long time, and I don't think I'll live that long." She stalked off and sat next to her mother until Keith came out again.

Keith hugged Ashley. "My parents will be here in three days. My mom says her only regret is living in New York, so far away from her granddaughter. Thank you for being here for me, Ash. And you, too, Marcus."

All Ashley could do was nod her head.

When Ashley woke up the morning after her granddaughter was born, she knew there was something she had to do. Her life was settling a bit in the last month. She still worked long hours, mostly seven days a week, but she was getting to know herself since she had started living alone. When she was married, her family was always first in her life, but now she knew exactly what she wanted in life. And now she wanted to meet her brother. There was a void in that part of her life that needed closing, and he could certainly answer some questions. After all, Jason was her brother. So she would give the lawyer a call first thing Monday morning for Jason's phone number.

Ashley went into the kitchen and opened the cabinet door, grabbed the jar of instant decaffeinated coffee, and placed the kettle on the stove. She stood in her pajamas looking out the patio door.

The phone rang, and it was Vanessa. "Hello there, Grandma."

Ashley laughed out loud. "You just shut up, Vanessa. Anyway, she's beautiful."

"Does she have a name yet?"

"Yes, Lori called me this morning. Her name is Callie. Isn't that cute?"

"Callie? Yes, it does have a certain ring to it. How did you and Marcus get along at the hospital?"

"Oh, girl, we had very little to say. Would you believe he had the nerve to ask if we could be friends since we are grandparents? I have no intentions of being his friend. Hell, I don't even feel comfortable being in the same room with him," she said, as she wrote herself a note on her list of things to do, which was to call the lawyer. She placed the pad on the table in front of her.

"Well, I called to invite you to go to Las Vegas with Gary and me next weekend."

"But, I—"

"But I nothing, Ash. You need to enjoy yourself. The dress shop will be there when you get back. Helen is doing a book signing there. Robert, Elliott and Janet may come along, too. But lately, you never know about them. Their marriage is so strange. Anyway, it'll be fun."

"When are you all leaving?" she asked, still undecided. She was thinking of a hundred things that she had to do. And Lori and the baby would be home.

"Friday morning. That gives you a chance to tie up any loose ends at the dress shop. You need to get away, Ash." Vanessa could hear her sigh. "Well, what is it?"

"Nothing, nothing at all. I'll go and you're right. I need to get away. Mother and Cora can help Lori out while I'm away. It's only one weekend."

"If I know Lori, she won't need help very long. She's just like you, Ash, independent. But good, I'll make your reservation along with Gary's and mine. We're not making that long-ass drive either. Now, start packing, girl. Las Vegas, here we come."

Ashley laughed. She wished that she were more like Vanessa. She was always happy and free spirited.

"Mother, are you ready?" Ashley yelled, standing in the door of the living room. She walked all the way inside as she heard footsteps coming down the hallway.

"I'm ready. I was just waiting for Cora to finish combing that wig of hers."

"And what's wrong with my wig?" Cora bellowed. She was walking into the living room with her brown purse hanging on her arm. Like a model, she stepped in the center of the room and turned around in a circle. "Now, how do I look?"

"You look fine, Aunt Cora, but we're only going shopping. You didn't have to dress so fancy," Ashley said, looking at the green suit Cora had worn to church. Ashley looked at Doris, who was dressed casually in a blue dress that she had made for her. But it wasn't as fancy as Cora's suit.

Ashley looked at her watch; it was eleven-thirty.

"Ashley, is it okay if we go to South Bay Galleria?" Doris asked. "I saw a sweater at a women's store, but I can't remember the name of it."

"Girl, your memories ain't no longer than your nose," Cora said, laughing.

"Are you ladies ready?" Ashley asked. "After we finish shopping for baby clothes, I'll take you ladies to lunch."

"Thank you, Ashley. Daniel used to take me out to eat almost every Sunday," Doris said sadly. Sometimes the pain of losing him stabbed fresh at her heart.

They shopped at the Del Amo Mall in Torrance. Ashley spent more than four hundred dollars on baby clothes for her granddaughter.

"Ashley, Callie is going to grow out of all those clothes before she wears them." Doris patted Ashley on her shoulder. "Your first grandchild, honey. Just don't buy her a car when she's only ten years old."

Ashley smiled. "I won't, Mother. Now, where can we go for brunch?"

"What about the Olive Garden? It's not far from here," Doris suggested.

On Monday morning Lori was released from the hospital. Getting out of the car, Keith held her with one hand and grabbed her overnight bag with the other.

Ashley ran out and took the baby from Lori's arms. "I'm glad you feel better today, Lori. And I know that you didn't want to stay the extra day in the hospital." Once they were inside, Lori went straight to her bedroom and Ashley followed her. She watched as little Callie opened her eyes, but only for a moment.

"What smells so good, Mom?" Lori asked, sniffing the aroma from the kitchen.

"I cooked a pan of lasagna and made a salad, enough for two days. I also stopped and bought an apple pie, too."

"I was so excited about coming home that I didn't sleep well last night," Lori said, and kissed her baby on top of her head. "Mom, do you feel different since you are a grandmother?"

"Yes, actually. I didn't know you could love a grandchild so much, and I feel I have so much to look forward to. When you told me you were pregnant, I felt so old. But not anymore."

Ashley stood against the long dresser and watched mother and daughter lay across the king size bed. Lori was lucky to have a husband who loved her so much. Ashley and Marcus knew the moment Lori brought Keith home that he would make their daughter happy.

Keith was recruited when he was still in college at UCLA as an engineer at TRW in Redondo Beach. He did such a good job, and had been promoted twice from supervisor to manager, which paid an outstanding salary that made it possible for Lori to stay home until Callie gets older.

"Can I get you anything, honey?" Ashley asked, as she leaned against one of the bedposts that was on each side of the antique wooden bed. Ashley opened the blinds and sat on the corner of the bed next to Lori and the baby.

"No, Mom. I don't want anything right now."

"Not even a glass of juice?" Ashley asked.

"Okay. I'll take a glass of orange juice."

Keith walked in as Ashley was about to walk out. "Can I get you anything, baby?" he asked, and bounced on the bed beside his wife.

"I was just going to get her a glass of juice, Keith. Would you like a glass, too?"

"No thanks, Ash. I'm okay now that my wife and daughter are home." He smiled and kissed Lori on the cheek.

Ashley smiled, too. "God, please let them stay in love," she whispered, walking into the kitchen. She still thought of Marcus, and when she did it still hurt. It didn't matter how much better she looked, how well her business was doing, it still hurt her. And like a part of her body, the hurt stayed with her everywhere she went.

"Here you go, Lori. I'll set it next to the bed," Ashley said. Keith heard the doorbell and went into the living room. It was Doris and Cora.

"Oh, let me see my granddaughter." Doris bent over as Lori lay the baby in her arms. "Just look at her, Cora. Isn't she a doll?"

"Beautiful, like her mother and grandmother," Keith said.

"I agree," Marcus said, his voice resonating through the room.

Ashley felt her body tense when she heard his voice. She looked around. Marcus was staring at her. He had eased into the room without anyone hearing him.

What a pain in the ass, Ashley thought to herself.

"How are you, Ash?" he asked.

"I'm good, Marcus." She was surprised that he hadn't

brought his fiancée, but Ashley figured he would ease her in slowly.

Keith had left the room and returned with glasses and a bottle of champagne in his hand. "Everyone, we're going to make a toast to Callie." He poured the champagne. Keith raised his glass first. "To my daughter."

"Here, here," Ashley said. "A new addition to our family."

Glasses clicked, and everyone raised their glasses to their mouth. Ashley felt the tears burning her eyes and thought of Daniel and the way life used to be. For a precious occasion such as this one, she and Marcus should be together. They had a daughter and now a granddaughter. But they didn't have it all together. Life certainly takes on changes.

When Ashley wasn't looking, Marcus would glance at her. Although he was getting married, and was in love, he wondered why all of a sudden he was so captivated with Ashley. She had changed in every way. Even the perfume she wore was different. Today, she was wearing a long dress, and it looked sexy with high heel sandals. Her hair was shorter now, and stylish, and silky, and what was wrong with him? It was that damn green dress with the split in back just high enough to make any man want it higher. And she looked everywhere, at everyone, except at him.

"Going so soon, Dad?"

Ashley went to the kitchen but she overheard Lori and Marcus, and quietly felt the tension leaving her body. She was more than happy to see him leave, wondering how many more times they would run into each other. She sighed and went back with the others.

"Take care, Ash."

"I will, Marcus," she answered, and turned her back to him. She could feel Doris and Cora's eyes on her, then on Marcus. Ashley took the baby from Lori's arms and kissed her on her forehead.

Chapter 25

Ashley stuck her head out the door to see how cold it was. She placed her brown boots beside the suitcase in the living room. Their flight to Vegas would be leaving at eleven that morning. She stood with both hands on her hips and looked inside her closet for another thick sweater. She pulled out a brown sweater the same color brown as her boots.

Ashley felt a hint of guilt for leaving when she knew how much work she had to do. But she needed to laugh, eat whatever she wanted, stay up as late as she wanted, and sleep late the next morning.

Ashley went into the kitchen, poured herself a cup of coffee, and sat at the table in the kitchen and dialed Lori's number.

Thelma, Lori's mother-in-law, answered the phone. Her high-pitched voice shrilled through loudly. It was ir-ritating to Ashley first thing in the morning. Ashley rolled her eyes up at the ceiling and frowned.

"Good morning, Thelma, are you enjoying your vacation?"

"Oh yes, Ashley. But I'm enjoying my beautiful grand-daughter better. Allen is going to spoil her rotten like he did our daughter. He was hoping it would be a girl all along."

"I'm just glad you're here with Lori," Ashley answered.

"Look, Ashley, go to Vegas and have a good time. Lord

knows you deserve it. And I'm so sorry about you and Marcus. It's his loss."

"Thank you. And I'm all right, Thelma. I have enough to keep me busy, and I enjoy having a business of my own. Now I'm finally making a profit," Ashley said, and looked at the empty coffee cup in front of her. She let the phone rest on her shoulder as she continued to talk, and placed the cup in the dishwasher. "I thought it would take me at least a year to accomplish what I have. It was hard, but I did it."

"Good, girl. We're all proud of you, Ashley."

"Tell Lori I'll call her when I get to Vegas. My mom and aunt will be over today to see if you need any help with anything."

"It'll be good to see them again," Thelma answered.

Ashley hung up and went outside to get her newspaper. She stood outside feeling the fresh air, and waved at her neighbor across the street. She went back to the kitchen and took a seat at the table. She sipped a glass of orange juice but made no attempt to read the paper. And out of the blue there was Marcus in front of her. It was as though he was always with her, in her thoughts, her dreams. And now since they had a granddaughter, one way or another, he would always be in her life forever, it seemed. It just wasn't fair. But life wasn't fair either. Finally, she opened the newspaper to see what the temperature was in Vegas. Thirty-nine degrees, she read. "Oops," she said. She went to get her leather gloves out the dresser drawer. She looked at the clock on the wall; Vanessa and Gary will be here any minute now, she thought.

Ashley rushed into her room, slipped on her boots, and took her black leather suitcase into the living room.

By the time she got her long black leather coat from the closet, Gary was ringing her doorbell. Ashley slipped into her coat and answered the door.

"Hey, baby," Gary said. I see you're ready to go. Here, I'll take your luggage to the car for you."

Ashley smiled. "It's a little heavy, Gary."

He picked it up. "Not as heavy as Vanessa's, I assure you." He was outside the door before she could say another word. She watched him as he walked back to the car. He walked fast and cool, as though he was always in a hurry.

Ashley went into her bedroom and switched on the answering machine, looked around her living room one last time, and dashed out the door.

Gary was outside waiting for her with the car door open. She got into the backseat. "What a gentleman you are, Gary."

"You mean my wife hasn't told you that before?" he said, and winked at Vanessa as he got in the car.

They chatted all the way to LAX. "We still have an hour and a half, Ash. But since there's so much security, it takes longer to check in since 9/11," Gary said.

"I understand," Ashley said. "I want them to take all the time that's needed."

"I heard that, girl," Vanessa said, turning around to face Ashley. "Anyway, Helen and Robert left last night. Helen had a book signing at some women's organization at breakfast. We are going to have fun, Ash. You'll be happy you came. It's about time you got out that house for a weekend."

"I guess," Ashley answered. "I'm really excited about it, too."

Gary parked in the airport parking lot and left his car for the weekend. It took only fifteen minutes to get to the airport and an hour to check in. The lines were long but moved fast.

The three of them sat together, and the flight to Vegas took only forty minutes. As soon as they got on the plane it seemed as though they were getting off.

They went to pick up their luggage, and Gary flagged

down a taxi that had pulled up as soon as they stepped outside.

As they walked into New York-New York Casino to check into the hotel, the casino was busy with joyous sounds of ringing slot machines, laughter, and voices high with thrill and excitement, with people ordering drinks from the waitresses and rushing from one slot machine to another.

They went to the tenth floor. Ashley's room was two doors from Vanessa and Gary's.

"Why don't we meet in an hour and go to lunch? After lunch we can hit the casinos," Gary said.

"Sounds like a plan to me," Ashley answered.

Once Ashley was inside her room, she hung her clothes neatly inside the closet. Leisurely walking around her room, Ashley stopped and looked out the window. Once it got dark the view from her window would be beautiful, with bright lights that would bring the city even more alive and joyous.

As Ashley walked around her room, she placed her *Ebony, Jet,* and *Fashion* Magazines on the small table. She still had time before meeting Vanessa and Gary, and sat at the table, and flipped through the pages of *Ebony,* stopping to read small articles. Just as Ashley was beginning to feel sleepy, it was time to leave.

Stepping out of the elevator, Ashley saw Gary and Vanessa talking to a gentleman as though they were old friends. Looking at the man from the back Ashley noticed his shoulders were wide; he could have played football. As she got closer she stopped, then smiled, holding her breath. Could it be Elliott?

Vanessa saw Ashley coming toward them. Gary and Elliott turned around, too. Elliott smiled as she got closer.

She was a sight for sore eyes, Elliott thought.

"Hello, Ashley," he said, his voice was warm and smooth. "For a moment you looked as though you didn't recognize me."

"I didn't at first, but it's good to see you again. I had no idea you and Janet were coming."

As cold as it was her smile warmed his heart. He looked at the red lipstick applied evenly over her full sexy mouth. He wondered why every time he saw her he looked at her mouth, wondering what it would feel like against his. "Janet couldn't come this trip. When I did decide to come she had already made plans to go to Detroit with her sisters." Going to Vegas with him was not her idea of having a good time. The romance had evaporated long ago into a living arrangement of convenience and Elliott's money.

"Now, that's a woman on the go," Vanessa commented.

Again Ashley sensed that he wasn't entirely happy. And being unhappy or lonely wasn't good for a marriage, she knew. His beautiful, light brown eyes were lifeless, but as he talked and looked at her his smile broadened. He was dressed in a pair of jeans, a black sweater, and a leather jacket.

"Hey, I'm starved," Gary said. He saw the long, admiring look Elliott had given Ashley and tried to break the tension in the air. Maybe Ashley wasn't aware of Elliott's feelings for her. Knowing Ash, she wouldn't, Gary was sure. But the man cares about her. And considering what Vanessa had told him about Elliott and Janet's marriage, this could be an interesting weekend. Gary decided to sit back and watch what happened next. Maybe some way, he and Vanessa could manage to leave them alone. Gary looked at Elliott again. On second thought, Elliott would get Ashley alone himself.

"Now, let's have lunch," Gary said, and grabbed his wife's hand. Vanessa giggled.

"There's a new soul food restaurant around the corner," Elliott said, as he held one hand out to Ashley. "Shall we go, ladies?"

Vanessa and Gary walked in front and Elliott and Ashley in back. "What made you decide to come to Vegas this weekend, Elliott?" Ashley asked him.

"Robert convinced me to put the pen and papers away. And now I'm glad I did."

"I'm glad you did, too, Elliott." The corner of her lips turned up into a smile as she looked up at him.

"Helen and Robert have a suite at Caesar's Palace. We'll drop by later today," Vanessa said, and looked back at the couple.

But Elliott had already made up his mind; he was going to spend this weekend in Ashley's company. He wanted her all to himself.

They arrived at the restaurant and ordered lunch. "I'm going to eat whatever looks good to me and worry about my weight on Monday," Ashley said, looking at the menu.

"Ashley, I don't see any problem with your weight, darling. You look fit, slender, and very attractive," Elliott said, his eyes lingering on Ashley's face. He was a gentleman, and married, and had to keep his true feelings intact, but every time he looked at her she looked more attractive than she did the time before. Every time he saw her, he felt a longing that tore at his heart for days after, a loneliness that haunted him wherever he went. Looking at her sitting opposite him, he knew that he would think of her again, want her for weeks after the weekend was over.

But for now, he would settle for her company. He took so much pleasure in being close to her, inhaling her perfume, watching her push her silky hair off her forehead.

Ashley ordered fried catfish, mashed potatoes, and a small salad. Elliott ordered the same, but instead of mashed potatoes he ordered potato salad.

They chatted during lunch. And Elliott ordered a nice bottle of wine to go with their meal. It had been a long time since Ashley felt so alive—excited about the weekend and happy that she decided to come. She felt like a young girl on her first trip away from home.

Vanessa folded her white napkin and placed it neatly on the table beside her plate. "This was just what I needed." She looked at her half-empty plate. "Now, I'm ready to hit the streets."

Gary grabbed her hand. "Why don't we go to the MGM Grand Casino? That's where I won three thousand dollars the last time I played blackjack."

"And you, Ashley? Want to tag along with us?"

"What are you going to do while Gary's playing blackjack?" Ashley asked.

"Girl, you know I love the slot machines," Vanessa answered.

Ashley didn't play blackjack and she knew that she would get tired of playing the slot machines after a while, especially after she lost her money. Marcus would always take her to a show at night since he would gamble all day and leave her to herself. Then after the show she would go to their room and he would go back to the casino and continue gambling.

"Ashley, why don't we hang out together? We can always think of something to do," Elliott suggested. He wanted to talk, laugh, and enjoy being close to her. He wanted to get to know more about this woman—her favorite color, movie, food, or which side of the bed she likes to sleep on.

"Sounds like a plan to me," Ashley answered. She started to stand but Elliott touched her hand.

"Let's stay awhile." He looked up and Gary and Vanessa were standing and ready to leave. "I'll pay for lunch. You two take off and have fun," Elliott answered.

"Good. Why don't we meet up later for dinner," Vanessa suggested. She and Gary flounced out, hand in hand like young lovers.

"I don't think I've ever seen one without the other," Elliott commented, watching them strolling out the door.

"You probably won't either. It's been that way with them since they first got together." Ashley looked sad for a moment, and as she looked deeply into Elliott's eyes she could see his loneliness as well. Lonely eyes were so familiar as though they connected with someone of their own kind. Like hers.

Elliott asked for the check and left the tip on the table.

They walked out into the chilly streets, the sky was clear, the weather was clean and brisk—with excitement thick in the air and the anticipation of having a good time, the freedom to stay up as late as one desired or to sleep away the chosen hours.

As they approached the corner Elliott stopped. "A friend of mine owns the bar across the street." He pointed at the small brown building where a couple was walking out.

"There's a nice jazz band that plays there on the weekends. We could go in and sit for a while, Ashley. But if you would rather go to a casino, I don't mind."

"Elliott, this weekend I'll go wherever the wind blows me."

"Good attitude," he replied. He looked at her shiny dark hair. The wind started to blow and she gently pushed her slender fingers through one side of it.

They walked inside the bar and went to a table at the window. Elliott helped her out of her long black leather coat. Underneath she wore taupe slacks and a matching sweater. Her brown ankle boots shined as though they were new.

"Can I get you two something to drink?" the waitress asked, dressed in a short black dress with a red apron, the same color as the tablecloths. Red candles were centered on each table.

"What would you like, Ashley?" Elliott asked.

"I think I'll settle for a ginger ale."

"The same for me, too," Elliott said to the waitress. She threw back her long, gold-colored French braids, and smiled with perfectly painted red lips.

"Is Bill here yet?" Elliott asked.

"No. Not yet. Bill called in and said he would be a little late, but he'll be here soon." She gave Elliott a warm smile, turned on her heels, and strolled away.

"I've known Bill since we were in college. Both of us had planned to be lawyers and practice together, but Bill didn't make it."

"What happened?" Ashley asked with interest. She was sitting opposite him, her face cupped in her hands and elbows resting on the table. Being with him was always so easy, so serene. And it made her forget the sad corners of her life.

"Bill loved to party and chase women, and he was abusing too much alcohol and missing too many classes. After a while it just caught up with him. What were you like as a child, Ashley?" he asked.

She sipped her ginger ale and ran her tongue over her bottom lip. It tasted sweet. "Well, I was an only child, which can be lonely sometimes. But my mother gave me lots of attention. At least I thought I was an only child, for a while, anyway."

Elliott's brows furrowed. Ready to listen, he set his glass on the table.

Ashley had to laugh. "I know it sounds crazy but I'll get to it." Ashley told her story from the beginning to the end. She stopped and took a deep breath.

Elliott placed one hand over hers. "We can talk about something else, you know."

"No, really. I'm all right. It's time I talked about this." She finished by telling the story of her father's infidelity.

Elliott cleared his throat and sat up straight in his chair. "Well, that was a load," was all he managed to say.

And over two tall glasses of ginger ale, Ashley told him about her childhood.

Gently, Elliott placed her fingers against his lips and kissed her hand.

For a few seconds, Ashley was sure her heart had

stopped; her blood turned warm as she felt it creeping up her toes and lingering at her heart. This moment would live with her for the rest of her life.

"Can I get you guys anything?" the waitress asked. She was sure they hadn't heard her as she walked to their table.

Feeling as though she had just come out of a dream-like state, Ashley slid her hand from Elliott's.

"Two glasses of Dom Perignon," Elliott answered. "Is that okay with you, Ashley?"

"Perfect." From the corner of her eyes, Ashley saw a man watching them. He was sitting at the bar when they arrived.

The waitress left the table and was back in a matter of minutes.

"Enjoy. Just call me Heather." She sighed, threw her braids back, and ambled away.

"Now, where were we?" Elliott asked, and they both laughed out loud.

"How's life treating you, Elliott?"

His eyes scanned her face as he nodded his head. It would take an entire weekend to explain his life, his marriage that had fallen into pieces like shattered glass.

"Life isn't treating me too well, Ashley. I have a lot of thinking to do about my marriage, and what I'm going to do about it." He looked out the window at a group of people who had just gotten off a tour bus and were all walking into the casino across the street.

Ashley didn't want to push him any further. This was supposed to be a fun weekend, after all. She wondered where Gary and Vanessa had disappeared to. Wherever they were she was certain they were enjoying themselves.

Ashley placed her napkin on the table. "Excuse me, Elliott. I'm going to the restroom." Elliott started to stand up but Ashley stopped him. "Please, don't get up."

"Okay. If Bill isn't here soon after you get back we'll leave and find the rest of the group."

"Okay, Elliott." Ashley went past the bar to a long, dark hallway. Seeing the ladies room sign, she made a right turn and went inside.

At the same time Bill was walking into the bar and took long strides in Elliott's direction; the waitress had pointed him out.

After Ashley came out of the stall, she washed her hands, and pulled out a stick of light red lipstick from her purse. She looked into the mirror, pushed her hair back, and bent over and cupped both hands full of cold water to rinse her mouth out. Ashley reached for a paper towel and glanced into the mirror again. She jumped and turned around; a low scream came from her mouth. Ashley's eyes met with the same dark brawny looking man that had been sitting alone at the bar.

"You've made a mistake. This is the ladies room, not the men's," she said, hearing her own voice tremble and high-pitched, unrecognizable as though it were someone else's.

His face was pitch black. Beads of sweat had formed across his wide forehead. He licked his pink tongue across his full bottom lip and laughed out loud. The loud roar caused Ashley to jump, and her purse fell from her hand and landed on her foot.

He came closer, and she knew that she was in trouble. No good would come from this, she thought. And she knew that she had to think fast.

"I ain't looking for no men's room, sweetie. I was looking for you, and here you are." He licked his bottom lip from side to side. This time in a suggestive, slow movement, his large eyes resting on her breasts.

Ashley looked at the door. She was sure this big, ugly bastard was going to hurt her, and maybe even kill her once he finishes. The bar was almost empty and it might be a while before anyone walked in. It could be too late for her.

"Please, I have money in my wallet. You can have it all.

Just please don't hurt me, mister." Without taking her eyes off him, she eased down, and with one hand picked up her purse. She pulled out a black leather wallet, letting her purse fall back to the floor, contents spattering. "Here, take it all. I won't say anything . . . to anyone . . . ." she pleaded.

He was so close she could feel his pot-bellied stomach rubbing against her in a slow movement, purposely touching her, enjoying the shock in her eyes and the feel of her body.

"I only came to rob you, but since we are here alone so cozy and all, well, when I finish with you, sweetie, you'll want to pay me for more. You see, that pretty-faced boy out there, all gentlemanlike, can't do to you what I can do. He's no man. Ain't nothin' but a pretty face. Now, take all your money out of your wallet and start counting."

Ashley could feel her entire body fidgeting. Her stomach felt as though it were tied in knots. If only she had kept her purse in her hand. At least she had a fingernail file in it. But he probably would kill her if she didn't kill him first. And a fingernail file couldn't kill or harm him enough so she could run. She had all intentions of fighting. If he killed her, at least she'd die fighting.

"Look, let me—" he grumbled.

Before Ashley could speak he grabbed a fistful of her hair, and his other hand pushed roughly under her sweater. He felt Ashley trying to pull at his hand, but he only jerked her hair tighter. He was breathing fast, hard, and his breath reeked of stale beer and food. His stomach was hard, pinning Ashley to the sink so she couldn't move.

Ashley was sick, and tried to hold her breath to prevent smelling him. She fought to pull her face away as she felt his long tongue against the side of her face, pushing inside her ear. She bit him on the arm. Her head jerked back from his backhand slap across her face, so hard she felt dizzy. She still pushed at him, kicked, cried, and when she screamed he covered her mouth roughly with his hand.

"You stop fighting and give me your money, and I can finish quicker," he whispered. "Now, pretty lady, get down on your knees, it's time."

"No! Never! Hell no" she hissed between closed teeth. She would not stop fighting. She had too much to live for, and what if she didn't fight? How could she be certain that he wouldn't kill her anyway? Ashley balled both fists, her breathing labored. And no, she would not get down on her knees. "You go to hell."

He laughed out loud, kissed her hard, his tongue pushing all the way in back of her mouth. Oh, God. What do I do? she thought.

Like a flash of lightning, the big brawny man was jerked away from her and kicked in his stomach. He reeled, and fell against the wall. And in a swift flurry of motion, he was kicked again, and again, and finished off with another swift spinning kick that caused him to land flat on his back, mouth open, as he fell out of consciousness.

Elliott shoved the man with his foot, but he was out cold. He looked at Ashley; the waitress had run in and was holding Ashley in her arms and led her outside. Bill called the police so they could take the man away.

Elliott could feel Ashley's pain as the two police officers questioned her. She cried, trembling, cold, holding her coat closed around her, her appearance disheveled, her hair in disarray. She kept her back to the man, afraid to look at him.

Curtis, as it turns out, was wanted for robbing and raping a woman near the bar a week ago.

"You won't see another bar for a long time," the officers told him, as they pushed him out the door.

Once the officers took Ashley's report and left, they all stayed in the back office. The waitress gave Ashley and

Elliott each a glass of brandy. Bill pulled up a chair opposite the sofa where Elliott and Ashley were sitting.

"It was like a nightmare," Ashley was saying. "Out of
nowhere he was just standing there watching me." She
stopped and held her hands to her face. "I'm sure if you
wouldn't have come in he would have killed me, Elliott.
He was so vicious and rote-gut, from the bottom of the
barrel." She dabbed at her eyes with a tissue. "I'll never
forget his face." Ashley took deep swallows of the brandy
and coughed. "And where did you learn to fight like
that?" she asked, turning to face Elliott.

"Yeah, Elliott. You still got it, man. I haven't since we
were in school. Elliott put a boot in my ass a time or two
when we were in college," Bill said. His eyes lit up. He
was medium height, brown skin with a small scar in the
middle of his forehead. One would say he needed a hair-
cut but he had been wearing his natural since the style
first came out. He wore faded blue jeans, white sneakers,
and a white sweater. The deep lines in his face made him
appear older than Elliott. Ashley figured it was the late
hours in the bar, or a life that was moving too fast.

"Knowing karate comes in handy when you're a
lawyer. I go every once and a while to brush up. Lord, it
came in handy tonight."

"You bet it did. That was a big, mean dude," Bill said. "I
think I better go for a brush up myself. It gets rough in
here sometimes and I can't always get to my gun in time."

The waitress walked back in. "Can I get you all anything?" she asked, and smiled at Bill.

"No, thank you," Elliott answered. "I'm taking Ashley
back to the hotel. She's had a long day."

Ashley looked at Judy, the waitress. It didn't take a
rocket scientist to see that Bill and Judy were having an
affair. Judy couldn't keep her eyes off him.

"Sweetheart, call a taxi for my friends," Bill told her.

"Sure thing. I'll call you when one gets here." She

walked out. Fifteen minutes later, she was back again. "The taxi is waiting."

The ride back to the hotel was quiet. Ashley lay her head on Elliott's shoulder and her eyes were closed. Elliott pulled her close to him and held her hand.

Her right temple throbbed relentlessly, and she suspected it would be there for the remainder of the night, reminding her of the unfortunate experience she had had only an hour ago.

"Sweetheart, you're still trembling," Elliott said. "We should be at the hotel in about two minutes. I'm so sorry for everything, Ashley."

She looked up at him. "I know, Elliott. I think I'll stay in tonight. I can have dinner in my room. My head is killing me."

"Are you sure you wouldn't feel better if you were around people?"

"No. It's just been too much for me today. I thought my life was over."

"I know, Ashley. So I'm going to have dinner with you. I won't leave you alone, if you don't mind, and if it would make you feel better." He squeezed her hand.

"No, I don't mind. And it would make me feel better. Now that I think of it, I think I'll feel better if someone was with me until I go to sleep. I really appreciate your friendship, Elliott. I'm lucky." She squeezed his hand in return.

He just looked at her for a few moments before saying anything. "I don't think anyone has ever said anything so nice to me before, Ashley. I'm the lucky one." With his heart sinking, from that moment on, he knew without a doubt that one day she would be his wife. He loved the way she looked and sounded, and he had fallen in love with every inch of her.

When they walked inside the hotel, Vanessa and

Helen were playing a slot machine. Vanessa looked toward the door as though she was waiting for them. She picked up her quarters, dropping a roll in her purse.

As Vanessa got closer she could see Ashley's face clearly. "Ash! Ash, what's wrong with you? You look ill." Vanessa looked at Ashley's red eyes and knew instantly that she had been crying. She looked at Elliott for answers, but he was holding Ashley close to him.

Helen, Robert, and Gary came walking toward them. "Ready for dinner everyone?" Gary said. "I could eat a cow I'm so hungry." He stopped when he felt Vanessa push at his arm.

"What is it, Ash?" Vanessa asked again. She looked at Ashley's coat as she held it tightly around her, as though she was freezing.

"Ashley had a bad experience today," Elliott answered.

"What do you mean 'bad experience'?" Vanessa asked. Robert and Gary looked at each other.

"Why don't we go to Ashley's room and get to the bottom of this," Helen suggested. And they all looked terrified when Ashley begin sobbing as her weight crumpled against Elliott. Elliott took her arm and led her to the elevator.

Vanessa and Helen walked ahead, but Vanessa stopped again. "Look, someone has to tell me now. What happened to Ashley?" she demanded, and looked at Elliott with daggers in her eyes. He had some explaining to do.

The elevator door opened but it was empty, and they were all relieved that they were the only ones that went inside.

"We stopped at my friend's bar today and Ashley went to the restroom. A man went in behind her and assaulted her. After he was in there he decided to try and rape Ashley. He also struck her twice before I got in there and kicked his ass. The cops came and took him to jail," Elliott said in a rush of words, an angry edge in the tone of his voice. "It's been one hell of a day."

"Oh God, Ash." Vanessa hugged her. Helen sighed deeply and placed one hand over her mouth.

They got to Ashley's room, and Helen called for room service to order aspirin and ginger ale for Ashley. Besides her head hurting she was also having stomach cramps.

"Robert, why don't we go out and get enough food for all of us?" Helen suggested. "Ashley, honey, we can all eat up here with you."

Robert sat on the bed next to Ashley. "Did the police take an accurate report, Ash?"

Ashley shook her head in response. "I think so."

"They did, Robert. Ashley and I gave them all the information they needed to lock him up. Besides, he also had priors," Elliott interjected.

"Well, you're a lawyer, Elliott. I'm sure you knew what to do."

"You haven't eaten anything, Ashley. What would you like to eat?" Elliott asked.

"We'll stay here with Ashley or we can go to our suite and eat there. It's bigger, the table is large enough for all of us to sit down together," Helen said. She wanted to cry for Ashley, and wondered how would she have handled herself in the same situation. And then she shivered as she thought of Elaine. Her sister was held all night by a man she had met in a bar, who took her to his house and raped her. But Elaine is happily married and living a life that has helped her get over the early years when she was terribly dejected and lonely. As Helen thought of it, all the women in her family had an unhappy childhood, thanks to her parents.

The men left. Vanessa and Helen stayed in the room with Ashley. They sat on the bed and waited while Ashley showered and changed into some fresh clothing. When she finished, they went to Helen's room, and the three women sat at the table and talked about what happened. As Ashley told them what happened, Helen couldn't move, Vanessa cried.

"I talked you into this trip and look what happened," Vanessa said.

"Don't say that, Vanessa. You only wanted me to get out and have a nice weekend for a change. And I was until that, that incident happened." She sighed.

Helen patted Vanessa's hand. "No, don't blame yourself for that, Vanessa. Things like that we can't always control."

"Thank God Elliott was with you," Vanessa said, and dabbed at her eyes with a tissue.

"He is undeniably a gentlemen. Can you imagine what would have happened to me if he weren't there? I have never been so frightened in all my life. And he does karate like a champ."

Ashley closed her eyes and held both hands on each side of her temple, feeling the pain in her head finally subsiding. "You know, you never think something so blasted terrible could happen to you. The suddenness of my father's death had been the hardest for me. What would my mother do had she experienced two deaths? I didn't want her to hurt that badly. I thought of that when I was sure he would kill me. I had to fight for my mother, Lori, and my grandchild. You know, I also wanted to live for myself. I've been so depressed about my marriage that I hadn't realized until now how very lucky I am. And I lived through it, and without the help of Marcus."

Helen moved her chair closer to Ashley and placed her arm around her shoulder. "I know how you feel. I lost my oldest sister and a very close friend. That was five years ago and I'm still not over it. If it weren't for Robert, God, what can I say? The man was there for me every step of the way. You see, Harriet, my sister had been married to Robert before I was." Helen grimaced at the thought of the day her sister died.

Ashley's ears perked. "Both you and your sister were married to Robert?"

Looking at the expression on Ashley's face, Helen and Vanessa hooted with laughter. Vanessa already knew the history behind Robert and Helen's marriage.

"Yes, we were," Helen answered. "When I was in high school, Robert and I were dating. We were just getting close when Harriet decided she wanted him for herself. She didn't love him, she just loathed me. We were sisters but she hated my guts. She was evil in her younger days. My dad died and my mom favored Harriet over Elaine and me, and in doing that, she neglected the two of us. She had such adoration for Harriet. Anyway, poor Harriet overheard an argument between our mom and dad. During that argument, she found out he wasn't her real father. That's what started the jealousy, the competition, when there shouldn't have been any. My parents handled the situation poorly." Helen shook her head in dismay. "I ended up marrying Thomas. And you know how that old story goes. We had a child together: Lynn. Thomas met another woman and left me. He tried to come back years later, but only for my money. Robert and Harriet got a divorce. Robert and I got back together again and, finally, got married. It's a happy-ever-after ending, except for poor Harriet."

"Gee, we're sitting around here like three old hens about to cry the night away," Vanessa said, and looked around as the men opened the door. All three women sighed in relief.

Robert placed the food on the table, and Elliott called for room service to deliver champagne.

They ate, laughed, and talked until after one o'clock.

Elliott walked Ashley to her room. "Are you going to

be all right, Ashley? He grabbed her hand and closed his hand tightly around hers.

"I guess I haven't completely settled down yet." She stood in the door looking up at him. Feeling his hand around hers, she felt lucky that he was with her. How could his wife let a man like Elliott go away on a trip without her? He was so attentive and so gentle, his deep-set, penetrating brown eyes that seemed to be carrying the weight of the world.

"Give me your key." He unlocked the door and walked inside behind her. "Now, I'm not getting fresh with you. But why don't you get into whatever you sleep in and get in bed. When you are sound asleep I'll go to my room."

She cocked her head to one side and gave him a soft, long smile. "Okay. I'll do just that. Have a seat." She pulled out a pair of bright blue pajamas and went into the bathroom.

As Elliott waited for her he looked through a magazine with clothing and models. He was sure that Ashley had brought it with her to look at different styles of clothing for her business. He closed the magazine and thought of the entire day. She was doing quite well for a woman who had just been attacked. She had been protected all her life, moved from her parents' house and into marriage, but Elliott could see a reserve strength in her that had been hidden away, and little by little was coming out. She was blooming into her own woman and didn't know it yet. The relationship he had with Ashley was different. Because he was her lawyer, her adviser, he knew more about her than she knew about him. Most couples didn't know about each other's life the way he knew about Ashley's. He respected their friendship, and would never jeopardize it by letting her know what he really felt for her. But one day, she would. And it was giving him a better life to look forward to, a future with a woman he loved.

She came out the bathroom wearing her pajamas,

nothing fancy that might appear to Elliott that she was trying to entice him or give him the smallest indication she was trying to lure him into her bed. But if he was single, circumstances might be different.

"Get into bed and close your eyes, Ashley. If the memory of what happened today drifts back, push it out of your head and relax."

He pulled the covers up to her shoulders as if she were a child and went back to the table. He was sitting in a chair that faced her bed.

Ashley tossed and turned in bed. Every time she opened her eyes, Elliott was there, watching her, jumping to every sound she made, every movement.

Enough, Ashley thought. She sat up in bed, and Elliott jumped from his chair and rushed to her side.

"Is there anything I can get you, Ashley? Maybe if I call room service and order some warm milk it may help you sleep. Are you cold, can I—?"

"Are you going to sit there all night and stare me in the face while I try and sleep?"

"I'm sorry, Ashley." He looked hurt.

"You're a very sweet, considerate man for doing this." She moved aside and placed her hand on the pillow next to her. "You must be exhausted, Elliott. Come lie next to me." She saw the shocked expression on his face and almost laughed out loud. But she trusted him, she trusted Elliott with her life.

He got up, and his bones ached, but he would never let her know that. Looking as though he didn't understand what she had suggested, all he could say was, "Pardon me?"

"On top of the covers, of course. This way I can fall asleep faster and you can get some sleep as well."

He thought about it for a few seconds, and nodded his head in agreement. To invite a man to lie next to her in bed—the woman was completely unaware of how attractive she really was. He wanted to laugh, but instead, he took off his shoes and in two strides, he was on the other side of the bed.

Elliott lay on his back next to Ashley, looking up at the ceiling, his hands folded behind his head.

"There. Now isn't this better than watching me while you're sitting in a hard chair, at two in the morning?" she asked, fluffing her pillow, placing it under her head. "Elliott, would you like to use the phone in case your wife might phone your room and you're not there?"

"That won't be necessary, Ashley. She won't call," was all he said. It had been years since Janet had called him when he was out of town. That was a sure sign that the love in their marriage had forsaken them a long time ago.

Ashley looked at Elliott and tried not to change the expression on her face. But how could a woman in her right mind let a man as handsome as Elliott go on an entire weekend without her? Then she wondered, how many weekends had Marcus gone on his business trips alone?

Elliott looked over at Ashley, and turned his back. "You wouldn't understand, Ashley. That's just the kind of marriage I've got."

Ashley sat up, resting on her elbow and looked down at Elliott again. "I think I would understand. I understand more than I had before my divorce."

"I guess you do know. It's lonely out there, isn't it?"

"Tell me about it. My business keeps me busy, but after I go home alone every night, it does get lonely, and it gives me too much time to think. And there's so much I would like to forget." Elliott was someone she could be with, talk to, and worst of all, wondering what it could have been for them if they had met twenty-five years earlier. But she knew just the thought of it was swimming in dangerous waters.

They talked some more until they fell asleep. Ashley jumped, and Elliott grabbed her, cuddled her in his arms. "It's all right, baby. I'm still here, right beside you," he whispered in her ear.

His warm breath against her ear sent waves through her soul. She closed her eyes, relaxed, and lay her head against his shoulder. She was close to him, and she was safe.

When they awakened the next morning, they were in the same position, cuddled close, his free arm around her waist.

They looked into each other's eyes; he kissed her forehead, and her heart froze. She yearned to feel his lips touch hers, her body mold into his. She loved this unfamiliar thrill of excitement that made her burn with desire. But the sound of his voice made her heart jerk back into reality. *He was a married man.*

"I better go to my room before anyone comes to check on you and sees me still here. No one would ever believe we just slept all night." He got up and slipped into his shoes.

Ashley started to get up but Elliott told her not to. "Thanks for staying with me, Elliott. It was nice," she said with a shy smile.

He was sitting on the edge of the bed looking at her hair spilling onto her face. Even with pajamas on, her hair in disarray, she was still a sexy woman. He was sure that she wasn't aware of the effect that she had on him. "It was nice," he said, and bent over to kiss the top of her head.

Elliott had left Ashley lying in bed. This was the way she would always remember him, in a warm place in her heart. She turned on her side and fell back into a deep sleep.

At nine, Ashley opened her eyes to the sunlight creeping through the corner of the drapes, illuminating the room to a bright orange. She got out of bed and opened the drapes wider, stood at the window, and stretched her

body, feeling the sun warming against her. She did a few
bends before going into the bathroom to shower.

When she finished, she slipped into her purple
bathrobe, called room service and ordered a half grapefruit, wheat toast, and coffee. She decided to skip the
butter. She had to remember her cholesterol.

Ashley was sitting at the table going through a fashion
magazine when she spotted a long black satin evening
gown. The back cut low in a V-shape that stopped at the
waist. Ashley carefully read the description and wondered how it would look if the back were draped and
dropped into a cowl-neck. She looked at it from every
angle. Did she dare wear this gown? Maybe, just maybe,
she thought. Yes, she would. She would make this dress
for herself, and wear it, she thought, her features relaxing into a mischievous chuckle. Why not, hell, she had
the body. She stood in front of the mirror and turned
from side to side.

There was a knock on the door. She folded the page
and closed the book. At the same time, the phone rang.
Ashley opened the door and ran to answer the phone.
She rested the receiver on her shoulder and grabbed
her wallet out of her purse, pulled out three dollars. She
gave it as a tip to the young girl.

"I'm all right, Gary. I got a good night's sleep," she
said, sitting down at the table. If only Gary knew why. *Elliott*, she thought, and closed her eyes.

"We'll meet you in the lobby at eleven-thirty, Ash. The
plane leaves at one."

"I'll be ready, Gary." She hung up and opened the
magazine again, and started to eat her breakfast. She was
famished.

At eleven, she was in the lobby standing in line to
check out.

"My, you look great this morning."

She smiled at the sound of Elliott's voice. "Thanks.
With all things considered, I feel great this morning."

His eyes looked dreamlike, as though he was enthralled, memorizing every inch of her, locking her into
his heart, his mind. She was wearing green jeans and a
matching sweater, her long leather coat folded neatly
across her arm.

"What time are you leaving, Elliott?" she asked, looking up at him. He looked tired. She knew it was because
of her. Sleeping fully dressed on top of the covers wasn't
comfortable, especially if you're not used to it.

"Actually, I was up early and met Bill for breakfast. I
checked out a half hour ago. But I was hoping that I
would see you before I left." He looked toward the door.
"I was waiting for a taxi when I saw you in line."

"Thank you for yesterday, Elliott, and last night."

"Last night was great. I just hated the circumstances
behind it. You're a nice lady to spend the night with."
They both laughed. He kissed her on the check. "My taxi
is here, love."

She couldn't understand it, but she felt sad, and had
to force the tears back. She didn't want him to go. But
she was glad they had had the chance to say their good-
byes privately.

"Have a safe trip, Elliott, and take care of yourself."

"You, too, sweetheart." He rushed toward the door,
and she could see him as he climbed into the yellow taxi.

After Ashley finished checking out and got out of line,
she saw Vanessa and Gary getting out the elevator with
luggage in their hands. Ashley went to give them a hand,
but Gary was placing the luggage in a corner.

"You ladies stay here," he said, more to Vanessa than
Ashley. "Don't disappear at no slot machines, woman."

"Oh go on already, Gary," Vanessa said, and waved her
hand.

Vanessa took Ashley's hand. "Are you really all right,
Ash?"

"Yes, I'm fine. Just looking forward to going home,
that's all."

"So am I," Vanessa answered.

"I've got so much to do, Vanessa." She held up the fashion magazine she was holding in her hand. "I saw a dress in this magazine I want to make. And guess what?"

"What, Ash?"

"It's sexy, and I'm making it for myself. I don't think I've worn anything sexy for a long time. I must have been a very boring person when I was married."

"You've changed, Ash. Just be sure and wear it somewhere where Marcus could see you."

Ashley laughed out loud. "You're the devil, you know that?"

"Yes, Ash. I know that. You should try it sometime."

"Maybe I will," Ashley said, and nudged Vanessa against her arm.

"Elliott's a nice fellow, don't you think?" Vanessa asked, sounding as though she was prying.

"Very nice. His wife is a lucky woman." Ashley changed the subject by asking Vanessa if she had won any money. She didn't want to discuss Elliott. Besides, she could never have him.

"Eight hundred dollars, let me tell you. And I only lost seventy-five dollars trying to win it."

"You're kidding me."

"No, not at all. And I'm taking every penny of it home, too."

Ashley looked at Gary, who was still in line. "While Gary is checking out, I'm going to the gift shop. It's right in the next room and I can be out before he finishes."

"For what?" Vanessa asked.

"My granddaughter of course," Ashley answered and smiled.

When she got back, Gary and Vanessa were patiently waiting. Ten minutes later the taxi was waiting for them and they were on their way to the airport.

Robert and Helen walked outside the hotel for their

taxi. She took her husband's hand. "It's a bad time for Janet to stray away and leave Elliott alone," Helen said.

Robert looked at her. "Why do you say that, darling?" he asked, but could guess what she was referring to.

"It's obvious that he's in love with Ashley. Although I doubt if Ashley knows, but he is Robert, and you know it. His face softens every time he looks at her. What do you think will happen, Robert?"

Robert kissed her on the cheek. "I don't know, but we can enjoy watching and see if anything develops, dear."

"I just hope Ashley doesn't get hurt."

"She won't, Helen. Elliott would rather not involve Ashley in a nasty divorce. He would never hurt anyone. Besides, who knows if they will ever get together. The taxi is waiting," Robert said to his wife.

Chapter 26

"Hi, Mom. Did you have a good time in Vegas?" Lori asked. Ashley looked tired so she must have enjoyed herself.

"Yes, I had a terrific time." There was no way Ashley would tell her family what happened to her. "Where's Callie?"

"She's asleep, Ashley," Keith answered. "My mom and dad have already spoiled her. Can you believe she's spoiled so soon?"

"Yes. A baby so beautiful can easily be spoiled." Ashley followed Lori to the nursery. Lori had decorated the room in pink and light blue.

Ashley picked up the baby from her crib and cradled her in her arms, remembering when Lori was a newborn. "She looks just like you, Lori."

"That's what dad said yesterday."

At the mention of Marcus's name, Ashley pulled her eyes away from the baby. Her brows furrowed. "Was he here yesterday, too?" she asked hastily.

"Yes. He gave me a hundred dollar bond for her. He's really good with her, too, Mom."

"I'm sure he is. He was good with you, too." She wanted to ask Lori if Marcus came alone, was he still going to marry that woman he had left her for, or did he ask about her? There were so many questions she wanted to ask.

"Tell me about Vegas, Mom."

Ashley was sitting at the foot of the bed and Lori was sitting next to her.

"It was cold but at least it didn't rain. We had so much fun. By the way, where's Keith parents? I know they didn't leave so soon."

"No. His aunt was having them over for dinner. I told Keith to go but he didn't want to leave me alone. He doesn't think I know enough about babies yet."

Ashley kissed the baby on her forehead. "I guess I should go and see if Mother and Aunt Cora are all right."

Lori lay the baby inside her crib. She followed Ashley back to the living room, where Keith was watching a western on TV.

"Leaving so soon, Ash?" Keith asked, as he got up to walk her outside.

"Yes. But I had to come over and see my granddaughter." She kissed Lori on her cheek. "Don't do too much, dear. And remember not to lift anything too heavy."

"Don't worry, Ash. With my parents around, Lori has nothing to do but take care of Callie." He walked Ashley outside to her car and said good-bye.

"Where is Mother?" Ashley asked Cora.

"Come in the den with me, Ash. Doris went to the supermarket to get a few things. Did you win any money in Vegas?"

"No, not a cent. When I go to Vegas all I do is play the slot machines, eat too much, and walk around."

"And?"

"And what?" Ashley asked, and took a seat on the sofa next to Cora.

"That's all you did in Vegas? Gee, Ashley. I'll bet your mind was on work the whole time you were there." Cora grabbed a stick of gum from the coffee table, folded it three times, and stuck it in her mouth. "Girl, in my younger days when I was home I was all over the city. Couldn't stay in one place too long, you know."

"Aunt Cora, I had a good time, and no, I didn't think of work, and I didn't stay in my room. Oh, and Elliott, my friend the lawyer, was there, too."

"What lawyer are you speaking of, Ash?"

"You know, the lawyer that handled my divorce. But his wife wasn't there with him." Ashley picked up a peppermint that was kept in the crystal bowl. "Elliott is such a nice man, so easy to talk to and be with, Aunt Cora."

Cora watched Ashley's eyes. They were dancing, and her features began to relax as she spoke of Elliott.

"Why wasn't the man's wife in Vegas with him?"

"She was in Detroit."

They heard the back door open and close. Doris called from the kitchen.

"I'm in here, Mother. Let me see if she needs me to get anything out the car." Ashley went to the kitchen. She kissed Doris on her cheek, took the heavy bag she was carrying, and set it on the table. "Is there anything left in the car?"

"No. I only got a few things. I missed you, honey," Doris said, as Ashley helped her out of her coat.

"I went to see Lori and the baby before I came here."

"We were over there yesterday. Marcus had just left. And I was glad, too. I didn't want to look at his face. He sure did disappoint me. He didn't know what a real woman he had, Ashley."

Ashley was surprised to hear Doris say that. They had gotten closer since Daniel had died. "You used to think Marcus couldn't do anything wrong."

"That was before he hurt you and decided to marry some hussy," Doris said with a bite in her voice.

Cora walked in. "And I bet my bottom dollar that's one marriage won't take place anytime soon," Cora said. "Marcus is going to drift from woman to woman before he gets married again."

"Why do you say that, Aunt Cora?"

"I see the way he looks at you, Ash. He's all mixed up in the head now. I believe he hates that he left you, but he's not ready to admit it yet. So he's going to go from one woman to another until he clears his head. And there's nothing worse than a man walking around with lose screws in his head."

Trying to make sense out of what Cora had said, Ashley pondered over it. "Let's stop all the talk of Marcus." Hearing his name was still a sore spot in her heart. But after this weekend she was sure the wound wouldn't be as deep. It was strange that somehow the trip to Vegas had made her change even stronger. All she wanted was to get over Marcus and get on with her life.

They were standing in the kitchen. Ashley opened the cabinet to get a glass, picked the tall green glass that Daniel used. No one else used it but him. She looked at it for a few seconds and decided to put it back and get another one. Thinking of her father made her think of Jason. Sooner or later she would call him. It was time to clear the air and talk about their parents. Maybe Jason had questions that she could answer about their father. And there was so much that Ashley wanted to know about Ruby, and Jason was the only person left who knew her. It had been months since they last saw each other, maybe they could get past the anger and hate. They were sister and brother, after all.

Chapter 27

"Here, let me show you a picture of a dress I'm going to make." Ashley laid the magazine open on the table. She explained how she would make the front and back differently from the one in the book.

"So you want to reverse the front and back?" Joan asked.

The phone rang and Ashley answered. "Yes, this is Ashley Lake, how may I help you?"

"Mrs. Lake, my name is Fern Joseph. I'm calling from Detroit. I went to Helen Graham's book signing a month ago here in Detroit. She was wearing a beautiful suit and said you made it for her. It's my understanding that you are a dress designer and have your own business?"

Holding the phone, Ashley took a seat at the table. She had never heard of this woman. Ashley looked at Joan, but she was still looking at the picture in the magazine.

"Yes, that's correct," Ashley answered.

"Mrs. Lake, my partner, Mr. Jackson, and I are opening four clothing stores—in L.A., Detroit, Dallas, and Houston. I think we can do some business together. We're looking for something different that is not in other clothing chains."

Ashley listened intensely. She waved her hand at Joan, motioning for her not to leave the room. God, you've answered my prayer, she thought.

"I'll be in Los Angeles Wednesday, Mrs. Lake. Perhaps

I can come to your shop and take a look at what you've designed."

"Wednesday will be fine, Miss Joseph. I'm here from seven to five in the evenings. What time would you like to come?"

"We can be there after one, if that's all right with you?"

"Yes, certainly. I'll see you on Wednesday."

Ashley hung up and jumped out her seat. "Can you believe it, Joan?"

"What, what, Ashley? Who was that?"

"A lady and her partner saw a pantsuit I made for Helen when she was in Detroit, and they are opening up four stores and want our business. I'm on my way, baby, big time."

Joan hugged Ashley, and both of them ran to a line of clothing that was hanging on a long rack. Ashley started picking out dresses, blouses, pantsuits, slacks, everything she thought they would like in their stores.

"I'll tell you what, Joan. Let's finish the jackets where we left off on Thursday. Tomorrow we will have the entire day to do this. And when Miss Joseph and her partner get here we can be ready for business." Ashley started to walk away. "Oh, I forgot, Helen's daughter has a friend named Maria that wants to design clothing and start a business of her own. She's coming to work with us for the experience. And just in time, I might add."

"We need all the help that we can get, Ashley. It's a good thing this place has lots of space. You won't have to get another place to expand," Joan said, and looked at the bare corner that two more machines could take up.

The day flew by fast. Ashley and Joan did finish the jackets they were working on. Joan left at five that evening but Ashley stayed until seven-thirty.

When Ashley got home the first thing she did was call Lori to check on the baby; then she called Doris and gave her the good news.

She went into her bedroom and slipped into a long robe and a pair of socks, opened a can of tomato soup, and sat at the table in the kitchen and read the newspaper. Excitement took over; she couldn't concentrate on what she was reading. She folded the paper and pushed it aside. So many things to do. She needed another sewing machine; another body besides Maria and Joan, hoping that Renee would be back next week. The phone rang again and she flopped down on the couch and answered.

"Mother, you sound so serious. Is there anything wrong?" she asked before Doris could get another word out.

"No, dear. It's just that me and Cora could give you a hand at the shop until you get enough help. We would be glad to give you a hand. After you told me about the large order, Cora and I agreed that we could help."

Ashley held the phone to her ear for a moment. "Mother, I can't ask you to do that. Besides, Dad wouldn't let you work a day during your marriage."

"Listen Ashley, Daniel is gone. Cora and I sit around this house all day and do nothing but cook, or shop at the mall, and watch all the ridiculous court shows all day. It would do us good to do something concrete for a change. You don't even have to pay us."

"Mother, do you guys really want to do this?"

"Yes, and Cora wants to as much as I do. We'll do anything to help you fill your order. Ash, we want your business to be successful."

"Okay, I'll tell you what. After Miss Joseph leaves on Wednesday I'll have a realistic idea as to how many people I can use. But, I won't let you two work without pay. Paying you is the only way I'll agree."

"Okay, call us on Wednesday."

Ashley hung up and curled her feet under her, and closed her eyes. When she opened them again it was past midnight.

Chapter 28

Wednesday morning Ashley woke up in a frenzy. At eleven that morning, a tall, dark, handsome man opened the door to Ashley's shop and held it open for Fern Joseph, who was also tall, and leggy. She was dressed in a short brown leather suit and brown boots, a brown Gucci purse swinging on her shoulder. Her eyes were slanted, wide apart, and her small lips were lined with dark brown liner, filled in with red lipstick.

"Mrs. Lake, I'm Fern and this is my partner, Lee."

Ashley extended her hand to Fern and smiled at Lee. "Just call me Ashley and this is Joan. Why don't we go inside my office? You can give me an idea of what you're looking for." Ashley led them to her office and motioned for them to sit in the two chairs in front of her desk. "Would you like coffee, tea, or a cold drink?"

"No, thank you," they both answered. "You have a cute shop, Ashley," Lee complimented.

Ashley looked in his eyes, which were a piercing light brown, set deeply into his dark brown face. "Thanks. I liked this place as soon as I saw it."

Fern spoke up. "Like I was saying, Ashley. We are in the midst of opening four stores and want something different to sell to women. They can always go into one of the big department stores if they want something that everyone else is wearing."

"I agree," Ashley said calmly.

"But we need to be able to order whenever we need

to," Fern said. "You never know how much people will buy if it's something made differently from what they see in other stores."

"You can always place an order and we'll fill it on time. But before I have hundreds of the same style made, I need to know what will sell. I haven't been in business long enough to be stuck with clothes that don't sell." Ashley placed her hands flat on the desk in front of her. "You can always give me heads-up on what's selling the most, and we can make more and keep extra ones on hand."

Lee cleared his throat. "That should work. But in the beginning we can have you make at least five different colors and sizes. When we think we are about to sell out, we will make a bulk order at that time. But we won't leave you stuck with clothes we won't buy."

Fern looked at Lee and nodded her head in agreement. "No Ashley, we fully understand. Can you show us what you have? I also have a contract you may want to look over and also consult your lawyer." She placed the envelope on Ashley's desk. "Lee and I have known each other since we were kids. I told him that I had a good feeling after you and I spoke. I'm usually a good judge of people and I think we can do spectacular business together."

"Thank you, Fern. I had a good feeling about you, too. Now that we've met, I know we can do business together. Why don't we take a look at what I have." Ashley led them to the racks with all the different styles that she had designed. "Now, just take your time and look around."

"She's just one of your staff?" Lee asked, looking at Joan, then at Fern, with concern.

"I have four more people coming on, so please don't be concerned that I may not be able to fill your orders when needed."

"We'll need pretty big orders, Ashley." He smiled, flashing even white teeth.

"I'm looking forward to it," Ashley answered. It was difficult to talk with Lee without looking at all the gold jewelry he wore. It was a little too much for Ashley's taste, too flamboyant. Gold around his neck, gold bracelets on each wrist, gold rings, and even the band on his watch was gold. Even with his expensive gray tailored suit, which was cut perfectly, the jewelry did nothing to complement it.

Ashley watched the two discussing the blouses they were looking at. One could see they were more than business partners. And Ashley watched the intimate touches, the way their eyes met and lingered on each other.

As Ashley read the contract that was prepared by The Inn Clothing Store, Lee and Fern were busy looking from one rack to another.

An hour had passed; they were going over the list they had made for the four stores: sixteen blouses, plus evening gowns, pantsuits, slacks, and suits. As Ashley looked over the list, she felt her hands beginning to moisten, and she realized she desperately needed more help. She was filling the biggest order at one time that she could imagine. But she managed to keep her expression passive and appear calm. "This is great. Your order will be ready on time," she said, not realizing her legs were shaking against the table. Oh, God, she thought.

Ashley walked them outside and said good-bye. When she came back inside Joan jumped from her chair and they hugged, laughed, and danced around each other like children on a school playground. "I guess I should call my mother and aunt to inform them that they have a job. Good thing Maria starts tomorrow, too. But I don't know how soon she will leave to start her own business."

Joan went back to the cutting table and Vanessa walked in as Ashley was going over the contract.

"Hi Joan, Ash. I smell coffee." She breezed in like a

gust of wind. Vanessa always walked fast even when she wasn't in a hurry.

"I'll get you a cup," Ashley said and laid the contract on the small table in the corner. As she walked into the small kitchen, Vanessa followed.

"You looked so preoccupied when I walked in." Vanessa stood in the doorway. "Are you all right, Ash?" she asked with concern.

"I've been worrying about my business lately. It's doing all right, but it's slowed down. Maria will be here tomorrow and I didn't have a lot for her to do."

"What exactly are you saying, Ash?" Vanessa asked, and took a seat at the table.

"I hadn't said anything about it, but just yesterday I wondered if I had made a mistake by leaving my job at the health care company so soon. Marcus always thought that I wasn't smart enough to go into business for myself. And I prayed that I wouldn't lose everything I own because of my impulsiveness to quit my job and go on my own. But guess what?" she asked with a triumphant smile. She squared her shoulders and held her head high with pride.

"Oh, Ashley. Are you sure you're all right?" Vanessa looked truly concerned and placed her cup on the table.

Ashley grinned. "Am I all right? Yes, girl, for once, everything is all right. I was going over a contract with Fern Joseph and her partner, Lee Jackson. They're opening four stores, Vanessa, four stores," she said, holding up four fingers. "And want me to do business with them. You've got to see the order they just gave me for all four stores."

Vanessa looked at Ashley in astonishment. "Oh, Ash, how awesome. Where are the stores located?"

"Detroit, Dallas, Houston, and one here. And they've already selected what they want."

Vanessa reached over and grabbed Ashley's hand.

"Vanessa, finally, my designs will be seen in different states. This should open lots of doors for me."

"'Ash, if anyone deserves it, you do. I'm just so happy. Show me what they picked out. What type of people are they?"

"Here's the rack they spent most of their time at. They loved all the blouses. Hey, and the red one I made last month, they simply loved it."

"What type of people are they? You're speaking so fast that you can't hear me."

Ashley laughed. "Okay, they're just the opposite of each other. She's nice-looking and so is he, but he dresses a little flashy. She was well dressed, light brown hair in a cute short cut, about forty years old."

"I'll bet he's from Detroit or Chicago," Vanessa said.

"It's Detroit, and they still live there," Joan interjected.

Ashley turned around to face Joan. "You heard more than I did, Joan."

"That's because I was out here when they were selecting what they wanted. You were nervous and don't remember, especially when they gave you the list of what they wanted," Joan chuckled.

"I got so excited I left my coffee in the kitchen," Vanessa said, and went back into the kitchen. She came right back with her coffee cup in hand. Ashley was reading the contract when Vanessa walked in.

"What's that?" Vanessa asked as she peered over her cup.

"The contract they left. It says they will pay for the merchandise upon arrival." Ashley lifted one brow. "I'm not too sure about that."

"You'd better take that contract to Elliott and have him take a look at it. I mean you never know if there is something you may misunderstand that can bite you in the ass later."

"Can he advise me with something like this? I was

under the impression he only handles divorce cases," Ashley said.

"I'm sure he can read a contract, Ash. And if he can't, there are others in the firm that can handle it. Lesson number one, while you're in business, always, but always, have a lawyer look over even the simplest contracts."

"You're right. Now I have to go shopping this week for another sewing machine, material, and other supplies. Well, a little of everything, really. Mother and Aunt Cora are going to help. Plus I'm expecting Maria to start tomorrow morning."

"I sure would like to see your aunt helping out." Vanessa laughed at the idea.

"She's going to run me crazy, girl," Ashley said. "But I need the extra help."

"Have you heard anything from Elliott since we returned from Vegas?" Vanessa asked.

"No, why would I? We never talk unless I need legal advice."

Vanessa stood and looked at Ashley. She shook her head, surprised that Ashley still had no inkling of what Elliott felt for her. "Ash, does he say anything about Janet at all? It must be pretty bad at home when a man and wife always go their separate ways." They had gone back into the kitchen and Vanessa refilled her cup with coffee.

"He did mention it briefly. That marriage is over, but you know some couples live that way forever."

"I know, Ash. It's just that he's such a nice fellow. But you're right of course."

"I feel so good, Vanessa. Do you know that since I got back I haven't thought of Marcus quite as much as I used to, and of course I've been really busy." She placed her cup on the table in front of her. Ashley thought of Elliott again. Why does it happen that all the nice people are the ones who get hurt?

Vanessa looked at her watch. "I better be going. I'm going to get my hair trimmed and you know how Charlie gets if you're late. I don't know how his wife tolerates him."

It was four that afternoon, and Ashley left the shop the same time as Joan. She couldn't wait to tell her mother and aunt about her contract.

Doris opened the door. "Come in, Ashley. I was just hemming my dress to wear to church Sunday." Doris led her into the den where Cora was watching *Judge Judy* on TV. She looked up as Ashley and Doris walked in.

"Hi, Ashley. You have a busy day today."

"Not too busy, Aunt Cora. But I will be in a week. I am hiring you and Mom to work with me for awhile."

"Honey, I was hoping you would ask us. It will give us something to do different for a change," Doris said.

"Yeah, and we can cook every night and take enough for everyone the next day. Oh yeah, I can bake that cake I saw in a magazine last week. Never tried it, but it looked delicious," Cora said, her eyes gleaming with delight.

Ashley looked at Doris and back at Cora again. "Aunt Cora, I doubt very much if you will feel like cooking every night when you and Mother get home."

Cora waved her hand. "Honey, you know I like to cook. I cook almost everyday. Don't I, Doris?"

"Yes, almost every day." Doris grabbed the cookbook from the coffee table and held it up so Ashley could see it. She smiled and sat back on the sofa next to Ashley.

Ashley looked at the cookbook on the table in front of her, her brows furrowed. Oh Lord, she thought. What have I done? "I'm going home and figure out how much material I have to buy. We have lots of work to do." She stood up with her purse in her hand and pulled out her car keys.

"Now, Ashley, don't you worry about a thing. Doris and I will be there when you need us," Cora said as she changed the channel on TV. "Working for you is going to be fun."

"Yeah, sure, Aunt Cora," Fun, Ashley thought. Goodness, what have I done? she repeated to herself. Ashley kissed her mother on the cheek and walked out slowly.

Ashley looked at her watch as she was driving to her house. It was five-forty. Maybe Mr. Browne was still in his office. Her purse was placed in the seat, and with her left hand she fumbled into her purse and pulled out her phone, dialed Mr. Browne's number, and waited for someone to answer. Ashley was ready to hang up when she heard his assistant's voice on the other end.

"Hi, this is Ashley Lake. Is Mr. Browne still in the office?"

"Hold on, Mrs. Lake. I'll check and see if he has left already."

Ashley held the phone, knowing the woman on the other end knew if Mr. Browne was still in his office or not. The man was a lawyer and she worked for him, so of course she knew.

"Ashley, how are you today?"

"I'm good, Edward."

"The reading of Daniel's will got pretty nasty when you all were here. I hope Doris is feeling better about it. I didn't get the chance to say I'm sorry you had to find out that way, Ashley. It was very unfortunate for Doris, too."

"Yes it was. But Mother is all right now, Edward. I would like to have my brother's phone number. I think it's about time we talked."

Edward held the phone for a few moments before he spoke again. Daniel had kept Ashley and Jason apart to prevent her from knowing that Doris wasn't her mother. But now she knows, and why shouldn't she get to know her brother? "Okay, Ashley, he is your brother, after all."

"What does Jason do for a living?"

"Jason is a high school principal, Ashley. But here, I have his phone number." He read the number off to Ashley, who scribbled it on a piece of paper. "Good luck, Ashley. I hope you and Jason become friends. Daniel told me Jason's a quiet man, like him." Edward hung up and Ashley stuck the paper inside her purse. Ten minutes later she drove into her driveway.

She finished eating dinner, showered, and sat in the den reading the *LA Times*.

Ashley curled up in the large chair and closed her eyes. Was she taking on too much? Was she ready for such large orders? Her eyes popped opened at the thought of failing. But she'd wanted this for so many years, and she would have done it before if only Marcus had had enough faith in her. Ashley was never as smart as he was, or so he thought. But now she had her own decisions to make, and her own mistakes. "Hell no," she whispered. She wasn't going to fail. She would fill this order and the order after this one. This was only the beginning.

Ashley pulled the small piece of paper out of her robe pocket and looked at it again. She picked up the phone and dialed the number, held her breath until she heard the man's voice on the other end. Her stomach clenched with apprehension and dread, and she started to hang up, but this was something she had to do.

"Hello," Jason answered.

Ashley sighed heavily. "Jason, it's Ashley . . . your sister." Ashley held the phone waiting for his response, immobilized. "I thought if you have the time this week, we could meet for lunch or even dinner. I would like to ask you some questions about our mother."

"What is it you need to know about her, Ashley?"

She squinted at the sound of his frosty voice, and once again, Ashley thought of the terrible day in the lawyer's office. Ashley rolled her eyes up at the ceiling as she heard him sigh. Give me patience, Lord, she thought to herself.

"Everything, Jason. I would like to know everything about her. She was my mother, too."

"Oh. Could have fooled me," he said with an edge of irritation in his voice.

"Look, Jason, what happened between our parents was no fault of ours. Why can't we get past this and get on with our lives?"

"Look, Ashley. I have gotten on with my life, and you're right. Don't think after all this time you can just make a phone call and everything will be all right. We owe each other nothing, and I like it the way it was. Now, if you would excuse me I have some work to do." He hung up on her.

Ashley held the phone in her hand, appalled by his bluntness. She looked at the phone for several moments before she placed it back onto its cradle. "That went well. But, at least I tried." Why doesn't he realize they need each other, or at least that she needed him? And she had to admit she wanted Jason to be the brother she never had. But now, she realized, it was too late. And as she thought of it, she felt tears spill from her eyes. Maybe having a brother would help fill the desperate void she felt in her life. Doris, Jason, and she had been cheated, thanks to Daniel. "Who does he think he is?" she murmured to herself and grabbed the phone. She was going to dial his number and tell him a thing or two for speaking to her as though he was better than she was. Ashley looked at the phone and hung up again. "We are strangers, after all," she murmured.

Jason was sitting at his desk going over the school budget. He completed it at home because there were no interruptions. At school there was always a student or teacher needing his attention. He leaned back in his chair and sprawled his long legs in front of him as he thought of Ashley. It had almost been a year since they had met in the lawyer's office.

Doris, the old woman, hated him and made no attempts to conceal it. So she got what she deserved. Under no other circumstances would he have told Ashley the truth about their mother. But when he looked into Doris's eyes and saw the raw hatred in them, he wanted to lash out and hurt her, make her feel the pain that he was left with. He was left without a mother or father.

As a child he used to wonder if he and Ashley would ever become friends. Now, Ashley and Lori were the only living relatives he had left.

Jason picked up the picture that was facing him on his desk. It was a picture of Diana. In two months they would be married. Diana was his friend and the woman he was deeply in love with. They had been dating for two years, had been friends for five. Jason's mind floated back to Ashley again. Maybe he was bitter, and what happened wasn't his and Ashley's fault. He picked up his pen again and started back to work. He didn't need his sister and didn't want to think of her. What's done is done.

The next day, Maria Garcia stood in front of Ashley's dress shop, staring at the beautiful clothes in the large glass window. She took a step closer to look at the cut of the long black silk dress, imagined it to be short with long sleeves and a wide-brimmed hat. She had to admit the dress was very detailed, and well made.

Maria had gone to school for fashion design and was ready to start her career as a dress designer. One day she would have a shop of her own. But for now, she would learn as much as she could by working in Ashley's dress shop. Lynn had told her that Ashley was a pleasant woman and had made clothes for Helen, her mother. And never delivered a day late, as promised.

Maria sighed and looked up at the sign with Ashley's name written in red capital letters. "Hope she's as nice as Lynn says she is," Maria whispered to herself. She remembered Lori when they attended USC, and Maria and Lynn had been roommates.

Maria walked inside and told Joan that she had an appointment with Ashley.

"She's in her office. What's your name?" Joan asked.

"Maria Garcia. She's expecting me," she answered in a soft voice.

"Yes, she is expecting you. Go inside and you'll see her." Joan pointed in the direction of Ashley's office.

Maria stood quietly in the door and cleared her throat. Ashley was sitting at her desk, a frown across her forehead, as she read an invoice.

Looking up at Maria, Ashley saw the largest, roundest, brown eyes staring back at her and motioned for her to come into her office. She couldn't take her eyes off the small young woman. Her hair was long, dark brown, cascading down her back.

"So, you are Maria?" Ashley asked.

"Yes. And I'm very happy to finally meet you. Thank you for giving me this opportunity to work in your shop, Mrs. Lake. I hear that you could use the extra help." Maria unfolded her hands and placed them in her lap.

"We have a large order to fill so you may not thank me when we finish."

"Oh, yes. I will. I don't mind hard work. The more I work the more I can learn, right?"

Ashley looked at her serious eyes and smiled. "That's a good scenario, Maria. Do you live near here?"

"Not far. My sister and I share an apartment in West L.A., and I have a car so you can depend on me, Mrs. Lake."

"Call me Ashley. Now I'll show you around. You've met

Joan already and my mother and aunt will be here to help. Also, Joan's sister should be back soon."

Ashley got up and walked around her desk. "We're like family here, Maria. You can use the phone here in my office for privacy or the one in the kitchen. There's always coffee, tea, or Cokes in the refrigerator. Whatever is in there everyone is welcome to it. On the weekends when I go shopping, I always grab cans of soup, Cokes, and cookies." Ashley showed Maria the racks of clothing she had made. She had been in business for only eleven months and couldn't believe she had made so many pieces of clothing, and they had sold well, too. They were made perfectly, and no dress sold for under two hundred dollars.

"I'm going to buy two more sewing machines so you will have one. Now, you can look around if you like and be back tomorrow morning at eight."

"I'll be here at eight sharp, Ashley. I'm so happy to have this opportunity." Maria smiled and walked to the machine where Joan was sewing.

"You can watch me if you like," Joan said. "I'm just glad we have more help." Joan gave her a cheerful smile and pulled her long French braids up into a ponytail.

"Are you sure it's okay for me to stand over you?" Maria asked softly.

"Sure, and you can pull up a chair next to me. How did you learn to sew?"

"I went to trade school and took dress designing. "But I need to learn the business side of it."

Ashley was standing near Joan's machine. "We can all learn from each other, Maria," Ashley said.

The phone rang. Rushing around her desk, Ashley reached for it. "Hello," she answered. For a few moments no one answered, and instantly she knew who it was, in her heart she knew it was her brother.

"Ashley, it's Jason. If you are free for lunch today we can meet."

Ashley's hand gripped the receiver. "Yes, yes I would like that."

"Where can we meet that's not too far for you?" Jason asked.

Ashley was trying to think of a quiet place where they could talk. "How about my house?"

"Okay. What's the address?"

She gave him her address, and when she hung up she looked at her hands—they were trembling. She ran her fingers through her hair and looked at her watch. It was ten-thirty. She tried to think of something that she could get for lunch. "Damn, forgot to ask what kind of food he likes." Now she would have to go to the supermarket and buy something. Everyone eats a good salad. I'll pick up some freshly made garlic bread, and buy some crab to mix into the salad, or should I get chicken? Better be safe and buy chicken, she thought. Who doesn't like chicken in their salad? She looked at her watch again. It was only five minutes later than it was the last time she looked. She felt her insides jitter.

Ashley stayed in her office going over her contract. She had to call Elliott for legal advice before she signed it. Getting a white envelope from her desk drawer, she folded the contract and placed it inside.

Maria left and Ashley grabbed her purse and went into the sewing room where Joan was. "Joan, I have to leave to meet someone. I should be back before one. Keep making the pockets for the slacks until there's at least fifty completed, two pockets for each pair of slacks."

Joan smiled and turned around in her chair to face Ashley. "Take your time, Ash. I should be finished by the end of the day."

"Okay. See you soon." Ashley rushed out and stopped in Ralph's Market in the Ladera Heights shopping center. She felt like a child waiting for Christmas. At last, she could find out what had happened in her father's life that she never knew until his death. And the mother she never knew? What was she like? Ashley always felt guilty when she thought of her. In her heart, Doris was her mother. Doris must have felt entrapped so many times by living with a man who deceived her.

Ashley finished shopping, paid the cashier, and headed home. She turned on Slauson Avenue and glanced at the new construction going up. It was a fitness center owned by Magic Johnson. She pulled a pen from her purse and quickly wrote down the phone number. The light changed and she drove off.

The doorbell rang. Ashley looked at the clock and it was precisely twelve noon. Ashley untied her apron, folded it, and placed it on the chair.

Ashley ran to the door and Jason stood waiting, both hands pushed inside his pockets. He was a largely built man like their father, well dressed in a charcoal brown suit. He looked down at Ashley and forced a stiff, fixed smile, but his eyes were angry.

"Come in, Jason." Ashley moved aside so he could pass. "I'm glad you changed your mind, and I hope you're hungry," she said, motioning for him to follow her down the hall.

"Here, I'll take your coat." The material of his jacket was soft, and tailor-made. Ashley hung it in the hall closet on their way to the kitchen.

While Ashley was in the kitchen, Jason looked around the den and spotted a picture on the coffee table in front of the sofa. He was holding it in his hands when Ashley walked back in.

"That's my daughter and ex-husband."

"Ex-husband?"

"Yes, I'm afraid so."

"How long?" he asked, and placed the picture on the table and faced Ashley.

"My divorce was just final a couple of months ago."

She stood beside him. "Come, let's sit at the table. I thought this would be cozier and more private than sitting in a restaurant."

He smiled and nodded in agreement. "Tell me about my niece?" he asked as he followed Ashley.

Ashley took the warm bread out the oven and placed it in the center of the table. "Coke, water?"

"Coke sounds good. That's all I drink," he answered.

She turned around and smiled. "So do I. My mother tells me that I drink too many of them." Amazed, she looked at him again.

She filled two glasses with Coke. "Your niece's name is Lori. She graduated from USC and has a wonderful husband and a beautiful three-month-old daughter."

"You don't look like you have an adult daughter, and you certainly don't look like a grandmother."

"Thank you. Do you have any children, Jason?"

"No. I had a short marriage of one year. But I'm getting married again in two months."

"What's she like?" Ashley took a seat at the table.

"Pretty inside and out. She teaches school." He looked at Ashley and placed his fork on his plate and decided to cut to the chase.

"Our dad was a good man, Ashley. He had gotten himself mixed up with two women and had two children. But at least he was man enough to face up to his responsibilities. That's the way I would like to remember him. Sure, I think I hated you because you had him all the time. But after we talked yesterday, I began to think about all the years that I hated you and was jealous of you. He was there for you day and night and the times I needed to talk to a father, he wasn't there for me."

"I know, Jason. And yes, he was a good father to me. But there was something else, Jason."

"What, besides being a married man?"

"Yes, but that's just half of it. It's what he did to his wife, my mother. When my husband left me for another woman I became bitter and angry at the world. One day I was at my mother's house and the subject of my ex-husband came up between us. Mother and I were alone." Ashley sighed and sipped her Coke. "My mother started to defend him. I talked to her so badly that day and she cried. I had never seen my mother cry before." Ashley avoided the bread and picked at her salad. "As long as I could remember, my mother did everything our father told her to, and with no argument. He was always the one who raved and yelled, and she took it."

Jason had stopped eating and was facing Ashley. He picked up an olive from his plate and popped it into his mouth.

"I didn't know why she was that way until we saw you in Mr. Browne's office. When you told me about our mother, her heart must have broken in two."

Jason saw the tears begin to flow down Ashley's cheek and moved around uncomfortably in his chair. If there was anything he hated, it was to see a woman cry.

"Later, my mother and I discussed her life with my father. She couldn't leave him because it meant leaving me, too. I owe her so much."

"I thought about that day so many times but there wasn't anything I could do to take back what I said. I was hurt and angry over our father's death. I never really got to know him. After he died it left me with no family at all. I wasn't lucky enough to have any of his family in my life. And I was always jealous of you. I'm sorry that I hurt your mother."

"Did your mother . . . I mean, our mother, ever mention me?"

"Yes. She picked me up from high school one day and saw you up close. When we got inside the car she said that both of us looked like Dad. I knew that she had seen you many times before."

"I saw her in the Baldwin Hills mall one time but I never really looked at her. But when you told me who she was, I thought of that time and tried to remember her face. We were still in high school, but I remember. What was she like, Jason?"

"She wasn't at all the motherly type like Doris seems to be. She had lots of spark to her, young at heart and loved to party. She went out a lot and dated. My mother was always happy, or so I thought she was. She worked hard and took good care of me. With the help of our father's financial support, she was able to buy me nice clothes, and I got a good education, also paid for by Dad."

"She sounds very different from my mother. So my father did come around a lot?" Ashley held her breath waiting for Jason to answer her question.

"Sorry, but yes, he did come around a lot. It wasn't to be with my mom, but he was a man that took care of his responsibilities and I was it. You have to respect the man for that, Ashley. You know, I think you look more like mom." He gave Ashley a small white envelope with his left hand and picked up his fork with his right hand.

Ashley looked at him closely. "Are you ambidextrous, Jason?"

"Yes, I can use both hands evenly like Dad did."

Ashley tore the envelope open and pulled out a stack of photos. The first one was of Ashley when she was eight years old. "Where was this taken?" she asked in surprise.

"I have no idea. They were found in a box after she died." The other photos were of Ruby and Jason.

"She was really an attractive woman. I'll always keep these, Jason. I appreciate you giving them to me," she said, and touched his hand, but he gently pulled it away. "I think she did care after all. Maybe not enough to have kept me, but she must have cared."

He looked at Ashley's face, the same face as their mother's. Jason felt a sense of relief since he decided to return Ashley's call.

As Ashley looked at Jason, she wished he would articulate what he was thinking.

It was beyond belief that they were sitting at the same table and talking as though they had grown up as brother and sister all the years as children. Memories flooded her mind of the day in the lawyer's office. She looked at Ruby's photo again and held it close to her heart.

"I would like to meet Lori one day, if you don't mind."

"Jason, of course I don't mind. I'm sure that Lori would love it." Ashley noticed he didn't include Doris, but she could understand why. After all, her father married Doris, not his mother. She wouldn't dare ask him anything about that. For now, she just wanted to get to know him better.

Their meeting had been deeper than he had anticipated, and he had to get out her house, get some air. "It's been nice, Ashley. But I better get back to school." He wiped his mouth with the white cloth napkin and placed it beside his plate.

"You make a mean salad." Jason got up and followed Ashley to the living room. He stood there while Ashley got his jacket.

Ashley opened the door and he started to walk out and stopped.

"Hey, I would really like it if you come to my wedding. I'll mail you an invitation."

"Yes, please mail it and I'll be there."

Jason nodded and walked outside to his car.

Ashley watched as he drove off. She went back inside and rinsed the dishes, and was putting them in the dishwasher when the phone rang.

"Hi Mom, I thought you would be at your shop. But guess what?" Lori asked.

"What, Lori?"

"Dad called me this morning and said his wedding plans have changed. He sounds indecisive about getting married now."

Ashley was holding a dish in her hand, placed it in the sink, and took a seat at the counter.

"I wonder why?" Ashley answered. "Did he sound unhappy?"

"Actually, he was very quiet. I'd say that maybe he was sad, or maybe they had an argument. Who knows?"

Ashley knew that after Marcus had been bragging to everyone about getting married so something pretty serious had to have happened for him to cancel, or change the date. He would have been getting married in two months. She was surprised that she actually felt happy about it. Then she smiled. Let him brag about that.

Lori hesitated. "Mom, he asked about you. He even asked if you were happy and if your business was going well. Why do you think he wants to know?" Lori asked.

"Hell if I know. I hope you told him that I'm happy. What the hell does he think, that I would always be unhappy without him? Things change, people change." She was getting upset. Did he think because he doesn't want her that no one would? Now she was pissed off.

"I told him you landed a big contract, and yes, that you are happy."

"Good. Keep me posted."

"Mom, what if he has realized that he was wrong and wants to come home?"

"Sorry, but I don't want him, Lori. After all, I do have some pride left. He didn't take *that* with him."

From the tone of Ashley's voice, Lori knew that she meant it. Ashley no longer wanted her father. Sure, she would love to see them reconcile their differences, and get together again in spite of what her father had done. But she had to agree with her mother. She still had some pride left, and her father couldn't just walk in and out of Ashley's life whenever he wanted to. Ashley had changed. She looked ten years younger and could stand on her own, start a business, and make a profit. Her father leaving made Ashley independent, and she had found the woman that she didn't know was inside her. You go, Mom, Lori thought to herself, and smiled.

Chapter 29

Elliott walked into his study and slammed his briefcase on the desk. He took off his jacket and hung it in the closet, then sighed as he stood at the window. It was May, and the gray clouds looked dark enough to rain. He watched the green leaves from the tall tree blow onto his lawn. The gardener would be cutting the grass tomorrow and would rake up the leaves.

He rolled up his sleeves, and noticed an ink spot on his white shirt. He switched the TV to the five o'clock news and shook his head in disgust as he heard about another kidnapped child.

"My, don't we look woeful today. Bad day at the office, dear?" Janet asked.

"Yes, Terri took a two-and-a-half-hour lunch today. The paralegal is on vacation and won't be back until Thursday. Robert is even thinking about firing that damn receptionist and I fully agree. The only reason she's been there this long is because she works well when she is there."

Janet sat on the arm of the chair. "Don't you think that's a little drastic, Elliott? Why fire her because she was late? Maybe the poor girl had some important business to take care of."

"This is not her first time, Janet. She pulls this little trick a little too often, and when we need her the most."

"So she's late once in awhile. Is that a crime?"

"When you are a lawyer and have others depending on you, yes, that's a crime."

"But Elliott, the firm should have two receptionists in case one is out ill. You know Terri is good. Why are you picking on her?"

Elliott looked at his wife and wondered why was she so interested in the way his office was run. And to imply that he was picking on the girl was ridiculous. All she really cared about was how much money he made. So what does she want from him?

"Why are you concerned about the way the office is run, Janet? It's not taking money out of your pockets, or stopping you from going on another vacation, buying expensive clothing." He waved his hand at her, wishing she would leave. "I can do without the fictitious attitude. Gee, you're a damn good actor."

He sat behind his desk and started going over a divorce agreement that he didn't have a chance to go over earlier.

"Elliott!"

He looked at Janet again. "What now?"

"I spoke with my sister today. She and Ted are getting a divorce. What do you think about that? Married for twenty-six years and getting a divorce."

"I think if there isn't enough love between two people they should get a divorce. Which reminds me, we're not sleeping together or living as man and wife, why don't you want a divorce, Janet? I'm willing to be fair, and give you half of what we have together, even though I worked hard for it."

"Have you met another woman, Elliott? If you have, she'll never have you. I like our life as it is. Why would I want a divorce? When you need sex you come to my bed. Don't I make you welcome? You can come and go as you please. Have I ever complained?"

Elliott placed both hands flat on his desk. "How can you stand there and really believe what you're saying? I don't love you, Janet, and you don't love me. Sex is just sex. No love between us, just sex. Now that I think of it, I haven't been to your bed in weeks. I can do without you, Janet. Besides, you can do very well without having sex with me. You seem to sleep through it anyway." He picked up the papers again and continued to read.

She flinched, frowning from the cold, calculating chill in his voice. He had never spoken to her that way before. "I'm sorry you feel that way, Elliott. Maybe the last time we made love I wasn't feeling well. We can always give it another try."

"I'm sorry, too, love. But I don't have all night to try and arouse you," he said, without looking at her.

She walked to the door, stopped, and turned around to face him. "I'll be in bed if you need me, Elliott."

"Sleep well, Janet," he yelled behind her.

She just stood and looked at him. Finally she flounced out.

As Janet walked away, Elliott looked at her. The peach-colored dress she was wearing was thin. He could see through it well enough to see that she was wearing a pair of dark-colored bikini panties and no bra. He was certain the talk of sex had excited her, her nipples stood straight up beneath the dress, but how long would she feel that way? Her little tricks no longer excited him, and he had no desire to have sex with her. Their marriage had died years ago. He didn't even remember when it had happened.

"You look lovely today, Ashley, as always."

"Thank you, Elliott," Ashley said, feeling the heat in her cheeks. She pulled the contract from her purse. "It's only a standard contract, but I'll feel better getting an expert's opinion of it. I don't want to be sorry later."

"You're smart. Ask Robert or me go over any of the contracts before you sign them. You never know what some of the small print means, or what it could cost you later if you don't understand. Anyway, I haven't had coffee yet. Why don't we go downstairs and get a cup at Starbucks?"

"Good. I could use a cup, too," she said, and went to the window while Elliott got his jacket.

Elliott watched her from the back. He couldn't take his eyes off Ashley. She was facing the window, her back was straight, her slacks fit every curve of her slender hips, and her red sweater accentuated the size of her breasts. It was getting very difficult to be so close and not touch her. He was so in love with her. *How could she not know?* he wondered. But he couldn't tell her. There were so many things he wanted to do with her: make love to her an entire night, hold her hand when they're just talking, or stroke her soft face with the back of his hand. He sighed and slipped into his jacket. "Ready?"

"Yes, I'm ready."

The sun was warm, and the clouds had disappeared. Century Park Avenue was busy, men and women dressed in suits, carrying briefcases and walking fast past tall green plants and waterfalls in front of the beautiful tall glass buildings.

As they walked across the street, Ashley looked back at the tall gray building she had just left. It had fifteen floors and Elliott's office was on the tenth.

Elliott held her arm as they crossed the street to secure her safety. It seemed so natural, so safe and real to protect the woman he had fallen in love with.

Starbucks was still crowded. Elliott and Ashley selected their coffee and took it back to his office. As they were walking inside, Robert was giving Terri instructions for phone calls that he needed her to make.

Robert turned around as Elliott and Ashley walked inside. "Ashley, it's good to see you. Is Elliott taking good care of you?" he asked, flashing her a smile.

Ashley noticed his manicured nails and shiny briefcase

with his initials engraved in gold. "How are you Robert? And yes, Elliott takes good care of me. Tell Helen I said hello."

"I sure will. Helen has decided not to write a new book this year. So we are going on vacation in a couple of weeks. I should have the case I'm working on wrapped up by then."

He picked up his briefcase off Terri's desk and strolled out the door.

Elliott and Ashley went back into his office. He went over the contract one last time while Ashley sat in front of his desk, watching him concentrate. His brows furrowed in a scowl as though there was something questionable on the contract. Ashley looked at the soft gray hair at his temples and wondered how it would feel against her fingers. His skin was a tan brown; his lips were full and turned up at the corners as he smiled and placed the contract on his desk. Ashley felt as though she was in a dreamlike state while looking at him. She could even imagine him sitting behind his desk in his home office, wearing a T-shirt and shorts. Were his long legs muscular, hairy? And his chest, was it hairy, too? If he kissed her, would she melt in his arms, mold her body into his? God, what was she thinking? But she knew. She had fought the urges since the night they spent together in Vegas and she awoke in his arms, his body close to hers. And God, he's wearing the same cologne.

"There's only one change, have half the payments up front to buy all your materials to fill your orders, Ashley. What if you complete an order for a company that goes out of business before you are paid? You can sell the order, but you won't know how long it takes to recuperate the money spent on supplies."

She nodded in agreement. "Silly me, I only thought of that this morning."

"I can amend it on the second page while you're here."

"Please do, Elliott," she answered.

"Also, I'll keep a copy of the contract here in your file. Can't be too careful, you know." He took the contract down the hall to the paralegal.

When Elliott returned Ashley was facing the wall in front of a law certificate that was framed in dark wood. Looking at her took his breath away. He cleared his throat and took his seat behind his desk.

Ashley sat back down in her chair, too. "Elliott, I'm so excited and a little frightened. This order is like a dream come true. Everything has to be done just right," she said, and exhaled deeply.

She looked so sweet, so delicate; Elliott placed a hand over hers. "You'll do well, darling. If anyone can, it's you, Ashley."

Feeling her heart swelling inside her chest, Ashley couldn't move her hand from under his, but placed her free hand on top of his. It was an intimate, warm, and re-assuring moment for both of them.

The paralegal was back and handed Elliott a white envelope with the contract enclosed.

Driving out of the parking lot, Ashley put on her sunglasses. "What just happened between Elliott and me?" she murmured. "And why does every little thing keep sending me back to him?" Holding his hand made her insides warm, brought alive every feeling that had died on the night Marcus walked out of her life.

Chapter 30

For the next few weeks Ashley was busier than she'd ever been in her entire life. She had rearranged the shop to make more space for three more sewing machines, had shopped for different fabrics and other sewing supplies needed to fill the order. The days were too short for all she had to accomplish, and Ashley worked well into the night.

Doris and Cora had started to work at Ashley's shop and loved it. They had the TV on all day so they wouldn't miss *The View* or *Judge Joe Brown*. Once the court TV shows went off, they turned the TV off. Everyone else wondered how Doris and Cora could work so well and watch TV at the same time. Renee was back and everyone was happy for her help.

Maria was great and everyone loved her. Most evenings she worked by Ashley's side until she and Ashley went home, which was always at night except one particular Thursday. Ashley sent everyone home at four. Her employees had been coming in early with no complaints. They loved Ashley and wanted her business to be successful.

That Thursday evening after everyone had left, as Ashley walked around the shop, she went to the kitchen to see if the coffeemaker was switched off. Ashley usually locked the door as soon as everyone left. But she was overworked, tired, and was in her office when the last person left. She was still in the kitchen when she heard the door open, then close. She went to see who it was and stopped in her tracks. Her eyes blinked, surprised to see him standing there.

"Hello, Ashley. You look wonderful in your tight jeans and T-shirt. Reminds me of the old days when we were younger."

Ashley turned the lights back on and walked into the room, "What do you want, Marcus? I was just closing for the day," she asked, cool and calm, trying to keep her voice level. She would not give him the satisfaction of knowing how nervous she really was. Meeting his stare, she looked him square in his eyes.

"I'm only asking for a few minutes of your time, Ash."

Ashley sat in a chair at one of the machines and motioned for him to sit, too. "Okay, Marcus, what is it?"

Marcus looked around at what had to be a full day's work. Material was stacked high on top of the tables, some spread out to be cut into a pattern. This was the first time he had been in her shop, and he had to admit, he was impressed.

"Lori says you have a big order to fill."

"Yes, but you didn't come to see me about an order, right?" She crossed her legs and waited.

"No. And I was wrong the years I kept you from starting your own business. I can see that now." He took off his jacket and folded it over his lap.

Still waiting for the reason why Marcus was there, Ashley sipped on a Coke that she had opened an hour ago. She looked at Marcus's face, he looked unhappy. And she wondered if it had anything to do with him postponing his wedding.

"I've been thinking a lot, Ash. We have a granddaughter together. You have changed so much in the short time we've been apart. Your appearance is much younger; you've grown into a different person than the woman I married. I was wondering if we could become friends again and see what happens between us? I mean, who knows what could happen?" he asked, as though he was nervous and pleading for his old life back.

Ashley felt her body freezing stiff all over. How long had she waited for this moment, dreamed of it, envisioned it a hundred times in a hundred different ways? Whenever she imagined it, she imagined herself crying and running into his arms. He would be home again in their bed, they would be whispering their love for each other, telling each other how much they were missed, and making love until morning. And now she felt her eyes burning with tears, her heart swelling. Marcus wanted her back.

Ashley sighed and looked him directly in his eyes, but managed to stay calm, and prayed that she would. She kept her hands folded in her lap for fear that she would shake like a leaf and fall apart. She had worked so hard to hate Marcus, worked so hard to forget the life she had had with him before he left her. *For another woman,* she had to keep reminding herself. He had humiliated her, stepped all over her pride, *for another woman.* But now he was back, and he wanted her.

"I can't do that, Marcus. I can't take you back." She stood up and walked to the other end of the room to get her jacket off the hanger.

Marcus stood up. "Wait, Ash. That's all you have to say? We were married for twenty-five years, and that's all you have to say?" He looked disappointed, angry, and overwhelmed by her reply.

Ashley slipped into her jacket and turned around to face him. "We were married for twenty-five years when you walked out on me, but that didn't seem to mean anything to you. Now, I've had a long day and have another one tomorrow. Please leave, Marcus." She picked up her purse and stood at the door. All of a sudden the tension and shock had disappeared, leaving her feeling free of the weight she'd been carrying on her shoulders. And she knew that she had made the right decision. She was free of Marcus and the life they had had together. *Finally.*

"Ash, give me a break. We loved each other once. How can you stand here and turn me down for one mistake? I miss you so much, Ash. Come on, give me a chance." He reached out to grab her but Ashley was too fast and stepped back before he had a hold on her.

"How dare you leave me for another woman and think you can just waltz back into my life again. I'm appalled that you would even try, Marcus. Now, get this straight, I don't need you anymore, Marcus. But I do thank you in a way."

"What do you mean?" He looked confused. She had gotten strong and he hardly knew her any more.

"If you wouldn't have left me, I wouldn't have all this, Marcus." She looked around at what she had accomplished without him. "I would still be in the kitchen cooking your dinner every evening, pleasing your every wish. I had lost my identity, Marcus, and had lost track of who I was before we were married. You said that I wasn't smart enough to have a business of my own. I do thank you for that, from the bottom of my heart." She opened the door for him. "Good night, Marcus."

Marcus started to say more but when he looked into her eyes, he knew it would be a waste of time. She had done well without him, and she was right. She didn't need him. He looked at her one last time and walked out. Once they were outside, Marcus watched her until she was safely inside her car, never looking back at him.

Marcus was shaken, but he liked the new Ashley. He could still see the cold brown eyes when she looked at him as though she was meeting him for the first time. And in a way she had. She was not the old Ashley that he had married.

Once Ashley got home, she saw a red Mustang drive slowly past her house. She stopped, turning to look at the car. She could have sworn the same car was parked across the street from her shop, but who knows. She was so nervous when she walked out, her eyes were probably crossed.

She ran into the bathroom and began spewing until her stomach was empty. Everything she ate gushed out. Once she finished, she brushed her teeth, cupped her hands to fill them with cold water, and splashed it on her face. Taking deep breaths, Ashley wet a small towel and placed it against her face, went to her room, and lay across the bed. Her nerves were eating her alive, but she knew she had made the right decision, and one she would have to live with. Apparently, Marcus's life was not going the way he had planned, so he came running back to her, she thought. How could he possibly think that she could forget all the pain and humiliation he had caused her? Ashley stretched her hands out in front of herself: they were steady.

Ashley poured herself a glass of wine and decided to go into the den. She sipped and heard the doorbell ring. As she started to the door she stopped. "Oh no, it couldn't be Marcus again," she said out loud. But when she opened the door it was Vanessa, and Ashley sighed with relief.

"Hey. I'm surprised to see you home so early. And it's not even dark yet," Vanessa said and looked at her watch. "I was a few blocks away and took a chance that you might be here."

"Come to the den."

Vanessa followed her into the den. Ashley sipped her wine. "Want a glass?"

"Yes, thanks." Vanessa took a seat on the sofa and placed her purse on the table in front of her. "I'm surprised to see you drinking anything but a Coke, Ash." She looked closely at Ashley. "Are you feeling all right? Your eyes are red."

Ashley came back with Vanessa's glass and sat in the leather chair opposite her. "Just an upset stomach." Marcus came to the shop just when I was about to leave. I was checking the coffeemaker in the kitchen to make sure it was off. I heard the door open and close. It was Marcus, just standing there looking around the shop."

Vanessa placed her glass on the table. "You've got to be joking, Ash. No wonder you look ill. What did he want?"

"He wants me back," Ashley said, matter of factly. "You know I told you his wedding was postponed. It may not happen at all," Ashley said, and wiped the moisture off her forehead.

Vanessa laughed out loud. "Get out of here. I can't believe that man." Vanessa threw her hands up in the air. "Well, what did you say to the jerk?"

"Girl, I was so nervous that I came home and had to run into the bathroom to prevent emptying my stomach in the living room. I never let on just how nervous I was."

"And? What answer did you give him, Ash?" Vanessa asked impatiently. "Don't keep me in suspense."

"I told him I couldn't do that. You would have been proud of me. I was so cool and calm, I didn't know myself. I wasn't angry, so I guess that means it's really over. Though it was over the day he walked out, but someplace deep inside, I always wanted him to ask if he could come back, just so I could put him through hell. You know, talk bad before I said yes." She leaned forward and picked up her glass again. "But I wasn't angry. I just wanted him out of my face. He was totally surprised at my answer. I really believe that he thought I would jump at the chance to get him back." She sipped her wine and set the glass on the coffee table. "I've come too far for that. Now, what do you think, Vanessa?"

"Come sit next to me, Ash."

Ashley got up and refilled her glass before going to the sofa. When she sat down, Vanessa turned around to face her.

"You've answered yourself already, Ash, and listening to you, I'll say you made the right decision. Let it go, Ash. You're right, you've come too far to turn around now.

And I wish I could have seen his face. Were you wearing those tight jeans you have on now?"

Ashley looked down as though she had forgotten what she was wearing. "Yes, I was wearing the jeans and T-shirt."

"Good. I hope those nice-fitting jeans made him eat his heart out." They both laughed and hugged each other.

"It was so weird, Vanessa. I thought if this day ever came, I would take him back in a heartbeat. But looking at him, I couldn't imagine it. Those days are gone."

"Are you still in love with him, Ash?"

"I'm not sure anymore." And then as she closed her eyes, Elliott's face appeared in front of her. And she remembered him holding her hand as they rushed across the busy streets in Vegas. What was she feeling for him, and why was she daydreaming about someone she could never have?

"Did you take your contract to Elliott so he could go over it?" Vanessa asked.

"Yes, and as always, he gave me some good advice. He made one change that made a lot of sense."

"Good. He's a good man. Why he stays home, I don't know."

"Maybe it's because he's comfortable there, and maybe he's still in love with his wife."

"You never know," Vanessa answered, and stood up and stretched. She looked at her watch. "I better be going. Gary should be home by the time I get there."

Ashley walked Vanessa to the door.

"Ash, I have to ask again, have you ever noticed the way Elliott looks at you?"

Ashley laughed out loud. "No. I think he looks at me like he does everyone. Why do you ask?"

"I asked because he doesn't look at you as he does everyone. I think he's in love with you. I mean really in love with you. You've never got the feeling that he cares about you?" Vanessa asked, knowing full well that Ashley would be the last to know. Elliott would have to tell her before she knows.

"He's a married man, Vanessa."

"I know he's married, Ash. That's probably the only reason he hasn't said anything to you yet. Anyway, just keep it in mind. Now, when did you start caring about him, Ash?"

Ashley felt exposed as though Vanessa knew exactly what was going on in her head. For a few moments she couldn't get the words out of her mouth. "I didn't say that. I mean . . . I never said I liked Elliott for anything except a friend."

"No, you didn't say so, and you don't have to. We've only been knowing each other forever."

Ashley shook her head. There was no winning with Vanessa. "I guess it started in Vegas. He was so caring. And I would be lying if I said that I hadn't noticed what a good-looking man he is. But that's all, Vanessa. I would never have an affair with him." She folded her arms in front of her, then let them fall to her sides. "It's like we've formed some kind of a bond between us. And it's still there. I could feel it when I went to take him my contract. It wasn't a sexual feeling, just mental. Well, yes, maybe it's that, too. It's strange, isn't it? I really do like him but he will never know it, at least as long as he's married."

"You can control it, Ash, and you are feeling like a woman again. At least you're among the living now. Normal people do have desires. If it's meant to happen it will."

Ashley waved her hand. "Oh, go home to your husband."

Vanessa smiled and sashayed out the door.

When Ashley went back to the den, she took both wineglasses and put them in the dishwasher, opened a can of tomato soup, and pulled out a box of crackers from the cabinet.

Early that night, Ashley showered and crawled into bed. It had indeed been a long, interesting day.

* * *

The weeks went by fast, too fast for Ashley. She worked hard and quickly to complete the order. She was at her shop at five every morning. Maria was there at seven; Joan, Renee, Doris, and Cora at eight-thirty or nine. Doris and Cora made sure that since Ashley wasn't getting enough rest, at least they would see to her eating one full-course meal every day.

Fern and Lee had agreed on paying Ashley for half of the order up front. And the last orders Ashley had gotten were filled a week earlier than scheduled. Having the extra help was what she needed, but how long could she depend on her mother and aunt?

After they had completed Fern's order, Ashley felt like celebrating and invited everyone to her house for dinner that following Sunday. Lori, the baby, and Keith also came. Gary had to go out of town for a couple of days so Vanessa went alone.

Ashley had dinner catered in from M & M's soul food restaurant. She played music and everyone chatted about the order they had filled. Helen and Robert came over and brought her roses.

Ashley had gone into the kitchen and Lori went behind her.

"Mom, Dad and I had a long talk last night."

"Oh. How is your dad?" Ashley asked, and wondered if he had said anything about her.

"He's good, but sounded a little disappointed because you wouldn't forgive him and take him back."

"And he discussed that with you?" Ashley was taking more glasses from the cabinet.

"Yes. I'm old enough, Mom."

Ashley was facing the sink and turned around to face Lori. She wondered what was she thinking. "What do you think about the answer I gave him?"

"I think it's strictly up to you, Mom. I just want you

two happy, either together or apart. That's all I want for both of you."

"Thank you, Lori. But it will have to be apart." Ashley picked up the dishtowel and dried her hands, folded the towel, and placed it back on the counter.

"I understand, Mom. Now, why don't we join the rest of the party," Lori said, and wrapped her arm around Ashley's waist.

When Ashley and Lori went back into the den, Maria was playing with Callie.

"Maria told Lori that she was very happy about working with you, Ashley," Helen said. She and Ashley took a seat on the sofa. Everyone else was either in the dining room or the kitchen refilling their plates with food.

"Maria is very good, Helen. But now both of us know how much work it is to run a business, and the work you have to put into it. We are thinking of going into business together, and I'm delighted. I have the sewing machines and the place, and Maria has the knowledge, besides, she works her ass off. I've also been thinking about renting a larger place and using the front as a dress shop and the back to make the clothes. And of course I'll need to hire a salesgirl. But it will be a while before I expand that far."

"You have a good head for business, Ashley. And I knew you and Maria would get along well." Helen looked at her watch. "On the way home, Robert promised Elliott that he would drop a file off at his house. So we'll have to leave soon."

"Elliott helped me with my contract. The first time I met Elliott and his wife was at your house. I wasn't too impressed with her. She had a snobbish attitude," Ashley said, and was sorry as soon as the words came out her mouth. But it was too late to take back what she had said. It was true, so why should she take it back?

Helen smiled. "Let me tell you about her, Ashley. She's a country girl who came from a very poor family. She has three sisters and has more than any of them, so she thinks she is better than they are. Elliott gave her whatever she wanted. Well, at least he used to. Frankly, I don't think he gives a damn anymore."

"Why do you suppose he stays in the marriage if he doesn't love her?" Ashley asked.

"From what Robert told me, he has asked her more than once for a divorce. She's threatened to take everything the poor man has worked for. She called me a few weeks ago but I didn't return her call. I'm cutting all ties with that depraved bitch . . . oops, my husband has scolded me about my mouth," she said with two fingers against her lips. "Curse words just seem to flow out my mouth. My late sister, Harriet, hated it."

"Helen, it's time to go, darling," Robert said as he stepped down into the den.

"Coming, love. We had a nice time, Ashley. Maybe we can continue this conversation at a later date. Anyway, congratulations." Helen followed her husband out the door.

It was late evening, and everyone had left except Doris, Cora, Keith, and Lori. Doris was holding Callie in her arms while Lori helped Ashley in the kitchen. After the paper plates and cups were taken outside and placed into the trash can, the five of them chatted about Ashley's future plans for her business.

"Mother, can I see you in my bedroom for a minute?" Ashley asked.

Wondering about the somber expression on Ashley's face, Doris followed her to the bedroom.

"Mother, have a seat," Ashley said and sat on the bed beside Doris. "You haven't said anything about my invitation to Jason's wedding or the day he came over for lunch. How do you feel about it?"

Doris had wondered when the conversation would come up. She didn't like the idea of Ashley associating with the man but what could she say? After all, he was her brother.

"There's nothing much for me to say, Ashley. He was rude and mean at the reading of Daniel's will. I just don't want him to hurt you again. I hope he's becoming a brother to you because he wants to from the goodness of his heart. You know nothing about that man, Ashley."

"I know, Mother. But I really believe he's sincere. I'm the only real family he has left. You will always be my real mother, and I wouldn't do anything to hurt you. Knowing that Jason and I have the same mother would never change my love for you. You are my real mother," she repeated, "but he is my brother. I just want to give it a chance and see if it works out for us, if we can really be sister and brother. Can you understand that, Mother?" Ashley played with Callie as she waited for Doris's answer.

Doris held Ashley's hand in hers. "If that's the way you feel, I hope the best for you and Jason." She wiped a tear from her eyes and thought about Daniel. This is what he would have wanted for both of his children. Doris had wished a thousand times that she could have birthed Ashley instead of Ruby. But it's too late for that now. Ashley was hers and she was very happy to know that Ashley still felt the same for her. And Doris knew they had become even closer.

"Grandma, are you sure you will be all right?" Lori asked, as she watched Doris hold the baby against her shoulder so she would burp. "She cries when she's sleepy."

"Look, I was taking care of babies before you were born, you know. Who do you think took care of you when your parents went on vacations? It was me," Doris pointed out to Lori.

"And now it's two of us," Cora interrupted. "It's good having a baby around this house."

"Okay. Come on Keith. We'll be late and Mom wouldn't like that at all." They started to walk out and

Lori stopped again. "Grandma, don't forget to place her milk in the refrigerator."

Doris laughed and waved her hand. "Get out of here, girl."

When Keith and Lori got to the Radisson Huntley Hotel in Santa Monica, Ashley was parking her car. They waited so they could be seated together.

"Your mom looks beautiful, Lori. And I'm noticing for the first time, you look a lot like her." Keith held Lori's hand as they waited for Ashley.

Ashley was dressed in a light blue dress that she had made and a pair of shoes the same color. Her pearl earrings dangled against her ears, and her hair was swept up in back.

"You two look nice today," Ashley said, and smiled at the young couple who complemented each other.

"I can't wait to meet my new uncle, and I hope I don't cry. You know I cry at weddings," Lori said.

"Cry?" Ashley said. "You don't even know the couple yet. What a beautiful day for a wedding." The sun was warm and everyone was dressed for summer. They passed the room where the reception would be held. "Come on, the wedding is in the garden. I know where it is because Marcus and I were here for a wedding two years ago," Ashley said, and led the way.

At least one hundred people were seated in the garden. Jason was talking to his best man when he saw Ashley and excused himself.

"So, this must be my beautiful niece, Lori?" Jason asked, and extended his hand.

"Yes, it is," Lori answered. "And this is my husband, Keith."

The two men shook hands. "All three of you look so nice, Ashley. Diane can't wait to meet you. I told her all about you," he said proudly.

"Good. We can meet after the wedding. Are you nervous?" Ashley asked.

"You just can't imagine how nervous I really am. Come on, I have a seat up front for you three. After all, you are my family." Jason seemed so happy and Ashley wondered if she would cry at this wedding. She wanted to laugh as she thought of what she had told Lori about crying. Could it be that coming to a wedding so soon after her divorce explained the despondency she was beginning to feel? *Okay, girl,* she thought to herself. *You can do this, you can smile and pretend you are happy for this special day. If not for yourself, do it for your brother.*

They took their seats and twenty minutes later six bridesmaids were marching in beautiful pink dresses into the center of the patio. The music started to play, and the bride walked in. Ashley had to admit, she was undeniably a beautiful woman.

After the wedding ceremony everyone went inside the hotel and took their seats at the tables. Again, Jason had selected a table in the front for Ashley and her guests. And before dinner was served, Jason and the bride came over to Ashley's table and included her in all the pictures. It was as though they had been like brother and sister all their lives. She met Diane's family, who were all friendly, including Diane's Uncle Matt, who couldn't seem to take his eyes off Ashley.

Ashley danced with Matt, twice. When she returned to her table, Lori and Keith teased her. It was clear that Matt was attracted to Ashley.

Before Ashley left, Matt gave her his business card. But by the time she had gotten home, the business card, left in her dress pocket, was forgotten.

Chapter 31

Monday, business was as usual. Ashley had ideas for other dresses she wanted to design. Joan needed a day off, and Renee was hemming a pair of slacks.

Maria helped Ashley and gave her suggestions that would be profitable for her business. Doris and Cora weren't needed every day, but Ashley did use them three days a week.

Ashley was folding some material when Maria told her that Fern was on the phone. Ashley hadn't talked to Fern since the last order was picked up. "Hello, Fern. How is business?" Ashley asked.

"It's all good, Ashley. The order came out beautifully, but I think we need more blouses. Everyone loves them."

"Which ones, Fern?"

"The ones with the wide-flared sleeves. They were a big hit. I'm almost out. How about forty blouses in different colors? Maybe ten of them can be made with printed material. I'll leave the selection of colors to you, Ashley. Oh, and we need twenty of the silk dresses. The ones with the slanted pockets on each side."

"That's no problem," Ashley answered.

"We'll be doing lots of business together, Ashley. I'll put a check in the mail tomorrow."

"It's all good, Fern." Ashley hung up and turned to face Maria.

"Looks like we did a good job," Maria said. "I'm going

across the street and buy a couple of bran muffins. Want a cup of coffee?"

"Yes," Ashley answered. "I could use a cup."

"What about you, Renee?"

"No thanks, Maria." Renee picked up her purse. "I'll be here early tomorrow morning to make the time up."

"Don't worry about it, Renee. You told me last week that you would leave early today," Ashley said.

"I'm going to miss Miss Doris and Miss Cora bringing us food every day," Maria said, and pulled out her wallet. "Both of them are so nice to me."

"Thanks, Maria. I miss them, too," Ashley admitted. "But they will be here tomorrow and feed us again three days a week, and every day next week to help fill Fern's new order." Ashley laughed and placed the folded material on the cutting table in front of her. "I've put on about six pounds, too. So you know what that means?"

"Yeah. You have to run an extra mile in the mornings to get it off," Maria said.

Maria left to buy coffee and muffins. When she returned, Ashley was on the phone. They worked side by side that day, and at four Ashley locked up the shop.

Ashley was tired when she got home. She had a slight headache and wondered if her blood pressure had gone up. Her doctor had taken her off the medication, but lately, she had gone off her diet. Now she had to start running again and get herself back in shape. She undressed, looked in the mirror, and pinned up her hair. It was time to get it trimmed again, she thought.

After Ashley got out the shower, she looked in the refrigerator and grabbed a Coke, went to the den, and flopped down in her favorite chair. Now she understood why Marcus called it his chair. It was comfortable. She turned up the control so she could lift her legs, her arms locked around her knees.

Ashley closed her eyes and remembered her conversation with Helen about Elliott's marriage. Why doesn't he leave? she wondered. But now she realized there wasn't love in her marriage either, only an illusion that she believed in.

She felt Elliott's arm around her waist, his lips warm against hers, his tongue the taste of sweet wine as he kissed her until she was dizzy. Piece by piece, her clothing dropped to the floor, circling her bare feet until she was naked. He guided her to a bedroom that she had never seen before; the scent of his cologne made her want to taste his naked body. They made love and Ashley couldn't get enough of him, his taste, the feel of his hands, so warm against her.

The phone rang and woke Ashley with a start. "Where am I?" she asked out loud. She ran her fingers through her hair and wondered how many times the phone had rung before she woke up.

"Hello," she whispered, still remembering the dream she had had before the phone woke her. It was Doris. "Oh, Mother, how are you?"

"I'm all right, Ashley. You sound as though you are out of breath. Did you just come in?"

Ashley heard the concern in Doris voice. "I'm out of breath. But no, I didn't just come in. I had fallen asleep in the chair. Glad you woke me, Mother." She sighed. But no, she wasn't glad. The dream was so real, as beautiful as the love stories she read in novels. And for a moment she wondered if it could really be so beautiful. "I still need you and Aunt Cora tomorrow, and every day next week. I'll see you tomorrow, Mother." She looked at the clock; she had slept for an hour.

It had gotten dark and she closed the blinds and sat back in the chair, but this time she did watch the news. Unable to concentrate, she got up and got a glass of warm milk. She was still thinking of the dream she had had of Elliott, and she was still sleepy, but the milk would help. It was possible that being alone made her have the ridiculous dream. But was it really the loneliness, or was she falling in love with Elliott?

The next morning after a good night's sleep, Ashley felt rested and laughed as she stood in the shower and thought of the dream she had had the night before. She had to forget, put it out of her mind. It was just a ridiculous dream, that's all.

Maria was already there with bran muffins and coffee from Starbucks. She was threading the sewing machine when Ashley walked in. "You look fresh. Did you have a good night's sleep?"

"Yes, I slept soundly last night." Ashley passed Maria and took her purse to her office. The fragrant coffee met her as she went back to the sewing room. "The coffee smells delicious. Thanks for buying me a cup." She smiled as she looked in the big beautiful brown eyes. "I got an idea." Ashley placed both hands on her hips with a gleam in her eyes.

"What?" Maria asked, and placed her cup down on the sewing machine in front of her.

"It's hot, but it's a beautiful day. Why don't we shop for material today? We were stuck in here when we had that big order to fill, and you were so helpful to me, Maria. So let's lock up and go shopping when we finish. I'll call Mother, and they can stay home today. She and Aunt Cora can finish what they started day before yesterday. Besides, Joan and Renee won't be in today. Today is the one-year anniversary of their mother's death. They want to place flowers on her grave. But we'll have to work like hell tomorrow."

Ashley and Maria finished the muffins and coffee, and went shopping until three-thirty. Then they went back to the shop and went home at four-thirty.

Gee, where did the year go so fast? Elliott wondered, flipping the pages of the calendar back to September.

The days were long and warm, but he had a lot to do. After Helen's book signing, she and Robert would get a midnight flight and go on vacation. Elliott had inherited two of Robert's cases. Janet and her sister were on a seven-day cruise. But what else was new, Elliott thought. She was always gone. Lately, he was beginning to like it that way. There were no more arguments between them, no more coming home to an empty house and getting angry about it. Elliott wasn't sure when it happened, but he looked forward to Janet going away.

Elliott walked through his house, then stopped and stared out the kitchen window, hands in pockets as he looked at the view up the hill from his backyard. It was Saturday, another weekend he was alone. Why had he bought a four-bedroom house? There were no children, no animals, just he and Janet in a marriage with no love between them.

In the beginning they were so much in love. And Janet actually wanted children. But as the years passed, she found one excuse after another, and had never gotten pregnant. So she spent money ridiculously. Maybe it was her way of buying happiness that he couldn't give her. Now she doesn't associate with any of their friends, such as Robert and Helen. Just a year ago she attended a dinner party at Helen's house. But now she makes excuses to stay away.

Elliott needed a distraction from the case that he was working on. He wanted to hear himself laugh out loud, feel alive again. Such a beautiful day, and he was alone. Whenever he thought of happiness, he thought of Ashley. He shook his head, pushed his hands back into his pockets and went back to his office. But instead of going back to work, he decided to go to Helen's book signing, grab a bite to eat, and be back early.

* * *

Ashley was humming a song in the shower. This was a Saturday that she had decided to do whatever she wanted to. She didn't get out of bed until ten, had a full-course breakfast, and read half of Helen's new novel. How she comes up with the plots she writes, one would never know, Ashley thought. In novels you fall in love, get married, and live happily ever after. Well, not in this lifetime. She stepped out the shower, water dripping down her long legs as she wrapped a large white towel around her wet, lean body. She pulled the shower cap off her head and shook her hair lose.

In the kitchen, Ashley set two of her plants in the sink and ran water on them. She picked up the morning paper and sat outside on the patio. The warmth felt good, rays of sun streaming their way onto the shaded patio. Her bathrobe was short and she could feel the warmth against her legs. As she read the paper she wondered what she would do the rest of the day.

Ashley turned the page, and saw a dress on sale at Nordstrom's and couldn't resist wondering how it would look if she made it, converting it from a summer to a long winter dress, and cut lower at the neck. But she wouldn't even think of making it until she finished with Fern's order.

It was four when Ashley decided to go and have Helen sign her book. Besides, it was an excuse to get out the house, and not stay inside placing sleeves in a dress or hemming a pair of slacks. Maybe on her way home she would drop in on Doris and Cora, or even catch a movie at Magic Johnson's theater.

Still humming, she took her time and dressed in a sleeveless red dress. She combed her hair back into a French roll, and put round gold earrings in her ears. Ashley stood in front of the full mirror and turned side to side. There, she was ready to go.

* * *

As usual, the line was long, but Ashley didn't mind. She liked the Beverly Center Mall. As the line slowly moved, she was finally inside the bookstore. Helen looked beautiful in the purple dress that Ashley had made for her vacation.

"You look very pretty in red, Ashley," Helen whispered, as she signed her book.

"And you look equally pretty in your purple dress." After Ashley's book was signed, she saw Elliott, and her stare was fixed on his face. And he stopped talking to Robert as his eyes met hers.

Elliott saw her walking in his direction. Deep inside, he was hoping she would be at the book signing but he didn't dare call her. As she got closer, he couldn't move or look away. She looked so young, her eyes were smiling, and her red lipstick was glossy and made her lips look full and sexy. God, he wanted to kiss her until the lipstick was gone. It had been so long since he ached to be with a woman, ached so much that it hurt.

"Good to see you, Ashley," Robert said, and kissed her on her cheek.

"Same here," Elliott said, and casually embraced her.

"Helen always brings in the big crowds, but her writing is extraordinary. I was reading her book this morning," Ashley said, and flashed Elliott a dazzling smile.

"Yes, my wife is good." Robert turned to Elliott. "Now, Elliott, do you have any questions about the two cases I gave you?"

"No. They're pretty straightforward. And the temp we have for a receptionist seems to be catching on quickly."

"What happened to your receptionist?" Ashley asked. They moved to the corner so that customers could pass.

"She's on vacation, too," Elliott answered. "But she'll be back next week."

Ashley nodded, and as she looked at Elliott she remembered the dream. It was so clear, as though it was today. She remembered the slow smile in the corner of his mouth when he looked at her naked body, his warm hands gently touching her, kissing her and pulling her closer. Stop! Why can't I forget? She turned her head as though he knew what she was thinking.

"Well, I just wanted to get my book signed and wish you and Helen well on your vacation," Ashley said. Maybe this wasn't such a good idea after all, she pondered.

"Thanks for coming, Ashley," Robert said with a smile.

"I'll walk you to your car, Ashley. Wouldn't want someone to grab you and take you away," Elliott teased.

The parking lot was full, and they had to take the elevator to P-3. Elliott unlocked the door for Ashley. She got in and rolled the window down. "I appreciate you walking me out, Elliott."

Her arm was on the door and he touched it. "My pleasure."

Ashley turned the key in the ignition three times, but her car wouldn't start. "I wonder what's wrong? It started right up when I left."

"Try again," Elliott suggested.

Ashley tried again, but all they heard was the turning of the key.

"I think you need a new battery, Ashley. You want to call the automobile club or can I take you home?"

She sighed and pulled the key out. "I don't really feel like standing around this late in the day. You mind taking me home?"

"I would like nothing better. Besides, I haven't anything to do today." He smiled, opened the door and helped her out the car. "Come on, my car is right on the other side of the parking lot."

As Ashley and Elliott walked to his car there was another crowd getting on the elevator. Ashley saw some people carrying Helen Graham's novel.

Driving to Ashley's house, the weather was still warm. Ashley looked across at Elliott. It seemed they were always thrown together and left alone. But as she looked at him his smile softened, and she was sure her heart stopped.

"Make a right at the corner, Elliott, then a left at the next light," she instructed.

"How are you going to get your car tomorrow, Ashley?"

"I'll call my mother and aunt." She smiled. "They do everything together. I'll call the auto club and have them meet me there. Here, you can park in the driveway."

Elliott stopped the car, hating that their time together had ended. He would settle for just talking and looking at her.

"I have a bottle of wine in the refrigerator, Elliott. Would you like to come in and have a drink with me?" Ashley asked, hoping he would say yes. It was still early, and she felt lonely and wanted someone to talk to. The weekends were the worst because she was home and the house seemed so big, so lonely with no one to share it. Sometimes she went back to the shop and worked.

"I would love to, Ashley. Nobody's waiting for me at home." He didn't mean to say that but because it was true and he had gotten used to it, it tumbled out so naturally.

They walked inside; Ashley excused herself and went to her bedroom. When she came out Elliott was sitting on the sofa in the living room.

"You have a beautiful home, Ashley. It has your touch."

"Thanks. Let's go into the den and I'll open the patio doors." She led the way, he followed, and stopped at the glass patio doors as she opened them.

"Nice." He stepped outside while Ashley went to the kitchen and got two crystal glasses from the cabinet and the bottle of Chardonnay from the refrigerator. As she placed it on the coffee table, Elliott walked back inside.

"Have a seat." She motioned for him to sit on the sofa

next to her. "What do you do on the weekends, Elliott?" she asked, handing him his glass.

"First, what are we going to drink to?" He held his glass up.

Ashley picked up hers. "What about a long friendship?" Their glasses clicked, and they sipped their wine.

"Now, what I do on weekends is work, stay home, and watch TV because I never get to watch it during the week. When I get home, I'm either in my study working or reading a book. It's boring, but it's my life. What do you do, Ashley?"

"I've been bringing work home but this weekend I promised myself that I would read, relax, and do nothing. Sometimes I go and see my granddaughter."

"I still can't believe you are a grandmother, but you're a beautiful grandmother."

She felt her cheeks burn with embarrassment. She wasn't used to hearing a man compliment her by saying she was beautiful. "Tell me about your childhood, Elliott. Were you born here?"

He refilled their glasses. "Yes, I was born here. My mom and dad moved here from New Orleans when she was six months pregnant with me. I had one brother who was hit by a car when he was eight years old. I was six at the time but I can remember."

"I'm so sorry." Ashley squeezed his hand.

"My parents didn't have any more children. I think my dad wanted another one, but my mom didn't. After my brother died she went to night school, then went to work. Boy, it was a long time ago but I think of him almost every day."

"Well, I told you before that I was an only child until now," Ashley said. "In a way, even though I know my brother, it's like I'm still an only child."

"You seem to have had a happy childhood."

"I did. Everyone in my old neighborhood knew each other."

"I had lots of friends and I played football in high school, majored in law. My parents still live in Carson where I grew up. They've seen kids grow from babies to adults, and now they see their kids. Every time I go over there my dad tries to make me remember someone that was there when I was a kid. That's the story of my life." He smiled as he watched Ashley.

"Are you hungry, Ashley? We can go out and grab a bite to eat."

"I can always fix something here, Elliott. Are you hungry?"

"No. But if I get hungry, I'll let you know."

"I'm glad you came over tonight, Elliott. I didn't feel like being alone. I lived at home with my parents before Marcus and I were married. Until Marcus left, I never lived alone. But I think I'm doing all right by myself." She relaxed and curled her legs underneath her.

"You know, Ashley, my wife and I share the same house, but in a way, I live alone just as you do. When you have no one to share your dreams with, or talk to about how your day went, even complain about something, you're alone."

"I hadn't looked at it that way. Come on in the kitchen with me so we can see what's in the refrigerator to snack on."

They went into the kitchen and Ashley got a plate and crackers out of the cabinet. Elliott got a spoon and knife from the drawer.

"I remember the early years of my marriage when I used to help my wife cook. The kitchen was almost too small for two but I would get right in there and help," he said, handing her the knife to slice the cheese. He picked up a small flowerpot that was sculpted into a black woman wearing a black-and-white flowered dress and hat, smiling with full red lips. "This is cute," Elliott complimented, and gently set it back on the corner of the sink.

"I remember in the early years of my marriage when Marcus would get home before me and surprise me by cooking dinner. But before he left me, sometimes he'd have dinner before he came home, which means I ate alone."

They both sighed, as each thought about the happier years in their lives.

They were standing close together, and their eyes met and locked. It seemed so natural and yet beyond belief that at the same time they freed their hands of what they were holding, took a step forward, and with their eyes still locked his arms slowly wrapped around her waist and her arms around his neck. Their lips touched, their hearts racing, and their arms locking tighter as though they would never let go, never be apart again. And the only sounds were their hearts beating rapidly inside their chests.

They had gotten to the bedroom, and Ashley held back and looked at him. She wanted to see Elliott's face, not imagine it was Marcus. No, this was a man that she'd wondered about for months. What would it feel like to be held in his arms? Not the way he held her in Vegas, but to make love to her. It was wrong, she knew, but just this once she had to know, to experience his touch, his kiss. Just one night of love that would be bliss and explode on a hot, sultry night, like now, like tonight. Just this once . . .

For a moment Elliott started to step away. *Have I frightened her, will she kick me out?* But his smiled softened as she placed her hands around his neck, her warm lips brushing against his face and neck.

Sending chills up his back, Elliott cupped her face in his hands. "I love you, Ashley. I've always loved you," he whispered. His eyes were blazing on her lips, and he kissed her hard and passionately, feeling her respond. He felt her gently pull back and stepped out of her shoes; her red dress slid off her shoulders and down her hips. His eyes met hers and blazed with desire. He watched her step over her dress as she stood in red lace panties, and he saw her honey-brown skin and perfectly round curves, just as he had envisioned her.

She lay on her back, waiting for him, wanting . . . her body tingling with anticipation.

Elliott was naked, splendidly and beautifully naked. He lay beside her and cupped her face with exquisite tenderness, his lips moving down her neck, working swiftly, feverishly, draining her of strength as his tongue parted her lips to plunge inside and taste the wine on her breath. He kissed her breast, electrifying her hard, brown nipple that stood up like a rosebud. Then, as he shifted to one side, he took the other sensitive breast into his mouth and moaned, feeling the urgency building inside him, a fierce hunger, a desperate need to be inside her as he felt her twist and turn until she was underneath him.

Feeling Elliott's warm mouth on her nipple, Ashley's breath came out in a low moan. This passion was one she had never felt before, had never needed so urgently, and she was shocked at her brazen movements. She wanted him to take her even higher, make her float deliriously into a different world where she had never been. And he did, where just the two of them would always be together in their souls and their memories. There was no interference, and no other world but theirs. Just the two of them, a secret they would share and take with them wherever they were. For the first time, she would take what she wanted, needed. And for the first time she felt sexy, beautiful, and she wanted Elliott to have it.

Her body was scalding hot as she clung to him, welcoming him. She lurched upward, only to feel him thrust inside her, lifting her as he moved deeper, drawn into her pleasure.

Panting, she lay in his arms feeling the soft, cool

breeze over their naked bodies. Their eyes closed, and they fell into a deep, peaceful sleep.

It was morning, and the birds were singing on the window ledge. Ashley was the first to wake up. She opened her eyes and closed them again. The sun was too bright. Elliott stirred; his feet touched her leg. She remembered the night before and her eyes blinked wide open.

Ashley turned slightly and looked over at him, but he was still asleep. God, what had she done? she thought. Was it the wine? No. She knew better. It wasn't the wine, and she wasn't making any excuses. It was her, her body and her needs, and her love for Elliott. What would she say when he awoke?

Ashley quietly got out of bed and tiptoed into the shower in the other bedroom. She didn't want to wake him until she could think of something to say. One thing she knew for certain, they could never be alone again.

As Ashley stood in the shower she heard a voice, Marcus's voice. *You hated me for leaving you for another woman, and you slept with a married man. Yes, Miss good, wholesome Ashley, look what you've done.* Ashley shook her head from side to side. "No," she whispered, "Marcus will never know." She stepped out the shower, dried off, and went to the kitchen to make coffee, and took two cups from the cabinet.

The aroma from the steaming coffee tingled at his nose. Elliott dressed and went to the kitchen, where he found Ashley wearing a short white bathrobe.

Standing at the window, her hair lay on the back of her neck. Ashley heard Elliott and turned around to face him. Her eyes were sad, her pouted bottom lip quivered.

The moment he saw her face, he knew she regretted what had happened between them the night before.

"Good morning. Why don't you have a seat," she said. "Cream and sugar in your coffee?"

"No. I take it black." He watched as she filled the cup to the brim. Her bathrobe stopped above the knees, and she was barefoot, with no makeup, and her hair was brushed back. But she was still a lovely sight, Elliott thought. A man could easily get used to seeing her in the early mornings. "How are you feeling this morning, Ashley?" Elliott asked tentatively.

Ashley sat in the chair opposite him, forcing a smile. Damn, he looked sexy so early. His deep voice reminded her of last night and she felt a tremor down her back. "I'm all right, Elliott."

"How do you really feel, Ashley? You don't look happy at all."

"I'm not exactly unhappy. But I'm old enough to know what I did last night was wrong. It can never happen again." Looking at the hurt in his eyes, she laid her hand on top of his.

"I'm sorry, Ashley. And it's not what *you* did was wrong. It's what *we* did. You didn't do it alone."

She nodded in agreement. "It was beautiful, Elliott." Just as it was in her dream, she remembered. But she couldn't tell him that.

He placed his cup on the table. The coffee was just the way he loved it, strong and black. "I was lying when I said that I was sorry. And I don't want you to feel guilty, Ashley. We knew what we wanted, and needed."

"I know, but it doesn't make it right, Elliott." She slightly pulled her hand away. She knew that she would weaken and lead him back into her bed. "Are you hungry? I could cook breakfast."

"And after breakfast?" he asked. "No, I better leave now while it's safe for both of us." He took her hand and led her into the living room. They stood at the door. "You are a beautiful woman, Ashley. If only things were different."

Ashley looked up at him. Wasn't that what most married men would say? *If only things were different. If only we would have met earlier.* She was not the kind of woman to date a married man. If she couldn't have first place, she could never settle for second place in any man's life.

"If only things were different, we wouldn't be standing here," she said, and kissed him on the cheek.

Elliott took her hand and placed it against his lips. He looked her straight in her eyes. "Do you love me, Ashley?"

She was so aghast—her eyes widened and she opened her mouth to speak but no words emerged. "What?" Her intake of breath sounded like a hiss.

"Do you love me? A simple yes or no will do." He took a step closer, and she took a step back.

"What good would it do for me to love you, Elliott? There's nothing either one of us can do about it."

"I love you, Ashley. And if you love me, then maybe there is something that can be done about it."

Her legs were weakening under her, she wasn't sure if she could stand much longer. And she felt as though her life depended on her answer. "Yes, yes, I do love you. But—"

"No buts. One day I'll come back. One day soon, Ash. When I ring your doorbell again, it will be you and me. No one else, Ashley. Just the two of us." She opened her mouth to speak but Elliott placed two fingers against her lips and kissed her on the cheek before she could say another word. He walked out the door, closing it quietly behind him.

Ashley stared at the closed door until she heard his car drive out the driveway.

She made her bed and sat on the edge with her elbows rested on her thighs, both hands covering her face. Then she looked at the clock on the nightstand; it was still early, only eight o'clock. Gary was out of town and she knew Vanessa was always up early. She went to the kitchen and poured a second cup of coffee and went back to her bedroom. Lying back across her bed, she thought of Elliott. Why did he ask if she loved him? In spite of everything, she had to tell him the truth. She did love him. But he said he loved her, too. Did he really? And what difference does it make?

Ashley reached over to her nightstand and grabbed the phone. "Vanessa, are you up?"

"Yes, Ash. I just got out the shower. What are you doing?"

"Nothing. I need a ride to the Beverly Center. My car is there. Elliott brought me home from Helen's book signing yesterday." She looked at the side of the bed where he had slept.

"I can take you. Let me slip into a pair of jeans and I'll be over."

"Good. I have to get dressed myself."

"Look, I have no food in my refrigerator and I'm hungry. What do you have to eat?"

Ashley laughed. "I'll have breakfast cooked by the time you get here." Ashley hung up and went to the kitchen.

Standing in front of the refrigerator, Ashley opened the freezer and pulled out packages of breakfast sausage and hash browns, along with a can of biscuits and three eggs from the refrigerator. *Just what I need for my cholesterol, but at least the sausage is turkey. And one egg shouldn't harm me.*

She went back to her bedroom and slipped into a pair of red jogging pants and a red sleeveless T-shirt.

By the time Vanessa arrived, Ashley only had to scramble the eggs. Vanessa looked at her and knew instantly that something was bothering her. She could always tell because Ashley's brows squinted together into a scowl.

"Are you worried about your car, Ash? If you are there's no need to be. You can call the auto club when we're almost there. It's probably just your battery," Vanessa said as she helped herself to a cup of coffee and noticed two empty cups in the sink.

"It's not the car." Ashley placed their plates on the table and took her seat.

"Looks delicious, too, Ash," Vanessa said, and sprinkled black pepper on her soft scrambled eggs. "So, what's bothering you, honey?" she asked between bites.

"I did a stupid thing last night."

Vanessa placed her folk on her plate when she heard Ashley's voice tremble. "What did you do, Ash?"

"Like I said on the phone, my car wouldn't start and Elliott brought me home." Ashley cleared her throat. "We slept together and he didn't leave until this morning. Right before I phoned you."

At first Vanessa choked, coughed, then dropped her fork on her plate and laughed out loud. "Get out of here. You did a wonderfully stupid thing, if you ask me. Damn, I'll bet he's good, too. He has large hands and feet, and you know what's said about that. But you can't always judge by it. I slept with a man that wore a size twelve shoe and was no longer than my middle finger. And I slept with one that had short, fat fingers. Girl, I thought that man was pulling out a slab of salami. Oh, and he wore a size eight shoe. You never can tell these days." Vanessa laughed out loud again.

"Vanessa, it's not that funny, not funny at all, under the current circumstances."

"Are you regretting it, Ash? And you didn't answer my question."

"Well yes! I mean, no. Damn, Vanessa, it was wrong but I can't say that I regret all of it. Oh, I'm so confused." She looked at Vanessa's face and a smile jerked at her mouth. "Yes, he's all that and more, much more." This time Ashley's smile was wide.

"I know how you feel. You regret the fact that he's married. But you two were good together and that's what you don't regret. Right?"

"Yes, that's what I mean. And it doesn't matter, I'm the one that's here alone and he's the one that has a wife.

The holidays, my birthday, and all the important days, Elliott will be home with Janet, his wife, and his work, he'll never have time for me," she said remorsefully. "I should have never let it happen."

Vanessa sighed. "You're absolutely right. But you only made a human mistake. You just got caught up in the moment, and this hot, sultry weather just makes you want to tear off your clothes, desire flares, builds up, and flows deep inside—"

"Stop it, you fool," Ashley, said, laughing for the first time that morning. She was glad that she called Vanessa to come over.

"At least I made you laugh. So what are you going to do about it, Ash?"

Ashley threw both hands up in midair. "Nothing. Absolutely nothing. Just make sure it doesn't happen again. What else can I do?" She opened her mouth to tell Vanessa what Elliott had said about ringing her doorbell one day but changed her mind. What good would it do to tell anyone? False hope, no, she wouldn't put herself through that kind of drama. But she would never let it happen again.

They were sitting at the table, finished with breakfast. "I'll put the dishes in the dishwasher and we can leave," Ashley said.

"Sure, don't rush," Vanessa remarked. "I'm going to see Lori one day this week, Ash. I bought the baby the prettiest dress yesterday. It's all white trimmed in pink. She'll look like a doll in it."

"She's growing. I usually stop by during the week on my way home. I just can't see her enough."

They were standing in front of the sink and with a frown across her forehead, Ashley seemed preoccupied.

"Ash, you're much too hard on yourself. Elliott is a handsome and nice man. From the beginning you two have had some sort of magnetism that keeps pulling you two together. That man's been in love with you from the first time you met."

"Vanessa, it's just that Elliott will always be with me." She placed her hand against her heart. "I'll always want a man I can't have. Anyway, I'm going to comb my hair so we can get out of here. Enough about Elliott."

Vanessa watched Ashley amble out the kitchen. A man that Ashley would always want and can't have, as she put it. But with Elliott being the man, she wasn't sure about that. No, she wasn't sure about that at all.

Chapter 32

For the next few weeks, Ashley threw herself into her work, went to church twice with Doris and Cora, had dinner at Lori's house, and went to a movie alone. She worked vigorously, drawing and creating new designs for a fashion show that she decided to do as a way of marketing her new creations. Maria designed four blouses for the show.

With her profits and some of the money that she had inherited from her father, she decided to have the fashion show at the Marriott Hotel on Century Boulevard near the airport. She had even hired another person, anticipating that her business would increase after the show.

It was Sunday, the day of the show, and Ashley was so nervous that her stomach ached. She wore an eggshell-colored pantsuit and matching open-toe heels. Her hair was pulled back, and she wore white pearl earrings each with a diamond in the middle. She looked like a breath of fresh air sweeping through the room.

The tickets were thirty-five dollars each, including lunch. She used Helen, Vanessa, Lori, Lynn, and Maria as models. Joan and Renee helped with all the preparations, such as selecting the food and centerpiece for each table. There was an open bar for drinks.

The fashion show started at precisely one o'clock, and the room was completely filled with people Ashley knew and some she didn't know. Doris and Cora had a table in the front. Ashley invited Jason and his wife, but they hadn't arrived.

Ashley noticed three beautiful women at a front table as they laughed out loud. It seemed they were having a good time. And as she looked at their faces there was something faintly familiar about one of the women, but Ashley couldn't remember where she had seen her.

Legs trembling, Ashley stood in front of the microphone to introduce herself. She spotted Marcus standing at the door and paused for a moment, then continued. But after she started talking, she relaxed enough so no one would notice. After she finished, Ashley stood in back of the room and watched the show with Elaine, Helen's sister. Charlie and his wife, Gwen, were the announcers who described what the models were wearing. Gwen had been a model when she was younger.

Marcus walked up behind Ashley. "I see there's no stopping you, Ash. Congratulations."

Ashley turned around to face him, but when Charlie announced what Lori was wearing, Ashley looked at the runway. She and Marcus watched their daughter until she was behind the curtain. "Thanks, Marcus. See anything you may be interested in for the wife-to-be?"

"No, that's not why I came." Marcus started to speak again, but Ashley walked off as though he wasn't there. She was too busy to give one person very much attention.

Marcus watched her back as though she was someone he didn't know, and wished he did. And for the first time, he had to admit that leaving Ashley was a mistake. If only she had changed while they were married. Maybe if he had stayed and tried to work out their differences they would still be together. But instead he turned his back on her.

After the fashion show people were still eating. There were sliced turkey, pastas, salads, breads, coffee, and tea.

"The show was wonderful, Ashley," Helen complimented.

"Yes, Ash. You outdid yourself," Vanessa said.

"Helen, who are the women sitting at the front table? I don't want to point at them."

"Ashley, you don't recognize at least one of them?" Helen asked.

"No, but I'm sure I've seen the one in the orange."

"That's Carolyn London, Tyra Banks's mom, and her sister and cousin. I ran into Carolyn in New York a year ago. From time to time we see each other when I'm in New York."

"She's very pretty, but all three of them have such pretty faces," Ashley said.

"They seem to be having a wonderful time," Vanessa interjected. "I would like to meet them."

"Come on. I'll introduce you guys," Helen said, and led the way.

As soon as Ashley, Helen, and Vanessa got to the table, Carolyn spoke before anyone else had a chance. It did not go unnoticed that she was used to taking charge. "Ashley, we were going to see you before we left. Honey, I want four suits and a long gown. Tyra is always preaching to me about buying more clothes."

"And I'm Jacqueline Baker, Carolyn's cousin. I want a blouse like the blue one, and two suits, and my husband is always preaching at me for buying too many clothes," she said, as she looked at Carolyn and burst out laughing.

"Hey, don't leave me out," the third woman said. "Ashley, I'm Bernetta London, Carolyn's sister."

"I'm honored to meet you ladies," Ashley said. "This is Vanessa and Helen Graham."

"Wait, wait, wait. Ashley, I need two pantsuits, and you can charge it to Carolyn's bill," Bernetta teased. She spoke up before Carolyn could take charge again.

Carolyn spun around in her chair and faced Bernetta.

"How can you tell someone to add something to my bill, Bernetta? Are you out your mind? Did you hear me say I would pay for your clothes?"

"Put a sock in it, Carolyn," Bernetta hissed.

Ashley was waiting for the three to start swinging, but instead all three of them whooped with laughter.

"We don't see each other very often, so when we're together we get a little crazy, as you can see," Jacqueline explained.

"I'm happy you guys are having a good time," Ashley said, and laughed out loud with Vanessa and Helen.

"Ashley, I'm leaving for New York tomorrow, but as soon as I get back I'll call you so we can go to your shop to be fitted. I love your work, and will use you often," Carolyn said. She stood up and embraced Ashley.

"When you ladies are ready, just call. I'll set aside an afternoon so I can get measurements, and we can take our time and go over some more drawings you may want to select from."

"And don't forget to pick me up, Carolyn," Jacqueline reminded her.

"Girl, no one is going to forget about you."

"Listening to you three having so much fun and laughing makes me wish that I had sisters and cousins," Ashley said.

"Ashley, I have three other friends that are writers," Helen said. "Come on so you can meet them and get some business, girl."

"There's still food left so eat and have fun, ladies."

"Helen, how many tickets did you sell?" Vanessa asked.

"Ten of them."

Ashley and Vanessa followed Helen to a table in the middle of the room.

"Ladies, this is Ashley. Ash, this is Victoria Christopher Murray, Maxine Thompson, and Marissa Monteilh. They are wonderful writers. Maxine also hosts an Internet radio show."

"Ashley, when can I set up an appointment with you?" Marissa asked, pulling out a business card from her purse and flipping it over. "You see, I wrote down the name of the suit I want. Is it all right if I call you tomorrow? I go on tour in two days."

"Call me tomorrow, we can set an appointment."

Maxine and Victoria spoke at the same time. "Sorry, go on Maxine."

"I want a nice pantsuit. I'll call tomorrow and make an appointment for my measurements."

"I can call you tomorrow, too, Ashley," Victoria said. "You've got my business."

Ashley clapped her hands together. "I'm so excited about meeting so many exciting people, and thanks for coming. I'll look forward to seeing you guys soon."

"Vanessa, Helen, you two are truly good friends. I'm so happy. I wasn't able to eat all week because I didn't know if I would have a good turnout." They went to each table and chatted with the other guests.

The show lasted from one o'clock to five. After the guests left, Ashley and her friends and family met up at Ashley's house.

Ashley, Vanessa, and Helen were in the kitchen preparing cold drinks and cake. "I see Marcus stopped in, Ash. That man can't get over what you can do without him," Vanessa said. "You see, Helen, when Ash was married her husband took charge and did everything."

Ashley placed the cake knife in the sink. "She's absolutely right, Helen. Now he's surprised that I have a mind of my own."

"And you are doing so well, Ashley," Helen complimented. "That's why I invited guests to come today. You've worked so hard."

"I have worked hard. As a matter of fact, next week I'll be working on the possibility of opening a boutique in front of my shop. We can make clothes for other shops and at the same time sell at my boutique. After all, it's large enough."

"Oh, Ash, that's wonderful," Helen said. "But won't it be too much work? You don't want to overtire yourself."

Ashley smiled. "I got it all covered. I have Maria, Joan, and Renee working as seamstresses. I hired another person to help and interviewed two more. Charlie was telling me about someone who sews when I got my hair trimmed last week. And when Maria decides to leave and start her own business, I'll just have to replace her. But she is going to be hard to replace."

Vanessa kissed Ashley on the cheek. "That's my girl. You have all my support, honey."

"Mom, we're leaving. Callie is tired," Lori said as she stood in the door.

Ashley walked over to Lori and placed her hand over her shoulder, and walked her back into the living room. She took Callie out of Doris's arms and gave her a kiss on her forehead.

Right after Lori and Keith left, everyone else said good night and left Ashley at home to rest.

As Ashley was undressing she thought of the fashion show. It had been a long day but profitable. And to think well-known authors and Tyra Banks's mom wants her business. Feeling happy-headed she smiled, then laughed.

Ashley was up until eleven that night hanging clothes on hangers; some she had given to her models. Going over her books for the boutique, she was on her way. She felt deliriously high, on a roll to better days.

The year had passed fast but Ashley had gone beyond her expectation with her business. She and Maria shopped for clothes racks and hangers, and selected dark green carpet for the floor. All the sewing machines were placed in back of the shop. The fashion show had brought in more business. Now she had to hire a sales-person for the boutique. Lori could help her there.

Helen and Robert had returned from their vacation, and Vanessa and Gary had gone on vacation to Hawaii. She hadn't seen or heard a word from Elliott, and it was beyond comprehension why she was disappointed. She missed him desperately. But somehow, missing Elliott kept her mind off Marcus. What was it that Aunt Cora said, "one way to forget one man was to lay under an-other"? She had never felt the way she had when Elliott made love to her. So electrifying, she thought, her body quivering. Hadn't she told him that sleeping together would never happen again? So it was back to business as usual. So why was she so lonely, disappointed? And why couldn't she just forget him? She was just so tired of being alone, had never wanted to be single in the first place.

Another week had passed and it was Sunday morning. Ashley was sitting on the patio reading her Sunday *Los Angeles Times*, a tall glass of orange juice on the table in front of her, when she heard the doorbell ring.

As she rushed into the living room she looked at the wooden clock on the wall. It was only nine-thirty, and she wondered who it was so early. She pulled her bathrobe tighter around her, ran her fingers quickly through her hair, and opened the door.

"Marcus! What on earth are you doing here?" she asked, surprised.

He looked at her, stunned; she was a sight for sore eyes. Her hair was tumbled in curls, and her white bathrobe was above her knees. He looked at her bare feet, toes manicured and painted bright red.

Ashley stepped back as he walked past her as though it was still his house.

"I know it's early, Ash. But I need to talk to you."

She clicked her tongue at the roof of her mouth. "Come on, we can talk in the den," she said, with a hint

of annoyance in her voice. She almost stopped when Elliott came to mind. Funny she should think of Elliott at
this very moment. And what does Marcus want to talk to
her about, anyway? she pondered.

Ashley sat on the couch; it was discomforting when
Marcus sat next to her.

"What do you want, Marcus?"

"The same as the last time we talked. I want my wife
back, Ash." He stopped and looked at her. For her age
she couldn't possibly look any younger.

"Why do you want me back, Marcus? I'm forty-six, and
I've grown up. Bullshit means nothing to me anymore. I
can smell it a mile away. So let's discuss this for the last
time." She stood up, but just as fast Marcus stood up beside her.

"You have to listen to me, Ash."

She shook her head, noticing his red shirt. He didn't
have that shirt or brown slacks when he was home. She
assumed Marcus must have bought new clothes after he
left her. "I take it life isn't working out as you planned?
She doesn't have your dinner cooked when you get
home, or doesn't she pick your clothes up from the
cleaners, or is it just that she doesn't jump whenever you
call her name? What's not working out for you, Marcus?"
she asked, and stood in front of him.

He looked down at her as she stared brazenly into
his eyes, hands on her hips, feet apart. For space he
took a step back. "Just listen, Ash. I made a mistake
and a fool of myself. We have a daughter and granddaughter together." He took her in his arms as he felt
her arms circle around his neck, and he relaxed. His
blood ran hot. He had her back. All it took was a firm
hand, and he had her back. There was no doubt that
she had been playing hard to get. But he knew Ash;
she wasn't the kind of woman to play games, especially
with someone she loved.

Ashley closed her eyes. Was he as lonely as she was? Was he really sincere?

"I love you, Ash. Please believe me, baby."

"Please believe me, Marcus. I love you, too." Eyes still closed, she felt his strong arms holding her tighter, massaging the middle of her back. His touch was so familiar, so serene. "I love you too, Marcus. But I'm no longer in love with you." She felt his body stiffen, his arms fell from her back as though all life had drained from them.

Marcus pulled away and took a step back to look at her face. Had he heard her correctly?

"And you are right. We do have a daughter together, Marcus. But she's an adult now with a family of her own. I'm only forty-six, Marcus. I want to be in love and happy the second half of my life. I never understood what you tried to explain the day you left me, until now. I understand perfectly what you were trying to explain to me. Thank you for that, Marcus. It gave me my life back, and a better one at that. It gave me a chance to get to know and like Ashley."

He discovered his arms were still hanging lifeless at his sides and stuck his hands in his pockets. At that very moment Marcus realized he and Ashley were now strangers. He didn't know her as the woman he had been married to for twenty-five years. She didn't want him anymore, it was unbelievable, but she really didn't want him. His shoulders slumped as he saw the earnestness and determination in her eyes. She stood straight, her shoulders back.

"All right, Ash. I guess you've said it all." He turned his head away so she couldn't see tears forming in his eyes. And it was hard to stop the stabbing in his chest.

Ashley followed Marcus to the door. "Good luck, Marcus," she said, and touched his shoulder.

Marcus opened the door, unable to say anything. He nodded, walked out, and gently closed the door behind him. Once Marcus was outside, he looked back at the house that was once his.

Ashley stood behind the blinds and watched Marcus as he drove off. Just as she turned to leave the window, she saw the red Mustang. She thought of the night that Marcus was in the shop, and she wasn't sure if she had seen it before, but now she was sure, she had seen the car. It was possible that the woman was following Marcus.

On her way back to the patio, she grabbed the phone and carried it out with her. She sat at the table and picked up her newspaper.

As Ashley was driving to the shop, she decided to drive around the bank that she had moved her accounts from. When she drove to the back of the bank, she saw the parking lot and drove around it twice. As she was driving out she looked into her rearview mirror and saw the Mustang. It was Marcus's girlfriend's. She had been following Marcus. And now she knows where Ashley lives. Ashley waited until Monique got out her car and went inside the bank. Ashley drove behind her car and wrote down the license plate number.

Ashley's next stop was at the Los Angeles Police Department, where she filed a compliant against Monique for harassment. She told the police officer that she knew who the woman was and was afraid for her safety. The officer said they would send someone to speak with the woman today.

Ashley felt a surge of excitement as she drove to her office. She was sure that Marcus and Monique were having a problem and she only wanted to follow Marcus. Well, Ashley thought. She wrecked her home, and that was harassment, too, as far as Ashley was concerned.

As Ashley walked into the shop, Joan, Renee, and Maria were already working on the new dresses that she had made patterns for. "Good morning, ladies. As you can see, I'm running late but I have Starbucks coffee for all of us," she said, walking to the lunchroom.

"Come on, Allison," Ashley said. Allison was hired two weeks ago and was doing well.

"Ashley, I drew a picture of a suit I want you to see today. Maybe you can add more style to it," Maria said, feeling the hot coffee going down. It was sweet and good. Maria and Ashley were still planning to go into business together. Joan and Renee agreed to stay on and work for them. Ashley was even looking into some health insurance for her employees.

They worked straight through, eating lunch at their machines, and when Ashley looked at her watch it was already two-thirty. "I'm beat and Charlie said he can squeeze me in if I leave now."

"Go on, Ash," Maria answered. "You worked till eight at night all week long."

Ashley was walking into the beauty salon when she saw Charlie getting a Pepsi from the vending machine.

"Well, that's the way jeans are supposed to fit. You look as though you've lost more weight. And check out the red, red lipstick you're wearing," Charlie complimented.

Ashley laughed but she was embarrassed when she saw the other three operators and their customers peering at her.

"My weight fluctuates, and because of the long hours I work, I skip meals. There's just not enough time in a day. If I go home early one day, I work later the next day. And that's a beautiful purple shirt you're wearing, Charlie."

"My wife picked it out when she went shopping last week. No matter what she buys she always picks something up for me, too. She's a good wife, mother, and partner. I'm a lucky man to have her. Come on, so I can shampoo your hair and pretty you up."

* * *

The phone was ringing as Ashley walked inside her house. She dropped her purse on the sofa and answered it.

"Ash, what in hell are you trying to prove?" Marcus yelled through the phone. "You are making my life a living hell."

"What are you talking about, Marcus?"

"Don't be coy with me, Ash. Why did you go to the Police Department and file a complaint against Monique. That wasn't right, Ash, and you know it. How in hell was she harassing you?"

"She's been driving down the street where I live, and I saw her the night you came to my shop. She wrecked my marriage and broke up my home, now I would say that's a good case of harassment, wouldn't you?"

"Look, don't piss in my ear and tell me it's raining, Ash. This is your way of getting even. Monique wasn't harassing you. And you know it."

"Look, Marcus. Take care of your business." She hung up, and picked up her purse and went to her bedroom. Ashley shook her head and laughed.

Chapter 33

"Come in, Ashley. Doris is down in the cellar," Cora said.

"Is that Ashley's voice I hear up there?"

"Yes, Mother, it's me." Ashley went to the cellar door and stuck her head in. "What are you doing down there?" she yelled.

Doris went back upstairs. "I called you at the shop but Joan said you had left early for the beauty shop."

"After I left the beauty salon I decided to go to the store and buy some food instead of waiting for the weekend. The weatherman says we may get some rain. If it rains I want to stay in my pajamas all day."

"Have you made anything new lately?" Doris asked.

"Yes, I have. That's another thing I want to do on the weekend. Grab my drawing board and come up with some new ideas."

"Ashley, Brother Jones wants to know when you're going to church with us again. I think that man likes you," Cora teased.

"Come into the living room. No use standing here in the hall," Doris said, leading the way and stopping to pick up the remote control to turn on the television.

"What do you guys want to see?" Doris asked.

"I don't care, Mother."

"Ashley, you didn't answer me. When are you going back to church with us?" Cora asked.

"Aunt Cora, I don't like that old bale-headed Brother

Jones. Besides, he looks at every woman in the church.
I wouldn't be surprised if he hasn't already dated half
the women there."

Cora laughed, and pulled the side of her wig up to
rub her head. "Honey, half the women in the church
wouldn't want that man. I was just teasing with you, Ashley." Cora and Doris laughed.

"His head is too big anyway," Doris said, laughing. "Big
and empty."

"Are you dating anyone at all, Ashley?" Cora asked.

"No, Aunt Cora, I'm too busy."

"Now Cora, don't go harping on Ashley about dating.
She'll date when she's ready." Doris interjected. "We
went to see Lori and the baby yesterday, Ashley. And
guess what?"

"What, Mother?"

"Lori told us about a senior citizen bus trip to Vegas.
We called and made arrangements and now we're going.
But we'll be back to work at the shop on Wednesday."

"That should be fun, Mother. You and Aunt Cora
should enjoy the trip. It's about time you guys do something different besides helping me and staying home."

"Ashley, how is Jason?" Doris asked. She still couldn't
bring herself to say Jason was Ashley's brother. It was like
opening old wounds again.

"I don't know. Since he returned from his honeymoon
I called, but he doesn't return any of my calls. I think it's
because of his wife. When she answers, she's very cold. I
leave a message, but he doesn't call me back. But it's all
right, Mother. Jason has his life and I have mine."

"If it's not meant to be, Ash, then it won't. I cooked
some chili and cornbread. Would you like a bowl?" Doris
asked. She just wanted to change the conversation about
Jason, and fast. Mentioning Jason's name in her own
house was so strange. And she couldn't forget the evil in
the man's eyes and the sarcasm in his voice. The truth

was, she didn't want Ashley socializing with the dreadful man. He's poison just like his no-good mama was.

"No thanks, Mother. I eat lightly in the evenings. But I'll take a bowl home for my lunch tomorrow. I think I'll go fix it now. We don't have good lunches when you and Aunt Cora have a day off."

"You sit, Ashley. You've been working all day. I'll fix it," Doris said standing up.

As Doris walked out, for the first time Ashley noticed that she looked happier and more content since Cora was living with her permanently. And maybe it was because the truth had finally unraveled, freed her from the lies she had lived for forty-five years.

Doris came out carrying a brown bag in her hand and handed it to Ashley.

Ashley hugged Doris and kissed her cheek. For a moment she felt a strong urge to hold her mother tightly in her arms, thank her for being the loving mother she had always been.

"You ladies have a good evening. As for me, I'm going home and crawl into bed."

It was getting dark and Doris and Cora walked Ashley outside to her car. They stood there until she drove off.

Once Ashley got home she changed into a long terrycloth bathrobe. It wasn't chilly inside but she felt cold and tightened the belt around her waist. She went into the kitchen, placed the chili into the refrigerator, made a cup of chamomile tea, and curled up in a chair. Before finishing the tea, Ashley laid her head back and fell asleep.

When Ashley awoke it was completely dark. A sharp pain in her temple and a sore throat explained why she felt so cold. With so much work, all she needed was the flu. But flu or not, tomorrow she had to go to work. She turned off the lamp and took two aspirins.

The next morning, Ashley climbed out of bed. Every bone in her body hurt, but at least the headache was gone. She could work as long as her head wasn't pounding.

Ashley stood in the shower, feeling the hot water soothing her aching body. She got out and went back to her bedroom, lay across the bed, and fell back into a deep sleep.

Ashley jumped with a start when she heard the phone ringing and looked at the large bath towel still wrapped around her.

"Ash, it's Joan, are you all right?" Joan asked with concern.

"Yes, but I'll be late. I fell back to sleep," she said, clearing her throat. It burned and she coughed.

"Honey, are you sure you're all right? I asked Maria if you were going to be late, but she said you didn't tell her."

"I know," Ashley said and cleared her throat again. "I have a sore throat, but I'll be there within the hour." As she talked, she went to the closet and pulled out a pair of jeans with her free hand. She sneezed, coughed, and this time her throat burned like hell.

"Are you sure that you should come in today, Ash? We can handle the work ourselves."

"Thanks, Joan, but I'll be all right." Ashley slipped into her jeans, grabbed a sweatshirt from her drawer, and brushed her hair back.

As the day wore on, Ashley felt worse. She went into her office and interviewed two young girls as saleswomen for the boutique. One was a young married woman with two children. She wanted to work only four hours a day. Ashley hired the other young woman. Her name was Kendra. She was twenty-one and lived at home with her mother.

By six Ashley locked up the shop and went home. She planned to brew a hot cup of tea and crawl into bed.

Chapter 34

"Absolutely no divorce, Elliott. Don't you think I've noticed how you've been moping around for the last few weeks? You snap at everything I say. What happened, is your woman pressuring you to divorce me and marry her?" Janet asked, her voice smothering with sarcasm.

"I'm amazed you noticed, Janet," Elliott answered. "Just when did you find the time to notice anything I do?"

"Oh, I've noticed, Elliott. Don't think I'm stupid."

Elliott and Janet were standing in the kitchen. Elliott had gotten a bottle of beer from the refrigerator and Janet had followed him from the second bedroom that he now occupied.

Elliott brushed past Janet as he went back to his office, and slammed the door behind him, but Janet followed him anyway. She swung the door open and entered, now angrier than before.

"I have work to do, Janet, so get the hell out my office. Don't you have someplace to go?" he snapped, never looking up at her.

She brought on a passive voice. "No, I don't. I thought we could have a quiet evening together." She was standing at the door waiting for his response, hoping that he would soften. She had gotten her silky black hair cut into a shorter style, and was dressed in green jeans and a black low-cut sweater with nothing underneath.

"So, what do you say, Elliott?"

"I say I'm busy, and I've forgotten what it's like to spend a quiet evening with you, Janet. Besides, I haven't the appetite for it anymore." He leaned back in his chair and took a long swallow of his beer, feeling the bubbles tingling down his throat. It was cold and just what he needed. She had tried to get him in bed before and it didn't work. Maybe tonight would be her last try.

"I'm trying, Elliott. Help me out here," Janet said.

"Help you out, Janet? You can't make everything right again in one night. Too much has gone bad between us, too much time has past." He put on his reading glasses and opened a folder. "I'm filing for a divorce tomorrow."

She stepped closer to his desk. "I'll take you for everything, Elliott. I swear I will."

"I'm sure you'll try. Now, if you don't mind, get the hell out of my office," he said, waving his hand as though she was dismissed.

Janet took another step forward. "Get out of your office," she repeated. "When did you decide this office belongs to you? Everything in this house belongs to us, Elliott. Us! That's the way it's been and that's the way it is until we go to court and it all becomes mine," she exclaimed, her hands on her hips. She looked around as though she was looking for something to strike him with, but stopped when she looked into his cold, calculating eyes. A folder lay open on his desk and he rested his hands in front of him.

Elliott rubbed his hand across his forehead. "You ask when I decided this office was mine? The same time I decided the other bedroom was mine."

"I'm keeping this house, Elliott." She held her ground just to prepare him for the fight he had ahead of him. If he leaves, it would just be with his clothes.

"Fine, keep the house. I'll agree to that. I'll even pay for it."

"You'll be left with nothing, Elliott, I'm warning you."

"We'll find out soon enough. Since you're not sensible, you'll just have to wait until you're served to see what I agree to. Better yet, you should go and get a lawyer as soon as possible. That is the last piece of sensible advice you'll get from me. I'll start looking for a place to live this week."

"You'll be sorry for this, Elliott," she yelled. "For your information, I'm going to travel and spend your money as always, married or not. Don't be foolish enough to think that I will live any differently because you want a divorce."

"Leave my office," he said, just above a whisper. Elliott got up and grabbed her arm, led her to the door, then pushed her out, slamming the door in her face.

Janet saw something different in his eyes. Determination was what she saw, and he was cold, which was out of character for Elliott. Janet was shaken by his words, and this time she believed him. He was not one to issue idle threats. He was a lawyer and might know of a way to keep everything for himself.

As Janet sat on the sofa staring at the empty glass in her hand, she thought of a way to get one of the best divorce lawyers. She and Terri, Elliott's cute little receptionist, got along well together. She could call her tomorrow while Elliott was in court and ask her for a list of the best lawyers. After all, Elliott would not be available for the entire day, and she could be getting the information for anyone. Triumphant, she felt a fierce surge of satisfaction, smiled, grabbed her purse, and walked out.

"Mr. Douglas, I need the Garfield file, since he will be in at three today," Rose said.

She was the best temporary receptionist they had hired, unlike Terri, who was never on time and scatterbrained. Today, like so many times, she had requested an extra hour for lunch to enroll in night school.

"Damn," Elliott said out loud. "You know what, Rose? I was going over the Garfield file at home and left it in my office. It'll only take forty-five minutes to go home and get it."

"I'm sorry, Mr. Douglas."

"Don't be." Elliott looked at the wire-rimmed glasses resting on her nose. She was a tall woman, a grand-mother in her early fifties, and always dressed very pro-fessionally in a suit. Rose had been working as a temp for the company for a month, and Elliott had spoken to the other partners about hiring her full time. He rushed out of his office.

As Elliott pulled into his driveway, Janet's car was there. All he wanted was to get the file without another altercation about a divorce. And since he had made up his mind to divorce her, he felt a sense of relief as though a dark cloud had lifted from his shoulders. Who needs a divorce at fifty years old? But it couldn't be helped. Getting a divorce should be sad, but instead it gave him hope.

Elliott went inside his office and the file lay open on the corner of the desk. Walking out the office, he felt lucky that Janet didn't want to face him any more than he wanted her to. She probably went into her bedroom when she heard his car pull into the driveway.

In the living room, Elliott opened the door to leave and stopped when he heard a sound as though Janet was groaning. Could she be ill? He rushed to her room. The door was open, and he stopped in his tracks, the file falling from his hand as papers scattered on the floor. He wanted to turn and walk away, but his legs wouldn't move.

Janet was lying naked on her back, legs spread apart, her eyes closed. Her body twisted and turned in plea-sure, her hands above her head balled into fists. She raised her legs, opened them wider as if she couldn't get enough.

The young woman's face was buried between Janet's thighs, her long black hair covering the middle of Janet's body, while one hand caressed Janet's thigh. Her long legs were hanging off the foot of the king size bed, and she tilted her head just high enough so that the tip of her tongue teased Janet's hot, mahogany colored flesh. As though she felt an intruder in the room, abruptly the young woman raised her head.

"Oh, dear God," Elliott whispered. No wonder Terri needed the extra hour, but obviously it wasn't to enroll in school. The seven-day cruise Janet went on while Terri was on vacation at the same time. It all began to fall into place. The four-day trip to Vegas a month ago—Terri had called in sick that Friday—apparently they were together. What a fool he'd been. He had been supporting both of them. All the time he had thought Janet had a lover . . . another man, but this was beyond belief.

Feeling the perspiration forming on his forehead, Elliott thought he would vomit, but he managed to keep it down. He stood against the doorframe, one hand in his pocket, and waited.

Terri gulped, muttered something moronic, jumped from between Janet's legs, and grabbed the sheet to cover herself. Janet screamed, jumped out the bed, and grabbed her robe.

"Elliott, what the hell are you doing here?" she yelled, her voice quivering as though she was gasping for air. "I mean . . . why are you here?"

"Get dressed, Terri," Elliott ordered. Ignoring his wife, he turned on his heels and stormed back into the living room, giving the two women privacy to get decent.

Elliott flopped down on the sofa. He rested his elbows on his knees and held his face in both hands. He was ill, stung, and couldn't get the vision out his mind.

"Elliott!" Janet sat next to him and grabbed his arm, but he pushed her away.

"Elliott, please, let me explain. We haven't been seeing each other long."

Elliott moved away from her as though she was dirty. "Get that little boy-bitch out my house." He got up, went to the bar, and poured a glass of Jack Daniels. He took a long swallow, hoping it would help calm the anger.

Elliott looked at Janet long and hard. All of a sudden he knew that he had found the answer to his problem. He would use this misfortune as a way to end his marriage under his conditions. He watched Janet as she left the room.

In five minutes, Janet had returned and sat next to him. Apparently, Terri had taken the back door out. "She's gone, Elliott. I'm so sorry you had to walk in on that. I never meant for you to find out." Unable to look at his face, she lowered her eyes. "Please don't hate me, Elliott." Again she reached for his hand, and he quickly pulled away from her as though she would dirty his clothes.

"Have you always been gay, Janet?" he asked, his voice cold. "And how many? Or are you sleeping with men and women these days?"

"Oh, Elliott, she's only the second one," Janet murmured. "The first didn't last very long."

He threw back his head and emptied his glass. He set the glass on the table and faced Janet. "Okay, here's how it's going to be. I know you believe seriously in appearances. You wouldn't want your family, especially your mother, and your one hundred-member golf club, not to mention friends like Helen and Robert—"

Her head jerked up and her heart beat rapidly. "What are you getting at, Elliott?"

"Agree to my terms of the divorce or I'll have to divorce you because you're a lesbian. I'll file for a divorce

tomorrow. So what do you say, Janet? My terms or everyone that you know finds out about you."

"You jerk, you blackmailing, no-good jerk. How could
you stoop so low?" She stood up so fast that Elliott had
to grab her arm to keep her from falling over the coffee
table. He pulled her back down on the sofa.

"Sit down and shut up," he demanded through closed
teeth.

She was tired and felt dirty, her chest hurt, and Elliott
stared through her like a burning dagger.

"You can have the house. I'll pay off the mortgage so
it will be free and clear. If you're smart, you'll sell it and
buy yourself a nice townhouse and bank the rest, at least
two hundred and fifty thousand dollars. You can also
have the large bank account that pays a considerable
amount of interest each month, and I'll pay you not a
damn dollar more. You're healthy and can take care of
yourself. Besides, you're lucky, you have men *and* women
to help take care of you," he snapped with sarcasm.

For seconds she couldn't speak and couldn't believe
he would cheat her out of everything. Suddenly Janet
threw her body against him, and raised her fist to strike
him, but he caught it in midair and pushed her hard
against the sofa. "I won't agree to it, Elliott. You can't
make me," she hissed.

"Okay. It's your choice." Elliott got up and grabbed
the phone. He dialed a number and waited for an answer. "Hello Margaret, it's your son-in law."

Janet jumped in front of him and grabbed the phone
from his hand. "Mama, someone is at the door. I'll call
you back later." She hung up. She was beaten, she knew.
Her mother's weak heart would give out for sure if she
knew, and what would her sisters say? "Okay. I'll agree,
but you'll be sorry for this, Elliott." She jumped up and
stomped her foot. "You will be sorry."

"Are you threatening me, Janet? That's not wise, but
anyway, you made the right choice."

He got up and went to his bedroom. When he came out again, he was carrying his suitcase and overnight bag, and took both to his car. Elliott came back inside again, went back to his room, and returned carrying five suits. "I'll be back next week to get the rest of my clothes." On his way out he stopped and picked up the file he needed.

Feeling deflated, Janet didn't look at him, didn't answer. She was beaten. It was over.

Later that day Elliott checked into the Park Hyatt Hotel near his office on Avenue of the Stars in Century City.

Hanging his clothes in the closet, he could still imagine Janet and Terri. Boy, Janet had had him fooled. Well, it was over with, he thought, arranging his suits on the hangers. He undressed and hung his suit in the closet, and slipped into his navy blue bathrobe. His room was large, with a nice desk that he could work on. Elliott opened a file he needed to read, closed it, and decided to dress again and go to the hotel restaurant for dinner.

He ate dinner alone and thought of Ashley, but he would wait before he called her. First, he had to find an apartment and start his divorce procedures.

"Sure honey. I'm in for the evening, so come on over," Ashley said. She hung up and switched on the TV until Lori's arrival. It was seven and getting dark. Ashley closed the blinds and went into the kitchen to pour a glass of apple juice. She was over that terrible cold and had been working late again. In the last few weeks, the boutique was doing well and she had hired another seamstress and also another saleswoman to work on Saturdays. She was planning to open another boutique soon. In her wildest dreams Ashley never imagined making such a profit by opening the boutique. As the company grew, she planned on having enough people so that she could cut down on her hours, relax, and live a little.

She curled up in her chair, her eyes closed, and relaxed until she heard the doorbell ring. She rushed into the living room, and anticipating seeing her granddaughter, swung open the door.

"Elliott," Ashley whispered. Unable to say another word, she stared at him, feeling as though her heart was flipping over and over inside her chest, and was sure her legs wouldn't hold her up much longer. The phone rang, and she jumped. "Come in and have a seat. I have to get the phone."

With a hundred thoughts going through her head, Ashley ran to the den and answered on the fourth ring.

"Mom, I'm so sorry but the baby is still sleeping. The little angel, we hate to wake her."

"I understand, honey. Let her sleep. It's Friday night and I can see her sometime this weekend." She could still feel her heart hammering inside.

"Okay, Mom. Keith was talking about you today. He said we see more of you since you have a granddaughter. Mom, are you all right?"

"Yes, yes, I'm sorry, Lori. I'll see you on the weekend." Looking toward the living room where Elliott was seated, Ashley couldn't concentrate. She hung up and hurried into the bathroom to see if her hair needed combing, and put on some fresh lipstick. She looked into the mirror one last time, took a deep breath, and went back into the living room where Elliott was patiently waiting.

"You really surprised me, Elliott. Would you like a glass of wine, Coke?" She could hear her voice trembling and tried to keep it level.

"No. Not right now. Please, sit down, Ashley."

She didn't know why, but she hesitated for a moment before sitting next to him. He seemed so serious.

"To tell you the truth, I surprised myself. I had no intentions of coming to see you so soon." He stopped and
stared at her. She was so breathtaking, he couldn't speak
for a moment. "I left my wife two weeks ago and went to
see a lawyer to start my divorce procedures. Janet and I
have already agreed on a settlement so it should go
pretty smoothly. Darling, do you remember the last conversation we had?"

She nodded. "How could I forget?"

"I asked you if you loved me, and I told you that I
loved you. More than that, I'm in love with you. If you'll
have me, it will be just you and me, Ashley." He waited
for her response.

Ashley felt as though she was on the edge and that one
push would make her explode into a sea of tears. "You
really meant it. I never thought you'd be back, and I was
afraid to wish. Oh Elliott, I don't know what to say."

"I love you, Ashley. If you love me, then you can start
by saying it."

Elliott held his hand out to her, and moving closer to
him she took it.

"I think we can have a terrific life together, Ashley.
What do you think?" he asked in a low whisper.

She lay her head on his shoulder. "I'm in love with
you, Elliott. But I never thought this would happen. I
never thought I could fall so deeply and completely in
love again."

"I'm here forever if you'll have me," he said, his lips
brushing against hers.

"How do you want your coffee in the morning?" she
asked.

"Black. No cream. No sugar."

"And your eggs?' she whispered in his ear.

"Over easy, sweetheart. Everything about me is easy,
Ashley."

She turned off the lamp, and hand in hand they went

to her bedroom, knowing the second half of their lives had begun.

"Black? No, cream, no sugar, huh?"

He stopped her in the hall, they embraced, kissed, and before they reached the bedroom, they were already undressed.

Chapter 35

October 2004

The enlargement of Ashley's shop was successfully completed by two construction workers that Raymond had used previously to enlarge another space. The place next door to Ashley's shop was small and empty. The walls were knocked down so that she could expand her boutique. The back of her shop was still used as a small sewing factory, with eight seamstresses, and Maria agreed to stay on as Ashley's business partner. Elliott drew up the contract between Ashley and Maria.

Ashley was still doing business with Fern, but most of the clothes were made for her boutique and quickly sold. The profits were increasing, and in a year and a half, what she had been striving for was victoriously achieved.

In her quiet office, Ashley sat behind her desk. She smiled, thinking of the night before and the morning she had spent at Elliott's apartment. They had made love, and it was like magic, like a silky breeze that touched her very soul. Without a doubt, she was content and completely in love with him. He had gotten his own apartment and they were together every night. Tonight, she was invited to his apartment for dinner; it was his turn to cook. Ashley almost laughed out loud as she thought of it. The last time it was his turn, he ordered in Chinese food.

How many times had she invited him to her house for dinner and they ended up kissing all the way to her bedroom, then undressed and went to bed? Dinner always came later, sometimes much later.

Ashley looked at her watch; it was after four. She decided to go home and shower, slip on a pair of jeans, and head for Elliott's house.

She had gone over an invoice from Fern, but she could finish tomorrow. It was Friday, and Ashley went into the sewing room and told the girls to pack up and go home. They got up to leave just as Marcus walked in and followed Ashley to her office. She didn't sit down but leaned against her desk as though she was impatient. She was in a hurry to be with Elliott.

Ashley looked at her watch. "What can I do for you, Marcus? I'm in a hurry and don't want to be late for my date."

"Date?" he asked, as though he was surprised that she was dating. "Is that why you wouldn't accept my marriage proposal?" he demanded, and stood against her desk in front of her.

"No, it's not the reason. I thought I made it clear the last time we discussed it." She looked at her watch again and picked up her purse.

When she turned around he grabbed her arm, hard. "What's gotten into you, Ash?"

"What's gotten into me? I'm a woman now, Marcus. That's what gotten into me."

She looked at his hand on her arm and jerked away. "Why are you here, Marcus?"

Angry with himself, Marcus shook his head. "I'm sorry, Ash. We were married for twenty-five years and this was the first time you mentioned a date. I know I have no right to feel this way after what I've done to you." He sighed. "I came to ask you one last time to marry me. I have to, Ash, because if you still say no, I'm going to marry . . . Well, I'm going to get married." He swallowed hard and watched the reaction on her face, but there was no change. No shock, anger, nothing. She just looked at him.

"Is it Monique?"

"Yes it's Monique," he answered.

"Well, that's why you left, isn't it? I thought it would have happened much sooner. Anyway, Marcus, you've told me. Now, I don't want to be late for my date." Again, she picked up her keys and purse, and walked him to the door.

Once Marcus opened the door, he turned and looked at her again, and gave her a quick kiss on the cheek. As he started to walk out Ashley called his name.

"I wish you all the happiness, Marcus. I really do." She felt tears in her eyes. What a touching moment, she thought. Who would have thought in a hundred years that she and Marcus would each be seeking happiness from someone else?

He wiped tears from his eyes, and turned around and held her once more, and kissed her on the forehead. "Thank you, Ash," he managed to say.

Ashley stood and stared at the door for a few moments before she heard Maria coming in from the kitchen. She sighed and took a deep breath. This time she said good-bye properly to Marcus. Their twenty-five years was gone forever. Funny, she thought, as she stood there. She felt relieved of all the hurt and suffering she had felt. And now she could go forward with her life.

"Are you all right, Ashley?" Maria asked and stood in front of her.

"Yes, surprising enough, I am all right. Really all right." But deep inside she felt a hint of jealousy; Marcus was marrying the woman that he had left her for.

But now she had a man she loved and he loved her.

"Maria, it was good of you to wait for me, but let's get out of here."

Maria nodded in agreement. "What are you doing this weekend, Ashley?" Maria asked.

"I'll be at the boutique from ten to two, and Kendra will be here until six. She can close and lock up. After I leave, I'm doing absolutely nothing. What do you think about making Joan a supervisor? She works hard and I trust her."

"I agree. There's no one better."

Maria picked up her purse and they walked out. Maria stood by Ashley while she locked the door to the shop.

Ashley got home and showered, watered her plants, and opened her mail. It was early so she dressed in a blue jean skirt and red sweater with a deep V in front. Standing in front of her dresser, she carefully combed her hair and looked at herself from side to side in the mirror. The evening had begun eventfully, but being with Elliott would make her forget. They were so evenly yoked, and had so much in common that it had gotten so easy and comfortable to be together. And now Ashley had a life after work to look forward to.

Ashley picked up her purse, went into the den to lock the glass patio door, and got her keys. Again she thought of Marcus. He was getting married again. Was he as much in love with Monique as she was with Elliott? she wondered. But she had to admit that if it weren't for her love for Elliott, she probably would be crying about Marcus's marriage. "Thank you Elliott," she whispered.

Ashley walked out the door and looked at the bright stars, inhaled the fresh air, and decided she wouldn't think of Marcus anymore this evening.

* * *

Elliott greeted her with a long, sweet and gentle kiss. She held onto him, and all she could concentrate on was the love they shared.

"Come in, darling, and see what I cooked for us." Ashley stopped when she saw fresh flowers in the center of the table, a bottle of chilled champagne, and two glasses.

"Everything is so beautiful, Elliott. How did you find time to do this?" She grabbed his hand as they talked.

"I left a little early today. I wanted dinner to be special tonight, Ashley." He looked into her eyes and kissed her again. "Today I'm a single man. My divorce is final. Now, my dear, your dinner is ready. You sit down and I'll get dinner."

"Can't I help?" she asked, and started to get up again.

"No, you may not. Everything is ready." Elliott went to the kitchen and came back with a thick steak on each plate and placed one in front of her. He went back to the kitchen and came back with a garden salad.

Ashley watched him as he pulled out his chair. He looked sexy in his jeans and white T-shirt. He had moved into his apartment two weeks after he left Janet. Ashley was with him when he found it. It was small and modern, located in Westwood not far from the law firm. And he was happy; Ashley could see it in his face. The sadness he used to have in his eyes was replaced with life and happiness.

Elliott filled their glasses with champagne and sat next to Ashley. He took her hand in his. "Close your eyes, Ash. I have something for you." He smiled as he watched the happiness on her face. "After all, I loved you soon after we met."

Her eyes were closed, but she still smiled. Ashley felt the ring slide on her finger and her eyes flew wide open.

Elliott placed her hand against his lips. "Will you marry me, Ashley? We could live in one place instead of you staying at my apartment one night and me at your house the next. I want to wake up every morning, baby, with you next to me." He saw a tear trickle down one cheek, felt the moisture in the palm of her small, delicate hand. With one finger, Elliott gently brushed the tear away.

She was afraid that if she spoke she would burst into tears. "I must be the luckiest woman alive. You are the love of my life, Elliott. You gave me a second chance, and I love you for that."

"Is that a 'yes,' darling?"

"Yes, yes, of course I will marry you." She fell into his arms.

As Elliott pulled her up, he felt her arms circle around his neck.

They ended up in his bedroom, and in his bed, and again, dinner would come later, much later, if they ate at all.

About the Author

Patricia Anne Phillips is also the author of *June in Winter* and *Something in Common*. Patricia lives in Los Angeles, California.

Her website is www.paphillipsbooks.com.